Kay Stephens was born and brought up in the West Riding of Yorkshire. She spent the first seven years of her working life as a librarian, and since then has written several novels as well as short stories. She now lives in the South of England and is currently working on her next novel, also based in Yorkshire.

North Riding

Kay Stephens

This edition published 1998 by Pan Books
an imprint of Macmillan Publishers Ltd,
25 Eccleston Place, London SW1W 9NF
and Basingstoke

Associated companies throughout the world

First published in 1990
by Century Hutchinson Ltd

First published in paperback in 1991
by HEADLINE BOOK PUBLISHING PLC

10 9 8 7 6 5 4 3 2

ISBN 0 330 37412 5

Printed and bound in Great Britain by
Mackays of Chatham plc, Chatham, Kent

For my aunt,
Ivy Jones,
a fine Yorkshirewoman

Prologue

The Great Exhibition: Crystal Palace, 1851

It was the best day of his life. Abel Falgrave gazed yet
again down the length of the great glass Palace, past the
ornamental fountain to the tree that surprised everyone by
being rooted within the building. Inhaling deeply, he savoured the vast range of colour, the sound of strange accents,
the soaring excitement. Queen Victoria and her Consort
were leaving the exhibition now, but the stimulation of their
presence remained. And she had paused to admire his
display of jet jewellery from the Falgrave workshop.

Those minutes were photographed on his memory, as
clear as anything taken by Daguerre or Fox Talbot. He had
been explaining to an elegant woman how jet was mined in
seams, either precariously by hewing into the very face of
the Yorkshire cliffs or by digging into the nearby hills, and
then with a swirl of full skirts she'd moved on, and he had
turned.

The approaching group exhilarated and unnerved him.
The ladies wore the finest silks he had seen, the men the
smartest morning-coats. Their bearing and their splendour
diminished the colour and the noise of visitors, exhibitors,
made the excesses of some displays appear unseemly. They
fanned out as they came nearer, and there the Queen was,
rather smaller than he expected, not so severe, more attractive than her portraits. Her brown hair gleamed in the light
from the arching glass overhead, her complexion resembled
delicately-tinted porcelain.

To Abel himself she gave no more than an acknowledging
nod, but to one of her ladies-in-waiting she exclaimed
delightedly over several of their dark glinting necklaces and
one, finely-carved cameo brooch.

He wished now that he'd had the presence of mind to
offer them to Her Majesty, though if all the exhibitors

did likewise the Queen and her retinue would soon be overburdened. Yet he was well satisfied – would never have believed when he forsook mining the jet that working on its transformation into jewellery would bring him to London for such a breathtaking occasion.

Noticing the diminutive figure now thrusting towards him amidst a throng of wide-skirted dresses, Abel smiled to himself. Maud would be astonished to learn that the Queen had admired their jewellery. She'd be chagrined, as well, because she had not been present.

'You're looking mightily pleased with yourself,' she observed. 'Having a good laugh, are you, because I've trailed this place end to end looking for Madam here?'

With a jerk of her hand she hauled their daughter Hester from behind her back and gave her a push towards him.

'Just you ask her where I found her this time . . .'

Hester gazed up into her father's eyes, brown like her own, and so filled with undisguised affection there could be no doubting his support. Even if she hadn't behaved like a little lady.

'I was sitting in the tree,' she confided. 'Only a little way up, I wouldn't have fallen.'

'You see,' Maud went on, before Abel could comment, 'worse than any lad, our Hester. Why can't she occupy a place on one of them red upholstered benches like those good children over there?'

She had dressed the girl in her first ankle-length gown, the miniature of her own. But worse than Hester's failure to conduct herself accordingly was this dread that she'd be lost. Maud would never admit to being overwhelmed by the Crystal Palace, its sheer size, the extent and confusion of galleries showing everything from furniture and chinaware to rich materials. Privately, she offered prayers that the three of them would survive the ordeal.

'It's such a lovely tree, Papa. I'm sure there's none in Whitby that grow inside a building.'

'She's the one we should have left at home. Seven years old, and still can't be trusted not to go wandering off.' Maud paused, adjusted the angle of the gold-coloured bonnet matching her gown, and glanced around. 'Not many people inspecting our things, are there? I saw the Arkwrights' display – bigger than the space we've been allocated *and* better positioned . . .'

'Did the Queen stop to see what they had on show, an' all?' Abel inquired casually. He'd been biding his time to tease his wife a little with what she had missed.

'You don't mean! Oh, did she really stop here to have a look?'

'Right where you are standing now.'

'You could have fetched me. You know how much I wanted . . . You knew how disappointed I was that we'd such a poor view of the opening ceremony. I've always dreamed of meeting royalty. And the Queen herself . . .'

'She paused for only a matter of moments, my dear. And as for fetching you . . .'

'I know, you couldn't have left the display unattended, specially while her party was here.' Maud smiled at last, possessed of too much Yorkshire sense to permit disappointment to alloy the gratification of having their jet receive royal approval.

'Go on then – tell us what she said,' she prompted her husband, after pausing long enough to give Hester's wrist a slap when she reached out to touch one of the glittering black bracelets.

'Hester love,' Abel said before replying, bending towards his daughter, 'we couldn't fetch all the polishing materials with us from Whitby, so if you put fingermarks all over things they'll be spoiled.'

'Sorry, Papa, it's just that they're all so sparkly.'

'I don't believe the Queen went anywhere near the Arkwrights' display, Abel. What *did* she say?'

'To me personally, nothing. She only smiled, like. But she was telling one of her ladies-in-waiting which pieces she considered finest . . .'

'Show me,' Maud interrupted, beaming. 'If they aren't similar to items I already possess, I must have them for myself. It's a good advertisement, as well you know, that I should wear stuff from our own workroom.'

'This bracelet is the one thing *I'd* really, really like,' breathed Hester wistfully.

9

'Jet's not suitable for little girls,' her mother began. And then she met Abel's glance. 'Aye, she is keen, I'll grant her that. Go on, love, we'll let you have the one you want. But only once the Exhibition's over.'

Selecting enough of their best pieces for the 1851 Exhibition had been a considerable task – but the rows of engraved brooches, elegantly-carved necklaces, bracelets, rings and sets of faceted buttons were a credit to the Falgrave works. Both Maud and Abel could sympathise with their daughter's urge to touch. Hadn't they loved the jet for the biggest part of their lives, weren't they both ceaselessly fascinated by watching jewels emerge from this rough gemstone formed in the earth while their own coastline lay beneath an ancient sea?

'Lambert would have liked that tree,' Hester announced, and they both looked down at her.

'Aye, I daresay he would,' her father agreed, then fell silent. Their eldest child, forceful for eleven years old, had declined the suggestion that he accompany them to the Great Exhibition.

Jet jewellery was daft, according to Lambert, of no interest to anyone but women and girls. I've a mind to show him how it begins, Abel reflected, take him round the mines, nothing soft there.

He slid one hand into a pocket and fingered the small piece of jet that he'd carried with him since the time he left mining. One face only of this fragment had been polished. Its touch was totally familiar, resurrected the oily smell that hung in the air when rough jet was broken. He didn't need to look to see the paler, brownish layers beneath its surface, the rings identifying it as fossilised wood. A part of the cliffs that were home.

Maud's voice broke in on his contemplation. 'I think I'll have a bit of a sit down.' Her excitement about the Queen had only temporarily obliterated the strain of locating their daughter.

Drawing out a chair for her, Abel observed that the high colour induced by her anxious quest had drained away, leaving her face almost as pale as her fair curly hair.

'That's right, love. Me and our Hester will have a look round.'

'Make sure you don't miss that massive cut-glass fountain, it's by a Yorkshire firm – Oslers' of Wakefield.'

While Abel was nodding a small hand sought his fingers, the face framed in dark ringlets upturned towards him.

'I've got something to show you,' he told her. 'I noticed it when I was hurrying in this morning.'

Hester trotted at his side as they passed all the big white statues that she thought quite boring. The people walking alongside and past them fascinated her – she kept turning round to gaze. As well as hundreds of ladies dressed in gowns of all hues, there were men and women who obviously were foreign. Mama had explained that other countries were showing all kinds of things that they manufactured.

'Here we are, love . . .'

Before she could even think about all the materials and ornaments and strange inventions surrounding them, her father was leading her to a small set piece.

Schoolmaster Severity, she read, and examined the group of furry creatures. Rabbits were the pupils, the teacher a slightly larger animal, maybe a stoat. She didn't like the realisation that they all were dead.

'Olive would think they were nice.' Her sister was only three, at home in Whitby with her nannie and Grandmother Falgrave.

Inwardly, Abel smiled at his own misjudgement. Hester was growing faster than he recognised.

'What shall we see next?' he asked her, gazing about Sir Joseph Paxton's mighty structure and marvelling how this design of ironwork and glass was inspired by the veins of a giant waterlily.

He explained this to Hester as they walked, and told how the former gardener's boy had matured at Chatsworth, creating a massive conservatory as a prelude to the revolutionary Crystal Palace. Ordinary people *could* achieve greatness – so long as they applied themselves, and worked hard.

'About that tree,' Hester began gravely. 'It's awfully big

– is that the kind that turns into jet in thousands and thousands of years?'

Abel's private smile emerged as a twitching of the lips beneath his dark moustache before it widened in delight.

'I'm not really sure,' he admitted, wondering at his child who amid all the opulence and technology of this Great Exhibition only seemed interested in the family occupation.

Would she keep this love of the jet, follow him into its crafting, share his ambition? Trade should widen after showing their goods here. There'd be scope beyond decorations for ladies' gowns and jewellery worn in mourning. Since the railway had been extended from Pickering to Whitby there'd been more visitors in the town, and the opening up of fresh lines would bring more still. Given another few years – ten, say – where might Falgraves be?

Chapter 1

Whitby, 1861

The moon silvered a track from the harbour wall across a tranquil sea to the cobalt sky. Overnight the fog had dispersed. Standing at the window of his house overshadowed by the abbey ruins, Abel Falgrave smiled. His friends among the fishermen would be safe, their craft soon secured at Whitby's quay. And on a day as fine as this he'd leave the brougham at home, would enjoy the walk to the workshop.

A gleam from the shifting fire glinted on the decorative brasswork of the bed in which Maud had given birth to all four of their children. It seemed nowhere near twenty-one years since their first. But Lambert would come of age this month, on the same day as Queen Victoria's daughter, the Princess Royal.

Another glimmer revealed the stillness that was Maud's sleeping face. Abel marvelled yet again at her capacity for rest. Too active of mind himself, with a body rarely inclined towards repose, he was well-acquainted with the hours that presaged dawn.

The November air was chill despite the fire, dank with yesterday's fog which permeated even the good York stone of Falgrave House. The air struck colder still from the large expanse of glass, but Abel never regretted the windows, installed ten years ago when their tax was repealed. Each day his sense of wonder was nourished by contemplating this wild seascape and a community established before the Viking invasion. Moon-washed now, the red roofs farther down the hill and across the harbour were angled curiously one against the other, their size, shape and height as diverse as the boats remaining at anchor.

Bare feet silent over the carpet, Abel crossed to stoke the fire. Grasping the poker, he paused with one foot on the brass fender, smiling once more. Gleaming like this, before

13

the flames snatched them, the coals shone as brilliantly as the jet that was his life.

From the next room he heard some sound, and was frowning as he returned to his wife in bed. These past six months their older daughter Hester had grown secretive. Last night he'd known she was troubled, but was uncertain how to approach her. Older than her seventeen years in the concentrated work she did, producing designs for their jet carvers, she was still his first little girl; he ached to help her.

On the other side of the stout wall, Hester felt relief slackening muscles tensed by hours of alarm. Jamie would be safe, sailing his father's boat into harbour over that flat calm sea. Awkwardly, her legs cramped from standing immobilised while she stared out beyond the darkened port, she finally moved towards the bed. Still wearing last evening's gown and too weary to struggle from its crinoline cage, she lay there, dark eyes closed, willing anxiety to cease. Somehow, she must regain sufficient energy for another day in the workshop.

Hester still hadn't slept when May Thorpe came in to place her hot water jug on the marble-topped washstand. She was too exhausted to care what the pert maid might think of her being dressed at five o'clock.

'Morning, Miss Hester. And a nice one it is, an' all. That nasty sea fret's gone.' May's plain face shone with her eager smile.

But it had only cleared during this past hour or two, thought Hester, or she'd have been less concerned for Jamie.

'That's good, May. Thank you,' she added, more sharply than usual. No sense in encouraging her to linger; the same age as herself, May risked asking questions. And servants, however obliging, talked.

Alone, Hester removed the pink silk gown with its black braid trimming, and extricated herself from the watch-spring steel foundation cage. The family workshop was no place for fancy clothes.

More self-confident than many of her contemporaries, she cared little that most days of the week she dressed less

14

well than some of the wives touting fish at the harbour. On occasions she even enjoyed her mother's reaction to her shabby garments.

Today when Hester had washed, dressed and hurried downstairs to breakfast, Maud Falgrave's glance travelled the length of the mahogany table and over her.

'Is that the best you can do with yourself? Your face looks as though you haven't slept – but if you have, that *thing* you've got on must have been with you in the bed.'

'There's another year's wear in this plaid, Mother. I think it's good enough for smothering in black dust.'

'You're still the boss's daughter, have you no pride?' Maud nibbled delicately at freshly-baked bread and honey. 'You'd not catch me showing myself in front of the workers with a skirt clinging round my ankles, looking like a dishrag.'

'Happen not, Mother, but I am doing a job there.' When you put in an appearance it's all for show, she added, but only to herself.

'Hester,' her father cautioned, but the girl was containing her thoughts. His brown eyes were tempered with understanding.

'Let her be, Abel,' said Maud with a tight smile. She liked her say, but didn't waste time over repetition. 'She's not as daft as she looks. And so long as *one* of us Falgraves shows them we have some standing I suppose we'll survive.'

'Standing matters a lot to your mother,' Abel confided to his daughter fifteen minutes later, after he had pulled on a double-breasted overcoat over his morning-coat and seized his new bowler hat.

Hester grinned. 'I do know that, Father. From the look of you today, it matters to you as well.'

Well-defined lips twitched beneath his moustache. 'I've an appointment at the bank, soon as I've checked all's well down yonder.'

They quickly left the drive of Falgrave House and were starting down the steep narrow street, between red-roofed houses that clutched the slopes, defying gravity which might topple them into the harbour at the mouth of the River Esk. It was only in snow, rain or hail that they used the brougham

15

bought nine years ago in 1852, when newly-introduced rubber tyres made Whitby's cobbles bearable.

Hester enjoyed the walk as much as her father, even on this keen November morning with frost as well as salt in the wind biting at face and fingers. Oil lamps glowed beyond windows lining gas-lit streets.

'Hester – ay, lass, thank goodness I've seen you!'

The woman darted from one of the many winding alleyways, so close to them that Hester almost stumbled into her. More agile than her bulk would suggest, and clad in an unfortunate red gown matching her fat cheeks, she continued backwards down the hill, still speaking.

'Did he tell you then, where he was making for?'

'Jamie?' Hester felt a surge of alarm. 'What's happened, Mrs Skelton? You'd better tell me.'

'I don't know, do I? That's what I'm saying. But he'd tell you, I know he allus does.'

And hadn't she been wishing all night long that Jamie didn't burden her with his plans? 'It'd help his dad, he said – help you all.'

'He's taken that smack out, hasn't he? I knew it. Dad would have it last night that the lad were gallivanting with his pals, but I knew different.'

'He's not home then?' Hester's early morning relief vanished.

'Would I be here if he were? I checked the boat an hour since – or where it's supposed to be moored.'

'He'll turn up, Mrs Skelton,' Abel Falgrave reassured her. 'The lad's handled yon smack since he was a nipper.'

Not on his own he hasn't, thought Hester grimly, wishing with all her heart that Jamie had less mettle and more sense.

'He thought to bring in a good catch,' she began, but Edna Skelton shrugged that away.

'We've managed somehow. All these weeks since my Archie broke his leg, we've managed. Jamie shouldn't ought to have gone risking his neck . . .'

'I'm sure there is no grave risk,' began Abel, but was interrupted by running footsteps. They all turned to face another twisting alleyway that they had just passed. 'What

16

do you bet that'll be the lad now, trying to make it home before you're up and doing.'

But the lad darting towards them was younger than Jamie Skelton – thin and ragged, his brown eyes wide with terror.

'Mister, come quick – there's a chap on t'cliffs. Stuck there, yelling his 'ead off.'

'Where? Show me . . .' Already Abel had turned and was haring off with the boy back along the alley.

A second's hesitation and Hester followed, blessing the men's boots she wore to work and skirts shortened to clear dusty floors.

'Nobody'll get at him from the bottom, you'll only reach him from top of t'cliff,' the lad panted, over his shoulder.

Inwardly, Abel groaned, hastening uphill between the last of the houses then striking off into the darkness to their left. The ground was uneven beneath his soles, its grass slithery with frost.

Silhouetted by the moon emerging from a cloud, the lad was pointing urgently as Abel, gasping, reached the headland.

'It's nobbut a bit of a narrow ledge where he's clung on . . .'

'Let's see.' Staggering a little over the rough turf, Abel caught up with him.

From above, the figure illuminated by moonlight was tiny, huddled into the cliff-face, one hand clawing repeatedly at rock and sparse vegetation, sending fragments scuttering down into the waves. And he'd ceased shouting for help. Abel guessed him almost finished by the cold, and by fright.

'Hester, Hester . . .' he called, urging her to hurry.

'Here, Father.'

Hypnotised by the hazard below, he spoke without turning. 'Fetch some ropes – there's that ship-chandler's in Church Street. Knock them up if they're not open. Quick, love, it's bad . . .'

Edna Skelton wouldn't leave her alone, chugged lumpily at her side. 'Is it him, is it?'

'I don't know, I'm sorry. And if I don't get a rope in time there's nobody will save him.'

17

In the chandler's Hester pushed past a couple of men provisioning for a voyage.

'Sorry, but there's trouble on the cliff. I need ropes and any help you can give.'

'Somebody been climbing again?' the proprietor asked, locating two strong ropes and thrusting them at her. 'I'll drop the latch, be after you in a tick.'

Jamie's mother had flopped on to a chair. Hester left her there, gathered breath again and chased along the cobbled street then, stumbling on tussocks, went out on to the headland.

Abel's overcoat, fashionable bowler and morning-coat were flung aside on the frosted grass. He was blowing on ice-numbed fingers.

'He's still hanging on,' he told her, snatching one rope.

'Is it . . . ?' she began, and stopped: she was better not knowing.

'I checked this rock while I was waiting,' Abel announced calmly, and began lashing the rope around a massive slab. 'We'll need help, though, you'll not hold my weight.'

'You could hold mine,' she suggested. 'That way, we'd manage.'

'Don't talk daft. As if I'd let you.'

'Well, you be careful, mind. Where's that boy gone?'

'Sent him for Dr Davidson.'

The chandler was coming anyway, breath rasping, as he hurtled towards them through the strong headwind.

'Young chap stuck, about a third of the way down,' Abel informed him, tying the rope around his middle. 'If you and our Hester lower me down, I'll transfer this rope to him. Once you've hauled him up you can take your time getting me to the top.'

'Oh, Father, do take care.' Suddenly this man who had loved her all her life was far more precious to Hester than any fellow part-way down that treacherous cliff, even Jamie Skelton.

But Abel was already out of sight, the rope tautening, burning their hands as it threatened to pull free.

'Hang on, I'll wind it round myself to take the strain,'

the chandler said. 'You just watch it isn't snaring on t'edge of t'cliff.'

Abel reached the ledge swiftly in a rush of stones and gravel, steadied himself, felt the rope slacken. 'Right,' he called, 'take up the slack, but not too tightly.'

He would need to manoeuvre the rope off himself and on to young Jamie. The easy way would have been to use the other rope, but Jamie was unconscious now, cold as a corpse already. Having the others secure the second rope would take minutes they dared not risk.

Just keep a steady head, that was all he must do – think only of this youngster who'd been his daughter's pal for years.

Rapidly, Abel loosened the noose that had worked up around his armpits, eased it over one arm and his head, then along the arm with which he leaned into the rock face.

Bending gingerly and praying the moon wouldn't disappear behind cloud, he raised first one of the lad's arms then the other, pushing the rope down firmly, tightening it over the saturated clothing about his waist. Pressing the entire side of his body into the cliff, he gradually inched himself clear of Jamie's insensible form.

'Right now,' he shouted. 'Start hauling.'

Awareness of waves breaking on the rocks far beneath came only once the inert lad was pulled upwards out of reach. Best not think of that, Abel silently cautioned himself, glancing up to watch Jamie's progress.

Grimy feet and ankles were all he could see now, as the others drew the lad over the cliff's edge. Abel shut his eyes, willed the ledge to hold out until the rope was lowered again.

The chunk of rock, dislodged as Jamie Skelton was dragged over and on to firm ground, struck Abel full on the shoulder. Falling, he heard Hester's scream soaring with the seagulls' screech.

Frank Clough sniffed, then wiped the sleeve of his blue smock across his face which already felt gritty with jet dust. He glanced sideways from the polishing wheel and raised an eyebrow at his father, Edwin.

'Not in yet, is she? Wondered how long it'd be before t'boss's lass started taking advantage . . .' Gentler treadling slowed the wheel.

'Nay, Frank, don't make your prejudice that obvious. She's worked here a good few years now, and toed the line – and well you know it.'

'Apprenticed, aye. Look what's happening now she's got a bit of freedom.' Legs working furiously, his treadle raced the wheel.

'Freedom? Nay, I doubt she'll get much of that. Abel Falgrave may be fair, but he's strict an' all. And as for t'missus . . .'

The other men laughed. Maud Falgrave was the one whose family had owned the jet workshop when it was opened up after the first few black pebbles were found on the beach and polished. Abel had bought into the business before their marriage, after being introduced there by the quantities of jet he'd mined, over at Runswick Bay.

'Happen we'd better look out,' Edwin Clough continued. 'If neither Mr Falgrave nor Miss Hester are coming in, you can bet your life Madam'll be checking on us.'

'Thought she concentrated on making that shop in Flowergate pay?' Wally Hardcastle remarked. A dour man, with grey hair and a complexion no more colourful, he liked to keep abreast of the situation. And was as incisive as the tool he used for faceting.

'Tha's reet,' Frank's younger brother Harold said, with a grin lighting green eyes. 'But they do employ a lass there nowadays, remember.'

'And you are not likely to forget that, eh?' his father baited him, without looking up from the pendant he was carving. 'Sally Drinkwater's as bonnie as any you'll see this side o' Scarborough.'

'Does our mam know you've noticed?' Frank chimed in, changing to polishing with the leather-covered shagboard.

Again, all the men laughed. Some choked afterwards, throats irritated this early in the day by dust from the jet they were honing.

'Drinkwater, you say?' somebody inquired. 'Not the Drinkwaters that come from Staithes?'

'Aye, they lived there once.'

'The family did well out of whaling – mind you, that were over thirty year since. Whaling's different now wi' them exploding harpoons.'

'And none of it going on round here nowadays.'

'The Drinkwaters set up fishing with just a couple of coble boats at after. 'Tisn't everybody allus benefits from change.'

'Happen not.' Edwin shook his head, not certain he approved of whaling anyway, despite all it had done for Whitby.

'I'm glad you're all at your benches or the wheels, any road, while you're gossiping like women mending their nets.'

Maud Falgrave's commanding voice was no less steady than normal, but when all attention in the workshop swung towards her, the silence was as potent as the loudest gasp. Maud Falgrave was broken. She'd never been even average in height, but today she'd shrivelled into a dot of a woman, old at forty. Her green shot-silk gown appeared to stand away from her, its crinoline skirt all that was holding her upright.

Edwin Clough remembered he was the foreman, and recovered sufficiently to find her a chair.

Maud dismissed it with a shake of her head, which loosened further the fair wisps of hair under her green beribboned bonnet. Very briefly, her lips worked, soundlessly. And then she swallowed.

'There – has been an accident. Mr Falgrave won't be in today.' Blue eyes searched Edwin's usual place, refocused, and located him still standing beside the chair he'd offered.

'I'm counting on you, Edwin Clough. Till we sort something out, this place'll have to run itself. I'll see wages are paid Friday, as usual, of course. Oh – and I'd be grateful if you'd send one of the apprentices down to the shop. I can't be spared to go tell the girl.'

Maud turned abruptly, bustled out of the workroom and down the stairs to the waiting carriage before the tears came.

'Get me home again, Kilner, fast as you can.'

It was because Abel wouldn't stop moithering that she'd consented to leave him in the doctor's care. Ever since he'd regained consciousness while they were bringing him into the house, he'd been worriting about the works. She couldn't have sent their Hester – the girl was incoherent with shock and distress. And besides, the doctor needed her answers to a lot of questions.

Kilner was slowing the horses outside the front portico of Falgrave House when Maud opened the door of the brougham.

'Madam, please – take care,' the elderly manservant began but Maud, staggering slightly as the carriage lurched, had already clambered down and was running for the steps.

Dr Jon Davidson met her in the oak-panelled hall, the expression in his blue eyes grave.

Maud clutched her throat, gulped. 'He's gone, hasn't he? I knew I should never have left him.' The words tumbled from lips so numb they no more belonged to her than the melodramatic speech they framed. But this was desperate, her man was . . .

'He's no worse than when you set out, my dear.' Taking her arm, the man who'd seen two of her four children into this world led Maud to the windowseat upholstered in red velvet.

'Unfortunately, though, he's no better either.'

'But – he will be, with time, care . . .' This was her Abel they were discussing, the man from whom she drew strength, the tireless spirit who infused her world with life.

Grimly, the doctor sighed, sought and failed to find phrases to ease the news. 'Your daughter told you where we found him?'

'The foot of the cliffs. Go on . . .' She could only hear it the once, though she sensed her entire life might not be long enough to learn to understand.

'The water there is but a foot or two deep, with nothing to break his fall.' He took her hand wishing, not for the first time, that doctors were granted some additional grace for imparting facts. 'It's his spine, my dear.'

'No, no!' She snatched from his grasp, covered her face. 'He'll not walk again, is that what you're saying?'

'I've requested another opinion, naturally. A specialist is on his way here now. But I think it's only sensible you should be prepared.'

'I'll see him now.'

To the doctor, Maud seemed to compose herself instantly. Tucking elusive strands of hair back into her bonnet, she erased the despairing lines that had wrinkled her face and straightened her shoulders. Walking behind her to the drawing room door, Jon Davidson failed to keep up.

'It'll be all right now, love,' Maud asserted, striding to the sofa where Abel lay immobile. 'The men were working already, as normal, and I've assured them they'll be paid on Friday. Later in the week, I'll see that stuff ready for sale is transferred into the shop. How are you feeling now, pet – any easier?'

Abel nodded. Even that hurt him, terrified him as well: his head was all he could move. 'Thanks, Maud love, you're a good 'un.'

She found his hand. It felt like cod straight from the fishmonger's marble slab, and had about as much strength to it. Severely, she willed herself to oust sentiment.

'Doctor tells me he's got a specialist coming. We'll soon have you up and about . . .'

Astonished, Abel was about to correct her, but happen she had to think this way. She was a strong woman, all right, but we all have our limits.

'Aye, aye. Most likely it's shock that's done it, shock to the system.'

The doctor noticed their daughter who'd sat, wordless, at her father's side since they'd brought him home. The girl was shaking so much he was surprised the chandelier above her head wasn't rattling. And her face was the waxy pallor of the candles it contained, a sharp contrast with her dark glossy hair. It was Hester's eyes that disturbed him the most, though. Their brown had turned as black as the jet the family worked.

'Hester – I want to talk to you.'

She couldn't rise without Dr Davidson's help, and a lump came into his throat. He'd always thought of himself as

23

bear-like and for once was glad of the bulk that could offer reassurance to this tall, slender girl.

'It's all my fault,' she blurted, once they were out in the cold hall.

'Nay, nay, Hester – don't.'

'But it is, it is. If I'd stopped Jamie taking the boat out, he'd never have gone aground in the fog, he'd not . . .'

'And since when did any young fellow take heed of a lass, even someone he's been friends with most of his life?'

'I could have made him listen, should have,' Hester persisted, as May Thorpe appeared and opened the parlour door.

'I think some tea is required for Miss Hester, don't you,' Jon Davidson suggested to the maid, as he led Hester through and to a sofa by the fire.

'He'd not have had to swim ashore, wouldn't have got himself stuck on the cliffs.'

'Aye, well – Jamie Skelton'll not forget that experience in a hurry. I've made him aware he's lucky to survive exposure as severe as last night's.'

'And but for my father he'd have been the one who plummeted into the sea.'

'Aye.' He sat beside her and managed a smile, albeit a grave one. 'That means you've a special role now, you know. There's only you can show your father that what he did justified the consequences. And it's you, as well, that must ease the lad of his guilt.'

'Me? There's no hope of that. I'm not the girl I was this morning, even though I'd spent the night pacing the room on account of Jamie. I've had the stuffing knocked out of me, it'll take some replacing. The Falgraves are finished, Doctor, that's how I see it.'

'Not surprising. Shock does terrible things. But the body has a marvellous way of reconstructing itself. And you're strong women – you and your mother, both. It's the two of you that'll carry the lot of you through this trouble.'

'My mother, yes. She's the size of two pennorth o'copper, but that's the only thing small about her. I'm not like her, Doctor. If you only knew – I'm the most anxious person there is.'

'Today, maybe, today. And that's excusable.'

'My father's not going to get better, is he?'

'It's not three hours since the accident, love . . .'

'All right, all right.' She closed her eyes, sighed. When she had swallowed, Hester spoke again. 'Will he live?'

'He must have a strong constitution to have survived this far.'

'One thing I can do is help look after him. That'll be my work from now on.'

'If that's what he and your mother wish. You'd not like to distress them, I'm sure.'

'There'll be nowt else, will there? The workshop will have to be sold.' In giving the works his name, Abel Falgrave had stamped his personality on the business. Hester had been told often enough that her mother's family had started it up, but could never really accept it had an existence without her father.

'Time will tell, my dear, time will tell. Now, you'll not waste this pot of tea, I'm hoping.'

May Thorpe was staggering in with a tray full of cakes, daintily buttered bread and scones, as well as the silver teapot and china. Hester tried to smile and nod appreciatively as her mother would have done, yet all the while she felt sick.

'Thank you, May.'

The girl's oval face was tear-streaked, her lip quivered, and she darted from the room.

Briefly, Hester itched to follow, to run and run until everything that had happened today was far behind her. Fighting for control, she gazed around. All she saw was the silk brocatelle curtains, the new armchairs with their elegantly-curved upholstery and thin metal frames, the marquetry tables. And all she wanted was to smash the lot, to stop its refinement mocking their catastrophe.

'Perhaps just the tea,' Jon Davidson said, 'and perhaps I'll pour.'

'Thank you. You see what a state my hands are in.'

'I'd order you to bed, if I didn't know you'd disobey me. But it'll be a long day, Hester, so don't be too hard on yourself.'

25

She recalled the doctor's words that evening when she and her mother sat at one end of the long dining table, each for the other's sake attempting to eat. Is this how it's going to be now, Hester wondered, with no one daring to voice their appalling thoughts. And with the empty chair where Abel Falgrave's spirited conversation had enlivened every meal.

A minute ago she'd nearly choked trying to check a sob, and only because she'd looked at the sideboard where the gas-light was glinting off the decanters and their stoppers. Each stopper was the figure of a small boy, perfectly crafted in silver; one holding grapes, another a pair of goblets and the third, a wine bottle. Her father had bought and treasured them.

'The children took it well,' Maud remarked. 'I'm thankful the doctor volunteered to tell them.' Olive was only thirteen and had cried when she came home from school to the news. Watching tears streaming from serious blue eyes would have cracked her own control.

'He's done a lot for us today, hardly left the house till tonight.'

'Our Bernard was a right little man . . .'

'Yes, for a lad of eleven, he has a lot of thought.'

He had come to his mother, taken her hand, and all the while his dark eyes were stretched wide against the tears. 'We'll manage, you'll see,' he'd asserted.

Both children had been less composed after seeing their father. In the room with him, though, they had listened seriously, nodding energetically when Abel roused sufficiently to assure them he wouldn't always be flat on his back.

'I just wish there'd been a bit of hope,' Maud confided to her daughter, as they pushed away half-full plates. 'I could have cried my eyes out when that specialist from the hospital came and went, and only confirmed what we feared.'

'Happen Dr Davidson would know of somebody in London who'd advise.'

'I never thought of that . . .' Tired eyes brightened in her mother's grey face.

'We haven't had much time for thinking yet – not sensibly, any road. I never imagined shock could make you so debilitated.'

'Lucky we're neither of us given to swooning, eh, Hester?'

'It is that! I just wish it didn't feel so nightmarish, like being trapped in the grim bits of a book by one of the Brontës or Dickens.'

'We'll have no time for reading now. Though why I should think of a daft thing like that tonight, I don't know. Nothing matters now save keeping the workshop going. And keeping your father as happy as . . .'

'Happy? Nay, Mother. We'll none of us ever be happy again.'

'That's defeatist talk and I won't have it, do you hear?'

Hester stood up, too exhausted to endure any more.

Maud Falgrave wasn't deterred. 'Your father's alive, that's what counts. And we're going to keep him alive. He's my husband – the man who's made you four with me,' she added, outspoken even for her. 'So long as there's breath in my body, I'll not let him go.' She paused, but only to gather in air. 'And I'll tell you another thing – I'll see he doesn't get downhearted. Because that would be the finish of him.'

Chapter 2

The covered barouche rumbled over the cobbled streets, its horses steaming in rain almost as drenching as if the North Sea itself were invading the land. At the drive of Falgrave House the coachman slowed but only in concession to the awkward curve, and presently reined in precisely that Cecil Arkwright might place his expensively-shod feet on the first of the steps leading up to the door.

'Wait there, Dobson,' Mr Arkwright ordered, pausing beneath the portico built in the style of Palladio which was the only relief to the austere lines of the house. This business would be concluded swiftly, he felt sure, and he did not mean to delay afterwards while his coachman was summoned from the servants' quarters.

The jangling bell brought a tired-looking maid to the door, a girl who hadn't troubled to disguise that she had been weeping.

'I am sorry to learn of the accident yesterday,' he told her, offering his calling card. 'If your mistress is at home, I would like a word with her. I shall not detain her long.'

May glanced around for the carved jet salver normally kept on the long walnut side-table. Unable to see it, she took the card as it was, invited him inside to wait and loped away to find the housekeeper, Mrs Richmond.

'There's a Mr Arkwright here, wants to see Madam. Whatever shall I tell him, Mrs Richmond?'

The middle-aged housekeeper sighed and pushed at her abnormally straggly hair. 'Ay, I wish I knew.' She had been confounded by the tragedy affecting the household. Nothing in all her years in service had prepared her for this. 'We can only ask her, I suppose. I'll have to do it. You get on with seeing to the beds.'

The master, although in considerable pain, was proving he still had a will of his own. Everyone else, the doctor included, had decided a bed should be made up in one of the downstairs rooms. There were enough of those, after all, and one reception room would not be missed.

Abel Falgrave had roared his disapproval. 'I'll sleep in my own bed of a night.' He'd not relinquish every scrap of the life he knew.

'And in the daytime?' his wife had ventured.

'We shall see. I'll accept that, for a day or two, rest must be the order. After that – well, I'll not be cooped up in any one room the remainder of my days. There's – there's that contraption hoists our meals up from the kitchens. We'll have it strengthened to take my weight, extended somehow to reach the upstairs landing. Get somebody in today, if you can, Maud, to start work.'

Maud Falgrave had come smiling from her husband's side, suddenly having found much that was recognisable in his strangely-inert form. This compensated for his new sharpness. Mrs Richmond was less delighted. She could imagine the mess constructing some kind of a hoist would make, and the havoc of having workmen about the place.

'What is it now?' Maude inquired wearily, looking up from the difficult letter she was writing to her favourite son, Lambert.

'It's Mr Arkwright, Madam, Mr Cecil Arkwright. He didn't say why he's here.'

Maud didn't trouble to glance at the proffered card. 'He doesn't need to say. I can guess.' She'd half-expected he would make an approach, though not this soon. Arkwrights' had been attempting to buy out the Falgraves since they'd both displayed jet jewellery ten years ago at the Great Exhibition. 'I'll see him, of course, but don't send in a tray. He'll not be stopping long enough for tea to brew.'

Cecil Arkwright's frockcoat and the top hat he surrendered to Mrs Richmond confirmed Maud's assumption that the visit was formal. He inquired about Abel immediately after greeting her, but there was no real pretence that concern was his reason for coming.

'Do sit down,' she suggested, and wasn't surprised that he didn't follow her example of taking the nearest chair.

From his prematurely white hair to his fashionable ankle boots, Mr Arkwright was a commanding figure. He wouldn't be unaware of this, and he'd never in the past failed to snatch the slenderest advantage. He economised now over the words expressing sympathy, and stated his purpose just as Maud was tempted to voice it for him.

'You'll not manage the works now, I'm thinking, and should be thankful to be relieved of one burden. I'll pay a fair price and guarantee all your workers their jobs. I could take the shop in Flowergate off your hands as well.'

'You might,' Maud responded, buckling a smile on to lips that still threatened to tremble. 'But for one consideration, you might do as you propose. The fact is, Mr Arkwright, we Falgraves have no intention of selling out, none whatsoever.'

'You'll never manage . . .'

'Oh, but we will. Even if his recovery proves incomplete, my husband will still control some aspects of the business. And for the rest – we're a family accustomed to hard work, and we work well together.'

Keen grey eyes narrowed as Arkwright tried to read beyond her resolute expression. 'Are you telling me your eldest son is coming home to assist, quitting his regiment?'

Momentarily, Maud lowered her eyelids. She'd not have Cecil Arkwright suspect she doubted Lambert's capacity for sacrifice. 'Whether or not our son decides that leaving the Grenadier Guards would be justified is a matter for the future. You will realise that twenty-four hours has not been long enough for the news to reach him.'

'So, you may be required to think again, if he remains where he is.'

'You cannot have understood me fully, Mr Arkwright. True Yorkshire folk are used to cutting their coat according to their cloth – and that applies equally to the resources available in pursuing their line of business. Some might call it making-do but I consider it exploiting everything and everybody accessible, to the limit.'

Ensuring that her smile was anchored in place, Maud rose to her full four feet and eleven inches.

'It was kind of you to call on us, Mr Arkwright, but I know you will forgive me now if I devote my time to more constructive matters.'

Willing her legs not to reveal her exhaustion, she hastened across to the watered silk bell-pull. She was thankful when Mrs Richmond herself reappeared to escort her visitor out. May Thorpe was a good enough girl, but hardly prepossessing.

'Sent him away with his smile wiped off his face,' Maud exclaimed a few minutes later when she joined Abel to familiarise him with events.

'Sent who away?' he asked. He had been dozing, trying to escape the pain which Jon Davidson's medication did not eradicate, but most of all avoiding the prospect of lifelong frustration.

'That Cecil Arkwright. I knew either him or his brother would jump at the chance to try and make us sell – though I thought they might have had the grace to allow us a day or so to sort ourselves out.'

'And you dispatched him with an incontrovertible "no".'

'I did that! It's the first thing I've enjoyed since yesterday morning.' She crossed to sit beside his makeshift bed.

'You do realise though, Maud, that continuing might prove impossible.'

'I'll need a lot of convincing. And besides, we don't know for sure that nothing can be done to set you on your feet again. It's far too early to look on the black side.'

'Someone responsible will have to keep an eye on the day-to-day running of the workshop, you know. Edwin Clough's a good foreman – I've no doubts about him opening the place and locking up, doling out the work to the others – but he'll not do more than that.'

'I'll be going there frequently, shan't I? I shall look in later today, once we've got you settled in that bed upstairs. And Hester's there every day, isn't she?'

'She's too young for assuming authority. And when she's working on a design she'd not notice anybody, not if they were standing on their head beside her.' He couldn't contemplate that lass of his taking on work that should rightly be his own.

'All the same, love, she'll *be there*. Family. The men'd not try owt on in front of her.'

If only Lambert would come home, his father thought,

but refrained from mentioning the possibility. Their eldest was ambitious, a young fellow to be proud of. It was unfortunate that his ambitions lay elsewhere. And Maud already cared too much, however privately, that Lambert chose to live away.

'Where's our Hester today?' He'd expected to see her before this.

'She's tired out by the look of her, so I let her sleep. She had a nasty shock as well, and she'd looked very pale yesterday first thing.'

'And you told May not to waken me, didn't you?' Hester was in the doorway now, her smile for them both brilliant. 'You needn't have, I'm quick to recover.'

She crossed swiftly to kiss each in turn, lingered with a slender hand behind her father's dark head.

'Any better, Papa? Any less pain?'

'Somewhat easier, thanks. But you're dressed for work – deserting us already?' He couldn't help resenting her being able to go there.

'If I go in, Mother isn't compelled to. It won't hurt for the men to have one Falgrave around.'

Her parents exchanged a glance and Maud smiled.

'You were hoping I would, weren't you?' Hester felt warm deep inside her because this was something she could do. The night had convinced her that rebellion against what had happened would help no one.

'Not precisely,' Abel told her. Hope was an emotion which he was learning could bear little relation to his circumstances.

Her mother interrupted. 'I'll admit to preferring to remain here, at least until the doctor's been again to ensure your father's safely installed upstairs . . .'

The bell by the main entrance jangled again as Hester went from the room into the hall.

Maud bustled after her. 'You'd best get back in there. We want no callers seeing you in your working clothes.'

Jamie Skelton was more miserable than he'd ever been in his life. Yesterday, he'd been sent home in somebody's carriage and, after the doctor's examination, ordered to rest.

Surprisingly, he had slept. Admittedly, there'd been dreams – a vivid re-living of trying to steer through the fog, of running the smack on to the rocks. Worse still, memory had reconstructed his impotent attempt at swimming in the cold of the North Sea with limbs so numb they felt dead. The rest of it, struggling to scramble up the cliffs, was still in as much of a fog within his head as the eerie white blanketing that had settled over the water. The one thing he wouldn't forget, ever, was that scream of Hester's when her old man plummeted downwards.

He was awake early today, went barefooted down the uncarpeted wooden stair from the large room shared by the nine Skelton children. His father Archie was still in the bed that had been made up in a corner of the living room since the day weeks ago when he'd been brought ashore with a broken leg.

His mother was at the stone scullery sink, washing hands, face, and the bit of neck that showed above her old red gown.

'Are you all right, love?' she inquired, drying herself on her coarsely woven apron as she turned from the sink.

'Aye, I expect so.' Why did she ask such *daft* questions? Couldn't she tell he'd never be right again. And never is eternity when you're nobbut seventeen.

'Why don't you ask how I am?' his father snapped from the bed. 'Wasn't being laid up enough? Did you have to break up my livelihood into t'bargain?'

'The boat mightn't have broken up . . .' Jamie ventured.

'That's all you know. Do you think I haven't found out? Do you really think I'd just sit here, wondering? While you were sleeping off t'effects of yon stupid trick . . . I might be stuck here wi' this lot, but I do have friends, tha knows. Us fishermen stick together when times are bad.'

Jamie swallowed, looking away from the man in a rumpled nightshirt. Crying like a lass wouldn't help, unless that was what his father wanted of him.

'Smashed her up proper, didn't you? Holed her right through till t'sea poured in and forced every plank of that boat apart. Aye, and t'rigging came crashing down through the lot, an' all. There isn't one bit of it worth fetching home for firewood.'

'I did say I'm sorry . . .'

'Sorry doesn't mend nowt.'

'Won't the insurance . . . ?'

'Insurance? Don't talk to me about insurance.'

Jamie caught his mother's warning glance. Sighing, he headed for the door. His father's wrath, however justifiable, was bad enough but infinitely harder to bear was the knowledge that the injury Hester's father had suffered was his responsibility.

'You're not going out without breakfast?'

His mother, bless her, still cared, if only automatically, because she'd done nothing else through the years that produced his five sisters and three small brothers.

'I don't want anything.'

'Give me a hand then, before you go. I can hear our Maurice on the stairs, the others'll not be far behind. With all your arguefying I've got nowt done.'

You're making me your excuse, thought Jamie, knowing that the household existed in a permanent state of disorganisation. And yet, until his father's accident the reigning chaos had been happy. Even now, the children running to take their places standing around the table were smiling.

Following Maurice who was four, Sylvie skipped on thin grubby feet, her gappy grin embracing the siblings coming after her. Only seven years old herself, she had a motherly way with all but the three oldest of the family, and watched over the children now as they pressed in closely together. Joanie was last again, but although she was nine she needed helping a lot.

Sylvie flashed her a smile across the table, but Harry on one side of her and Maisie on the other were leaning on Joanie's arms. There was little enough room as it was, now she struggled to thrust her solid body at the table edge. Her flattish face registered frustration, the rather oriental eyes dulled.

Jamie was also watching. 'Don't . . .' A firm hand on Maisie's shoulder, the other on Harry's collar, Jamie widened the space between them. 'There you are, Joanie.'

Sylvie beamed at him.

At least one person didn't altogether condemn him. That had been the worst thing, last night. As the others came upstairs and crossed the worn, splintering boards they had whispered, thinking he was asleep. Dollie was ten and had grasped most of what had happened, especially the fact that Jamie had destroyed their father's boat. To hear her talk, you'd have believed that was what he'd set out to do.

'I suppose I'll have to work even harder now, else we'll all starve.' That had been Jessie who worked curing herrings, hated the job, and insisted that she was going into service. Jamie hated Jess, prayed she would go quickly.

Now, Maurice reached scrawny arms across the table to the pile of bread already curled at the edges.

'Not yet, you don't!' Armed with a flannel in each hand, Edna Skelton missed nothing. ''Ere, you – make yoursen useful.'

Jamie found the slimy cloth thrust into his fingers. He was told to start with Nat. He didn't mind that – the baby of the family, Nat was, after Sylvie, Jamie's favourite. Perhaps because he hadn't endured so long of the Skelton frugal living, his limbs and the face upturned for washing were still rounded.

'Don't take all day, our Jamie,' Edna snapped. 'See to Harry now, and Joanie's picking her nose.'

Ignoring instructions, Jamie kissed Nat's firm red lips and stroked the glowing ginger hair that marked them all as kin.

'Where's the comb, Mother?' From the square at the top of the cellar steps that served as a scullery, Jessie addressed Edna in the voice she considered better-class, the voice she would use when welcoming smart visitors brought in a fine carriage to someone else's grand home.

'Ay, I don't know, love. Have a look on the bed, your father might have been . . .'

'What do I want combing my hair for? Unable to get about, and now no prospect of work if I do get better,' Archie Skelton sniffed, glanced around at his family, the rows of mucky little ankles and feet sticking out beneath frocks washed and handed down and washed again since

Jamie was put into breeches. 'What'll you do next, I wonder, James? How are you going to provide for your brothers and sisters now you've smashed up our livelihood?'

Jamie had crossed the stone flags and was out through the door before his father finished speaking. He would get work. Any kind, preferably on a merchant ship sailing today from Whitby, and he'd not keep a penny he earned for himself. First, though, before all that, he must tackle something more alarming.

He left behind the narrow house near the harbour, crammed in with others that were no more than hovels and all smelling of that same flooding occurring regularly. The alley smell was worse, centuries of chamberpots having drained through its gulleys. Today's downpour might have seemed a blessing, if he'd been wearing more than a shirt and breeches. But he'd not turn back now, might find seaboots at least in the Skelton boathouse.

Jamie's unhappiness deepened. It should have been so different. He'd pictured it all, the way he would come home with the biggest catch the Skeltons had set eyes on in years. He'd have made his father proud, would have watched Mam cooking as she never had before, but only after he'd sold the bulk of what he'd caught. That way he'd have taken home good money as well as the fresh, gleaming fish for their bellies.

Now he was on his own, disgraced, already missing the bright hair and eyes that cluttered up the house so's you could neither breathe nor think your own thoughts, missing the children that were his family. And the sea scared him. It never had in the past. Since he was a little lad, he'd put out in the Skelton boat, weathering high seas, storms, lightning that skimmed the waves towards him. But that was before he'd thought to put out on his own. Before he proved his own stupidity.

Captain James Cook had started in a small way too, though, so happen if Jamie really set his mind to it *he* might become somebody – somebody like his hero. But only if he managed, somehow, to conquer this new dread of the sea.

Turning left towards the quay, he entered the boathouse which was really no more than a shed where they kept their tackle. His own boots were gone with the wreck and his father's were too large, but an improvement on nothing.

Jamie struggled to pull them on over feet wet from the downpour. He was going to look like one of the chaps who dossed in doorways of shops or at the back of an inn. Did that matter, though? Hester'd never give him the time of day now, never mind continue their friendship.

And he'd miss that even more than he'd miss his brothers and sisters. They had met ten years ago when Hester attended a private school out towards Mulgrave Castle. One day she'd run away and he'd found her when he left the dame's school at tea-time. She'd been worn out with walking back into Whitby by that time, and determinedly *not* crying.

Looking back, Jamie realised that must have been one of the few occasions when he was presentably dressed. Hester's mother had been so relieved that her little girl was safe, she'd created no substantial obstructions to the unlikely friendship that developed between the pair during the years that followed. Jamie was never invited into Falgrave House, but had no regrets about that; the prospect alone would have alarmed him.

And Hester could be as inventive as he himself, when need be, so they'd always succeeded in contriving to meet, and more frequently than anyone suspected.

He wished today that he *had* been beyond the steps of Hester's home. He might not be so paralysed with dread now, numb right through with a chill even worse than the rain beating down from skies as black as the ruined abbey.

The house was in sight now, bigger than ten of his own put together. Furnished exquisitely, he'd heard, with expensive stuff. Its good solid stone held numerous windows – so t'Falgraves could look down on ordinary folk, his father always sneered. He'd known his father was wrong, hadn't needed Abel Falgrave to prove his concern yesterday.

It was too late now.

He opened one of the wrought-iron gates and began to walk up the drive. These boots leaked, letting in as much wet as they kept out, squelching with every step. But if he grew more inhibited by the picture he must present, he'd never get through that door.

There was an iron bellpull. Jamie hesitated, steeling himself, before disturbing the household with its clanging.

Hester herself opened the door. He'd never been more relieved.

'Jamie . . . you're wet through!'

'Doesn't matter. I came – ' Already he halted, choked. 'I've got to thank your father. That's if . . . how bad is he?'

'He's alive, Jamie, not much more. He's conscious, though. I'll see if . . .'

'He'll see you, lad.' Mrs Falgrave was in the doorway of one of the front rooms to the left of this large entrance hall. Far smaller than he was, she nevertheless made him feel as nervous as he'd been at the age of seven. 'This way, he's in here.'

'But . . .' He glanced down at his sodden boots. They were making grimy puddles on the marble floor. The other side of that burnished door there was carpet. If he took the boots off, they'd stare at his mucky feet.

'Well, are you coming, or aren't you?' Mrs Falgrave asked.

While he was finding words she spoke again, to Hester. 'Kilner will be waiting with the brougham. It's more than time you were down at the works.'

As Hester said goodbye to her mother and to Jamie, his alarm grew. He'd relied on speaking with her first, explaining to her his sorrow. Then he forgot his dripping garments, failed to notice the fine Wilton carpet that soaked up like sponge the water issued by his boots. Abel Falgrave might have been dead, he lay that still beneath the expensive-looking covers. And in a rush the memory came back to Jamie of how strong those arms had been, fixing the rope around his useless body. Until now, he hadn't considered that he'd been other than unconscious during that rescue. Now he knew he'd recognise again the grasp that had held him on that ledge on the cliffs, the touch of a finely-woven cuff as it brushed his wrist, the scent of a recent cigar.

'I've come to thank you,' he gabbled, 'and to say how –

38

how very sorry I am that it turned out the way it has. It –
I don't think it were owt I did as sent that rock falling . . .'

'I know that, lad, I know. You were in no fit state to help
yourself.' I've always loathed the cliff-face, Abel added to
himself, ever since the day I was made to dangle from a
rope, hacking into a seam of jet. Nobody ever persuaded
me to try that method of reaching it again.

'I wish there was summat I could do. Don't know what
to say.'

'Never mind. What's done's done.' *Saying* the necessary
words was easy enough, he didn't have to express what he
was feeling.

'But . . .'

'I appreciate your coming. T'wouldn't be easy.'

'If there's owt I can do . . .'

But Maud Falgrave had listened in the doorway. Her
blue silk crinoline brilliant against the dullness of the day,
she came into the room like a full-masted schooner.

'That will be all, James, for now. Mr Falgrave must be
permitted rest.'

In the hall, she closed the door of the room behind her
and glanced up at him, the eyes matching her dress hard.

'You will understand that we do not wish another visit
from you. In reconstructing our lives we look to avoid
reminders of what has happened.'

Hopes of finding some means of demonstrating his gratitude and his distress drained through the soles of Jamie's
feet. She had the front door open. He could only remove
himself from this embarrassment.

Hester was waiting in the brougham, having instructed
Kilner that they would drop off their visitor in the town.

Her voice was unchanged from the voice that had
charmed childhood and his teens, and he'd had more than
he could take already. Jamie could only clamp his lips together, shake his head and run.

He didn't slow to a walk till he was close to the quayside.
The alleys he'd taken were carefully chosen, too narrow for
any carriage.

Sam Grinsdale, one of his father's cronies, was putting
out in a dirty boat that bore witness to his shiftlessness.

'Need a hand?' Jamie shouted, unsurprised that nobody else would crew for the man. It got him out to sea again, made him face it.

Remains of the previous catch had seeped into the deck, deeper than the downpour might clear. The smell combined with his nervousness, making him sweat despite the sting of the rain. Before they were out of sight of the harbour mouth, and on the calmest water he'd experienced, Jamie was sick.

The men were singing against the noise of the treadles driving grinding wheels, polishing boards and brushes, as Hester began the climb up the steep stair to the workshop. Just for a while she resented their lightheartedness – didn't they understand about her father? But then they always were a cheerful bunch, or had cause to be these past few years. They'd done well since the Great Exhibition, better still with Queen Victoria wearing jet jewellery, even at a banquet, in mourning for her cousin.

The singing ceased before she reached the top and she regretted the change generated by the sound of her approach.

'It's only me,' she began, opening the wooden door and wondering if she'd always acknowledged in this way the common dread of her mother.

'How's Mr Falgrave then today, Miss Hester?' Edwin Clough inquired. Being foreman justified his being spokesman.

Hester smiled, and noticed how taut her face felt from the hours of suppressed emotion. 'He seems a little easier, thank you.'

'You'll tell him as how we was asking?'

'I will indeed.' Removing her dark brown cloak, she went to hang it in the narrow area partitioned off to serve as the office. She kept on her three year old bonnet, needing that as much as the assorted hats the men wore to protect their hair. 'That'll please him.'

Less pleasing would be the paperwork accumulating here on the brown wooden desk. It wasn't two days since the accident and already there were accounts to be settled for deliveries of jet from the mines. There were notes, as well, of completed jewellery transferred to the shop.

'Did you check in the fresh supplies, Mr Clough?' The rough jet wasn't necessarily all of the same quality, nor indeed from the same source. Usually discovered in horizontal seams no more than six inches thick, it was hewn with a pick: some from 'jet holes' deep in the local hills, some from the face of the cliffs themselves.

'I did and all, very particular like. We're not having anybody unloading any sort of old muck on us, just because Mr Falgrave's not here.'

'That's right. Thank you. And the stuff that went along to Flowergate?'

'Listed piece by piece, like it allus is. And checked and signed for by young Sally when our Harold delivered.'

'Good.' If the men managed as well as this, she and Mother would see to writing up the books, settling accounts. There was her designing, though. 'Have you started on those new beads, Jeff?'

Jeff Hardcastle was an apprentice, learning turning and about as agreeable as his father, Wally. He was more colourful, though, possessing a head of glorious hair the shade of the nearby sands.

'Aye – nearly finished 'em by now.' He hadn't, but he resented this lass no older than himself poking her nose in. Resented everything she was, come to that. Walking in here, after her private schooling, only serving a bit of an apprenticeship, because she was the boss's daughter. *And* because of that being allowed to work on the creative part of the job. He was being made to work under supervision at each of the different tasks in the workroom. What had he to look forward to? Once they were satisfied with his turning, he'd be tackling grinding. He'd like to see her muckying herself at the grinding wheel that gave each piece its shape.

He moved only fractionally aside so she could inspect his work. Just dare to criticise, he silently challenged her; it wouldn't take much to incite him to tell her what he thought. A man could do what she was doing here, a man who otherwise had no hope of earning.

41

'Satisfactory then?' he demanded, while she examined the beads he'd produced. Edwin Clough was giving him a look from the bench over yonder. Not that he cared – his father had the measure of Edwin Clough, foreman or not, if need be . . .

'They seem all right,' said Hester, determined not to enthuse over work grudgingly produced by a lad who hadn't the sense just to be glad he was learning a good craft. Didn't he appreciate that he was working *jet*? Surely he knew its long history, that even in the Bronze Age jet was used for adornment?

She noticed the dust then, all around Jeff, thicker than normal on all the sturdy benches, deeper still on the floor where its particles crunched beneath her boot soles.

'You haven't swept up, have you? I doubt if this place has been swept since my father was in.'

Frowning, Edwin Clough was following her gaze then looking straight at Jeff again.

Worried, Hester crossed to Edwin. 'Can I talk to you, please?'

They went into the office together and Hester closed the door. 'You know what my father would say, don't you?'

'Aye – and I've seen a fire that flared when jet dust caught light long afore I came to work here. I don't need telling it's a hazard.'

'But I thought it was your responsibility to see . . .'

'Look, Miss Falgrave – I've no quarrel with any of you. I'll do all I can to help now. But yesterday, like I said, I was checking in t'new supplies; after that, making sure the jewellery for the shop was all right.'

'Perhaps this is the time for someone else to share your duties.'

'There's no need for that,' Edwin told her firmly.

'I'm not insinuating you're not capable, you know,' said Hester gently. 'I'm only suggesting possible ways of easing your responsibility.' Some workshops had a second foreman.

'Aye – well, there'll be no need. I don't like sweeping up being overlooked any more nor you do. I'll see it's done regular.'

'Thank you, Mr Clough. Now, if there's any more invoices that require attention, I'll take them with these. I'm on my way down to Flowergate, as Mother hasn't time to see to the shop today. I might call back in here on my way up to the house,' she added, aware that she ought to have remained longer.

The men had unnerved her. She'd been conscious for some while that Wally Hardcastle and that son of his would never take to her designing any of the jewellery. Jeff, in common with many of the apprentices, had been encouraged to learn drawing as a means of developing any talent for designing. And Jeff was showing considerable aptitude.

The lad was obliged, nevertheless, to familiarise himself with all aspects of the work before Abel Falgrave would consider his attempting any diversification. Hester could understand the Hardcastles' resentment. She herself had served only a token apprenticeship. But where in the whole of Whitby had any other girl done more than work on the periphery of the industry? She knew, and the men knew, that if she hadn't been Maud Falgrave's daughter the situation would have been very different. Hadn't Maud's father started up the workshop, taught by a cousin who learned jet carving in the first workroom set up by Captain Tremlett in the early 1800s?

Although abnormally eager to get away, Hester paused for a moment, looking around her, trying to recapture the delight she'd always experienced just watching how skilfully the workers transformed the rough jet. Frank Clough was hand-engraving the polished surface of a brooch, his father carving a cameo pendant, in relief. Their knives looked similar from this distance, but the way they were held identified each separate task. Wally Hardcastle, using rouge on one of the wooden wheels, was gradually bringing a brilliant shine to a cross for a church in London.

Out in the street, Hester drew her cloak tightly around her. The rain was less heavy now, but still enough to produce a thorough wetting. And she had sent Kilner and the carriage back to the house. Her father seemed determined something would be done that day about installing some kind of contraption for conveying him from one floor to the next. No doubt by now her mother would be receiving instructions to locate someone capable of this task.

Hastening along narrow roads and down steep ginnels between all sizes of houses, shops and inns, Hester was in no mood for catching glimpses of the harbour with the sea beyond which normally delighted her, nor the ruined abbey dominating the East Cliff. Eventually, she passed the top of the alley where Jamie Skelton lived.

Her general unease intensified with this reminder of Jamie's arrival at the house that morning. And his swift departure. Knowing her mother, Hester could guess that she wouldn't have withheld her opinion as to why he should not call there again.

If only Jamie weren't so stubborn. If he'd consented to ride with her into the town here, she would have assured him that although naturally distressed by her father's accident she'd not condemn Jamie. Whatever her family might say, *she* had a mind of her own, would never stop seeing him.

Hadn't Jamie's spirit been the quality she'd most admired from that first day when they both were children? Visiting his home, she always came away marvelling that he'd not been crushed by the poverty, and such overcrowding that he seemed devoid of space in which to be himself. And only this week, despite intense anxiety caused by his taking out that boat alone, she'd been thrilled as well by the determination with which he was tackling a night's solitary fishing.

The familiar Falgrave shop, its windows glinting with their jewellery, jolted Hester back to the present and, not sorry to try and push Jamie's exploit to the back of her mind, she opened its door.

Sally Drinkwater beamed at her across the glass top of the display counter she was polishing.

'Hallo, Miss Falgrave – didn't expect to see you here today. I'll just finish this,' she added, breathing on the glass and giving it a final rub. Smiling, she nodded at Hester's greeting whilst replacing the mats of soft kid on which Falgraves showed their best pieces to clients.

'There's no hurry, Sally. I only thought to check that there are no problems here.'

'None as I know of, Miss – unless it's having no customers. But it's a real November day, isn't it.' Abruptly, Sally halted her chatter and sadness overtook her pretty china-doll features. 'But listen to me, going on and never asking . . . Is Mr Falgrave any better?'

Hester gnawed her lip, unsure how to answer. Sally was her own age and always seemed different from their other employees. Still, she must remember her position. If she said too much, news of the severity of her father's condition would spread to the workroom and might panic the men into leaving.

'He's in less pain, thank you, Sally. And he appeared brighter this morning.'

'I do hope as it won't be long before he's recovered. We all do, Miss Falgrave.'

Sally's azure eyes were riveted on Hester's face, their concern telling her that she knew full well how vain that hope might prove.

Hester straightened her shoulders and resisted the powerful urge to sink on to the chair reserved for customers.

'I meant to check the window display before coming in but my mind was occupied elsewhere. Now . . .'

'You can inspect it just as well here in the dry, can't you, Miss?' Smiling again, Sally opened up the wooden shutters separating the window from the shop itself.

Suddenly realising how exhausted she felt, Hester walked around the counter to join her.

Maud was anxious. No longer quite so alarmed about her husband's condition now that he had survived for well over twenty-four hours and was taking light nourishment, she was struggling with the difficulties of adapting themselves and their home to his needs.

Dr Davidson was trying to locate a live-in nurse, while Abel was obsessive about installing some kind of hoist to take him from floor to floor. As much to escape his vehemence as to ascertain what might be done, she had

45

come into town in the brougham, taking the unprecedented course of quizzing Kilner on what might be feasible.

Astonishment gagged the manservant for a time but eventually Maud's perseverance convinced him of her need for advice. After all, for over twenty years she had relied on Abel to attend to all matters that were not a lady's province. The abrupt withdrawal of his ability to do so left yet another part of her feeling bereft.

Kilner had suggested several small companies which might oblige with the construction they required. The first two visited had been of no assistance whatsoever. Disappointment, and the return of this abnormal tiredness plaguing her since yesterday, made Maud long to go back home. But she'd not contemplate that without some success to report. Abel was so abrupt about the thing he rather scared her.

Initially, when Kilner halted the swaying carriage, she prepared to alight and approach yet another tradesman with her scarcely-understood description of what they required.

Before she had turned the handle, Kilner was at the door. 'I wouldn't get out, Madam. You'd best take my advice and remain where you are.' His face was flushed with anxiety.

She saw then that they were outside the Falgrave works. At the foot of the stair leading to the room where their jet was worked, a small but rowdy crowd was gathering.

'Help me down, Kilner, quickly.'

'But, Madam, I'm sure the master wouldn't wish me to . . .'

'He's not here to decide,' she continued briskly, pushing with the door so that Kilner had no alternative but to hand her down on to the cobbled street.

At the entrance to the works stood Jeff Hardcastle. Over the heads of the men who had collected there, she spotted the grey hair of his father. A quick glance revealed that, to her relief, none of the others were Falgrave craftsmen.

Maud crossed the narrow pavement and separated the group with a determined thrust of her furled umbrella.

'Hardcastle, have you no work?'

Both men faced her. If she had been less alarmed, she might have enjoyed their shock.

'Well? What are you doing out here during working hours?'

A chortle came from the other men who, from their appearance to say nothing of the pots they held, were customers of the adjacent inn.

Jeff Hardcastle shifted from one boot to the other and turned his black-streaked face to his father.

Wally Hardcastle came straight to the point. 'We've withdrawn our labour, Mrs Falgrave, that's what.'

'Indeed? And your reason for jeopardising your positions?'

'Oh, I don't mind telling you that. We're not being ordered about by any bit of a girl.'

Every onlooker laughed, and two gave a cheer of encouragement. Maud sensed Kilner immediately behind her in the group, but willed herself neither to turn to him nor to permit him to speak for her.

'If you're both resigning, so be it,' she snapped. 'Leave my premises at once.' She gulped in air. 'But I'll see every jet workshop in Whitby learns of your disloyalty. If you are thinking again – the stairs are behind you. I'll see you both when you're at your benches.'

Water from a gap in the guttering above was pouring steadily down on to her bonnet and cloak, soaking through to her dress beneath. Maud did not flinch. She would not stir, not even to unfurl her umbrella, until she had outstared the pair of them.

Chapter 3

Maud stood in the centre of the workroom, breathing in the oily smell of freshly-broken jet, narrowing her eyes against the dark fog created by its particles suspended in air unchanged for days. With the windows closed to keep out the cold and rain, the place seemed unbearable, but she mustn't soften because the men endured a bit of discomfort. She glanced all around her, then at Wally Hardcastle and afterwards his son.

'The next time you wish to register a complaint, you will do so through Mr Clough or direct to my face. I'll not be so lenient again if anyone walks off the job. He will be dismissed, instantly. And I mean what I say – I'll ensure he doesn't work elsewhere in Whitby. Mr Clough, you were in charge – what was it about?'

'They were picking on our Jeff,' Wally Hardcastle began. 'I'll not see my own . . .'

Maud silenced him with a raised hand and looked to Edwin Clough for the explanation she'd requested.

Edwin cleared his throat, glanced longingly towards the office.

Maud would have none of that. 'Oh, no. This will be sorted out in front of you all. Then we'll have none of the workers in any doubt of the situation. You'd best tell me quickly, Mr Clough, those treadles have been stopped a full minute already.' And that meant, at least, that all stages of polishing along with any grinding were suspended.

'Well, it was on account of me having so much to see to really, Mrs Falgrave,' Edwin began slowly. 'I'd been covering for the boss, and hadn't rightly noticed how bad the dust were getting.'

'Mm. I can see for myself that sweeping's long overdue. And every man of you knows that's a hazard.' She turned to Jeff. 'I suppose that's your job?'

'While I'm the newest apprentice, yes.'

'And maybe you think it's a bit beneath your dignity. There's more than your dignity'll get hurt if this lot catches light. You can sweep up now, and I don't mean just shoving the dust out of sight under the benches.'

Maud watched, motionless, while Jeff Hardcastle fetched the brush and commenced. She then turned to his father. 'And if your lad's so slipshod that he can't notice when everywhere's smothered in muck, you'd best jog his mind. While Mr Clough's got more to see to, you lot should be able to manage to ensure routine's not neglected.'

She adjusted her cloak, checking a sigh as she saw how her saturated hem had collected a border of jet dust as messy as the coal it resembled.

'I don't hear any wheels starting up – get treadling! We don't pay you to stand idle.'

Still intrigued by the confrontation, two or three of the men failed to follow the lead of the conscientious ones whose treadling set grinding or polishing wheels whirring.

Maud glowered in their direction. 'I'll dock the pay of anybody who's not working jet when I count five.'

Jeff Hardcastle was sweeping so energetically that the broom was increasing the shifting black fog clouding the workroom.

I'll have to tell him about that and all, thought Maud. But not today. Even she must succumb some time to the exhaustion generated by yesterday's shock. And even to the tiredness sprung from this encounter. Everything was combining to wear her out.

Maud was emerging from the door at the foot of the stair when Hester spattered her way along the street towards the brougham.

'Everything all right in there? I've just come from the shop.'

'No thanks to you, if it is,' Maud retorted as Kilner held the door for them. 'Get in there, young lady, I want to talk to you.'

'Me? I did call in at the works first, before I went to Flowergate.'

'And don't we all know that! Did you have to go upsetting the men on only the second day we're without your father?'

'Upsetting? How?' She was puzzled as well as horrified.

Maud looked at her daughter. 'You don't know, do you? Happen I am being a bit hasty.' Grimly, she related what she had found.

'And all because I'd spoken up about the place not being swept.'

Wearily, her mother nodded. 'Another time, you'd better have a quiet word with Edwin Clough instead.'

'That's what I did.'

'But they still knew where the instruction had come from.'

'I'm sorry if I'm to blame for the trouble, Mother. We've enough with just coping day to day.'

'Aye, well – they'll have to learn, won't they? There's you and there's me, and we're the ones who'll be giving the orders.'

And *I'm* going to make certain Falgraves' survives, Hester decided. It's to my generation that the future belongs. And I'll ensure that it develops – I'll not have anybody ever thinking that I don't always give of my utmost.

'But they did listen to you. They did, didn't they?' she said aloud.

'This time.'

'Edwin, you look fair paid,' his wife Alice exclaimed. 'Been bad today, has it?'

Edwin Clough threw his overcoat on the hook at the back of the door that was warped by weather and age, and dropped his toolbag in one corner.

'On your own then, are you?' his wife continued when he said nothing.

'Aye, our Frank and Harold went for a drink when we finished. They said they'll not be long.'

Alice nodded, turning away from the table where she was giving their five youngest offspring supper. Crossing swiftly to Edwin she took hold of his shoulders, then drew him to her for a kiss.

'Steady on, lass. I'm not out of my mucky clothes yet, am I?'

'It'll not hurt.' Her grey eyes scrutinised the hazel ones

50

which seemed to stare out from his blackened features. 'What's gone wrong now?'

'Ay, I don't know. If this is how it's going to be from now on, I don't relish t'next few years.'

'Nay, don't talk like that. It were nobbut yesterday as Mr Falgrave had the accident.'

'Aye, and it's nobbut today that folk have started downing tools.'

'Never!'

Briefly, Edwin outlined what had occurred. 'I'm not all that keen on working for a pair of women myself, but I can't say owt, can I? All we can do is our best.'

'I'm sure that's what you are doing.' Alice returned to the table where the two youngest had abandoned their bread and jam. 'Herbert, Maggie – you'll eat that up, and then you're all off to bed.'

'You don't mean us as well,' Alfred piped up. He was ten and with Ida and Lydia at nine and eight was considered almost grown up in comparison with the two babies of the family.

'It's too soon, Mam,' Ida added.

'Your father wants a bath, doesn't he?'

'You can fill it for me in t'wash kitchen,' Edwin told her. 'Don't pack the bairns off soon as I come through t'door.'

He loved his children and, working as he did from six of a morning till six at night, saw little enough of them.

'You're really worried about things at the workshop, aren't you, love,' Alice said as she was ladling water into the bath.

'I'd like to be able to see what'll happen next.'

'You're not the first to think that way.'

'No, but with folk like the Hardcastles you can never tell which way they'll turn. Wouldn't surprise me if they were agitating for a union afore long.'

'What, for jet carvers? It's not a massive industry, Edwin.'

'Unions are springing up all over. I heard tell of trouble again in Sheffield, with t'saw grinders. Next news is – they'll be uniting.'

'Any road, unions help the workers, don't they? Get them a fair deal. Isn't that what they're for?'

51

'Run proper, aye. Without bigots getting a hold. Once that happens there's no knowing where it'll lead. They threaten folk as won't join, tha knows – smash their tools. Aye – *and* aren't above smashing heads an' all if it gets them their way.'

Alice returned to the living room, all her natural cheerfulness dispersed. Edwin was too conscientious, that was the trouble. He'd make himself poorly over the job, before he'd give in. And, when all was done and said, the responsibility was the Falgraves'.

She didn't envy Maud, despite that lovely big house and the money to keep it going. They had met quite often during the Crimean War, doing what they could for families left short of brass while their men were fighting at the front. And she'd liked Maud Falgrave, admired the way the little body made plans and saw they were carried out.

This, though, was a grimmer business. And how the poor woman could bear to see her husband injured so terribly, Alice couldn't imagine. Noting how exhausted Edwin looked tonight was taking it out of *her*.

And the children were making enough noise for ten, never mind five. It was always the way this time of year. It was too cold, and often too wet, to let them play in the bit of a courtyard at the back of the houses. If she let them out they only ended up crowding into the privy. And that wasn't nice when it was shared with the other four houses in the row.

Keeping them in meant they were all five under her feet. The scullery at the cellar-head was such a scuttering little place she was in danger of sending one of them flying down the stone steps if they wandered in behind her. When she went to do the washing they were into the tub, sloshing water about, or risking tiny fingers in the mangle.

'The house looks nice, love.'

Edwin had bathed swiftly in the ice chill of the outhouse, and was smiling as he buttoned up his clean shirt.

Alice beamed back at him. She had made an effort today, had dusted the oak sideboard, and the four matching chairs. And had put a fresh cover on the back of the sofa. None of her menfolk used fancy oil on their hair, but it protected one of her few good pieces of furniture from that clinging jet dust that sent them home as bad as miners.

The children looked clean as well, bless 'em. She tried every evening to wash their faces and hands and have their hair brushed for Edwin coming home. Today, they had cooperated. The three middle ones were reminding her, these days, of Frank and Harold at similar ages. They were good, as children went, and liked to help with their younger brother and sister.

'What time will them two be in for summat to eat?' Alice asked, with a glance towards the black marble clock on the mantelshelf.

'I don't think they'll be long. They went off to see their mates by t'pier rails after dinner. Can't have much left to say to 'em this evening.'

'I wonder.' Alice was uneasy. She'd been perturbed enough last night, speculating on the changes that might be forced on them because of Abel Falgrave's injuries – the gravity of which was being discussed throughout Whitby. Today, seeing Edwin's normally placid features darkened by the bother at the workshop she felt sickened with apprehension. He was trapped, wasn't he, between his workmates and the bosses. And both her eldest trapped along with him.

'There's no rush, love,' her husband told her, gazing down at his children and trying to will his affection for them to supplant anxiety about their future. 'Can't say as I've much appetite as yet.'

If there were no further signs just then that the rest of the men intended resisting authority now that Abel Falgrave was confined to his home, there were none either that they would help in running the place. Now that Maud had seen how easily routine might be neglected she dared not let a day go by without at least one visit.

The workers appeared to take exception to any comment Hester might make; in fairness to the girl, she mustn't yet expect too much of her daughter.

'You'd better stick to your designing as much as you can, love,' Maud had told her following several discussions on how they might most effectively manage the works. 'And you could keep an eye on Sally in the shop so's I don't have to go round there so often.'

Hester was never sorry to concentrate on devising new patterns for the glittering jet which so fascinated her. Currently, she was engaged in drawing matching sets. She had begun with faceted and carved jet buttons for the front-fastening bodices that were fashionable. These would link with the black trimming on sleeves and skirts so popular just now. To go with the buttons she had designed brooches, and since then had decided to go ahead with necklaces.

All these items might be sold separately, but if a similar design were featured on each some women would wish to acquire the set.

Roses were her favourite flower, but she planned to incorporate others in her future work, and was experimenting with sketches of tiny birds.

'Frank Clough reckons he can carve a seagull on a button,' she told her father when she was sitting beside Abel's bed one Sunday in early December. 'Do you think that'll sell?'

'Why not?' Abel replied. 'Frank's going to be one of the best carvers of intricate work in Whitby once he's got a few more years on his back.' He just wished he could be in the workshop to encourage that.

'He's good now,' Hester observed. 'His work's that fine.'

'I'm not saying it isn't. But give him a bit longer to develop his feel for the jet, to *know* it, and he'll amaze even them that's been in the trade for years.' He ached to have a hand in Frank's progress.

Hester nodded, aware of the truth in her father's thinking. One man might spend his life producing competent pieces, the next because of his attunement with the raw jet would create something brilliant.

'Bring some samples home, think on,' he continued, and made himself smile, determined Hester wouldn't learn how dearly lying here inactive was already costing him. How *galling* it was.

54

'I'll show you some of the designs now, if you want. I was making a start on them last night.'

Leaving the bedroom, Hester shivered. Away from the roar of a coal fire, the house was dreadfully cold. And the marble-floored hall was always full of draughts that wafted up the wide staircase.

This morning when she'd walked to St Mary's church, the first few flakes of this winter's snow had been falling. On her way home the wind was keening through the gaunt abbey ruins. Outdoors now, snow was being blown into drifts that glittered frostily in the early twilight.

In her own room, she paused for a while by the window, gazing down over the town huddled around the harbour. A lamplighter was moving between clustered houses, his progress marked by the sudden awakening to life of twisting streets and steep alleys. The snow beautified everything, concealing pungent fishy remains down by the harbour itself and, no doubt, disguising equally malodorous waste discarded by some households in its proximity.

Whatever the reality of Whitby's less salubrious aspects, though, she'd never cease to love her town. And she wasn't always entirely cushioned by the Falgraves' circumstances. Jamie Skelton might never have been welcomed here, but she'd been a regular visitor in their home. It would have taken more than the smell and the staining of repeated flooding to keep her from the house which was no more than two rooms set one over the other, above the rough-hewn cellar.

And in the past more would have been needed to keep her away than dread of her parents discovering where she spent so many hours. She'd always enjoyed the spice of wondering if this would be the day when further excursions were forbidden.

For more years than she could count with any accuracy, Hester had been escorted to and from her private school and on expeditions to the shops by Freda Blake, her nannie. Until the day, that is, when Maud Falgrave had discovered what Freda was really like and dismissed her. A distant relative of Mrs Richmond and in her twenties when first employed by the Falgraves, for a long time Freda was considered impeccable.

Hester, who even at six years of age had preferred her own will to Freda's, hadn't complained when the young woman frequently took her charge out of sight of Falgrave House and left her to her own devices. It had felt very grown up to have the trust of this flame-haired beauty and to be allowed to play unattended.

From the day that Hester first met Jamie Skelton, evading Freda Blake became a necessity. Jamie was the most exciting person Hester had ever met. His yarns of accompanying his father and the rest of the herring fleet, and his extensive knowledge of the adventures of his hero Captain James Cook kept her enthralled.

Even now Hester still experienced a thrill simply by calling her friend to mind. Nothing, not even the sad outcome of his last adventure, could extinguish her admiration of Jamie Skelton's spirit. If she met him tomorrow, she would be over the distress generated by his appearance at Falgrave House and his involvement in the accident. And if Jamie needed a modicum of caution to temper his wilder schemes, that would come with maturity. Maybe she herself was the person whose influence might effect that change in him.

Distracted by these thoughts, Hester delayed for several minutes before finding the designs and returning to the master bedroom. As she neared the closed door, she heard a girl's voice and smiled.

'Hallo, Olive. No, don't stop . . .'

Her younger sister had begun reading aloud another chapter of Charles Dickens' *Great Expectations*. Their father found holding a book impossible now, and even though the task of running the workshop had precluded much leisure reading, he had always retained a love of literature.

At first Olive stumbled over some of the words, acutely aware of Hester's presence. She admired her sister's skill as a designer and her new-found usefulness in helping to run the family business. Beside her, she felt dull and uninteresting. Inherently of a quiet disposition, Olive often felt that her young brother Bernard who was only eleven possessed more aplomb than she herself could muster.

Coming, as she had, into a family of a sound financial background, Olive had never needed to acquire much fighting spirit. What she did need still was the support and encouragement of her parents. Since last month that seemed denied her. She could see well enough that, with her father, there was some reversal of roles. Being able to complete small tasks for him in this way brought her into his company, and helped compensate for the loss of his protectiveness.

What she didn't understand was her mother's refusal to grant her much attention.

'So, that's where you are, young madam.' Thrusting into the room, her taffeta skirts swishing about her, Maud fixed Olive with glittering blue eyes. 'Go to your room at once, I'm sick of your defiance.'

Hester watched as, hurt like a puppy that has felt someone's heel, Olive closed the book she had been reading and scurried from the room.

'Would you mind, Hester,' her father said. 'Your mother and I need to talk.'

Following in Olive's wake, Hester thought to catch the slight girl with fair, curling hair and ask what had roused their mother's wrath. She was too late though, for the door of her sister's room shut with a slam that was followed by the rattle of a key.

'Olive's a good girl, you know. She often comes to read to me,' Abel began evenly. Maud had no cause to lose *her* patience.

'While she knows that'll get her away from me.'

'What has she done?' he inquired as his wife eased her wide skirts on to the chair beside the bed. Didn't Maud know he needed calm?

'You shouldn't have to ask, you encourage her. Wasn't she reading a novel, on a Sunday?'

'Sunday or otherwise, the days are all the same to me. I hadn't thought about it. And I can't honestly see what harm . . .'

'Hasn't the Good Book always been enough for you, as it has for me?'

'Not the Bible alone.'

'I'm talking about this one day of the week. There's little enough sacred . . .'

'Maud, for heaven's sake! Olive's a sweet girl.'

'You don't see her as I do.'

'No, I don't believe I do,' Abel observed.

'She's wilful is that one, if not underhand.'

'What *had* she done to anger you? Reading that novel was only since she'd come in here.' Maud was short of summat to grumble about.

'Oh, but it wasn't! That's the whole point, Abel. I had reprimanded her once, not fifteen minutes ago.'

'And she thought to evade your wrath by reading it to me.'

'Precisely. You've fathered a scheming little . . .'

Her husband's sharp chuckle interrupted her. 'Happen the girl's acquiring a bit of an understanding of how the mind works.'

'Fancy explanations don't make her behaviour any the better. Olive is growing intractable. This morning she bluntly refused to accompany Hester to St Mary's.'

'She told me that she felt unwell.'

'The girl's forever bemoaning aches and pains. If we listened to her, we'd be convinced she's a chronic invalid.'

'Poor Olive, she's at a difficult age.'

Maud gave her husband a look. 'What do you know about that?'

He hadn't lost all sense as well. 'She is our thirdborn . . .'

'You always were too soft with her,' Maud sniffed. 'And with the others as well. Lambert never learned the meaning of duty, that is for sure.'

'You've had word from him again?'

'Aye. Word I didn't want. But I shouldn't burden you with his shortcomings.'

'It is something I can share.' They kept leaving him out now.

'Well, since you know he's written, you may as well hear the rest. He'll not be home before this week's out either. *And* he makes plain the fact that he'll only be here for a short while. There's no hope he'll contemplate giving up the Grenadiers.'

'Did you think that there was?'

Maud glanced down at the fingers clenched in her lap. She'd no wish for Abel to read the disappointment in her eyes. She *had* hoped, though, had believed she might depend upon Lambert.

'Perhaps he will know of a local engineer who'd construct the hoist that'll allow me to take more of a share in our affairs. Since you couldn't manage to locate anyone.'

His wife faced him once more. 'I've had other things on my mind, haven't I? And Nurse Clapper considers you're better keeping to the one room.' Since the day the nurse arrived, Maud had been glad to rely on her for guidance regarding Abel's care.

'That woman has no concept of what is needful for me, or . . .'

'She is highly respected in her profession, Abel. You know we were told Miss Nightingale herself recommended . . .'

'For men at the front perhaps,' Abel interrupted. 'Where they're in her hands for a short while before they escape. That woman is a tyrant.'

Didn't he love Sundays now, not so much for his family gathered about him, but for the Clapper woman's absence?

Afraid suddenly that the nurse hired but three weeks ago might be despatched, leaving her to battle with additional difficulties, Maud nearly insisted that Abel must try to adapt to having Nurse Clapper's help. But then she saw his expression, read in his brown eyes the grim reality that took too much facing.

Heavily, for all her tiny frame, Maud rose. Moving closer to the bed, she brushed her husband's cheek with the back of her fingers and bent to kiss his lips.

'We'll find a way,' she said gently. 'Don't you fret, we'll find one.'

'I'm determined on that. Especially for some means of releasing me from this confinement. I read some few years ago of a safety lift demonstrated in America by a man called Otis. You could find out more for me, discover if such a thing is available over here.'

Inwardly, Maud groaned. No good would come of Abel's

insistence on moving about the house. Hadn't it taken both Kilner and Dr Davidson to carry him bodily from that room downstairs?

Once out of their bedroom she sighed and pushed at her hair in front of the lace cap. Her head, these days, seemed to ache perpetually. And that was nothing to the deeper ache inside her. All day long and far into many a night she was plagued by her body. Abel had insisted that she still share his bed. She wished to God there were some means of quieting the expectations of the part of her that had rejoiced in his taking possession.

She was forty years old, but still experienced the urgent pulsing that had awakened to Abel's first caress. She had been glad then, had gloried in the sensations that were so much more than the anticipated wifely obligation. Now, she only wished all feeling removed from her.

Startled, embarrassed by her private emotions, Maud glanced upwards at a sudden bumping and clattering from the darkened stairs that led towards the servants' attics.

'Who's there?' she demanded. 'What're you . . . ?'

Something hurtled between the banisters, skimmed past one side of her face, glanced off her shoulder and hit the carpeted floor. Looking down, Maud recognised the worn toy cart.

'Bernard!'

His laugh blended with her shout. Two steps at a time he scampered down to her side. Brown eyes laughed into her own.

'I made you jump, didn't I, Mama?'

'I'll take that smile off your face. And it'll be his belt your father will take to . . .' Remembering, she checked, and drew in a slow breath that failed to compose her. 'You're taking advantage, that's what. You and your sister, both . . .'

'Hester, you mean?' Bernard suggested innocently.

He was so like his father when first she'd known him that Maud ached to draw him near for a hug. But he was growing into a heedless lad – another month of this regime and there'd be no controlling him.

'You're quite aware I don't mean Hester. You and Olive try my patience week in and week out. Please remember what day it is and put that away this instant, together with any other toys. You're much too old, any road, to be playing with such babyish things whatever day of the week. I'll have May Thorpe sort through your cupboard. There's many a lad in the hovels down by the harbour who'll be glad of just one item of the toys you've outgrown.'

Horrified, Bernard stood motionless, dark head bent as he gazed down at the treasured miniature cart. He could see as well all the dozens of toys equally treasured. He *needed* them all, couldn't contemplate an existence without them. Especially now.

'It was only because there's nothing to do here,' he protested in a voice half its normal power. 'Mightn't you reconsider . . . ?'

'You're forbidden the servants' landing, too, had you overlooked that as well? I'll not have an undisciplined boy rampaging as you do through the entire house.'

Bernard said nothing. His teeth were clamped on the soft inner side of a lip that he'd not permit to tremble.

'Is this some new insolence?' snapped Maud, baffled by the absence of his usual repeated pleas for lenience.

'I just hate Sundays,' Bernard said at last. 'Not that the rest of the week's much better. Nobody cares any longer.'

'Oh, no? That's why I'm working my fingers to the bone, is it, because I don't care? Who else'll see the business continues to flourish so's we keep a roof over our heads and good food inside you all.' I'm sounding like one of the fisherwomen down on the quay, Maud realised, loathing herself for that but lacking the strength to stop.

Bernard turned from her swiftly, but not so swiftly that she missed the single tear escaping his compressed eyelids. Maud swallowed, and extended a loving hand to haul him back to her side. Sensing her intent, the boy began running and was into the bedroom and at his father's side before she lowered her hand.

Again she swallowed, appalled by what was happening to them. Within minutes she had antagonised each of her younger children. In no time at all they would hate her as much as Abel hated that nurse. They were both tyrants.

But Sundays were sacred, weren't they, to the Lord and

61

to family. Only so recently they had been a family, gathering around the piano in the drawing room, singing hymns. Normally, at this time in December, they'd be practising carols. But nothing was normal, never again would be . . . She couldn't bear it a day longer.

Slowly, Maud walked back to the foot of the upper staircase, arranged her bulky crinoline cage, and sat there. Why am I doing all this, she wondered. Why am I steeling myself to keep the workshop going? Why in the world am I risking my children's affection, consigning my husband's care to a nurse whom he hates, making myself so busy that I've ceased to behave like a mother or a wife?

Edwin Clough was a good man, as were his eldest sons. Although it was only a little after six of the icy December morning, he had already allocated the pieces of rough jet to all the workers and, with Frank and Harold, was singing as he carved.

Reaching the top of the stairs, Maud smiled. 'I'll swear there's nobody in Whitby has a more cheerful band of men in their shop!' Even Wally Hardcastle appeared less dour today. When she looked around for his son Jeff, though, she couldn't see him.

'Is your Jeff not well then, Wally?' she inquired.

'He's terrible bad, Mrs Falgrave, with the ague.'

'I'm sorry to hear that. I hope he's soon recovered.'

Removing the tiny bonnet that she wore well forward over her face, Maud tucked into her lace cap the strands of pale hair which had been caught by the wind whirling snow at her as she'd left the brougham. She asked Edwin Clough if he'd ensured some other apprentice would keep the workroom swept in Jeff's absence, and nodded her approval when he confirmed that it was arranged.

Taking off her dark red cloak, she went to hang it in the office. Before sitting at the desk, Maud straightened her skirt and shook its lower folds to rid herself of some of the particles of black dust. Abel had declared her blue-green shot silk too elaborate for the workshop, but Abel didn't understand. She had an appointment at noon with another Falgrave.

62

Isaac was the cousin of Abel's who'd taken on his share of the jet mine twenty odd years ago. That had been at the time shortly before their marriage, when Abel bought into what had been her family's workshop. They had continued to buy the bulk of their raw material from Isaac, and this was the first business meeting at which she was replacing her husband. The way Isaac saw her mattered a great deal to Maud. Being family didn't entitle anyone to pity her circumstances.

The stomping of feet and laboured breathing made her glance through the door that was still ajar. Appearing over the top stair was Kilner's face, florid now between grey mutton-chop whiskers.

'You're in poor shape, Kilner,' she observed, but with a smile. She liked their manservant, an obliging fellow who never forgot his place. 'What's brought you toiling up here?'

'A message from Miss Hester, Madam.' He had taken her in the carriage as far as the shop in Flowergate. 'The shop-girl won't be in till late. Her grandmother's passed on in the night and Sally's mother insists the lass helps lay the old lady out.'

'So Miss Hester's minding the shop.'

'That's so, Mrs Falgrave. And she said to tell you she'll be working on them designs of hers an' all.'

'I hope she will, indeed. There'll be precious few customers at this hour of a winter Monday.'

With his mistress's reminder of her noon appointment, Kilner went clattering down the stairs. Maud looked out of the window that gave on to the workshop, wondering what had changed since her arrival. Recognising that all she heard now was the whirring of the wheels and the steady rhythm of the treadles that worked them, she realised that all singing had ceased. Briefly, she wished the men had felt able to continue, even that she knew how to encourage them to do so.

Was it she herself, perhaps, who turned their enjoyment of work to this seemingly numb repetition? Hadn't she only yesterday stifled all enjoyment in her children?

Forget that – you're here now so just concentrate, she told herself. Each time she glanced down to the documents on

Abel's desk, though, her eyes wandered again to the window that linked with their workers.

Could it be envy she felt for those men beyond that square of glass where the black dust being swept from the floor added yet another layer to the dark glitter on a long-established cobweb? They had their understanding of one another, gleaned from crafts that were as interdependent as beads in the necklaces they produced. The carvers would be lost without the grinding that filled the place with its inky fog, just as engraving would be nothing on jet that had no polish.

The men were as different from each other as any group in Whitby, but when a complex order came in they buckled to together. Those who were expert at cutting the brittle jet without it shattering would prepare pieces to size. Bob Dunsdale and other quiet workers like him would turn their hand to anything, even hours of laborious polishing. Or, if a lot of engraving was required, they'd do the simpler parts of a design then pass the piece over to one of the Cloughs for the more intricate details. They were a real team.

And here was she, no more popular than in her own home ... Oh, Lord, if only she could forget how Olive and Bernard always turned to their father now. Wielding authority had never seemed offensive while it was shared. Abel had a way with their offspring, was firm without antagonising. She supposed his approach here was imbued with similar characteristics. In the old days she'd never been here long enough to observe how he achieved a good rate of production and kept a contented workforce. If only *she* liked one thing about being in charge here.

Maud's feeling about her position intensified before the day was little more than half over. She emerged from the meeting with Abel's cousin Isaac with the deal she had wanted for purchase of their next supply of rough jet. In the process, though, she had felt trampled by Isaac's attempts to uplift the price. If she hadn't known from Abel of the difficulties always entailed in reaching the strata of jet lying beneath alum rock, she might have been led to believe the problems of hewing it out with picks were increased.

Ultimately, she had convinced Isaac that she'd not accept

any higher price as justified. But the battle had been hard, and had left her feeling hardened.

Sitting back in the carriage, as Kilner drove them away from Isaac's house at Sandsend, Maud willed herself to relax. Tonight, Abel would commend the deal she'd secured and she'd make time to win back her two youngest children's affection.

Even her reflections didn't prevent her from noticing the young fellow on the shore. Calling to Kilner to slow the brougham, she looked more closely for confirmation of what she suspected he was about. Convinced she was right, she alighted swiftly and hurried through a flurry of snowflakes, approaching him from behind as he halted again, gathering something from the beach.

'Is this a new remedy then for the ague, Jeff Hardcastle? Or is it that you've heard there's jet to be had for the picking here today? Jet which you'll either sell to the trade or, worse, will turn on my machines, covertly . . .'

He swung round, but without neglecting to pocket the dark pieces he'd collected from among others surrounding them, washed clean by the tide.

His expression changed swiftly from surprise to challenge. 'Will you be taking them from me, Mrs Falgrave?'

'I'd not demean myself. But you'll not work that jet in our shop then sell it privately. It's your job I'm taking.'

'You can't. It's *Mr* Falgrave I'm promised to.'

'Do you think I don't know your agreement's with him? But I'm the one who's administering the workshop now, and this is the second time you've absented yourself without cause. I overlooked the previous occasion because it was fleeting, but you'll lack the opportunity to try me with a third.'

Before she could flinch under the menace in Jeff Hardcastle's eyes, Maud turned and, trying to walk with dignity over the loose sand, hastened to the carriage. Kilner had been watching the encounter from where he stood at the horse's head. She had to will herself not to seek his support.

'Are you all right, Mrs Falgrave?'

She tried to nod calmly. 'Thank you, Kilner. Back to the works now.'

Even after consideration, Maud knew that she'd taken the only possible action. If Jeff Hardcastle was starting to deal in whatever rough jet he could pick up, that had to be stopped. It was no more acceptable than having him use their workroom for fashioning stuff to sell on the side. But the episode gnawed into her for days, increasing her dissatisfaction with her new role, alerting her to the impossibility of maintaining discipline and being liked.

Never before had Maud considered whether or not people liked her – maybe she hadn't needed to, for she hadn't been unpopular. And somehow she still hadn't succeeded in winning back the unconditional love of her children. Since that Sunday, Olive and Bernard appeared to have devised a new contest – a striving for her attention. The one who felt it was withheld reacted like the spoiled child she'd believed them not to be. The one who received it gloated until she saw they were no better.

Below stairs, Joseph Kilner confided in Mrs Richmond his dread that the accident to the master would twist and harden the natures of every member of the family.

"Tisn't natural the mistress should have to take so much upon her. I've seen how she's had to steel herself to be firm wi' folk.' He'd always been protective of master and mistress alike, though it was Abel who best understood Kilner's true history.

Once employed in a rival jet works, Joseph Kilner had lost three fingers when the grindstone shattered while he was shaping a jet nugget. Fearing questions regarding their safety standards, his employers had blamed him for the accident and dismissed him.

Still unmarried at turned fifty and with no living relatives, Kilner had managed to exist by driving pack-horses across the bleak moors and doing a bit of poaching. His first encounter with the Falgraves had been while Abel was inspecting the horses delivered for his fine new brougham.

The poacher he caught in the grounds surprised him with his knowledge of these beautiful animals which were a bit of a mystery to him. And the jet talisman the man wore aroused his interest.

'It's to ward off dogs – lots of poachers wear them,'

Kilner had explained wryly. They'd laughed together across the bristling back of a terrier whose barking had drawn Abel to this intruder in the bushes.

'It strikes me that you and me's going to have to gentle 'em all,' Kilner added now to the housekeeper who was giving him the silent look which, he'd learned these past ten years, signified her reservations.

But Mrs Richmond was wishing she'd been first to voice these feelings. Hadn't the Falgraves been *her* family since she was widowed at twenty?

They both were right, Maud *was* worn down by the difficulties.

Something would have to be done. If only she weren't exhausted beyond belief and plagued by so many problems, she might arrive at an answer.

When May Thorpe came running, as she had been forbidden to do, with her cap all awry on her mouse-coloured hair and a rent in the white apron tied around her dark dress, Maud anticipated catastrophe. But the maid's haste was due to no more than the unexpected arrival of Mr Cecil Arkwright.

'He particularly wishes to speak with you, Madam. He says it's urgent.'

And when would he admit otherwise, thought Maud, but couldn't sate her curiosity if she dispatched him unseen.

She merely half-listened through his greeting, and the subsequent inquiries after her health and Abel's. As usual, he wasn't slow to reach the point.

'We're into the second week in December, as you're well aware. It is some weeks now since your husband's unfortunate accident – and I'll warrant those weeks haven't been easy.'

'Ease, Mr Arkwright, is a luxury for some who relish an idle life. The rest of us find satisfaction in accomplishing something worthwhile.'

Eyes glinting, he smoothed his lovely white hair. 'Aye, I'll not argue with that. And I'm glad to note you retain your good Yorkshire straightforwardness. I've been thinking as well that you'll not have lost your inherent carefulness.

That's why I've considered long and hard, and have come up with an offer you'd be daft to resist.'

The offer was staggering. Arkwright had so increased the sum he would pay for the Falgrave business that not staring open-mouthed required all Maud's willpower.

As before, she responded coolly, but this time his offer did deserve considered reflection. He was still guaranteeing that their men would stay in work, and seemed eager to make no changes in the qualities that rendered the Falgrave works unique. If they sold out, Hester would continue designing the jet jewellery that she loved. And she herself would have time for Abel, time to explore the possibility of having the lift he'd set his heart on installed. She might manage somehow to prevent the frustration, which he often failed to conceal now, from becoming worse. She would have time for Olive and young Bernard, might preclude their feeling neglected . . .

Time, though, was precisely what she needed now – time in which to weigh all aspects of the offer Cecil Arkwright was making. And time to discover why intuition was hammering away at her, insisting that something in his manner indicated the deal might be most opportune for *him*.

'I'll need your bid in writing, you'll realise that. And we'll need time to discuss all its implications. Neither Abel nor I will be hurried over this, Mr Arkwright.'

Chapter 4

'You're useless, young Skelton, that's what. I'm putting in for the neet...' the skipper shouted, glancing sideways from the helm.

'No, no. I'll be well again in a minute,' Jamie protested, determined he'd not give in to the sickness nor to the terror.

'You said that hours sin' and look at you. Puking like a lass that's never seen a boat.'

'Please, Mr Grinsdale, don't go ashore yet.'

Sam Grinsdale laughed, leaning close to Jamie and increasing the boy's nausea with the smell from his rotting teeth, which momentarily overpowered the stench of the ill-kept boat.

''Fraid to go home, that it, eh?'

'I'd just prefer to remain at sea. It – it's a good night for the fish – you'd not wish to be wasting that?'

'And how would I do otherwise, Skelton, with *you* taking my attention every five minutes? Never knowing whether you're leaning over the side disposing of your guts, or if it's yourself that's gone over.'

'I'll be all right now, honest.' He couldn't go back, couldn't return to harbour with nothing to show for the day. And nothing to show either that he'd conquered this abominable dread of the water.

The snow had ceased around midday, driven off by a keen wind. Jamie's clothes, though, felt no drier for all that, drenched as he was in the sweat generated by his vomiting and the all-pervading agitation. And the wind, naturally, was whipping up the waves, creating a swell that only a few weeks ago would have excited him.

Now it only made him more aware of every creak of the decrepit boat, of each movement that, to him, seemed to forecast its destruction. A wave raced over the deck where, too weak for standing, he was cowering. With it hurtled

69

long-discarded fishy entrails, the gory mess that Sam Grinsdale had accumulated.

No matter how he tried, Jamie couldn't contain the sourness rising within him yet again.

When he was in a state to glance up from the side of the boat, Whitby's abbey was dead ahead of them. This was the second time he'd come out with Grinsdale. That first trip had been even shorter, and he'd not be taken ashore in disgrace again.

'There's no wonder you lost your dad's vessel, is there, laddie?'

Being addressed as though he were a nipper goaded Jamie. Wiping his mouth on his tattered shirtsleeve, he stood upright, faced Sam Grinsdale.

'I'm not the first that's run aground in the foul weather off this coast.' Only last February the lifeboat had been lost in rough seas.

'Garn – you're a right lily!'

Jamie squared up to him. 'Say that again . . .'

The boatman only laughed. An easy life was all he wanted, or he'd go out more regularly with the herring fleet. He only need fend for himself and required no more than food enough to survive, and drink to make the surviving pleasant.

'Nay, Jamie, us'll not quarrel, eh?'

'But you'll let me prove I've not lost my nerve?'

'By staying out till we've a good catch? Well – happen that'd be no great hardship. For me.'

Again, he laughed, spattering Jamie with his foul spittle.

Setting his face, Jamie began taking in deep breaths of the icy wind that was buffeting them. 'I'll see to the nets.'

The rest of that day and all through the biting cold of the night the small boat ploughed through seas growing ever rougher. Sleet and snow drove across the decks, numbing their fingers, combining with the salt in the spray to make their faces raw.

Somehow, though, Jamie controlled his heaving insides, compelling himself to haul in the catch, even to gut some of the fish ready for market.

A blizzard was raging as they steered back to port where

Whitby appeared ethereal, uncannily beautiful. Seen through the haze of snowflakes and with the pristine covering softening the cluster of buildings, it seemed an enchanted place rising out of the sea.

'You can take the helm while we go in.' Not an unkind man, Sam had been surprised by Jamie's spirit, had warmed to the will with which the lad had worked.

Over in Flowergate, inside the Falgrave shop, Sally was leaning on the glass-topped counter, laughing up into brilliant green eyes.

'Come on then, Harold, into the back room. Just for a while . . .'

Harold Clough hesitated, glanced towards the shop door.

Sally giggled. 'There'll be nobody come, not in all this snow.'

'And what if Miss Hester walks through that door?'

'She won't, will she? She sent you round with all this new stuff.'

'All the same . . .' Harold tried to ignore the invitation in wide blue eyes and moist lips that on occasions had stirred eagerly beneath his own. Sally was a lovely-looking girl whose interest flattered him, but his job meant more; he'd not jeopardise that.

'Give us a kiss then, just so's I don't forget . . .'

Her lips were tantalisingly pursed, offered towards him in blatant appeal. One kiss might be all right, but would it stop at one?

'We'll neither of us forget. But this isn't the place, Sally.'

He'd be missed at the works. Having his own father as foreman often meant sharper discipline, not less. And he *wanted* to get back to his bench. He'd spent ages on the messy process of leading a piece of jet, using the flat of the wheel and 'rotten stone' – abrasive river mud from Derbyshire – to remove scores and grinding scratches. Then he'd carefully executed a diamond-cut pattern with the edge of the same lead-wheel. He'd been itching to polish up the brooch, to see how good it was turning out, when he'd been sent round here.

'When will I see you then?' Sally persisted.

Meetings weren't readily arranged. Her father was strict, would never allow her out with a man unchaperoned. And right now Harold was in no mood for concentrating on organising anything but his job.

'Tonight,' she said firmly, recalling something. 'I've got to go round to my grandmother's house. Mam's busy preparing for the funeral and the rent man wants Gran's place empty by the end of the week.'

'Where is it?' Harold inquired cautiously. He might manage an hour or so with Sally, on the pretext of drinking with his friends.

'Just outside Sandsend. I could be right quick sorting out her stuff, then we'd have time to ourselves.'

Harold sighed. 'Sorry, love, don't think I can manage to get out there and back.' He didn't want to go into explanations at home – not with an older brother and a dad who relished tormenting him about young Sally. And what if any of her family turned up at her gran's?

'You do still like me, don't you?'

Her plaintive voice and the slight quiver of her pointed little chin filled him with affection. Wordlessly, he drew her with him towards the back room that served as a store for the jet jewellery.

He pulled her sharply into his arms, slid both hands down the tight silk at the back of her bodice, and clamped his lips vigorously on to her mouth.

'What are you going to do at Christmas?' Sally asked when he'd released her lips and despite his reservations was gazing into her eyes, his own like glittering emeralds.

Harold smiled. 'I don't know yet, do I? Ask me nearer the time.' Alarm rattled at the back of his mind, dulling any excitement she'd generated. He'd to master his craft, hadn't he – that came before making plans for a day or two off. Couldn't she understand how it was to love the jet so much that he was longing now to get busy with the pig's-bristle brush, the first stage of that final polishing? He'd been given a new walrus-hide wheel for using later on . . .

'Sorry I asked,' Sally snapped, hurt by his refusal to make firm plans. Did he think she wasn't good enough for him?

Who was he, anyhow? His dad was nobbut t'foreman at the workshop!

The shop doorbell made the pair of them start. Sally was swifter to recover and emerged from the storeroom as Hester came through the door shaking snow from her cloak.

'I was just showing Harold Clough how full up with stock we are – don't know where we'll put the stuff he's brought today.'

Hester smiled as she furled her umbrella and placed it in the wrought-iron stand by the door.

'If this snow really sets in that is going to be a problem. No one will be coming out to the shops. Then again, it might be to our advantage,' she added, considering. 'People might buy presents in Whitby who'd otherwise think of shopping further afield.'

'Let's hope they do,' said Harold, composed now and crossing through the shop to the door. 'The way we're working, we'll have to let more stuff go to our other outlets.'

'Huh – hark at him,' Sally exclaimed as the door closed behind Harold. 'Does he think I'm not doing my job right, or summat?'

Hester smiled. 'I'm sure it's not that. And, anyway, you know we sell wholesale to other shops elsewhere, and do special orders.'

'But the shop is paying, isn't it?'

'It's no good asking that, not yet, Sally. I'm not let in on how we're doing, either here or at the works.' That smarted, as well. Since Cecil Arkwright's last visit her parents had spent hours in earnest discussion, from which she had been excluded.

Seeing that Sally still looked perturbed, Hester reassured her. 'You needn't start worrying yet. And besides, there's Christmas to look forward to.'

'With my grandmother just dead? That *will* be a cheery time.'

'Sorry, I . . . that was careless of me. And that was the reason for coming round here, and all. I meant to get Harold Clough to ask you – when will the funeral be, Sally? I've told Mother I'll look after the shop if you've to help at home with feeding folk.'

'I don't rightly know. I'll tell you soon as the parson fixes it all.' She did know really, but might find it useful to absent herself for longer, if only Harold could get away.

'Very well.' The shop bell rang. 'Here's one customer, any road,' Hester began, then stared amazedly at the tall young fellow who'd entered. 'Jamie!'

'Thought it was you I'd spotted.' He had been positive, in fact, having watched Hester pass the top of the alley as he hurried up the icy cobbles from his home. He'd been determined to meet her.

'Just put in with a good catch,' he told her, beaming.

'Oh? Who took you on then?'

Jamie's smile dissolved. 'Not you an' all – does nobody in Whitby think I'm any use now?' His mother's first words had been almost the same, while his father had wanted to know which of the other fishermen was wrong in his head.

'I didn't mean it like that.' Awkwardly, Hester shrugged. She could hardly say that, knowing he'd lost his dad's boat, she simply wondered what he had taken to sea in.

'Doesn't matter whose boat it was, does it? We brought in a grand catch, and he gave me a fair share.'

Jamie was bursting with the satisfaction of having taken in fine fish, enough to feed them all and money as well from the sale of the rest.

'That's nice,' said Hester, glancing up at the clock. She had reserved this morning for completing several designs and had already lost precious time by coming round to Flowergate.

'I'm having dinner at the inn to celebrate. Come with me, Hester.' Now he was over the seasickness his belly was cleaved in. He couldn't remember when last he'd had money in his pocket. And decent clothes to house the pocket, as well. He'd stopped to buy a shirt and trousers, and a coat also. They were not new, but the pawnbroker who was a good friend to the Skeltons liked to get rid of stuff when their owners had passed over to where clothes no longer served them.

'Sorry, Jamie, but it'll have to be another time. I'm working, aren't I? I've left a lot of designs half-finished. You can walk me back to the workshop if you like.'

Thank you very much, thought Jamie. Did she suppose he'd nowt better to do? He'd been aching to tell her how he'd mastered his fear of the sea, if only for the time being. She'd always understood before about any fears he'd had. Not that there'd been many of those – but he'd kept nothing from her.

'Doesn't matter,' he responded lightly. 'See you some other day.' He didn't know how or when, but she'd not see that it mattered to him. He'd kept away from her, meticulously, until he'd proved what he could do and now . . .

'Yes. Goodbye for now, then. Goodbye, Sally.'

Resolutely, Jamie avoided watching her walk away from the shop. It felt like the end of their friendship, when he'd meant it to be its regeneration. Only on his return to shore had he permitted himself to contemplate the possibility of seeing her again, of overcoming the obstacle of that catastrophe on the cliffs.

'Did you want something?' Sally was in no mood for customers. Harold had reawakened exhilarating pulses just by kissing her again; having him leave resulted in the strangest pain deep inside her which nothing could ease.

The girl was as fair as Hester was dark and, if her face was rather characterless by comparison, it was far prettier. When he was little their Jessie had cried for a doll in one of the shop windows. This lass might have been used as its model.

Her blue eyes were friendly, as well, made him smile back despite his recent dissatisfaction.

'I might.' He'd never flirted in his life, wouldn't have known what the word meant, and certainly hadn't been other than utterly straightforward with Hester. But this lass aroused in him a playfulness he'd never tried on girls unrelated to him. It had nothing to do, either, with the rough-and-tumble games of that cramped house by the harbour.

'So you're a friend of Miss Hester's, are you?' He looked personable enough, even if he sounded no more refined than Sally herself. 'Looking for company, are you, to have your dinner with?' she added on impulse. As she said it, she wondered at her own reason. She couldn't leave the shop, could she?

'If you like.'

Grinning, Sally shook her head. 'Can't shut up shop, can I? But I don't mind if you want to stay here in the warm for a bit . . .'

He had lovely-looking hair, the most brilliant red she'd ever set eyes on. And his eyes crinkled at the corners as if he did a lot of laughing. But maybe the way he was built was the best thing about him, broad across those brown-clad shoulders, then tapering downwards to close-fitting checked trousers.

'You approve, do you?'

Sally flushed. Her scrutiny had been noticed. But why should she let that perturb her?

Smiling, she nodded. 'Yes, I do, as a matter of fact.' Having reached his face, her gaze lingered there.

Jamie grinned back, delighted that such a pretty girl was so evidently interested. 'Are you sure you're not allowed to go out at dinnertime?'

''Fraid so. I bring sandwiches with me, eat them in the back.'

'And what do you do when you shut up shop in an evening?'

His eyes were unusual, with flecks of green, brown and grey which glinted even in this poor light inside the shop. With a start, Sally realised that he had spoken, and grinned self-consciously.

'Oh, you know. Go home, have my tea . . .'

'Every night? Don't you go anywhere else?'

'Like tonight, you mean? I've got to go to my grandmother's. She died, you see.'

'I'm sorry,' Jamie said swiftly, thankful he knew how to respond.

'And I've got to go and clear out her home. The landlord wants all her stuff out, sharpish.'

'Just you on your own – won't you be upset?' He'd been thinking she looked as dainty and as sparkling as the jewellery surrounding her.

'I'll just have to get on with it, shan't I?'

'You shouldn't ought to have to do that on your own.' He'd felt like this before, years ago when Hester was little and lost. The urge to protect altered the casualness of the encounter. 'Someone ought to go with you.'

'Are you volunteering?' She could see again the picture she'd conjured before of having somebody with her in that tiny grey cottage. It seemed not to matter that the fellow wouldn't be Harold.

'So long as we make time first for summat to eat.'

'Thanks ever so much,' she replied before he could change his mind.

'Mr Falgrave, you're not taking one bit of notice of anything I've said.' Arms folded across her sombrely-encased bosom, Nurse Clapper regarded her patient as though he were a naughty nine year old. 'You'll never get better if you don't cooperate, will you now?'

I'll never get better, thought Abel. One day he would say it – why on earth need he restrain himself with her? It was bad enough keeping his feelings back with his children.

'You've left more than you've eaten of this luncheon.'

'Sorry. I'm not hungry. I've a lot on my mind.' He could be honest about that, any road. Ever since he'd read the news in today's *Daily Telegraph* he'd been able to think of nothing else. If only Maud were here, if only he knew when she'd be home . . .

He'd never felt more helpless, never so certain of what he wished to be done and yet unable to put it into effect. If he lived to be a hundred he'd never grow accustomed to relying so much on other folk.

Where *was* Maud? She hadn't said she intended remaining at the workshop all day.

He must leave the decision to her, much as that went against his inclinations. She was the one who would be most affected by the way they chose. He half-wished that nothing had occurred to alter their earlier way of thinking. He hated the tiredness and strain so evident, these days, in her once placid features – *almost* as much as he hated being flat on his back. He'd been looking forward to having her about the house more often, to having her attention while she was at home, without its being diverted to business matters. He had decided how they might best invest the proceeds of selling the works to provide a secure future. And he'd relished the prospect of sending Nurse Clapper packing.

Was that the brougham turning into the drive? His ears were attuned now to its arrival. Abel smiled slightly, at last, hearing Maud's light feet on the outer steps, then the door opening. She crossed the hall, ran up the long staircase.

'Hallo, Abel love – have you heard?'

'About the Prince Consort? Aye, it's in the *Telegraph*. It's a bad do. Especially for our poor lady Queen. She's only about our age.'

'I never dreamed his illness were that serious.'

'I don't suppose any of us did.' What a lovely way to go, though – swiftly, with no prospect of prolonged discomfort or being balked . . .

'All bar one, happen. I'll wager Cecil Arkwright had a good idea. Else why would he be in such a hurry to buy us out? We're not selling, of course. The Queen was enthusiastic already about jet, wasn't she? There's no other jewellery she'll wear for mourning. Other folk'll follow suit, naturally. No, we're not selling. Trade will multiply. We'll not relinquish Falgraves' potential now.'

Abel said nothing. Perturbed, Maud looked more keenly at him.

Wryly, he was smiling. 'And to think I'd been worrying that you might see it differently! I might have wanted you at home more, with less responsibility, but we don't chuck chances like this away.' Briefly, Abel was grave. 'You are certain, Maud, that you're prepared to tackle even more hard work?'

Smiling back, she nodded. 'What have I just said? Thank goodness that's settled.' She was sorry for the Queen, though. Somehow, the reminder of how fortunate she was that Abel had survived strengthened her to face the task ahead.

'The shop's well-stocked, anyway,' Abel continued after a moment's consideration. 'That'll give you a chance to step up production ready for the demand we anticipate.'

'We might have to take on more men.'

'Aye – well, the brass is there when we have to. You've not replaced Jeff Hardcastle yet, have you?'

Maud shook her head. She hadn't liked to. Abel hadn't commented when she'd told him how she'd been obliged to dismiss the apprentice. She had wondered since if he had disapproved of her action.

'After Christmas there'll like as not be more lads seeking work,' he said.

'Pity none of the Cloughs' young 'uns are old enough.'

'Now, Maud, you're being too cautious. There's others in t'workshop as you can rely on. Bob Dunsdale's a good, quiet worker. Hasn't he got a son Silas as is coming up to the right age?'

'I'll find out tomorrow. If that's so and the lad has any inclination, we can arrange for them to come here to see you.'

'What's wrong with you setting him on?'

'Oh, Abel . . .'

He saw how troubled she was by further responsibility. 'We'll have to see. And you're not to go worriting on about it. Now we have decided what we intend I'm going to ensure you relax more.'

Maud raised a fair eyebrow. He did talk daft, had he forgotten how much work there was? 'Oh, aye – and how do you reckon you'll do that?'

'Starting with Christmas, there's going to be a bit of enjoyment in this place again.'

'Christmas? But I thought, now that Prince Albert's died . . .' In fact, long before the Prince Consort's illness Maud had considered that their Christmas, this year, would scarcely be a celebration.

'The court will go into mourning, of course. That doesn't include folk like us. And wasn't Prince Albert the one who introduced many of the festivities? Christmas trees and suchlike.'

'I suppose so, but . . .'

'Mrs Richmond is capable enough, there's no reason she shouldn't be given a free hand. Christmas dinner will just be family. The rest of the time, though, I'd like us to keep an open door, Maud. It's weeks now since I saw any of my friends. Sidney Etherington and his wife could come, you've always got on well with Sadie. And if they're invited we can't not ask the Crabtrees. Then there's Leslie Melbeck – he can't want to stop in that great barn of a house on his own.'

'You'd better draw up a list, make sure we don't miss anybody out.'

'Our Hester can help with asking folk. It'll give her something else to think about besides work.' The girl talked of nowt else, these days. Couldn't she understand that was only rubbing it in?

'Poor lass, she doesn't get much time to herself now.'

Abel gave his wife a look. 'Has she been grumbling?'

'No, never a word. Unless it's because her designing's taking second place.'

'Didn't think, somehow, that she'd have said owt. Much like you, is our Hester.' And like me and all, he thought, *now*. When all he could do was endure one day and then the next, counting the hours sometimes, even the minutes, to get through without screaming aloud this feeling of sheer futility.

'Oh?' Maud was astonished, and not at all sure she thought the comparison a compliment. *She'd* never forget herself and appear at the workshop in such unseemly clothes. And some days Hester evidently gave no thought to her hair, scraping it back that tightly from her centre parting until her eyes looked to be leaping out of her pale little face.

'Hester and me – I mean and *I* – are going to take a few hours off before Christmas is upon us. A new gown is what we'll buy her, Abel. And if I don't take her there myself, there's no knowing what she'll select.'

'You ought to be thankful she isn't always primping in front of the glass, lots of mothers would be. All the same, she shall have something to brighten her up . . .'

Only the other day the doctor had been inquiring of him if Hester was unwell. Jon Davidson had caught sight of her as she hurried between the works and the Flowergate shop. Abel didn't like being told how exhausted the girl looked,

80

especially when he felt he was the cause of her additional work.

'We must ask Jon Davidson to call on us over Christmas as well.'

'And to bring his wife, what's her name – Ruth?'

'He's an ideal practitioner, couldn't have been more attentive to our needs.'

'We're lucky, Abel, that's what we are.' Maud's blue eyes misted. 'That's what I knew the minute I heard about Queen Victoria's bereavement.'

Lucky was anything but the term he'd choose. It was easy for her to talk, she wasn't locked in this confounded room on this dratted bed, day in and day out. Still, he'd bottled that up for many a day now and would keep it that way for a while longer, till after Christmas.

'I'll bet the Queen has more sorting out than this to do, now she's got to get rid of her husband's things.'

Sally was kneeling on the rag rug in front of her grandmother's oak chest. They had emptied every item of furniture and the tall cupboards beside the fireplace, pausing only to examine the old jet cross fastened to the newel-post to ward off evil.

Jamie had helped a lot by being there, as well as by deftly packing items into cardboard boxes. They only had the upstairs room to clear now, and that wouldn't take long. Her grandmother had possessed only one change of clothes and the two nightgowns that had gone with her when she was taken into the Drinkwater home.

'What's happening to the furniture?' asked Jamie as they went up the bare stone stair.

'Our Dennis has spoken for that. He got wed last summer, and him and Lizzie have got nowt to speak of. He's fetching a cart tomorrow to shift it all.'

'It's a good bed,' Jamie exclaimed, eyes widening. Having shared a lumpy old iron bed with his brothers in the one cramped bedroom of the house down by the harbour, he could appreciate a grand brass bed.

'She's kept it nice, hasn't she?' Smiling wistfully, Sally went to stand at its foot, ran affectionate fingers over the cold metal knob. 'House-proud, Grandmother was, even though she never had nowt much.' Her lip quivered, she swallowed, but couldn't restrain the tears. 'Ay, she did look little when we laid her out, and that thin . . .' Her voice faltered. 'I'd never seen anybody dead before . . .'

In two strides Jamie was at her side and put both arms round her. 'You have a nice cry,' he said, and noticed how this brought brief amusement to her lips while the tears still coursed down her pink and white cheeks.

'You must think I'm proper daft,' Sally exclaimed after a time, when composure was returning.

He shook his head. She saw how his hair shone with coppery red glints in the sparse glow from the rush-light.

'I've seen tears and all sorts, tha knows. I've got five sisters . . .' Jamie told her.

'*Five?*' Sally interrupted. 'That's a lot. Any brothers as well?'

'Three.'

'What a crowd of you! You must live in a very big house.'

He laughed, sharply. 'About as big as this, down by Whitby harbour.'

'They all must be nice, though, like you are.'

Spoken so seriously, with teardrops glistening on her pale lashes, the words moved him deeply. In a few hours Jamie had grown fond of this attractive girl, felt easy with her. Kissing her began as the affectionate gesture he used frequently with his kin, but changed almost at once into something more expressive, intense.

'You didn't stop me,' he began when his lips finally left hers.

'I didn't think to.'

She sounded as breathless as he felt, and rather awed by what was happening so swiftly between them.

'Have you got a sweetheart, Sally?'

She shook her head. There was nothing serious between her and Harold Clough, was there? And besides, Harold had disappointed her today.

'What about you, Jamie? Are you promised to Miss Hester?'

His laugh startled her. 'Garn, don't talk daft! We're fri-

82

ends, that's all, since we were little. Hester'll not wed the likes of me. Any road, I'll not be getting married.'

'Everybody does.'

'One day, happen. When I've made up to my father for wrecking the boat, when the little 'uns are all out earning.'

'Some prospect! What'll you do, meanwhile?'

His green-brown eyes lit up and the well-defined mouth approached her own. The hint of a moustache on Jamie's upper lip tingled against Sally's skin, arousing within her the urgency that had been awakened earlier that day, and left unanswered.

'I'll have to go home soon,' Sally asserted, but moved not an inch from the warmth of arms that insulated her from the closeness of death.

'Soon,' Jamie agreed. 'I'll see you there safely.'

First, though, he held her nearer still, found her mouth again, was surprised when the point of her tongue teased his lips apart. Tentatively, one hand traced her breast, remained there when she did not protest.

Desire was flowing through him, urging that he press ever closer to this yielding young person. And the bed was beside them – he was too much the man to ignore it.

With a small cry Sally sank backwards on to the feather mattress, but did not slip away before he joined her. With all his nerve endings yammering for release of the escalating pressure within him, he bore down upon her, a knee instinctively going to the front opening of her crinoline cage.

'No, Jamie, I hardly know you . . .'

'All right, love, all right. Just let me hold you.'

His mouth was feverish on hers, his tongue darting rapidly between her teeth. The ale he had drunk when they stopped to eat at the inn was sharp, but she savoured it nonetheless, as she ached to sample the whole of him. Harold had aroused her in the past, but never so violently. Deep inside her was a kind of screaming. A screaming for what, she did not fully understand, only that this young man was willing to give everything she needed.

Unlike Harold, Jamie did not wear a necktie. Sally's fingers explored within the open shirt, loosening an additional button or two when she couldn't resist his bare muscular chest with its generous expanse of coarse gingery hair.

'Ooh, Jamie,' she gasped, and giggled when the touch of her hand incited him to nibble at her earlobe.

Jamie, though, was inflamed by her caress and the need to learn how she might please him further. Kissing her more fiercely, he pressed again with his leg at the edges of her crinoline cage.

'Take the thing off,' he urged breathlessly.

'I'll do no such thing!' Pushing with both hands, Sally eased him a little away from her. 'There's fun, and there's ... expecting too much. And here you are, only today meeting me for the first time.'

'But such an exciting meeting,' Jamie insisted, his eyes agleam. 'And you so pale and ladylike among all the glittering jet. I'd not scare you, though, lass – specially if I'm to be promised I'll see you again.'

'I'll think about it.' Sally felt important, particularly when she recalled that Jamie was Miss Hester's friend. 'Though I don't know where we'll be able to go.' Her rare meetings with Harold Clough had taught her the need for discretion. Whitby was small enough for them to be seen. She'd not risk her father learning that she was alone with a man when he supposed her working late in the shop.

'There's Father's boathouse.' He would need to clean it out but if it were dry, it would shield off the wind and weather.

Sally considered. A boathouse sounded romantic, as adventurous as Jamie himself appeared. 'When?'

'Tomorrow when you close the shop. I'll be waiting.' Longer than that and he might be back at sea, couldn't afford to turn down a trip even for a lass as luscious as Sally.

Walking back along the narrow, snow-covered pavements to the workroom Hester was disturbed, her emotions churning. Telling Jamie that she had designs that must be completed had been the truth, for there never was sufficient time now. But she also knew deep inside her that she hadn't been entirely sorry to get away.

She had been wrong to suppose she had mastered the distress caused by her father's accident. Just seeing Jamie again *had* hurt, especially since he looked so pleased with himself.

A gap between the shops on either corner of a steep alley meandering down to the harbour offered a view across the water to the headland. Although partially coated with snow, the ruined walls of the abbey still stood out darkly against a sky heavy with the threat of another blizzard. Even from this distance she could distinguish the long line of the steps leading up the hill. Not far short of two hundred there were, and how she'd loved counting as she climbed when she was small. She yearned for that time, when she so easily had been happy. When she hadn't felt so alone and anxious.

Falgrave House was only a short distance below the abbey, most of it visible from where she stood. She'd often wished for a prettier home; its contours stolid and square with the portico its only adornment, it represented good Yorkshire sense without pretensions. Even now that its grey slate roof was blanketed with snow the place looked stern, more forbidding than the smaller houses lower down the slope. All packed in together, as if by some giant who could not collect enough of them, they appeared cheerful and indifferent to overcrowding. So familiar that they were a part of her.

The Cloughs lived in a cramped terraced house, only a street or two up from the quayside. The Skeltons in another that was tinier and closer to the water, where whaling folk once rendered blubber. But it was to be in that gaunt house near the abbey that she ached now, so fiercely that she had to will herself not to run all the way there.

Her parents had given her everything she possessed, she remembered firmly, walking on swiftly towards the workshop. She could love them best by suppressing the need for reassurance. From them, too, she had learned love of the jet – it was no hardship to experiment. She wanted to try figurines, a good contrast for the popular unglazed white porcelain.

The men were laughing together as they worked, telling her before she'd climbed the narrow stairs that her mother had left for home. Whilst she had been out at the Flowergate shop they had been promised higher piece-work rates to ensure greater production.

Wally Hardcastle alone saw that as less than a good inducement. 'Us legs'll drop off if we work these danged treadles any faster.'

'Nay, you've nowt to complain off, you allus win t'races when we have a contest in t'summer,' Bob Dunsdale reminded him.

'Only because my missus puts on a good table. It's nowt to do with treadling.'

'Bet you've muscles like an ox in them calves,' Harold Clough ventured.

'I've heard it's somewhat higher up where his strength lies,' one of the apprentices put in. Wally's first wife had died before she was forty, worn down by frequent childbearing. He'd taken a second wife no older than his son, Jeff, and had made the pair of them Whitby's talking point for a week or two.

Frank Clough checked his own laughter to jerk his head in Hester's direction. 'Better mind what we say, lads,' he warned under his breath, and surprised himself.

Still concentrating on the engraved brooch to which he was giving a final polish he glanced sideways as, removing her dark blue cloak, Hester crossed to hang it in the office. Since the moment he'd heard how severely Abel Falgrave was injured, his attitude towards Hester had altered. It was as if a layer of cloth had been whipped away, to reveal how mistaken he'd been in his earlier assessment. Gone was his resentment of what he'd considered her privileged position, but which he now saw was not so much privilege as natural progression.

Freed of his own prejudice, he'd found he was glad to acknowledge her innate gift for finding the best ways of showing the jet to advantage. Her designs were more innovative than most in the other workshops. He was invigorated by the intricacy of the patterns she expected him to transfer on to brooches like the one he was completing, or buttons so tiny that engraving anything on their face was a challenge. She made the work exciting.

There was excitement in more than the work, as well, though that must remain his secret. Outwardly, he was his old self with her, courteous – Mam had drilled courtesy into them – but that bit guarded, because of who Hester was. Inwardly, he seethed, not with anger but with a massive need.

It had begun that first day she'd returned to the works after her father's accident. She'd been standing by his bench, composed yet so pale he feared life was draining from her. Her interest in the jewellery he was fashioning to her design was no less genuine than before, her directions were expressed just as accurately. But all he'd been able to think was how he ached to comfort, to look after her.

That had been his undoing. Thinking to comfort was but a hair's breadth from thinking to hold. For once, he'd been glad of the loose blue smock they wore, beneath which his overheated body might suffer undetected. Even the black dust coating his face had its use, disguising his heightened colour.

'May I see, Frank?'

She was beside him now, not taking him by surprise – wasn't he always conscious of her movement about the workroom – but again bringing colour to his cheeks.

She was cool from the icy wind outdoors, but the fragrance of her hair as she bent towards him filled all his senses. Nothing could freeze out her loveliness. And nor could it diminish his response.

Her long fingers brushed his as she took the brooch from him, and Frank drew in a sharp breath as the surge within him sharpened to pain. No girl he'd met before had affected him this intensely.

'That's beautiful, Frank. Did you have a try at those buttons, the ones with the seagulls?'

'I did, but I'm not satisfied yet.'

'Ready to show me?'

He made a face and she chuckled. A light, pleasing sound close to his ear. Had she grown more delightful since her father's incapacity? Or had he never previously appreciated the absence of pressure that made working with her ecstasy.

'You can look if you want . . .'

He searched on the bench, rooted around in one of the trays among the layers of jet dust. 'Haven't polished any of them properly as yet, there's none good enough.'

'They're coming along, though.'

She was smiling, examining each tiny button in turn then comparing one with another, making a final selection. But suddenly she mixed them up again, mischievously.

'Which do you think's best, Frank?'

She cared for his opinion, and felt free enough with him to tease a little for his answer. And he was master of his craft, went unerringly to the best of these experimental buttons.

'Ah . . .'

Approval was in the warmth of her glorious brown eyes as they lit up, seeming far brighter to him than the light produced by gas to illuminate their workroom.

'Since we're agreed,' she continued, still smiling, 'you'll have no difficulty perfecting this. I should polish up the next you do. And I'll take samples to show Father. He always speaks highly of your work, you know. It's good to have my opinion confirmed.'

Her hand went to his shoulder, seemed to seal their continuing cooperation. And it burned through the grimy smock, the shirt he wore beneath, burned too through his skin until his being seemed ready to melt for her. If this was attraction, it was a fiery process. If it was more . . . unlikely though it seemed, Frank Clough was powerless to check the emotions she aroused in him.

Chapter 5

Jamie came striding into the shop while Sally was serving a fashionable young lady who, accompanied by her mother, was selecting a gift for her grandmother.

With her own grandmother's burial arranged for the following day, Sally had been feeling miserable but now that Jamie had arrived, smiling at her as though she were the only girl in Whitby, her sadness dispersed.

Her customers were taking their time but Sally wasn't entirely sorry about that. Jamie was standing behind them, half-turned from her as he scrutinised some of the jet displayed in the tall glass-fronted cases that lined three of the walls. His attention elsewhere, she had the opportunity to admire his powerful physique.

'What would you buy for yourself, Sally, if you had all the money you wanted?' he inquired as soon as they were alone.

'One of them pendants – in that case where you were looking. But that's daft talk, I'll never afford it.'

'I can, though.'

Jamie had been to sea again with Sam Grinsdale. He hadn't succumbed once to that wretched seasickness even if he'd still felt queasy and, although they'd only been out for a few hours, they'd brought in a good catch which had made a fair price.

'Nay, Jamie, I can't let you – I hardly know you, do I?'

'That's easy remedied, isn't it? And I meant as a Christmas present – that'd make it all right, wouldn't it?'

Sally was still uncertain. She'd been sensibly brought up, warned of the ways in which the accepting of gifts could be misinterpreted.

'Show me the one,' Jamie persisted, smiling. His hand went to her shoulder when she came out from behind the long counter and crossed swiftly to him.

The pendant was a cameo supported on a necklet of

small faceted beads that made it more delicate than many with heavier chains.

Taking it from her and instructing her to turn, Jamie fastened it about her neck.

Sally rushed to examine the effect in the mirror set one end of the counter. The pendant glinted in the light, brightening the dark dress she was obliged to wear on account of her grandmother.

'It is lovely on you,' Jamie was beside her again.

He particularly wanted to give her something, and he rarely had money in his pocket. He'd not be spending on anyone else for Christmas, as the Skeltons didn't waste brass on family presents. After this, most of what he earned would go to pay back his father.

He'd signed on with one of the trawler owners who fished in a big way. He'd be out tonight, which was the reason that he'd got Sam to put him ashore, and more often than not his trips out to sea now would be for days rather than hours. He already liked Sally a lot, needed to ensure she'd contrive to see him whenever he was in Whitby.

Sally felt torn. She'd tried on the pendant before when no one was around, had dreamed about wearing it, but there was a difference between life and dreams.

'Is that to be the one?' Jamie asked, taking coins from his pocket.

'It's nice and all that,' she replied swiftly, unfastening the clasp, 'but I'm not letting you pay all that for it. If you've got to replace your father's boat like you said, you'd do far better giving *him* your brass.' After a final glance at the pendant, she replaced it carefully in the display case and locked the glass door.

Jamie shrugged philosophically, and put his money away. He'd thought all lasses wanted a fellow to buy them things, but he'd not need telling twice that this lass thought differently. Happen in the long run it would turn out the same anyway. He intended seeing Sally whenever possible, and that might last until he'd squared things with his father. The immediate future was what had worried him, and he'd thought to sweeten the news of his protracted absences.

The clock struck the hour and Sally beamed. 'Time to

lock up, thank goodness.' It had been a busy day, but had seemed long just the same. 'I'm afraid I can't stay out late,' she told him as she began securing display cases and cupboards. 'I've told my mam that I have to work a bit later tonight, on account of having tomorrow off to help look after them that's coming for the funeral.'

'That's all right.' He'd be putting out on the next tide, and would have to change out of his good clothes first.

'Where are you taking me?' Sally inquired, as she checked the rear door was locked then crossed through towards the shop door.

Jamie stifled a sigh. All the time at sea he'd been thinking, and the only idea he had was the original one of going to the boathouse. When he told her, the smile that so enchanted him faded slightly.

'Aren't we going to have summat to eat first?'

He had thought of that as well, but wanted to avoid meeting either his own friends or cronies of his father. He might not have had much of a schooling, but the years that followed had instilled in him the dangers of taking a girl anywhere on his own. Anywhere they might be seen. His experience with Hester had shown that covert meetings were not only possible but the only sort he could manage.

'Have you a married sister or somebody then who'll come along, and maybe turn a blind eye afterwards when I'm compelled to kiss you?'

'Jamie Skelton, you do talk daft!' Sally interrupted, as they paused on the step while she locked the door after them. 'I haven't any older sisters.' She had brothers, though, and they along with her father would beat the living daylights out of any lad she was caught kissing.

'It'll be different once I've paid off that boat,' he told her confidently. He'd work twice as hard when the proceeds were for himself, when he'd be free to do as he liked. They'd both be a lot older then. He might even feel like buying an engagement ring.

Sally wasn't cheered. She didn't know how much boats cost, but she'd seen enough of scrimping and making do. The only time her family made a decent living was years ago in whaling. Fishing might replace that boat, but there'd not be much left over. Still, Jamie was handsome, she'd more sense than to let the future spoil tonight.

He had cleaned out the bit of a shed that served as the Skelton boathouse. He'd also been fortunate. On his way back ashore, he'd come across one of the Crabtree lasses, wrapped up against the cold as she put the last few knots in a net she was completing. He had stopped only long enough to pass the time of day and had been surprised when she started grumbling.

'I don't know how ever I'm going to manage. All I can think is that I'm going to have to lug this great thing up to the house for safekeeping.'

Evidently, her father had put out to sea with the key of the Crabtree boathouse on him. 'He'll murder me if I leave a new net out and it gets stolen. And he'll not be much better pleased either if he has to fetch it from home afterwards.'

The Skelton boathouse had been offered and accepted. Going inside now, Jamie smiled to himself, recalling how fortuitously he'd been provided with a substitute couch.

'Ooh, isn't it dark in here,' Sally exclaimed, but at least her first remark wasn't about the odour of fish. Either his cleaning had been thorough, or she was too familiar with fish for it to be obtrusive.

'I'll look after you, shan't I?' He hadn't needed an excuse to draw her against him, but wouldn't discard reason for tightening the arm about her shoulders. 'I just wish I didn't have a job that takes me away so much. I like looking after you, Sally.'

She had been wondering if she'd been foolish to decline the gift he'd offered to buy. Now he was talking like this, it seemed there was even hope of their friendship enduring.

'Yes, but you don't go off for more than a night or so at a time, do you? We'll manage to meet in between.' *He* wouldn't produce the same excuses as Harold Clough for not using that back room at the shop.

'Mm, well . . .' Haltingly, Jamie told her about the boat he'd signed on with, and how there'd be longer trips.

'I see.'

He felt her deflation in a physical slackening and gave

her a quick, impulsive hug. 'Come and sit down, Sally love, over here.' He drew her with him to the far wall where the folded net was waiting.

'Reminds me of when I were a little lass,' she said, a smile in her voice again. 'Me and my brothers used to help mend the nets – that was before I was took on to work in the shop, of course.' She neglected to mention the interim when she'd been in service to the parson's wife in Staithes. She had loathed every minute of skivvying.

'I'll bet you were a bonnie girl. I wish I'd known you then.'

'What's wrong with me now, then?' she demanded provocatively.

'Nothing, Sally love. You're perfect.'

His kiss was on her cheek first of all, but only because in the darkness he hadn't quite got it right. Seconds later, Jamie was gratified to find Sally's lips no less yielding than the previous evening. By his third kiss there was no mistaking her eagerness growing to match his own. His tongue was thrusting sharply between her teeth, eliciting a moan of what he hoped was ecstasy.

'Jamie,' she gasped when he swiftly drew in air, and her hand slid to the back of his neck, holding him more closely to her.

Encouraged, he found the opening of her cloak, explored the silk of her bodice where it swelled with a firm breast. His caress brought her alive in his arms, making her stir deliciously against him while her tongue teased his, inflaming him until the blood surged throughout his body.

That was what checked him. Jamie was scared. A fact he'd have admitted to no one, it was nevertheless unmistakable. While one part of him clamoured for the release he might find in possessing her, the other – that had harkened to young fellows compelled to wed the lass they had put in the family way – was terrified.

Life had been bad enough, hadn't it, when it seemed there was no means of paying off the massive debt to his father. Now he'd signed to crew on a long-haul boat that anxiety had eased. He'd not toss away a newly-quiet mind, no matter how exciting this lass was.

'What time do you have to be home?'

Sally was astonished, and considerably put out. Even Harold Clough had wanted more of her company than this. Last night Jamie had seemed different, had hardly listened when she said it was time for home.

'I don't know, I don't think I said an exact time.' She was just getting comfortable on the hard couch made of this folded net. Deep inside her she felt deliciously warm, simply because of knowing he wanted her.

'It's a tidy walk to t'far side of Sandsend.'

'I know that without your telling, don't I? I walk into Whitby and back every day.'

'We can talk as we go, love.'

Talking was nowhere near as exciting as kissing, and wouldn't do anything for this craving that Jamie created.

'When will I see you again then?' This evening was proving such an anticlimax she was desperate for something to look forward to.

'As soon as we put in again.' Sorry that he was the cause of her obvious disappointment, Jamie kissed her once more.

Her lips seemed to rivet themselves to his, the point of her tongue inserted between his teeth. Again desire seared straight through him and despite his resolve he pressed her backwards into the wooden wall of the boathouse.

Sally's head thumped into the wood. 'It's all right,' she told him swiftly with a giggle, for she'd not have him thinking she was ready to curtail the experience now it was becoming interesting. 'Why don't I sit on your knee?'

'With that stiff crinoline thing under your skirts?'

'I can take it off . . .'

'No, love, not now. Like I said, we've got to get you home.' And in time to ensure that he was back in Whitby and ready to sail with the tide.

This time Sally didn't argue. There was a long walk ahead, its only advantage the opportunity it would provide for talking him into seeing her, not only the minute he came ashore again but at Christmas as well. She had decided to abandon hope that she might rely on Harold to entertain her over the short holiday.

Sally was following Jamie out through the door when he

was stopped by a large man who stood outlined in the darkness against the slightly paler sky.

'My daughter says you've got yon new net of ours,' the man was saying.

'Aye, it's in here.'

As Jamie turned to go back inside Mr Crabtree noticed Sally. He chortled when Jamie re-emerged and handed over the bulky net.

'Nearly caught you at it, didn't I? I hope you've been careful, young Skelton – seems you've not been good.'

Jamie was mortified. There was no way he could reply. If he denied that he'd taken Sally he'd not be believed. That's the last time I bring her here, he resolved as they set off to climb through the town's narrow streets. He knew already in his heart, though, that there'd be other meetings, even in circumstances no more propitious. He'd never experienced such intense attraction: he meant to take more care than Mr Crabtree supposed, but was only human and couldn't entirely deny what was offered.

Bernard Falgrave bounded into the master bedroom, saw Nurse Clapper beside his father's bed, and halted.

'Good evening, Father. Good evening, Nurse . . .' He clamped his lips together over the merriment which must be suppressed. He'd made up a rhyme around the nurse's unfortunate name, a rhyme divulged only to two particular friends at school. He'd not have risked sharing the joke with Olive. She was altogether too silly for that kind of secret, and would have let it out to some member of the household within the hour.

'Master Bernard,' Nurse Clapper responded without enthusiasm to his greeting. The young members of the family might be tolerated in the patient's room, but only because she'd not yet developed reasons for their being excluded.

'Bernard, my boy – how was school?' Abel was beaming across behind the nurse's back. 'Come and tell me . . .' The lad and young Olive always succeeded in taking his mind off agonising imprisonment.

Making a wide arc around the nurse, Bernard hastened towards the bed and sat with a plomp in the chair nearby.

'We did local history again today. Did you know Robin Hood and Little John came to Whitby?'

'When they fired arrows from the tower of the abbey, you mean?'

'Arrows that landed at Whitby Laithes! You do know about it, I said you would . . .' He was discovering that his father had an intense interest in folklore.

'I've heard the story, of course. You do know it's only legend, Bernard?'

The boy nodded. 'Good, though, isn't it – to know they were associated with these parts.'

'What else have you learned today?'

Instead of going on to other subjects as his father anticipated, Bernard continued about the local legends that fascinated them both.

'All about the original castle at Mulgrave. How it was built by Wadda the giant. Him and his wife constructed a causeway and all. You can see some of the stones that she didn't chuck far enough – somewhere on the moors. I wish . . . oh, never mind.' He'd been about to say that he wished his father could take him there. But had learned these past few weeks the tactlessness of such remarks.

'Our Hester will take you maybe, when the better weather comes.'

'If she's got time,' Bernard said dourly.

'I would have thought there was history enough centred on Whitby itself,' Nurse Clapper observed. '*Real* history.'

'And my son's got a good grasp of that as well,' Abel announced with a covert grin for the lad which did not diminish the sharp tone of his words.

As he had hoped, Nurse Clapper strode out of the room. Like conspirators, father and son laughed quietly as the door closed. Both valued these times together, sometimes resented the presence of other members of the family, let alone the uniformed ogre.

Bernard was growing up fast and the process was aided by Abel's understanding of the lad's reaction to his mother's preoccupation with the business. It was to Abel that Bernard had confided his distress at the prospect of being obliged to dispose of many of his childhood toys. And, to Abel's astonishment, the boy had needed only a bit of encouragement to surrender enough of them to satisfy his mother's strictures.

'If it was me,' Abel had said that dreadful Sunday, 'I'd be terribly clever and select a few of the toys that no longer really mattered to me. Maybe that would ensure that she didn't order May Thorpe to make the selection.'

The idea had worked. When Bernard himself had suggested he might take the toys along to the vicar for distribution to children in the poorer houses near the harbour, Maud had considered that sufficient.

Abel had been as delighted as his young son. He loathed seeing Maud taking out her tiredness in harassment of the children for whom, he knew, she felt a love that equalled his own.

'Are there friends you wish to invite here during the Christmas holiday?' he asked Bernard now.

'I haven't thought about it actually. There might be. On the other hand . . .' Again, Bernard paused. He'd been going to say how much he always enjoyed family Christmases. 'Thanks, anyway,' he said swiftly. 'I'll think about it.'

'Tell your mother or Hester, will you, if there is anyone. They're organising our visitors. There'll be lots of people in and out, any road.' He told Bernard of the old friends who would gather there once more, and was glad simply to mention that it would be so. He'd never been so long without the company of people outside the immediate family.

Since invitations for the Christmas period had gone out, Sidney Etherington had called personally to say that he and Sadie would be pleased to join them. Evidently, he'd been reluctant to visit Falgrave House previously – Abel had been disturbed to learn that Sidney had feared friends would no longer be welcome.

'Whatever made you think that, Sid?' he'd asked.

'Oh, you know . . .' Sidney looked down at his large hands that always were red and raw. He owned several fishing vessels, but wasn't above taking one of them out himself.

And nothing he did running a profitable business armed him with ready words.

'Afraid, were you, that I'd not want folk seeing me like this?'

Sidney's denial had been vehement, so much so that Abel had realised this reason might apply to many of his friends. The notion saddened him. He could only be thankful that he was about to right that misconception – if misconception it was. He'd changed that much with being cooped up and frustrated, that he hardly knew himself.

'This danged treadle's giving out! Hark at the racket it's making now.'

Wally's expression had darkened even further since the day his son Jeff was dismissed. Every small fault in the equipment he used was fussed over and magnified until he was irritating Edwin Clough past all bearing.

'Doesn't sound any different from usual to me,' he told him now. 'Have you had a look to see if owt's wrong?'

'Owt wrong, owt wrong! Stuff we're expected to work wi' is falling apart, that's what.'

'I'll have a look mysen when I've finished this.' He was carving a likeness of the late Prince Consort, another of the brooches that Mrs Falgrave said would prove popular. Some were going into the shop, naturally, but the rest would be sent further afield, some abroad even. The Queen's deep mourning was spreading to the European courts – even ordinary folk over there were showing respect.

'Time somebody told Mrs Falgrave she'll have to lay out brass for a replacement.'

'I'll see she's told if there's any need – if nowt can be done.'

Wally glanced covertly around the workroom. Edwin's two sons were grinning for all they were worth. Some of the others, and all. Bob Dunsdale had his back to them as he worked and he would swear the fellow's shoulders were shaking with laughter.

This wasn't what he wanted at all. Did nobody appreciate what he intended? Better conditions were what he was after. The Falgraves were saving Jeff's wages – well, he'd see to it that brass was spent. And another thing, if there was all this additional work coming their way with the Prince Consort dying, now was the time to band the men together. Else the bosses'd take advantage.

Tackling any of the Cloughs was a waste of time; indoctrinated, they were, into thinking the Falgraves could do no wrong. But the rest of the men could be made to come round to his way of thinking. It was for their own good, after all, that they should have a show of strength.

Wally was fortunate when they stopped for their dinner break. Harold Clough went off to deliver goods to the Flowergate shop, and Frank and his father decided to meet their friends for a drink. Wally himself had a liking for beer, but readily sacrificed that to such a good opportunity.

'I've been thinking,' he began as, one by one, the treadles stopped and the workers reached for the food they'd brought with them. 'It's high time we armed ourselves for coping with all this additional work.'

'*Armed?*'

That was Bob Dunsdale; he might have known it would be.

'Only in a manner of speaking,' said Wally quickly, and stood up. He was over six feet tall and broad with it – might as well remind the others he was somebody to reckon with. 'We haven't a union, as yet, as well you know. But you've only to heed what's gone on in t'rest of t'country – aye, even i' other parts of Yorkshire – to see as it's unions as looks after t'workers' interests.'

'Nay, there's no need of a union here, Wally,' one of the old-timers protested in disgust.

Wally treated him to a prolonged stare. 'You might think that, Ned. And happen things'll remain all right, for your time here. It's young 'uns I'm concerned for. And the rest of us, of course. Specially now.'

'Now?'

Bob Dunsdale again. Wally swung his gaze towards him, made sure it didn't waver.

'With Mr Falgrave laid low, of course. You saw t'other day how his missus got rid of our Jeff. Without due cause.'

'I heard tell that he were caught gathering rough jet when he should have been at work,' an apprentice ventured.

'You know nowt about it, lad. It'll pay you to keep gossip and suchlike to yourself. And it's for lads like you that I'm doing this. You're the ones as'll be – be *exploited* in t'future.'

'Don't you think you might be going to extremes, Wally, calling for a union?' someone suggested. 'It's different from in factories.'

'I don't see how. There's the men, and there's them as pays their wages. It's same here, you know it is. And, like I said, we need some weight. The weight of not letting them divide us.'

Some of the men were listening, nodding now when they thought of how unions got folk better wages, and how by another Christmas they might not have to say no to so much that their wives and children were after. Before the Cloughs returned Wally had got most of the men behind him, and some of those who weren't for committing themselves so soon wouldn't take too much persuading. The only one who wouldn't say anything was Bob Dunsdale. Wally wasn't surprised about that, nor would he let it worry him. There were ways and means.

Hester had enjoyed the afternoon more than any since her father's accident. Considering that she had spent the time with her mother, returning to Falgrave House in excellent spirits was remarkable. For once, their tastes appeared to have converged. Her mother had not reproached her once for seeming unladylike, nor for failing to appreciate beautiful things.

And the gown her parents were giving her for Christmas was, indeed, beautiful. Intended more for summer perhaps than the sharp winters of Yorkshire's North Riding, it would nevertheless be warm enough for wearing indoors now. And as soon as she had glimpsed its exquisite flounces in the shop window, she had known she couldn't wait to wear such a deliciously feminine creation.

'You must try it on to show your father,' Maud had exclaimed as soon as Kilner set them down at the front steps.

Here they were now, in Hester's bedroom, both equally delighted as they unveiled the gown from its layers of tissue. A fine white cotton printed with sprigs of lilac-coloured flowers, its flounces had matching lilac trimming and its bodice was enhanced by openwork embroidery. With additional petticoats as well as the crinoline cage, the skirt swung out wide around Hester as she crossed the room for her dainty lilac shoes.

'You've a nice way of holding yourself when you can be bothered,' Maud observed approvingly.

Sitting carefully to put on her shoes, Hester glanced across and grinned. 'Glad I'm not entirely a disappointment to you.' Today, she felt she might say anything and get away with it. Her mother's commendation was rare enough to transform the day, and it had. She felt pleasure glowing through her, the result of so many hours without one cross word.

'You're so tall and slender,' Maud continued, smiling and still nodding to herself. 'That's elegant, you know. There'll be times when you'll gladly make use of that . . .'

Hester laughed. 'Oh, aye – down yonder, you mean?'

'You know I don't mean in the workshop. And many's the occasion when I've been saddened that you don't have an occupation permitting you to dress more attractively.'

'Well, we have to think of the work, haven't we,' Hester continued, straight-faced. 'There'd be none done at all if I startled the men by appearing in a pretty gown.'

Abel's delight showed in the warmth of his brown eyes the moment Hester followed his wife into the bedroom.

'By, but you're a bonnie lass, Hester.'

'Thank you, Father,' she said, going over to kiss him. 'And it's you that's provided all this finery to effect the transformation.'

'Happen it helps,' he conceded when she had thanked him for the gown, 'but you possess the face to do it justice.' And the figure, he added silently, awed by the maturity of his daughter and the appeal of such a neat v-shaped bodice with tiny tucks fanning out towards the shoulders.

'That's a dainty bit of cloth,' he went on, looking at the sleeve nearest to him which was shaped rather like a bell, but in two layers that widened towards the wrist where it revealed a plain white undersleeve.

'It's very becoming, isn't it, Abel,' said Maud from the other side of the bed.

'You've chosen well between you.' He was glad he could still delight his family, if only by providing the wherewithal. And was very glad also to see the pair of them so evidently in harmony. Maybe now that Hester was maturing so gracefully Maud would have fewer occasions to find fault with the girl.

Down in the kitchen, however, it was the strain between Abel and Maud that had been worrying the staff. Today, though, Kilner remarked on the pleasant outing as he entered the kitchen. 'It fair made me feel better, Mrs Richmond.'

'And not before time! You never know where you are, these days.'

Her affection for the family, which had always compensated for her own childlessness, had been tested recently by witnessing the most unprecedented storms. Only the other day she'd come upon Mr Falgrave berating his poor wife, and all because she was taking over charging wholesalers for goods supplied.

'You're behaving, Maud, for all the world as though I no longer exist.'

For once, Mrs Richmond had been glad to see the mistress stand up to him.

'And maybe I wouldn't if you still took a hand in the things you *can* assist with.'

That hadn't suited him at all. 'Assist, is it? You'd make an "assistant" of me now, would you – is that what I'm reduced to?'

'I only meant you could help by working out invoices and such like,' his wife had persisted calmly enough.

'Could I, indeed? And what other clerical tasks have you designated should be mine, eh?'

'I only meant that you're sharper at figures than . . .'

'Than I'll ever be at anything again!' he'd interrupted, twisting her words. 'I'll remind you I'm not done with yet – and until I am *I* say what goes. Here, and at the works.

I'm not going to be fobbed off by being given bits of jobs that someone thinks I can manage.'

Kilner and the housekeeper smiled at the voices they heard now.

'I must go and take this off and you'll have to hide it away, Mother, till Christmas Day.'

'We'll hang it in one of the wardrobes. I'm not risking the fullness of that skirt emerging all creased.'

Her mother's good humour extended through their meal that evening, making Hester almost regret their responsibilities at the works which precluded frequent outings together.

'I'm going to sit with your father this evening,' Maud announced when May Thorpe arrived to clear the table. Abel seemed less embittered today, happen she could prevent them all becoming soured by that accident. 'I'm going to set aside those invoices, even orders.' Abruptly, she checked herself and sighed. 'Oh, dear – there I go forgetting . . .'

'Forgetting what?'

'I promised our Bernard, Olive as well. While you were getting changed they came bursting into the room. Seemingly, your father had told Bernard he could invite a friend in at Christmas. Naturally, Olive will be treated the same. As it happens there's a family they're both friendly with – Jenkins, they're called. I know their mother, only slightly, but we've met. Any road, there's a lad Bernard's age and a girl in Olive's class. I said I'd have Kilner drive me over there tonight so's I can issue the invitation.'

'Would you like me to go instead?'

Her mother hadn't needed much persuading, and Hester wasn't sorry to be riding through Whitby. There had been another light fall of snow, replacing the earlier covering which had almost melted. The town looked so lovely with lamplight shining from some of the windows and the glow from gas lamps catching the frosty glint of the snow's crisp surface.

Between the houses, she caught occasional glimpses of the sea; even from inside the brougham could hear the rushing waves, smell the tang of brine. Nearing the harbour itself, she discerned the odour of fish but, muted by the carriage windows, it only increased the familiar atmosphere of the town.

The sound of shouting startled her. It was followed immediately by a scream, all the more alarming because it was a man's. A few streets away Hester could hear running feet. She must have just missed witnessing a fight; she hoped no one was badly injured.

Kilner seemed to be encouraging the horses to go faster, no doubt to have them well clear of any trouble. But then suddenly the carriage jerked, shuddered and jerked again. He was pulling hard on the reins, drawing them to a swaying halt.

In the alley to their left was what looked like an untidy mass of rags. Only it wasn't rags at all, it was moving, and blood was already staining the snow.

'You stop where you are, Miss Hester,' Kilner called as he stepped down.

She couldn't do as he advised. Somebody was badly hurt – two people were more use than one.

'By gum, he's copped it!'

Moving swiftly for an elderly person of considerable bulk, Kilner rushed to go down on one knee beside the man. When Hester reached them, he was turning him over, attempting to lay him flat.

'Well, I'll go to heck,' he exclaimed, using his handkerchief to wipe blood from the victim's face. 'Isn't he one of yourn?'

'I don't think – ' Hester checked when the man groaned and blue eyes opened in his battered face.

'Bob,' she said quickly, kneeling by Kilner in the snow. 'Mr Dunsdale . . . It's me – Hester Falgrave. Do you understand what I'm saying?'

Although the eyes trying to focus had a rather vacant look to them, he nodded.

'Sorry, Miss Hester. Don't want to put you to no trouble.' Bob reached the last few words with difficulty, then groaned.

'We'll get you to the hospital.'

'No. No, just let me rest for a bit and I'll be all right.'

'Certainly not, you need medical attention.'

'Miss Hester's right, you know, sir,' Kilner confirmed. 'And the carriage is at t'end of this alley.'

'Take me home instead then, please. My wife'll do whatever's necessary. She'd be expecting me long since, she'll be out of her mind with worry.'

'And not without cause by the look of you.' Kilner shifted his position to get one arm underneath Bob's and round his back. 'Do you reckon you can stand with a bit of help?'

Hester went to his other side and between them they got Bob to his feet and supported him as he shambled painfully in the direction of the brougham.

'Can you manage to tell us where you live?' Hester inquired when they finally succeeded in getting Bob into the carriage. 'Kilner will take you there, I'm going to fetch the doctor.'

'No, no – there's no call for that, Miss Hester.'

Doctors cost good money, she thought, and Christmas is an expensive time when there are youngsters at home.

She smiled at him. 'You're one of our men, aren't you – and must have been attacked on your way home from work. That makes it our responsibility.'

As soon as she had learned Bob Dunsdale's address she left Kilner to take the injured man home and set off along a short cut to Jon Davidson's house in Royal Crescent. Ever since the doctor and his wife had moved there just ten years ago when it was newly-completed, Hester had considered the surroundings compensated for the dread accompanying many a visit to a doctor. Today, though, she scarcely noticed the pleasing lines of the Crescent and had no time for admiring the attractive entrance to the house itself.

'Is the doctor in, please?' she asked the elderly housekeeper in a severe dark gown who opened the door.

'Yes, he's in, but him and the mistress have nobbut just had their dinner.' Keen grey eyes were assessing Hester, and plainly concluded that she wasn't in much need of medical attention.

'It's not for me,' she said hastily. 'One of our workers has been set on in the street. If I could have a word with the doctor . . .'

Jon Davidson had recognised Hester's voice. Emerging from a room to the rear of the hall, he strode towards her.

'Hester – what's to do? It's not your father?'

'No, he's – well, all right. It's one of our men from the workshop. We think he's been attacked. His face is all bashed about and bleeding. We just happened to find him lying in an alleyway.'

'Where's this?'

The doctor spoke over his shoulder as he turned to seize the bag standing ready on a table near the door, and to take his greatcoat from the hook.

'Oh, he's not there now,' Hester explained. 'Kilner's taking him home.'

'What's the man's name?' Jon Davidson inquired, guiding her through the door and across the pavement to where his landaulet waited, the horse tethered.

'Didn't I tell you? Bob Dunsdale.'

'Bob? Good Lord, I'd not have expected he'd find himself in trouble.'

'Is he one of your patients?'

'Aye, he is that. Not that you'd really know it. They're not a family for calling me in overmuch.'

'I rather think treatment might be a luxury to them. That's why I've told him now that Falgraves' will settle your bill. I know my father would wish . . .'

'Don't go worrying your head about that side of things, Hester.' The horse was travelling at a good pace now, and Jon Davidson glanced towards her, smiling. 'With folk that don't take advantage I've been known to overlook sending the odd account.'

This confirmed her liking for the amiable doctor who never seemed to spare himself when he was needed. Now, however, he looked tired and strained and she felt sorry there'd been cause to fetch him out.

When she said as much, she heard his sigh across the space between them. He was staring straight ahead now as if his attention was riveted on the grey mare's ears.

'It's not been a good day, I'm afraid. My wife's not at all well.'

'I'm sorry to hear that.' Ruth Davidson was a devoted

marriage partner who often ushered in patients or took messages. 'I hope she'll soon be better.'

Again, his sigh reached her. 'I'm afraid . . .' He checked abruptly, thanked her and was silent.

They had almost reached the Dunsdales' house in a terraced row on the hill at the back of the town where the road led out to Pickering. When he found the number they were seeking, Jon called to the horse and pulled on the reins.

For a man of his size, he sprang down lightly then turned to assist Hester. His blue eyes were troubled, she noticed, and again she regretted having to disturb him.

There was no sign of any reluctance, however, after he had knocked and they were admitted to the small but cheerful home. Bob's wife had settled her husband on an upright chair, its balloon back at right angles to the walnut table which had thick newspaper protecting its patterned chenille cover. She was bathing the appalling wounds that nearly covered Bob's face and had made an attempt at washing some of the blood from two gashes in his fair hair.

'Evening, Mrs Dunsdale. What's to do then, Bob?' Placing his bag on the table, Jon leaned over to take a look at the injuries.

'I were attacked from behind in the street,' Bob replied very quickly. 'Didn't get a look at who did it, on account of how quick it happened. T'were all over in a minute.'

'I see.' Removing his coat and placing it over the back of one of the other chairs, the doctor was busy thinking. An assailant approaching from the rear would hardly have inflicted so much damage to Bob's face. Still, the first priorities were ascertaining how extensive the injuries were and ensuring that they would heal.

Following closer examination, he approved the cleansing begun by Mrs Dunsdale and took over from her.

'You say the attack was unprovoked, then – no one that you knew?' he persisted while he worked.

'Aye, aye, that's reet.' Again, the reply came very swiftly.

'You were robbed, were you?'

'I don't carry owt of value, Doctor, not going back and forth to work.'

107

'So, we're to be glad the fellow was unlucky, eh? Teach him a lesson.'

'I certainly hope so,' Mrs Dunsdale agreed. 'What do folk want to go knocking decent family men about like this for, and just afore Christmas.'

Now that the doctor had taken charge Kilner moved quietly across the room. 'Might I suggest we were getting along, Miss Hester? If you don't wish to continue on and make your call, shouldn't we perhaps be heading for home?'

'In a moment, thank you.'

She went up to the table, addressed the other three. 'Is there anything I can do?'

Bob's wife smiled, if a little wearily. 'Thank you, love, but no. We're ever so grateful to you and Mr Kilner here for getting Bob home that quick. And for fetching the doctor.'

'You don't wish any messages? There's nobody you'd like to come . . .'

Mrs Dunsdale appeared as shattered as her husband by the sudden attack. Dazedly, she shook her head.

'Bless you, no. We'll just have a bit of a sit, after the doctor's finished.' She paused and nodded to two armchairs on the rag rug beside the blackleaded range. 'And then an early night for once won't do us any harm. Our eldest's still out, but we can leave the door on the sneck for him.'

Riding home in the brougham, Hester was perturbed and not solely for the Dunsdales. Jon Davidson had seemed his normal self only while he was attending to his patient. The rest of the time he was gravely troubled.

Finding Bob like that had been a shock, but the disturbance she felt owed more to her inability to be of any use. She wished she could have released the doctor so he might return more swiftly to his wife.

He was such a supportive man. Even those few minutes sitting with him in the landaulet had been reassuring. She'd not really had much time for thinking about marriage yet, but if she did ever get wed she'd hope for a man as kind as Jon Davidson, and for a relationship like theirs, with each partner so well fitted to care for the other.

Not, she reflected heavily, that she'd ever feel free to

change her name until, for her father's sake, she'd made Falgraves' even more notable – with the beautiful and original jet pieces that were her creation.

Chapter 6

'There's something wrong about all this, Frank.'

Hester had come to the Cloughs' home intending to speak to his father, but Edwin and his wife were out at choir practice. Frank was in charge of his young brothers and sisters, now all abed.

'I must admit it set me wondering this morning. It was a bit of a shaker seeing Bob come in like that, with his face and head all battered. Then there's the way his tools went missing.'

'He's the last person who'd be careless.'

'Specially with tools.' Each jet craftsman made his own, precisely for the job and to be used in the manner best suited to himself. He'd never part with them.

'I've asked him and so has Mother, yet Bob still denies having any tools with him when he was set on in that alley.'

'You think there's more than he's telling, don't you?'

'Don't *you*? Frank . . . have you noticed any animosity between him and any of the other workers?'

Frank hesitated, gave her a look. No matter how highly he thought of Hester now, she was still the boss's daughter. Near enough a boss herself, to his way of thinking.

'Well – there is Wally Hardcastle,' he admitted at last. 'Nowt's been said outright when any of us has been in t'workroom, just as it hasn't when you or Mrs Falgrave's there. But there's been hints. You can't keep folk quiet all the time.'

'And . . .' Hester prompted.

'Wally's after getting a union of sorts together. I know nowt no more than that he's trying for it. But unions have caused friction elsewhere, even i' Yorkshire.'

Badly shaken, Hester closed her eyes.

'Here – are you all right?'

Frank's anxious question made her look at him. She managed to smile. 'It was what you said. It wasn't exactly what I was hoping to hear. Not that I'm surprised about Wally Hardcastle stirring things up. I just hope to goodness he's had nowt to do with this.'

They were sitting on upright chairs drawn in to the table. Hester's hands were clasped in front of her, so tightly now that the dainty knuckles blanched. Instinctively, Frank reached out to cover them with his hand, realised what he was about when he was but an inch from her, and hastily withdrew.

Her smile warming those expressive brown eyes, Hester looked at him again. Frank felt emotion tighten his throat, was compelled to clear it.

'You can count on us Cloughs, you know, to stand by you. No matter what Hardcastle may do.'

'I know, Frank – thank you. It's just ... oh, it's all so new to me. Unions, and suchlike. And I don't want to go bothering my mother with every little thing.'

'She'll have to be told, though, about what Hardcastle's planning.'

'I suppose so. Do you know what I wish, what I keep wishing – that I were older. I'd be better equipped then for seeing to things that crop up.'

'Nay,' Frank protested fiercely, not wishing her any different. And then he grinned, selfconsciously.

Reluctantly, Hester rose. 'I'd better be getting back.' She had told no one where she was coming.

Standing with her, Frank searched despairingly for some means of detaining her. It seemed only moments since she'd astonished him by appearing at their door, and he'd done and said nothing. Nothing of the slightest use.

'Can't I offer you tea or something?'

'That'd be nice, thank you.'

She sat down again swiftly, convincing him that she'd been no more eager to leave than he to let her go.

She was watching as he crossed to fill the kettle in the tiny scullery at the cellar head. He was acutely conscious of her gaze, grew troubled by its probable cause.

'A bit smaller than what you're used to, I'll warrant,' he said quite sharply, setting the kettle to boil on the fire hob.

111

'I've seen far worse. Don't forget I've been in and out of Jamie Skelton's for the best part of eleven years.'

'Aye. I had forgotten.'

He wished he'd kept quiet. She was looking about her now – she was bound to see that the scullery had white-washed walls same as the cellar. And the living room wasn't much better with its walls bare of the wallpaper that people like the Falgraves must have in every room.

'Your mother keeps it clean and tidy,' Hester began, then recalled that it wasn't for her to pass on the information that Edna Skelton was a shiftless woman whose care for her offspring was curtailed after seeing they were fed.

'She does that. Even when the youngsters have been getting under her feet.'

'How old are they now?'

'Ay – I forget. Let's see ... Our Alfred's nine years younger than Harold, that makes him ten, then there's nobbut a year between him and Ida and t'same between her and Lydia. The two youngest, Herbert and Maggie, are two and three – summat like that.'

'Must make for a lively household.'

Frank came to sit at the table again while the kettle boiled. 'You could say that. I like it but Harold's less keen. He goes out a lot of a night.'

'And you don't?'

'Sometimes, straight after work, for a drink. Every now and again I'll go down to t'public house after I've got changed. This time of year, though, it doesn't always tempt you to set out again.'

'You've not got a young lady then, Frank?' As soon as he'd opened the door tonight she'd been struck by how attractive he was in his nice white shirt and a grey waistcoat that matched his trousers. But she didn't suppose wearing a hat to keep the jet dust out of that glossy brown hair, and having to have a shapeless blue smock did much for anybody.

His eyes were really beautiful; both he and Harold had green eyes. They glittered now in the glow from the oil lamp, making her feel warmed by his steady gaze. He had a kinder face than Harold.

'Sorry – I . . . No, there's nobody.' He'd been so taken up by the fact that she was scrutinising him that he'd ignored her question. And what could it matter to her, any road, whether or not he had a lass? He'd known from the start of the feelings she generated in him, that they were as impossible as they were illogical.

The kettle began singing and he went to take it from the fire. Ready to snatch this opportunity to escape Hester's penetrating eyes, he was overwhelmed by the impulse to remain close at her side. Talk about contrary!

While the tea was brewing in its pot he went to the sideboard and found two of his mother's best cups and saucers. They were Leeds Ware, of rare good value for anything owned by the Cloughs, and just as rare in their usage. Frank knew, nevertheless, that if his mother had been at home she wouldn't have hesitated to bring them out now.

'What lovely cups and saucers,' Hester exclaimed after Frank had wrestled with the problem of who ought to pour, and decided that tackling it himself saved finding the right words for suggesting she might wish to do so.

He grinned as he sat beside her again. 'That's why they're shut away. We thought Mam had gone raving mad when she bought them. It were when our Harold came home with his first wage packet. She said as how we'd managed in the past with only Dad's wage and mine, it wouldn't hurt to lash out. I daresay they cost far more nor an apprentice's weekly pay, but it is nice to have one or two bits of good stuff.'

'So long as it doesn't get out of hand,' Hester observed pensively.

Frank gave her a look.

She laughed, glancing sideways at him from beneath long dark lashes, making his heart surge, and other regions as well. When she spoke, though, her amusement at his surprise was tempered by seriousness.

'I've been thinking a lot these past few weeks about all the lovely things we've got at Falgrave House. They don't seem to have much purpose now.' Her eyes blurred, and all at once she was telling Frank about that first evening after her father's accident, how just looking at his silver decanter stoppers had made her feel like weeping.

'Aye, it's a bad do,' he said sympathetically. 'But at least he survived, it could have been worse.'

'I wonder . . .'

'Nay, don't say that.'

'I never have, not to anyone else. Promise you won't let on . . .' she paused, smiled a little no matter how sadly. 'But of course you won't, I know that. It's just . . . once or twice I've gone into his room when he hasn't been aware of my approach.'

Abruptly, she stood up and walked away to stare into the glowing fire in the homely range. 'Oh, Frank, he's looked that despairing . . .'

He was behind her now, his hand instinctively going to her shoulder. Hester leaned against him, rested her head. Gently, Frank turned her, his eyes earnest, dark and liquid like a woodland pool – somewhere bringing ease.

'You've shown such a lot of courage, you and your mother. It's only natural you should feel you just have to let go, now and again. Specially when there's problems at t'workshop on top of what you have to get used to at home. You're not on your own, though, you know. Like I said before, us Cloughs'll allus stand by what you do. And – and if you ever want to talk, like – well, like tonight, it won't go no further.'

Without thinking, she hugged him, just for a second let him hold her. And then she cleared her throat. There was mischief in her brown eyes when she met his glance.

'You want to watch out, making rash suggestions. I just might get a liking for confiding in you.'

Frank offered to walk her home when she'd finished her tea, but she pointed out that he was supposed to be looking after his brothers and sisters. And she needed to have a good think. Walking back up through the town would give her the chance.

'What you could do one day, Frank – if you've a mind – is to come and visit Father. He wants to see your seagull carvings on those new buttons, so why not come and show him yourself?'

She went on to tell him a bit about her idea for jet figurines. 'Shakespeare characters would sell. Othello would be magnificent, gleaming all black, wouldn't he?' She had seen the play when she was only seven, up in London with her parents for the Great Exhibition. She saw at once that Frank didn't understand. 'You could help explain what I intend to Father, tell him what you can manage.'

Frank made no promises about that but told Hester he would warn his father to keep an eye on Wally Hardcastle. Wally might have had nothing to do with the vicious attack on Bob Dunsdale, but if he had, he'd not manage to keep that from the rest of them for ever.

Bob wakened in the night, saturated in a sweat that was as cold as the air coming in through the gap between the window pane and its frame.

Had he cried out? He couldn't tell, prayed that he hadn't. Last night they'd had hardly any sleep, and Nellie had been really washed out today and still all on edge when he got in from work. However, she seemed to be still sleeping beside him; a fact which disappointed him before more than a few minutes had passed and his immediate concern for her had been displaced.

These dreams he kept having would make anybody long to share the terror. Not that he would consider sharing them with her, not while he was in his right mind. Trouble was, he couldn't be certain that there wasn't summat up with his head.

He hadn't believed the evidence of what he was seeing and hearing the other day; now it resurrected every time he shut his eyes he still hardly credited it was true.

They were almost the last to leave the workshop. There was only Edwin Clough behind them, and he was busy locking up. Bob followed Wally down the narrow stairs – you didn't push ahead of Wally Hardcastle even if you were there two paces before him. As he shut the outer door after them, though, he saw that Wally was hanging about. He was carrying something, not down at his side half-hidden as it might be by his coat, but with his arm partly extended. That was when Bob realised it was a bag of tools, *his tools*.

'Here, Wally – just a minute! I think you've made a bit of a mistake . . .'

Wally only shook his head, laughed, and began striding off up through the town. Bob was compelled to follow: those tools were his livelihood. Over the years, he'd made each one, all fitted to his hands, designed and crafted as meticulously as the jet that they enhanced. To his touch they were as familiar as his Nellie had grown.

'You've got my tools . . .'

It was a daft thing to call after a fellow like Wally Hardcastle. Didn't he know full well what he was doing? And the reason. Bob himself had been that unsuspecting he hadn't guessed. Not until he'd run panting and gasping after Hardcastle, all the way up those steps to St Mary's church and the abbey ruins. Only then had he understood this was more than just the man's desire to torment.

Against the snow, Wally appeared as black as the ruins themselves. Bob was so out of breath he could hardly control his legs and feet when he tried to run towards him.

The clanging began before he got there. One by one, Wally was hurling the carefully-crafted tools against the walls.

'For God's sake, man . . .' he pleaded.

The only response was a laugh. Wally lumbered onwards between sections of the old abbey. Following, Bob stopped each time he spotted anything lying in the snow. The first was his best engraving knife, its blade wrecked by the impact with the stone. Next he found a good carving tool, smashed beyond repair.

Emerging at the far end of the remains of the abbey, he saw Wally again, out on the cliff. He was throwing something over the edge. Bob heard a metallic rattle, distantly on rocks.

'That's enough, Wally,' he shouted. 'Give us the rest . . .'

To Bob's relief he turned, began striding back towards him. 'I will an' all! I'll teach you you're not that clever you're above falling into line.'

'Is that what this is about?' Bob was incredulous. 'Is it because I didn't jump at your idea of forming a union?'

'So, you haven't understood then,' Wally called. 'I'll soon learn you . . .'

Incensed, Bob had had enough. Wally might destroy his tools, but he'd not destroy him. Especially not here. Nobody knew the abbey better, for hadn't he been fascinated with the place since the central tower collapsed when he was a lad?

He swung round before Wally came any nearer, darted behind one section of wall, then scurried along and round the next corner. Warily, because of icy patches where snow-flakes had adhered and frozen, he began climbing. Presently, easing himself along the top of an archway, he paused, waiting.

Wally passed beneath the adjacent row of arches, sprinting, glancing to left and right. Bob remained where he was until he could discern a dark figure some way off, crossing the snow towards the top of the long column of steps.

He followed at a distance, keeping Wally in sight until they were in the steep narrow streets of the town. He lost him, as he had feared that he might, when they reached the network of ginnels.

That was when he took the chance and headed straight for home. Nellie would be out of her mind with anxiety already – he must get back to reassure her, even without his remaining tools.

Bob heard the feet behind him while he was in a darkened alley where there was no inn within shouting distance and nothing but rows of locked-up shops. He never doubted whose footsteps they were.

He started to run. Worn out already, he developed a stitch at once. He'd have to agree to whatever Wally was after, that was the only way.

'You win,' he said, turning. 'I'll join t'rest on you . . .'

'Garn – you don't think I'd take your word now, do you? It's not that easy. Another week or so, and you'd be going behind us back – siding wi' the bosses, running sneaking to 'em.'

Bob read in Wally's calculating eyes the determination to fetch blood. He saw in the hand he'd kept behind him some weapon far heavier than any jet worker's tool.

117

'Nay, Wally . . .'

The blows smashing into his face and head interrupted his protest, astonishing him more than frightening him, until he saw that Wally was enjoying the attack.

'And you'll tell nobody about this, remember? If you do say owt, you'll get far worse nor this. I'll see you're not fit for work again. And not only you, your missus and children . . .'

Nearly senseless, Bob could only groan.

'And don't forget,' Wally added finally, nudging his side with a heavy boot, 'as long as you stay at Falgraves' works, what I says goes.'

'You're having a bad night again, aren't you, love?' Nellie's gentle voice returned him to their bed, to the fact that he had survived that fright, had even got through the near-equal terror of facing Wally at work.

'Shall I fetch you another dose of the laudanum the doctor left for your pain?' she suggested, grasping his arm in the darkness.

'Nay, love, don't trouble yourself, thanks,' Bob answered. 'It's not hurting so bad.' He could endure the pain far more readily than accept that Wally seemed to have the upper hand. And if the candle was lit now that would lead to more questions from Nell. So far, he'd managed not to let on who was responsible for his injuries. For everyone's sake, that was how it must remain.

'Just go back to sleep, Nellie love. I'm all right.'

How much longer though, he thought despairingly – how much longer could he keep quiet about what had happened? He did not doubt that if anyone learned who had beaten him up, Wally would see that he paid for it.

One evening during the week before Christmas, Maud and her daughter returned together from the works and heard voices drifting down the staircase at Falgrave House.

'Lambert!' Maud exclaimed. 'Our Lambert's home!'

He met them at the door of the master bedroom, tall and imposing in his Guard's uniform, looking exceptionally well. He would be, naturally, thought Hester – for wasn't he doing exactly as he wished? She dismissed the thought instantly, was only a pace behind when maternal arms were flung wide for him.

He lifted their mother clear of the ground, swung her around as though she were a girl.

'You're back, love, you're back!' Maud exclaimed breathlessly, joyful tears awash in her blue eyes. 'How long can you stay?' she demanded when Lambert at last turned to embrace his sister.

'I have a whole fortnight's leave, Mother,' he answered.

Together, the three continued into the room to join Abel. Bernard and Olive were there as well, sitting on the far side of the large brass bed.

'Our Lambert's going to see I get fixed up with a lift so's I'm not stuck in this room much longer,' Abel announced. 'According to him, it shouldn't be difficult to arrange.'

Not so long as you're giving all your time to finding an engineer, thought Hester, and not seeing to a million and one other things to keep the business running. But I like Lambert, she silently asserted, I always have. It was wrong to find fault already, even privately.

'He'll give you both a hand with the business, and all,' Abel continued. 'See what can be done to pick up trade a bit.'

'We seem to be doing very nicely,' Maud put in, hurt by the insinuation that someone other than herself might do more. 'Like I said, with the Queen in mourning, there'll be other folk following suit. Them that lose their own husbands will notice how she dresses.'

Lambert smiled. 'Then you'll not refuse my assistance in ensuring that all your outlets are fully exploited.'

'Outlets,' his mother echoed. If Lambert had arrived during the early days of Abel's incapacity, she'd have welcomed loading responsibility on to him. Now – well, she felt that with Hester's help she had achieved a commendable degree of control.

Lambert was still smiling. 'You sell to those who supply other shops, no doubt, as well as to our own in Flowergate?'

'Of course we do,' Hester spoke up. 'And execute orders for wealthy folk who want something special, even some abroad.'

119

'Then there's scope aplenty for my following up your contacts. Doesn't hurt, you'll agree, to let them see a man's still involved.'

'What are you hesitating over, the pair of you?' Abel put in. 'Now Lambert's here, you should be glad of his suggestions.' Why were women so difficult? He himself recognised that since he'd been deprived of the ability to do everything necessary, Lambert would deputise very well.

'Of course, of course,' Maud agreed. Lambert's arrival was something she'd anticipated joyfully for a long time. She just wished Abel wasn't so ready to assume that they hadn't been managing well enough without her eldest son's intervention.

Hester looked up at Lambert. 'If Mother thinks it's a good idea I'll take you along to the shop tomorrow. Just about everything we make is on display there. You'd be able to familiarise yourself with the different kinds of things we're producing.'

'Is there much difference between the items? They're all black, surely, all jewellery.'

'That just shows how little you know,' Hester exclaimed, although she smiled. 'The simplest of pieces are turned and polished. Then there's some things that are faceted, diamond-cut. Cameos are carved, then there's engraving . . .'

'All right, all right, I don't need a lecture. I'll allow you've corrected me.'

'Happen you'd like to have a day in the workroom first, love,' his mother suggested.

'There's no need, thank you,' Lambert responded swiftly. He hadn't forgotten his rare glimpses of the place. It was so dusty and dirty, only one degree better than the mine which he'd never get out of his mind. 'I'll go along to the shop.'

'We'll go there first thing,' Hester began, but her brother interrupted.

'If you've other things to do with your time, I'll make my own way there.'

'I have, indeed. I much prefer getting on with my work.'

She was near completing sketches for the figure of Othello and wanted to discuss practical details with Frank Clough.

The morning was bright and clear. Overnight rain had disposed of the last of the snow, and the keen wind blowing over the town from the moors had dried red roofs as well as streets. Walking down into Whitby, though, on her way to open up the shop, Sally Drinkwater felt no brighter than the black dress her mother insisted she continue to wear in respect for her deceased grandmother.

It wasn't so much bereavement that was depressing her, though she'd loved the old lady, it was the thought of Christmas. Until just the other day, she'd been buoyed up by the prospect of at least one glorious party.

Her best friend from their Sunday School days, Margaret, had been married now for over a year, and had married well. Her husband was the only son of a family who'd made a small fortune out of mining alum, and they'd been determined to set him up in a house befitting their means. Margaret revelled in her new home at Staithes, and this year was planning a large gathering. 'Bring someone, won't you,' she'd told Sally. 'There'll be dancing far into the night.'

Sally had even persuaded her parents that, properly escorted, she might attend. The quiet Christmas they intended in consideration of their recent loss needn't be observed quite so strictly by their only daughter. Those of her brothers still living at home would go their own way, like as not, and that would be to the nearest inn. Sally was a good girl, they'd assured each other, not given to excesses.

The trouble was Margaret's stipulation that she should take someone with her. Initially, Sally had been excited, certain that either Harold Clough or Jamie would be as thrilled as she herself to attend. She had seen each of them once or twice in recent days, had grown to appreciate the secure feeling of having more than one lad to consider. Unfortunately, neither of them appeared to consider *her*.

She'd tried previously, of course, to get Harold to make some firm arrangement to meet during Christmas. When she tried again, beaming up into his lovely green eyes while he held her, she added the incentive of visiting this beautiful big house.

Harold was appalled. He'd never feel comfortable somewhere that large, among a lot of strangers, and with Sally's closest friend emphasising the bliss of being married. Then there was this question of dancing . . . when had he had the opportunity of learning how to dance? A perfect idiot, that's what he'd feel.

He'd blundered over his excuses, left the remainder of the snack they were sharing in the room at the back of the shop and almost at a run had bolted off, back to the workroom.

Sally wasn't daft – she'd understood his discomfort – and by the next time he came into the shop she was her usual friendly self with him. Harold wasn't a lad you could fall out with. And there was still Jamie.

Since the night when he'd been seen with Sally down by the boathouse, Jamie had had longer periods at sea – time to think and to make plans. The next time he appeared at the Flowergate shop it was with ale enough for two, and pies from the baker's on the next corner.

Sally was talked into picnicking in the back of the shop after she'd locked up. Afterwards, his kisses and caresses were no less exciting than before, and more than compensated for the lack of money for taking her out properly. She agreed readily to Jamie's suggestion that they do this again when next he was ashore. She admired his saving for that boat, and liked him and Harold equally – and Jamie wasn't scared of hanging around here.

'You've been that good to me, buying us stuff to eat and drink, all cosy here,' she said. 'And I'm planning a treat for you now.' But before she'd finished explaining about Margaret's party she had read in Jamie's gorgeous eyes a reluctance greater even than Harold's.

'I'm afraid I shan't be at home, Sally,' he began quickly, if rather awkwardly. 'I – you see, there's not many of us willing to put to sea over Christmas . . .'

'I'll bet there isn't,' she'd responded, all the time knowing that if there *were* such a fishing trip planned he'd only that minute decided to volunteer.

Maybe I've only myself to blame, Sally thought now, opening up the shop. I was too content to have both of them paying me attention. Harold with his friendliness, Jamie with his compliments, and both of them so attractive. One day she'd have to decide between them, she supposed. Still, except for being left high and dry at Christmas there was nowt wrong with liking them both.

She wouldn't go to Margaret's, though, not on her own. Even if she got one of her brothers to see her safely there, she'd not be left looking ridiculous with no one to partner her.

The prospect of more than a day or so stuck at home with all that quiet, that *mourning*, brought a lump to her throat. Nay, I'll not shed tears here, she resolved, blinking them back and going across the shop to unlock the shutters behind the window display.

The scarlet of his uniform tunic almost made her blink again, it was that dazzling through the glass with the sun streaming down on him. He was bareheaded, having removed his bearskin. His hair was shorter than was fashionable just now, but that hadn't spoiled its waviness and the colour was only a shade or so deeper than her own. In the sunlight, it gleamed like gold that had been spun.

For several minutes, Sally watched him, wondering why on earth this soldier was examining their jet so keenly. To keep an eye on him, as he moved she moved also, pretending she was polishing the glass counter. In certain positions the partially-closed shutters separating the window from the shop itself obstructed her view. But he seemed very interested, any road. She could expect he'd be inside in a minute, spending a guinea or two on somebody.

Smiling, Lambert finally marched into the shop.

Sally, scuttering round to her side of the counter, smiled back. 'Good morning, sir. Can I show you something perhaps?'

'Everything!' he exclaimed, and laughed at her surprised reaction.

He had a pleasing laugh, not a great bellow like her brothers, nor yet the false, affected laugh of folk that thought they were posh.

123

'I'd better explain, it's unfair of me not to. I'm Lambert Falgrave.' And he offered her his hand.

Sally shook it and almost bobbed her head in a curtsey. He was so polite he made her unsure what she was doing.

'You've heard of me perhaps?' he continued, while eyes that reminded her of his mother's held her gaze.

'Oh, yes – now and again, from Miss Hester.'

'I'm making myself useful whilst away from my regiment. I'm going to ensure that our jewellery sells to advantage.'

Sally nodded, rather overwhelmed by his sheer presence. He was so straight, so big, so splendid in that uniform.

'I have to admit I'm impressed by the window display here. I hadn't realised the sheer variety, nor the craftsmanship of the jet we're offering.'

'It's ever so beautiful, isn't it,' Sally enthused, glad to have something to say at last, on a subject that she knew. 'You were never in the company then, before you joined the army?'

'Hardly . . .' Reflecting, Lambert laughed again. 'Between ourselves, Miss – oh, what is your name?'

'Sally Drinkwater – they all call me Sally.'

'Well – Sally, fact is Father tried to indoctrinate me at an early age, but at the wrong end of the business. You know he began in mining the jet . . .'

He could see it now, and smell the oily stench as the jet broke. The clash of iron on rock resounded all about him, echoing, vibrating, as men with picks hewed out the substance no more interesting to him than common coal. The men had been smothered in its dust, he had felt it choking him, mingling with the pungence of their sweat in the sparse air. The only light was the miners' candles, he couldn't find the way back to the entrance. Panic and claustrophobia had overwhelmed him. Even the workers taking out their loads of jet and shale had to follow furrows in the ground cut for their barrows. His father had grinned at his distress, tried to encourage him to be a man. And him not twelve years old. *Feel the jet*, he'd been told, *handle it*. He'd wanted nothing to do with any substance that seemed so unclean.

Lambert noticed the concern in the girl's blue eyes and

came back to the present. He smiled again. 'It looks surprisingly good here.'

'When it's polished an' all that. I'd have hated mines as well.'

'It wasn't any better when we watched how it's recovered from the cliff-face. Not that we lingered overlong.' Abruptly he checked himself, realising that he was speaking to her as he never had to anyone of the early dread that had affected the rest of his life.

'So, you've made the army your career then?'

Amusement glinted in his eyes when her words continued his private reflections.

'And never regretted it – so far. It's an interesting life, Sally, keeps you on your mettle.'

'You'll get to see a lot of places . . .'

She sounded wistful. He wondered why, as the job must be congenial enough, and she was a pretty young thing – must have plenty of admirers.

'Any road,' she went on now, 'what have you come to look at?'

He considered for a moment. 'The variety of the jewellery that we sell, I suppose. I need to familiarise myself with it if I'm to help trade improve.'

'How're you going to do that?'

He didn't know, did he? He was no businessman. It was purely that, having felt obliged finally to come home, he'd had to suggest some purpose he might serve.

'I haven't worked out all the finer details yet.'

Sally stifled a giggle. He gave her a look, suspected she'd a good idea how unsure he was of his ground. Not a situation that he normally found agreeable. He was surprised he didn't mind more that he was concealing little from her.

First of all, he studied the items inside the glass counter display, then walked away and moved from one wall cupboard to the next, scrutinising everything behind the wooden framed panes. He was surprised when he saw how late the time was and told Sally he must be on his way.

'I've other matters needing attention. Somewhere I'm going to buy an invalid chair.'

'Oh.' Consternation drained the colour from her cheeks.

She'd heard rumours, of course, that Mr Falgrave mightn't ever be up and about.

'Is – is his condition very bad?' she asked in a whisper.

Lambert stared down at her. 'You've not been told? There's no hope, I'm afraid, that Father'll ever walk again.'

'Ay, I'm that sorry! I – I haven't liked to ask how serious it was.'

She was biting her lip, her eyes full of tears. Her emotion cracked his own composure. And, Lord knew, that hadn't been all that steady since his arrival yesterday. He'd been warned, naturally, but nothing could have prepared him for the shattering experience of seeing his father totally immobilised. To his alarm, he was compelled to swallow before speaking.

'He might have been dead, Sally, he was so still. Made me feel so useless. He's always been such an active man, never sitting down for more than a few moments except when he was occupied with some task. I was speechless at first, lost for something to say.'

'He'd be glad just to see you, though, thankful you'd come.'

'I suppose so.' That was another thing that hurt. After the initial welcome which had been unquestionably genuine, there'd been a new sourness on Abel Falgrave's tongue, overt dissatisfaction. Lambert had believed this was directed towards himself – justifiably, perhaps, on account of his delaying the return to Whitby. That was before he'd observed how his mother and sometimes even Hester were treated with this same acerbity.

And now he felt even more compelled to spend any free time in the family home. He'd not let those two bear that burden unsupported as well as running the business.

'Happen he'll perk up over Christmas,' Sally ventured, even though it seemed the season was doing nothing for her.

'I understand his old cronies are invited in, so the company might help.' And it would allow *him* to escape for a necessary break.

At that moment, two pairs of customers entered the shop, one a young lady and her brother, seeking a present for their mother. The other, an older woman and her son, wanted to order a carved inkstand to be made specially for another member of the family.

'Were you wanting it in time for Christmas?' Sally inquired, frowning. She doubted there'd be enough time for its completion.

'No, love,' the woman told her, smiling. 'It's for a birthday, not till the end of January.'

'If you can leave your name and address then, I'll see what can be done. Happen you'd like to see a sketch of how it will look, so's you can approve?' She knew this was done on occasions, when people wished to have something original.

'As a matter of fact, my son here has done a rough drawing.'

'If you'll leave that with me then.' She saw the address was written on the back of the paper. 'We'll be in touch with you in a day or two, tell you if this is feasible, how soon, and all that.'

After they had left Lambert came smiling towards her. 'You handled that well, Sally. I can see we've no cause to worry about the way things are run in here.'

Sally flushed and beamed at him. And then her smile grew mischievous. 'Did you have doubts about that, then?'

'Not once I had met you.'

He'd a lovely way of talking, and of looking at her, as if he was really interested in her as a person. It was a pity he was so saddened by what had happened to his dad. Each time she'd glanced up when he wasn't aware she was looking, he'd appeared shadowed, the skin around his eyes darkened. She bet he hadn't slept much last night.

'I really must be going . . .' Even as he moved towards the door, though, Lambert continued to feel this reluctance. He'd never in his life sought sympathy and finding it here had been unnerving.

'Where are you going to get that invalid chair?'

'Afraid I don't know.' He'd never dreamed he would have to search out anything of the kind. And besides, he'd been absent so long from Whitby, it scarcely felt like his home town.

'There's an old fellow out near where I live makes 'em. Used to be a boat-builder, I think. He's a bit of a cripple himself, he had to give up makin' boats. It's beautiful wood he uses, and he's learnt himself to upholster.'

They arranged that Sally would take him there after closing the shop that evening. He impressed upon her that the matter must be a secret – and that had clinched things as far as Sally was concerned. Keeping things secret made her feel warm inside, and bonded to the other person.

Chapter 7

Frank wasn't coming to the house. Hester was surprised by the depth of her disappointment. And yet, when suggesting he might show these samples to her father himself, she'd suspected he could be reluctant. So, here she was now bringing a set of beautifully-polished buttons, with seagulls so skilfully engraved they looked ready to take wing. She might show them to her father before dinner, together with her sketches of Othello.

She loved that figurine already, and it was still no more than her ideas on paper, and a piece of suitably-sized jet that Frank had picked out for her. He was a good worker, with all his father's enthusiasm and more besides. A couple of days after she'd mentioned the concept to him, he'd come to her when they were finishing for the day, had asked to see her drawings.

Nodding over them, he'd grinned. 'Aye, that's it, you've got him exact. He's got to be powerful, overwhelming almost. And that expression you've given him – he's just been told, hasn't he, about Desdemona's supposed disloyalty . . .'

He'd admitted then to getting hold of a copy of Shakespeare and reading the play. Something in his glance had told her he'd anticipated her amusement. She hadn't laughed, though. What he'd done was champion. If she'd wondered at first if his father ought to have a hand in the carving of Othello, she knew now Frank would be the only one.

As she walked up the drive to the house, slowly now for the long days, however interesting, were tiring, she saw Lambert stepping down from the brougham.

'Been somewhere nice?' she asked, catching him up in the hall as he unfastened his tunic while the carriage could be heard trundling off to be placed in the coach-house.

'Nowhere special,' he answered. Cagily, she thought.

'Business?' Hester persisted, removing her brown cloak.

129

She wasn't too happy about Lambert intruding on their affairs now. If he'd been here to help straight after the accident when they were all in shock, that might have been of use.

'Some of it, some a private matter.'

'Oh, I see – like that, is it? You've come back too grown up to confide in little sister any more.' She'd forced lightness into her tone, but there was too much uncertainty about Lambert's purpose here for her to feel genuinely easy with him yet.

'That's daft talk, Hester,' he responded, dropping the fine accent he'd picked up away from Yorkshire. 'I want us to be the friends we always were.'

She laughed. 'Like when you bullied me abominably?'

'You exaggerate, you always have. But I don't want us to lose that ease with each other.'

'Funny – I was just beginning to be frightened that we might have.'

'Don't say that, don't even think it.' Concerned, he placed a hand on each of her shoulders, gazed steadily into her expressive brown eyes. 'Whatever you might have thought of me for not coming home before this, don't doubt for one minute that we're all in this together. I think I know now how you must have felt, especially you and Mother, seeing him – well, yes, struck down like that. It's appalling, I know now. The worst thing I've ever faced. I'll never be the same since that first look at him yesterday.'

Hester slid her arms around him, thrust her head at his chest. 'Ay, Lambert, I don't know what to think. Some days, I believe it's going to be all right – Mother's a marvel, you know, keeping the workshop running. But then I see something that's wrong, speak up about it and nine times out of ten the men object.'

'You always were a lot older than your age.'

'I had to be, hadn't I, trying to catch up with you?' Briefly, there was a grin on her face, but her voice was laden with tears. 'And the trouble is the men don't know that, do they? They see me for what I am – a bit of a lass that half-knows what's involved in all the processes down there.'

'That's not my estimation. Sally pointed out a lot of the

stuff you've designed. You must have some knowledge or those designs wouldn't be practicable.'

'Happen. And happen them that carry them out cover up very well for me!' He *had* been to the shop then.

Lambert shook his head at her. 'I almost wish, for your sake even more than for the parents', that I felt I could quit the regiment permanently, take on full responsibility here. Fact is, Hester – just between you and me – even if I wished to, I couldn't live with seeing Father like that, day in and day out.'

'*We* have to.' She sighed. 'He's so frustrated by doing nothing, Lambert. And I don't know what to do.'

She was crying now, silently, but as she'd yearned to so many times since the day of that appalling accident.

'Take no notice,' she said at last, finding her cambric handkerchief. 'I don't make a habit of giving way.' There'd been that first time with Jon Davidson, and doctors were used to all sorts. Then that evening with Frank when she'd been so close to breaking. She wished that Frank had come home with her. Lambert was good, for a brother, but she needed somebody who was there day by day, seeing her at her worst as well as her best. Someone who took the trouble to read something up, because it mattered . . .

'You're doing too much, I suppose. Have you no young man to court you?'

That did make her laugh. 'When have I got time? Who's going to want to be bothered with somebody that's exhausted every evening?'

'There's nobody in the workshop interests you then?'

Ruefully, Hester smiled. 'It's evident you've not been near the place in many a long year. There is – there's several good craftsmen there who amaze me regularly by the quality of the stuff they turn out. But if you saw how dirty the job was you'd be able to guess what Mother would have to say if I got fond of any of them.'

'Do you go nowhere else, Hester?' Lambert inquired anxiously, unable to contemplate a life that had no space for amorous adventures. 'Don't you see Jamie Skelton now, because of what happened?'

'Not for that reason – Jamie couldn't help being the cause

131

of Father's accident. But I don't see him often, mostly because since he wrecked his father's boat he's been going on longer trips to sea.'

They were walking side by side up the staircase now on their way to call in on Abel.

'Good to see you both together again, come on in,' he greeted them. And then his smile faded, was replaced by frown lines which Hester realised were growing permanent. 'Your mother barely had time to say hallo before she needs must rush away to the kitchen. Don't know why I pay any staff here, if she can't rely on them.'

'I suppose there's a lot to organise, with Christmas almost upon us.'

'Are you saying I shouldn't be asking my friends in, on account of the extra work it'll cause? Don't you know I'm sick to bloody death of being stuck here with that bloomin' nurse.'

'I wasn't thinking anything of the kind, Papa.' Sitting beside the bed, she leaned across and kissed him.

'That Clapper woman doesn't approve of folk coming here, any road. Told me so the other day. Says so much company won't be good for me, indeed!'

Both Hester and Lambert looked towards the door as if they expected the nurse might walk in.

Abel snorted. 'You needn't fret, she's just this minute gone for a bite to eat. To hear her talk, you know, anybody'd think I were an old chap of ninety.' And many was the time that he wished that he were. It was the endlessness of this incapacity that was the most gruelling aspect.

Lambert came nearer to the bed. 'You'll soon be having more to interest you, anyway. Come the New Year, work'll be started on installing a lift.'

'At last! Thank God for that! Ay, lad, that's the best tonic I could have. Who've you found then to do the job?'

'No one you'll know. He isn't local. But one of my fellow officers comes from an engineering family. They were able to recommend a man who's studied that American's techniques . . .'

'Elisha Otis, aye . . .'

'I gather that this man they know has constructed quite a number of lifts already.'

'So he won't be experimenting on Falgrave House. Not that I'd have minded that even, so long as I get what's needed.'

Since the men appeared content to discuss the technicalities of lifts, Hester rose, about to go to her own room.

'Where're you off to?' her father demanded. 'You're getting as bad as your mother, barely showing your face then making off. You haven't told me how the day's gone. And I'm danged if it looks as if she intends to. Have you brought them buttons that you promised?'

'I have indeed – I tried to bring Frank Clough so's you could compliment him on them, but he . . .'

'Made some excuse, I'll be bound. Nobody wants to know now, they've all written me off.'

'That's nonsense, Father. If the truth were known, I believe Frank thought he'd find it a bit posh for him here.'

Briefly, Abel reflected. 'Yes, I daresay. Pity, though, a great pity. Unless our Bernard shows any aptitude for working jet, the Cloughs would be the most likely ones for taking over one day.'

And what about me, thought Hester, hurt. Don't I count at all, no matter how hard I work for the business?

'Maybe Hester will marry someone who has an interest in it,' Lambert suggested.

She quelled her groan. Not him as well! Did no man even contemplate the possibility that she might be capable enough to run the place?

Determined not to reveal her feelings, she unwrapped the glinting black buttons with their seagull engravings, and held them out for Abel's inspection.

'By, but they're bonnie – Frank has come on this last few weeks.'

'They are exquisite, aren't they?' she agreed, smiling again.

'May I see?' her brother asked, and nodded approvingly. 'Have to admit I've been pleasantly surprised by the quality of the jet in the shop.'

133

'You never looked at it before,' Abel reminded him dourly. 'You wouldn't have known.'

Lambert seemed intrigued as well by Hester's drawings for the Othello figurine. 'How long will it be before the first model's completed?'

'I don't know. Depends what else there is to get out, and bearing in mind the Christmas holiday. New stuff like this sometimes has to wait its turn while the men get on with what we know will sell.'

'That'll sell, right enough,' her father assured her. 'Those white Parian figures are popular – jet'll be more valuable, and better made.'

'More expensive, an' all,' Hester added with a grin.

'I'll help you fix a price once I see the finished article,' Abel told her. 'Think on now, keep a note of how long whoever it is takes over the job.'

'I know to do that with any new line. And it'll be Frank again.'

'Aye – well, you could do worse. Just watch you don't offend his dad, though. He always were our expert on carving.'

'He'll not mind, not with his own son. Anyway, Edwin Clough has enough on, these days.'

'Coping with work I ought to be doing, you mean. I didn't choose to be like this, you know.'

The sooner Christmas comes the better, thought Hester – it'll give you a change of company. With folk that aren't family you'll hardly be this tetchy.

On Christmas Eve, however, the presence of Sidney and Sadie Etherington who'd arrived with excitingly-wrapped parcels for all the family failed to make Abel entirely happy. The reason was Lambert's announcement that he would be out that evening, and again on the evening of Christmas Day itself.

'Trust him to spoil things,' he muttered to Sidney while Maud, Hester and Sadie Etherington headed towards the drawing room. 'I thought we'd got it all set up grand, never thought for a minute but what he'd have the grace to be stopping with us.'

Until Lambert's plans were divulged, Abel had been feeling better than at any time since the accident. Lambert and Kilner intended installing him in one of the downstairs rooms each day. And Nurse Clapper was away spending three days with her married sister.

No one understood how confining Lambert found Falgrave House now that he'd grown accustomed to his own way of life in the Grenadiers. Naturally there were restrictions but, for an officer, none which he considered too irksome. There was also the depressing effect of his father's incapacity: he had meant every word and more of the shock he'd mentioned to Hester. And he had found the ideal means of alleviating the stresses of their household.

He was at the reins of a carriage he had borrowed. Not the Falgrave brougham – he'd no wish to use a conveyance so readily recognised. Crispin Stansfield, the fellow officer whose engineer father had suggested someone for the installation of that lift, had offered the use of his travelling carriage. Fortunately for Lambert, Crispin and his wife were going with his parents to stay with a married sister near the border with Scotland.

What pleased Lambert even more greatly was the request that he might visit their empty house from time to time during his leave, to ensure that all was well there.

He went straight to their house this evening, unlocked the door then strode through to the sitting room and paused awhile at the windows, gazing out over the nearby edge of the cliff to the swell of the sea. Reluctantly, he drew across heavy blue velvet curtains. The view would charm anyone but, exposed as the place was, midway between Whitby and Staithes, he needs must keep out the chill wind blowing in off the North Sea.

Working swiftly, he laid and lit a fire in the iron grate, smiling in satisfaction as it began to draw at once and soon had not only kindling but coal as well blazing merrily.

He'd brought sherry with him and a bottle of port. There was fresh lemonade also which he'd coaxed out of May Thorpe whilst giving her a thorough kissing under the mistletoe in the hall at Falgrave House. He'd no intention

135

of having his companion the worse for drink; he'd never resorted to such tactics, had never had the cause.

He checked his appearance now, before leaving to meet her. And the tall uniformed figure, ablaze with scarlet tunic didn't disappoint. He was careful to keep his weight steady, even at times like this when deprived of the exercise sustained with his regiment. He'd never been sorry that he was blessed with the pale hair inherited from his mother, whilst the height which no doubt came from his father was enhanced by his military bearing.

Swiftly, he drew out and consulted his gold demi-hunter, smiling as he fingered the case then returning it to his pocket. His mother, bless her, had chosen this for his coming of age. She hadn't entirely been preoccupied with anxiety for Father and the business to the exclusion of choosing this gift for their eldest.

He must hurry now, though, or he'd be late. And he'd not forgive himself that. The girl was too young to be left waiting at the darkened junction of a road – that would be inexcusable.

He arrived as she came running down the lane from her father's cottage. Skirts held wide, and her dainty bonnet slithering back over glossy hair lighter even than his own, she suddenly appeared younger than seventeen.

'Hallo, Lambert.' Breathless with either haste or excitement, her voice sounded ethereal, nothing like it had in the shop. And she looked entirely different: previously she'd looked pretty, today she was ravishing.

She stood on tiptoe for his kiss, giggled when he assisted her up into the carriage.

'It's not your father's you've come in tonight then,' she remarked. She had adored riding in the Falgrave brougham when she'd shown him the workshop of the man who made invalid chairs.

Lambert grinned. 'No, and I've not brought Kilner with me either.'

He leaned into the carriage, tucked a rug over her skirts and kissed her again, but lightly. He was eager to reach the house.

'That means you can't ride inside with me though,' she

said, her blue eyes sparkling in the light from the carriage lamp.

'You'll need to be patient but five minutes,' he promised. 'It's only a short way over the hill.'

Contentedly, Sally settled back into the quilted upholstery of the interior. She could smell a perfume, lingering from the lady who normally sat on these cushions, and just a hint of a man's cigar. Briefly, she closed her eyes, sighing ecstatically. This was better by far than attending Margaret's party. And there was tomorrow evening as well to look forward to when today's excitement had to end.

She opened her eyes again and glanced out, watching the moon through the tracery of bare branches, feeling safe and cared for with Lambert handling the reins and the carriage keeping out the wind.

They certainly seemed to take only a few minutes to reach the house overlooking the sea. When he came to open the door and hand her down, Sally stared up at the Stansfields' home and thought how wealthy they must be. Although maybe only half the size of Falgrave House, this was owned by a couple who were only about five years older than herself.

Lambert escorted her up the few steps to the front door which he unlocked and pushed open for her.

'You go along inside. I won't be a moment – must see to the horses.'

Instead of doing as he suggested, though, Sally remained at the door to watch while he remounted the box of the smart black and gold carriage and with a flick of the reins started the horses in the direction of what she assumed must be the stable block.

Only then did she turn and walk through into the high-ceilinged entrance hall. Slowly, her smile widened and she twirled right around in sheer delight. Not only had she been brought out so that she might forget that she was ordinary Sally Drinkwater, who was always inhibited about not having an 'understanding' with a personable young man, she'd been granted a setting fit for any fine lady.

Lambert found her in the room he'd so recently prepared. Still wearing her blue wool cloak, she was standing with her hands extended to the blaze now sending sparks and satisfying flames up the wide chimney.

She had heard his approach, though, and faced him as he entered the room.

'Cold?' he inquired, thinking how fragile she looked.

Smiling, Sally shook her head. 'I was just enjoying the fire. With brothers the size of mine, you've got to be very determined to get anywhere near the hearth.'

'Come along, I'll show you where to hang your cloak.'

She went with him back into the hall, felt his hands gentle on her shoulders as he took the garment from her. And then, looking about her again, she pointed and exclaimed. 'How pretty . . .'

'The kissing bunch?' Lambert indicated the two hoops fixed to make a sphere and covered in mistletoe. Attached to it hung small apples and oranges. 'You've not seen one before?'

Sally shook her head. They had a tree at home, illuminated with wax tapers, but unless you counted the few bits of holly, that was their only decoration.

'Best not waste it then . . .'

Having found a hook for her cloak, he'd returned swiftly to her, no less determined than Sally herself to enjoy this house that was theirs so briefly. And she looked bridal in that gown of white gauze . . . he'd need to keep reminding himself that she wasn't his bride.

Lambert took her by both hands, brought each in turn to his lips, then slowly drew her close. Enchanted, Sally was smiling when he kissed her, felt her lips being moulded beneath his, then parted. His tongue probed, thrilling her with its insistence.

They had kissed the other day in the carriage, but only hastily, very conscious of Kilner's presence up front. This evening it seemed that she wasn't the only one glad to be away from all restraints.

His eyes closed, Lambert was pressing at the back of her slender waist, holding her to him so that even through his tunic she excited him. In the shop, wearing her dark dress, she had appeared strangely dignified in contrast with her evident innocence. Now, her flimsy youthful gown was complete allure – as entrancing as the perfect figure and features which had first attracted him.

'We must eat,' he said presently with a wry smile as he drew a little away from her. Later they would relax in the comfort of one of the sofas near the fire. 'Come – this way, Sally. And tell me what you'll have to drink.'

'Did your father mind you coming out tonight, and you only just arrived back home?' she asked while they were eating.

Lambert frowned. He wanted no reminder of the overt disappointment of both parents. Even though he'd meant not to spoil the occasion by mentioning one word of it, his sigh revealed his disturbance.

Sally nodded sympathetically. 'Can't be much fun in that big house, not any longer. Happen you'll feel better about it all when you've got more used to seeing your dad like that.'

He had set aside his knife and fork. Her hand reached across the highly-polished table and rested over his own. Lambert experienced again the unfamiliar emotion that so frequently since his return to Whitby threatened to choke him.

'Your Hester and your mother had to concentrate on getting on with running things, hadn't they? I'm sure having so much to do must have made it easier for them at first.'

'It isn't at all easy for any of us.'

'I know.'

He nodded. 'And *easier* was what you said. But I didn't meet you to dwell on the situation at Falgrave House.' He paused, swallowed, and remembered something he'd been meaning to ask. 'What did you tell your family about coming out like this?'

Her blue eyes sparkled, and the smile came back to her mouth. 'Just that somebody from Falgraves' was calling to take me to the home of their friends for the evening. It wasn't really an untruth,' she added quickly when she couldn't read the expression in his eyes.

Lambert laughed as they began eating again. 'And they didn't inquire any more closely?'

'Not when I said as how I'd be took home again safe,

and not too late either. I don't think they'd really wanted me to go to Margaret's at all this Christmas.'

'And you don't mind not going there?'

Sally chuckled. 'What did I tell you when you invited me? This is far more exciting. I can see Margaret any time.'

Gazing into her exquisite blue eyes, Lambert saw them cloud, understood that already she would be sorry when she couldn't regularly see *him*. He couldn't really comprehend how this could have come about so swiftly, especially since he felt so wearied with concern for his family, quite unlike himself.

She was more perceptive than he'd credited. 'Yes, I'll be sorry when you have to go back, but I'm not going to let that spoil tonight, nor tomorrow neither.'

Against all his preconceived notions, he was close to promising they would meet whenever he came to Falgrave House. And that would be most incautious, particularly before they'd been more than an hour or two in each other's company. Sally might not understand his friendship with his CO's daughter, could object to his visiting Mary near their barracks. And Sally wasn't at all suitable as a girl to court.

'You've gone serious an' all again,' she exclaimed, smiling into his eyes. 'You're not supposed to do that. We know this is just a bit of fun. We agreed, didn't we – just because we didn't neither of us want to be stuck at home . . .'

They had eaten some of the cold pie and ham that he'd brought with him, and were helping themselves to more of the freshly-baked bread and cheeses. They had drunk sherry before and with their first course, now Lambert opened the port.

'Do you like this, Sally?'

'Don't know as I've ever had any port. Can I try a drop?'

He poured a small amount into one of the crystal glasses and handed it across. Her fingers brushed his – he recognised the action as contrived but wasn't put off or even irritated.

'Tastes a bit strong, but I'll have a drop more if you don't mind.'

'It's all provided for you, my dear.'

Sally beamed, delighted. He was treating her like a proper lady an' no mistake. He was a lovely man. How she'd ever go back to liking Harold Clough or Jamie she didn't know.

When they had finished their meal Sally insisted on washing the dishes they had used. The kitchen was far bigger than any she had ever seen: if she'd been less alarmed about handling such delicate chinaware and glass, she'd have lingered. As it was, she was only too thankful when everything was safely washed and put away.

Lambert watched from the kitchen doorway, saying so little that Sally wondered if she'd ruined everything by insisting on completing this domestic task. When she turned away from rinsing the gleaming sink, however, she caught the pleasure in his expression.

He'd been strangely moved by how capable those small hands were, unable to prevent himself from picturing Sally in his own home. He ought to remind himself that when – or if – he had a home of his own it would be much like the Falgrave household, and its mistress would be occupied elsewhere than in the kitchen.

'You've earned a rest,' he told her as she came to his side.

The simple fragrance of her filled his nostrils as they crossed the hall and he turned aside briefly to extinguish the oil lamp and candles in the dining room.

The lamp on the sofa table in the drawing room was spluttering a little, so he leaned over it to inspect the wick.

'Why not turn it out?' Sally suggested. 'The firelight's so cosy.'

Lambert didn't argue. He'd willed himself all along to curb the urge to do more than set a scene that could induce romance. Sally might be a girl he'd chosen for her beauty and availability, but he'd been determined from the start not to take advantage. There was no sense, though, in quashing this atmosphere.

She was quick to sit on the sofa, and faced him the moment he joined her. Her kiss was full on his lips.

'Thank you, Lambert, for the lovely meal and for inviting me.'

He drew her into his arms again, pulling her with him

141

as he leaned into the corner of the sofa. She was warm, pliable through the thin material of her gown, making him ache for more than the touch of her bosom against his chest.

With some of the girls he knew he'd coaxed until they'd removed a wretched crinoline cage. How those contraptions contrived to frustrate a fellow! And he'd experienced the pressure of the length of young feminine limbs against his own. More than that he'd never attempted; with strange girls in an unfamiliar town, there'd been no way of ensuring that they hadn't been equally accommodating with other men. He'd not risk catching a disease that might mar the rest of his life.

There'd be no such risk with Sally, he felt sure, but he'd not chance with her the child that could ruin *her* life. Discipline, meanwhile, was not easy while she seemed hungry for his kisses, and with his own blood surging at each tantalising exploration of her delicate pointed tongue. Tasting of port, she was testing the sharpness of his teeth, all the crevices of his mouth.

He couldn't fail to be aroused, did not know how to curtail the fierce pulsing, nor to conceal the evidence of his need. His hand was at her breast, though he had not consciously moved. And now her mouth was utterly surrendered to his, opening for him, moist with promise.

When next the need of air enforced a pause, Lambert took out his watch. He frowned, feigning dismay.

'It's time I took you home, Sally my sweet. If you're later than you promised, they could prevent your coming tomorrow. I couldn't bear Christmas Day without you.'

A few more clinging kisses and she went meekly with him through the hall to take up her cloak. He would return alone to make the fire safe for the night. And, somehow, to accustom himself to this discomfort before going back to Falgrave House.

Hester greeted him at the door smiling, appearing delighted he was home earlier than expected.

'Papa has been so different this evening,' she whispered. 'So many people have called, he's scarcely ceased talking.'

142

'Then he'll be content if I go straight to my bed, and see him in the morning.'

'Happen he will, but Mother won't. Don't you know she wants to show you off to her friends? She's that proud of you, Lambert.'

'I thought rather that she totally disapproved of my not joining the jet business.'

'She'd have preferred it naturally if you had, but she's adept at adjusting her ideas before they prevent her showing off.'

Lambert raised an eyebrow, but decided against commenting on how his sister had changed from the girl who had appeared unquestioningly to accept their parents as they were.

'Where is Mother?'

'Oh – in the drawing room.'

'Come on, then.'

'Oh, no – I was busy in the sitting room.'

She returned there now, entering smiling and going towards the solemn-faced man who was sitting on the edge of one of the armchairs, looking uncharacteristically ill at ease.

'Sorry, Doctor,' she said swiftly, 'but I know how busy Mrs Richmond and May Thorpe are with preparations for tomorrow. Answering the door is little enough I can do.'

'And having it open on your smile is the nicest thing about coming here.'

Hester was astonished. 'Oh – thank you, Doctor. But you were telling me about your wife.'

'Mm.' Wearily, Jon Davidson glanced down at his hands as though he might find there the words for expressing the anxiety gnawing into him. 'As I was saying, I simply called here to say it's unlikely we'll be present for any part of your festivities. Ruth, alas, is no better.'

'What *is* the matter with her?'

'I wish I knew! That way, there might be some hope of a cure. The trouble is internal, and causes intense pain. Neither my colleague from Staithes who treats us both nor I can do more than guess, and try this medicine and the

143

other. And all the while Ruth seems to – to fade before my eyes.'

'I'm so sorry. And you've been that good to us these past few weeks. I wish there was some way we could help.'

Hester was so deeply concerned about Jon Davidson's wife that she slept quite badly that night. Morning came quickly, nevertheless, and she awakened to excited voices which reminded her it was Christmas. These sounds, moreover, did not come from young Bernard and Olive, but from her parents.

Wondering briefly if she had been correct in thinking the voices delighted, she got swiftly out of bed and hurried along to the staircase. Already Lambert and Kilner between them had carried Abel down to the hall. Her mother was actually *running* down the stairs to where, at the foot, Abel was being helped into an invalid chair.

'Lambert, my boy, this is the best present I could have. Thank you, Son, thank you!'

When she hastened down to join them Hester saw there were tears of joy streaming down her father's cheeks.

'You'll be able to show Nurse Clapper a thing or two now, when she returns,' she exclaimed, kissing his cheek.

'I will that, lass – I will an' all!'

Hester went to hug her brother. 'You've pleased us all equally, you know that, I hope? We ought to have thought of this weeks since.'

'So long as someone has,' Lambert responded quietly, moved by his father's emotion, and by the general approval of this family of his who, these days, made him fear they condemned him.

'Wherever did you get it?' Maud asked. 'Did you bring it all that way with you?'

Lambert shook his head. 'As a matter of fact, it was the girl in your shop who told me where I'd obtain a special chair like this.' He was determined it should be called a chair, even though it closely resembled a narrow bed with wheels, and was constructed with a sloping back to ensure that Abel needn't remain horizontal.

'Not young Sally?' Maud said, astonished.

'Sally, yes. When I was inspecting the shop I chanced to

mention what I was seeking. Fortunately, she was able to direct me to a man just outside the town who makes this kind of thing.'

He had mentioned her name, feeling eager to announce whose help he had received as well to – to introduce her into conversation. Now, though, he must remember this was an indulgence not to be repeated, otherwise in no time at all his secret would be known by everyone. And that would not do, for only by keeping it to themselves could any relationship between them continue.

Lambert's thoughtful gift enhanced the day. When Hester and her mother took the short walk to St Mary's for Matins, it was with hearts that soared beyond the distress that had troubled their recent weeks.

'With your father in that invalid chair, I can see as how it isn't that unreasonable to consider a lift between floors will greatly enrich life for him.'

'He'll be better able to examine the samples of jewellery that I bring home for approval,' Hester added.

'He should be capable of keeping an eye on the accounting, as well, even if one of us does have to write the figures down for him.'

'Papa will be able to see more from the windows,' Olive remarked, turning round from where she had been walking along demurely with her younger brother.

'He loves Whitby so much!' Bernard exclaimed. 'Even more than I do, and that's saying a lot.'

Only briefly, inside the church, did Hester's relief dim – when she recalled how seriously Jon Davidson had spoken of his wife's ill-health, and sensed his fear that nothing could be done for her.

Abel and Lambert were awaiting them afterwards in the dining room and were eager to begin the distribution of gifts. For Maud there was a splendid bodice ornament in the shape of a spray of flowers: fashioned of silver set with diamonds, some of its blooms were mounted on springs to form tremblers.

'Thought you ought to have summat for a bit of a change from all that dark stuff,' Abel explained. 'I told our Hester exactly what I wanted for you and I'm glad you think she's made a good job of choosing.'

Maud was overwhelmed. She'd never owned diamonds before, had been afraid that now her husband was incapacitated that would be the end of surprise presents.

Hester's new gown had been carried downstairs and when her mother handed it over Olive and Bernard added a necklace of seed pearls. Lambert gave her a skeleton clock.

'So you don't spend all your time lost in your designing,' he teased her.

For Abel there were books which came with offers from all the family to read to him. There were fine wines as well, and from his wife a brocade smoking jacket which he insisted must be donned immediately. While he was helped into this by Lambert, Maud opened the rest of her presents and Olive and Bernard were allowed at last to begin on theirs.

When Lambert finally was free to accept his gifts he was touched by the care and affection that had gone into their selection. From his parents came the chain to complete his birthday watch. Hester had bought silver frames and filled them with photographs of each member of the family. From Bernard there was a history of the Crimean war, from Olive a new sword-belt.

When the excitement diminished slightly, Hester went to her room and changed into the pretty gown she'd been given. She had resisted the temptation to take another look after the day it was chosen, and was astonished anew by the way it enhanced her. With the pearls about her throat, she felt transformed as she hurried downstairs again.

Jon Davidson was standing in the hall, surprising her, for she hadn't heard the clang of the bell.

'I was just telling your mother,' he began, then looked again at Hester and smiled despite his anxiety. 'Er – yes, I called by since I was in the vicinity – sickness is no respecter of Christmas and there's a neighbour of yours bad with the ague. Since Ruth definitely isn't up to coming over, I thought I'd bring you our seasonal good wishes.'

'If she's resting, mightn't you come on your own?' suggested Hester, reluctant to accept that he wouldn't be joining them, but then silently regretting her own selfishness.

'No thank you, my dear – I think perhaps not.' Declining was another sadness, though, for Hester suddenly looked so exquisite. Her delicately-coloured gown was such a perfect complement to her dark hair and eyes.

He was compelled to take leave of them, but not before Hester inquired if he had seen her father's chair.

Jon's smile now was wholehearted. 'Indeed, yes – he called to me from the room, and would have your brother wheel him out to greet me. It's a splendid idea, couldn't be bettered.'

No sooner had the doctor left than Mrs Richmond and May Thorpe began bringing in the dinner. They were to have turkey this year rather than the customary goose, preceded by turtle soup.

Throughout the meal, Abel appeared so delighted with the chair enabling him to be near the family table that if he minded the fact of needing assistance with his food he gave no sign of it.

There was port jelly between the turkey and plum pudding, with port to drink afterwards and Mrs Richmond's special fruit cup for Olive and Bernard.

Their two schoolfriends were brought to the house just as everyone was adjourning to the drawing room. Mr and Mrs Jenkins were introduced to all the family and stayed to drink a seasonal toast. Minutes after they departed, with instructions to their Belle and Cedric to behave well until they were collected that evening, the Etheringtons and Crabtrees arrived.

Everyone in turn exclaimed over Abel's new chair, and the change in his humour induced by his new mobility meant that Falgrave House was filled with the old conviviality.

With his old friends yarning about the sea, Abel was content. Bernard and Cedric left their games and came to listen. Olive was encouraged to play the piano. Since they had opened up the rarely-used music room the ladies left the men to talk undisturbed.

As Hester was following across the hall she noticed Lambert heading towards the stairs.

'Come and listen – Olive's not at all bad now. You mustn't feel awkward about joining us, if you're not interested in fishing tales.'

'I'm going out,' he said with a smile. 'Had you forgotten?'

She had, and the day passing in a euphoric haze altered abruptly.

'Is it to see the same friends as last night?' she asked, hating herself for envying her brother.

It seemed today that she had no real friends. At work, she might share a common enthusiasm for the jet with craftsmen like Frank Clough. She could even, as on that one occasion, visit his home and find there an extension of their good working relationship. At the church she met acquaintances among her contemporaries, exchanged cheery greetings. Ever since the last time that she'd seen Jamie Skelton, though, she had been missing the ease of their friendship, their ability always to take up where they had left off, and share their very different experiences.

I've a mind to walk with Lambert down into the town and call on Jamie, she thought. There was never any doubting her welcome from his mother, Edna, and the rest of the family always crowded round her.

'Hester, come along in and close the door on that draught,' her mother called. And she knew there would be no going down to the overcrowded Skelton house. There'd been no sign of Jamie, had there, no word from him either. She'd seen that look on his face when she'd left him high and dry while she rushed back to the works.

She'd admitted at last that she was lonely. The circumstances forced upon the family were partly to blame, but she knew in her heart that she hadn't learned enough about getting on with people.

Immediately after the accident she really had believed that keeping her father alive and the business running profitably were all that she wanted. Already, she knew they weren't sufficient. And she saw as plainly as if she had been told that to have the different life for which she yearned would entail a long, exhausting struggle.

Chapter 8

Christmas passed swiftly and Abel remained cheerful and interested in everything that was going on. Lambert looked out the Magic Lantern and entertained everyone with a show. Hester organised Charades and games of Forfeits for the children, and was pleased when visiting adults joined in. And there were many visitors to Falgrave House. It seemed that as soon as one or two people reported that there was no need to fear the accident had robbed Abel of his gregarious nature, all old friends lost their embarrassment about calling.

When the day came to reopen the workshop Hester and Maud both declared they would find returning there a restful change from the hectic few days in their own household. Both, though, were smiling as Kilner drove them down through the narrow streets. Good spirits had been restored, especially now that Abel was counting the days to the first Monday in the New Year, when work on the lift would commence.

'I ought to have known I could rely on Lambert to make everything start to come right,' Maud remarked as the brougham jolted over the cobbles.

Just for a moment Hester felt hurt again. She'd spent weeks, hadn't she, doing her best. It was hardly her fault that her achievements weren't nearly so spectacular as her brother's. She hovered on the point of risking their newfound contentment by speaking up. But Kilner was slowing the carriage now, and she wasn't sorry to have a reason for remaining silent. And she was looking forward to working with Frank on the Othello figurine.

Edwin Clough glanced up from distributing rough jet to the other workers and greetings were exchanged while Mrs Falgrave and Hester crossed from the top of the stair, removing their cloaks.

'I hope you've all had a nice Christmas,' said Maud, 'and that you're refreshed ready to get on with a lot of work.'

Only Wally Hardcastle sighed while the other men and lads chorused 'Aye', 'That's right', and 'Thank you, Mrs Falgrave'.

Their extra work had been rewarded with a handsome Christmas bonus. Now, according to the newspapers, the Queen had forbidden all jewellery but jet at court, and this was being followed in other courts abroad.

'We'll have to keep up supplies of our normal lines of jewellery,' Maud continued, 'but we're going to produce something entirely new as well. We're going to make figurines – in a big way.'

Surprised, Hester smiled. She hadn't known her mother was all that enthusiastic about the Othello figure.

'We're going in for figures of the Prince Consort. There's plenty of folk will want one in their homes as a mark of respect. It was our Lambert's idea.'

Hester felt the colour draining out of her face, had to will herself not to sit down abruptly on the nearest dusty stool. What right had Lambert to interfere? Hadn't he seen her sketches of Othello. Designing was *her* job. And she hadn't even been told.

Her mother was speaking mainly to Edwin Clough now, showing him photographs of Prince Albert which had evidently been selected by Lambert.

'You'll not need drawings, you can work straight from these.'

And that's cutting me right out of it, thought Hester grimly. There was nothing she could say in front of the men – not that saying owt would do any good, she knew her mother. She wasn't giving up the Othello idea, though, it was too good for that. She would have a word with Frank on the quiet, emphasise that this scheme of Lambert's didn't preclude everything else.

There was no opportunity to discuss anything in the workroom with her mother's bright blue eyes missing nothing. At dinnertime, however, she caught Frank up as he went hurrying down the steps and out into the street.

'Do you mind if we talk?' she said, feeling more helpless

than she had for weeks. Her mother's announcement had knocked so much stuffing out of her. 'Or were you going somewhere particular?'

Frank's hesitation had been due to surprise, not reluctance. He grinned down at her. 'Only for a drink with the lads. But I'd best go back and change this smock, if . . .'

'Don't talk daft, Frank. When did I care about a few streaks of polishing rouge and a bit of dust? Let's go this way.'

Hester set off at a swift pace down one of the ginnels that led towards the quay. She wanted to get well away from the works and all the others employed there; to sort out her own thoughts as much as to keep the conversation private.

'You probably saw I wasn't in on what my mother had to say this morning – about them figurines of the Prince. I just want you to know that I've every intention of still going ahead with the ones I planned of Othello.'

Glancing sideways, she noticed that Frank was beginning to smile, and was looking relieved. But he said nothing. She wasn't certain how to continue.

She walked on instead, starting along the quay itself now. It was a lovely day for winter, though the sun was hazed as it glimmered through banks of cloud. There were several tall ships tied alongside, their sails silhouetted darkly against the sky. The one nearest to them seemed to tower over her so that she felt very small and rather afraid. Walking through the long shadow cast by its sails, she shivered. She drew in a steadying breath, could taste the brine.

'I'll fight, if necessary, to produce the things I believe in – I'll have to. But I don't want any trouble.' Sighing, she paused. 'Can't you say something, Frank?'

'How can I? I believe in t'same things as you, Miss Hester, but . . .'

Miss? Oh, God – what a way to be with each other, when he was the only one she could count on to understand.

'My mother's more the boss than I'll ever be. *And* our Lambert an' all now, by the sound of it. They could have told me.'

'Aye, they could. That weren't nice.'

She'd been hurt, and had had pride in her work trampled

151

underfoot. And he was that fond of her it was all he could do not to stop in his tracks and hug her. And go on hugging.

'When does he go back?'

She laughed, if sharply. 'In just another day or two now. And only this morning on the way to work I was so pleased we'd had such a good Christmas. My father's been ever such a lot better – brighter, you know. And that was thanks to Lambert. He got him an invalid chair, and he's made arrangements for construction to start on a lift. Oh, I do wish you'd come up to the house, Frank. Father's so thrilled with the work of yours that I've shown him.' And I need somebody at the back of me, if I'm to stand up to them she thought.

'All right, then. You'll have to say when . . .'

'Ay, bless you! We'll have to make it when you've done the first Othello figure.'

'Aye.'

'You don't sound very happy about it.'

'I'm not – not about visiting Falgrave House, if you must know. But I'll stand by what you want. Only I can't help wondering what your mother'll think of me spending time on that when . . .'

'I know. That's what worries me. I'll not jeopardise your job, love, that wouldn't be right.'

She'd called him *love*. It might have just slipped out, most likely it had, but it wouldn't have done so if she'd never had the endearment in mind. Frank couldn't contain his smile.

'I'll work over, if you like, to get that figurine right.'

His promise and the enthusiasm from which it sprang were all she needed. 'You've made me feel a lot better already. I hope you realise that, Frank Clough.'

She knew now that she wouldn't get all her own way at the works, but she had one ally, if it came to a fight. When her mother made that announcement, she'd considered appealing to her father for authority to continue with the lines she herself was planning. But that would cause bother, something she constantly hoped to avoid.

The following day Hester arrived at the works determined

152

that she would be as obliging as she knew how. Every suggestion made by her mother would be carried out. Uncomplainingly.

All last evening she had been troubled by their differences, had reminded herself yet again of her original resolution that she would devote her life to caring for her father. Instead of that – and she was the first to admit now that she'd have found confinement to the home dreadfully frustrating – she was being granted the opportunity to practise her skills. Humouring her mother was a small price to pay. And by winning Maud round, Hester would eventually earn the goodwill that would lead to consideration of her own ideas.

They had travelled separately to the workroom. The day was dry enough for the walk that Hester always enjoyed, even with a keen frost like today's making Whitby's cobbles and narrow pavements treacherous.

Maud's first call had been at the shop. She'd come away feeling uneasy, though for no reason more substantial than Sally Drinkwater's sudden tendency to answer quite assertively when questioned on the smallest of details. The girl had even presumed to remind her that the weekly sales had not been analysed in the way that they normally were when Mr Falgrave had them in hand.

But *I've* always superintended that shop, Maud reflected, and wondered if Abel had, in fact, taken on much of that particular responsibility without her even realising.

She had an armful of documents now, anyway, and thumped the bundle down on to the desk at the works. Hester seemed to be playing around with her usual bits of paper, covered in drawings of buttons and beads, and a figure that couldn't be missed, but bore no resemblance whatsoever to Prince Albert.

'Just look at this lot!' Maud exclaimed. 'I've been told your father analyses each week's sales.' She didn't like admitting she had no idea at all how this was done.

'That's right,' said Hester. 'He likes to know which particular lines are most popular. And, I suppose, the most profitable.'

Removing her cloak and thrusting it at the hook on the

door, Maud stifled a grunt. Arithmetic had never been her strong point. In her day, girls weren't expected to require such knowledge. So long as they could run a household without bankrupting anybody, they were a success. She couldn't see why company business need be more elaborate. And she didn't take to Hester's apparent grasp of what was required here.

'Since you know all about it, you can get started on this lot then. I'm surprised your father hasn't been asking for figures by now. And when you've got the weekly sales sorted out, you'd better begin on the yearly ones.' Having Sally mention these had reminded her of something she did know – and that was Abel's determination to learn how they had done throughout the year by the earliest possible date after 31 December.

Hester sat gazing in horror at the heap of documents. Inwardly, she was containing anger, her throat tightening with the effort of *not* objecting to her mother's orders. Concentrating on routine patterns for run of the mill jewellery had grown monotonous already, but it was infinitely preferable to doing masses and masses of calculations.

'What's wrong now?' Maud demanded. 'Them patterns can be fitted in any time, this lot's urgent.'

'Can I just explain something, please,' Hester ventured, with a great effort keeping her voice very low. She had to swallow before she could continue, trying not to flinch beneath her mother's cold gaze. 'I was getting on with these to try to please you. You seemed to want me to produce no more than variations on our usual lines.'

'Yes? Oh, do come to the point, Hester . . .' Maud needed to get out into the workroom, away from all those sums. They stared up at her, accusing her of incomplete comprehension of the job.

'It'd just be nice, that's all, if I could get these drawings off my hands first,' Hester added lamely, hating herself for sounding ineffectual now, and all because she was controlling her indignation.

'It might be nice, but in case you haven't noticed we're no longer in a situation where we can pick and choose what we do. I might remind you, young lady, that if you don't

154

cooperate in running this place there'll soon be nowhere for all your fancy designs to be turned into jewellery.'

I'm not a total imbecile, Hester thought bitterly. She would do as her mother asked and avoid antagonising her further. But, come what may and regardless of Lambert's intervention, she would somehow ensure that Falgraves' produced from *her* patterns.

A short distance away in Flowergate Sally's heart lurched as the shop bell rang and she looked up to see the flare of scarlet uniform. She was serving an old lady who was buying necklaces and brooches for all the females in her family, and taking a long time in the process.

'They'll none of 'em want one that's like any of the others, but they'll all have an eye to how much each item's cost me!' she'd chuckled, seating herself heavily on the chair by the counter and settling to take half a day if necessary over the selection.

'Always a staunch royalist, that's me,' she told Sally now with a glance and a nod in Lambert's direction. 'I was surprised none of them gave black jewellery this Christmas, with the court being in full mourning, so I thought I'd put that right. There's not much I can spend my money on, these days, I don't want for owt. And I can't take it with me. Any road, it'll make sure that they're dressed proper when it's my turn, won't it? Save 'em a guinea or two then.'

Glancing again towards Sally, she jerked her head in Lambert's direction. 'Serve him if you want to, lass. He'll be quicker than me.'

'It's all right, madam,' said Lambert swiftly when Sally hesitated. 'I'm one of the Falgraves. I'll wait to discuss business with Miss Drinkwater.'

'Ay, you did make me sound important!' Sally exclaimed later when the old lady eventually was satisfied with her purchases and left.

'And important's what you are,' he responded, smiling into her eyes. Without Sally his leave would have been tedious indeed. There was no denying that her interest was good for his morale, counterbalancing the depressive effect of finding his father so crucially disabled.

'Come into the back,' she said breathily, excited already and Lambert still the other side of the counter. 'If anybody that knows us comes in, you're on business, after all, aren't you?'

He drew her to him the instant they were in the back room. On Christmas Day itself their meeting had been as circumspect as the previous evening's. Somehow, he knew not how, he had restrained his sexual needs. Now, though, they had grown to a force so insistent it was almost past ignoring.

Against him, Sally was no less passionate, her breasts pressing at him through the taut cloth of her bodice.

'How will I live,' he groaned, 'when I have to leave you?'

'I'll give you a lock of my hair.' She had dreamed for ages, hadn't she, of having someone care this much about her.

'I'll not stay away so long, Sally, never again. I'll be home to Whitby whenever it's humanly possible.'

The secrecy of their meetings suited him well – he'd never seriously contemplated the married life that could spoil his enjoyment of the army. And Sally was as attractive a girl as he'd met anywhere, and certainly delightfully uninhibited. He'd grown aware over this past few days that she'd not need much encouragement to surrender completely. Not that he'd be careless of her welfare – he knew from talk in the mess that there were means of avoiding unwanted complications.

His friends were returning to their home today, an unfortunate fact which denied him the availability of pleasant surroundings. But there'd be time for due preparation before his next visit to Whitby. He'd find them a suitable rendezvous.

'You're not going back yet, are you – not today?' Sally inquired.

'Not today, no.' He thought for a second. 'I'll tell Father I need the brougham. But not Kilner with it!'

'I'll see you tonight then,' she agreed. 'Only I'll have to let them know at home.'

'I'll call for you there,' he said recklessly, thinking her family would be reassured, but immediately thought better of it. 'No – I'll meet you at the corner of the lane, as before.' There was no sense in being recognised by the Falgrave carriage or, worse, being introduced to her family.

Sally cared not at all, anyway, and was delighted that evening to be rushing towards him once more, her heart bumping within her chest as her thin soles lurched over the stones.

'Mother says I'm to bring you in when we get back,' she whispered against his searching mouth as they stood beside the carriage. 'But I'll understand if you'd rather not.' Although hardly living in poverty – when her father's folk left the whaling they'd realised on the boats and equipment, invested in a couple of coble boats and put money by – theirs was still a tiny home. And everyone knew Falgrave House, proudly overlooking the town.

'We'll see, we'll see. Let's not even think about the evening ending. And isn't it more fun to keep our friendship private?'

When he'd settled her into the brougham, Lambert set a fine pace, up and over the moors in the direction of Pickering. They ate lavishly at a wayside inn where the kitchens appeared well-stocked still with Christmas fare. There was plenty of drink besides, calculated to warm them both for a carriage that would be cold until their bodies' heat raised its temperature.

He drove on afterwards farther still from the coast, pulled off the road and tethered the reins about a bare-branched tree. Sally extended a hand to draw him to her as he entered the brougham.

'Kiss me, Lambert, kiss me.' The drink had dispersed any faint inhibitions, but hadn't erased her dread of their eventual parting.

He'd had the forethought to bring plenty of rugs; some he had already piled about Sally, now he sat beside her and reached for the rest. Desire was a delicious tumult, accelerated by the pressure of her slender form as she leaned into him. Kissing became a torture, so pale a promise of what he needed. 'I want you so much, Sally.'

'I thought that happen you did,' she whispered dryly, her eyes wide and laughing.

157

Lambert's laugh was strong, appreciative. He hugged her closer than ever, exhilarated by her strange mixture of worldliness and innocence. But because he liked her more he'd less justification for taking her. No girl had ever intrigued him so. He'd be thinking her a coquette then she'd confound him by being a woman deserving respect.

'One day you'll know how much,' he swore, and meant it. It was his discomfort that such a day hadn't yet arrived. Somehow, he must summon sufficient containment to preserve their present relationship.

Sally, though, had less concern, and less experience too of the strength of desire. She was kissing him again, her young mouth moulding to his, her body's urgent pressure willing his coercion.

Across miles of moorland raved the wind, near to storm force now, wailing about them, rocking the carriage. To Lambert it seemed to warn of the ferocity he might release from within, to Sally it was the threat driving her to security in him.

'Hold me, Lambert, love me.'

Didn't he wish them to belong to each other? She'd love to be his – a special person, no longer the one girl in a family of lads. She'd been teased all her life, when she wasn't being ignored – until she'd gone into Falgraves' shop where she became a young lady, acquiring knowledge about those glittering black jewels.

It was like a dream that she was in the Falgrave carriage now, with their eldest son, and his arms about her, his lips within reach. Her kiss was hard, demanding.

Lambert returned the kiss slowly, passionately. And then he took her gently by the shoulders and held her a little away from him.

'Aren't I good enough for you?' she asked him wistfully.

He hugged her again, couldn't stop himself crushing her to him. 'You could be too good to me, do you understand? Do you, Sally? I've known you just a few days, you shouldn't . . .'

'I haven't, you know, not with anybody. I were brought up decent.'

'I know, I know.' And can't you see that is the whole

trouble? he thought. 'We will see each other again,' he reminded her. 'There's no need for us to use this night as though it were our last.'

'And how do I know you won't meet other girls when you go back, and think they're nicer than me?'

'You won't know it, not for sure, not until I'm home again and coming straight to you.' And let us hope, for your sake, that no untoward temptation awaits me elsewhere. Or hope, for his own, that seeing the CO's daughter again, or Mary who lived so conveniently close to his barracks, restored good sense.

Wasn't Sally a little too intense, the kind of girl who expected a romantic encounter to progress to the altar? He wasn't looking for permanent ties – he'd need to be more sure than this before he took her. She was employed by the family; there'd be no escape for him.

'Next time I'm in Whitby,' he told her, 'I'll find us somewhere more congenial than this carriage.'

And was the promise for her sake, he wondered, or for his own – a pact with the seething within him that it would be sated?

Abel's head ached. The whole of his body – paralysed as it was – pulsed with the noise of picks driving into stone. I can't stand much more of this, he thought, and yet this was only the first day's work on the lift for which he was so desperate.

He hadn't considered how it might be to live trapped in bed or chair within the four walls of this room, while the entire house shook and strange men's voices grated on each raw nerve. And Maud wouldn't be home until late. She had a meeting with his cousin Isaac Falgrave over at Sandsend, and Isaac's wife Bess had suggested Maud eat with them.

Nobody knows, that's the trouble, he thought bitterly – nobody on this earth knows what it's like to be stuck here. That woman was back an' all – Nurse Bloomin' Clapper. Full of her homilies, her nursery manner, her disapproval, she'd erased Christmas as though it had never taken place. And Lambert had returned to his regiment down south. In some ways, that seemed the hardest pill to swallow.

His eldest son had smiled down while he was saying goodbye, those blue eyes revealing relief because he was getting away while all the time his lips were forming words of regret.

Abel hadn't been fooled. But nor was he, these days, sufficiently in command to do other than respond as if the sentiment were genuine. Afterwards, privately, he could admit to feeling sloughted, and to missing his son. It wasn't only the lad's scarlet uniform that brightened this place – *when* he was around, Abel added silently, admitting now that Lambert had disappointed him by going out so much and by turning so secretive about it.

Not that he himself had expressed anything but the opinion that a young fellow must have his own friends. Maud, now, she had ranted on at the top of her voice about Lambert's absences from meals. Not to the man himself, mind – to her beloved son she was always unfailingly agreeable! And who was the one obliged to endure her complaining? Who was the one trapped by this infernal body, with no escape?

He heard the front door open, then Hester's voice in the hall downstairs, with a man's which he didn't immediately recognise. In the past, he would have been at the door of this room, out onto the landing, standing at the head of the stairs. He'd have known who had entered his house.

He wasn't trying to eavesdrop – why should he care what they were discussing? But the place was suddenly calm; evidently the workmen had packed up for the day. Voices did carry up from the hall, and they did tantalise when no more than the occasional word could be distinguished . . .

Why was Hester taking so long to come up to see him? Who had she brought with her? *Were* they coming to him? In the few days that the workshop had been open again since Christmas, Hester had changed. She had grown withdrawn, so obviously troubled that he had wondered if there was some involvement with Jamie Skelton again.

If that were the case, this evening with her mother out of the house was just the opportunity for her to bring that lad here. And if he should be their visitor, she'd do well to keep Skelton away from him. Being civilised about the

160

matter on that first occasion was all that could be expected of him, surely? Now he'd suffered weeks of this torture, he was entitled to have some feelings . . .

She was coming up the stairs now, but on her own – his ears had grown keen during his imprisonment.

'Hallo, Father.'

'Hester, love.'

'How's it been today?'

'I only hope them men are quick about fitting that lift, they make an infernal racket.'

'Oh, dear.' Smiling, she kissed him. 'I'm sure when it's finished you'll find it's been worth all the disturbance.'

'It had better be. Did your mother say what time she'd be in?'

'Afraid not. I don't suppose she knows.'

'Bess always put on a good table. And if I know our Isaac he'll take his time agreeing terms over that new seam of jet he's opened up.' He only hoped Maud had the wit not to give in to him. Isaac was always full of hard luck tales about mining the stuff. He needed somebody as would stand up to him. If only *he* could . . . Ay, but even thinking that way was useless. 'Who is it you've brought home with you?'

Hester looked at him, disconcerted. How had he known? Wryly, she smiled. 'Frank Clough – we want to show you something we've been working on.'

'Oh, aye – those figurines of the Prince Consort?'

'Not those, no. They're nowt to do with me.'

I see, thought Abel, so you haven't liked anybody else having ideas. Is that what's been making you so contrary, I wonder?

'It wasn't a bad idea, Hester love, even if you didn't think of it.'

'Have I said it was? All I want is the opportunity to develop some of the things I *do* happen to think of.'

'*Some*? Nay lass, be fair . . . Since long before I were – were like this, you've had virtually a free hand. How many of your designs have we turned down?'

He was right, of course, she had been fortunate indeed to have so many of her drawings adopted. Only . . . well, she'd believed it was more than good fortune that had ensured her work was acceptable.

'What is it, then, that you and Frank have come up with?'

'We'll show you, shall we?'

'Aye – call him in, love, go on.'

Frank came in rather awkwardly. The sight of his boss laid flat like that on his back horrified him so much he wanted to turn and run. He walked straight up to the invalid chair, however, and smiled down – although his face felt stiff enough to crack.

'Good evening, Mr Falgrave. Glad to see you're out of bed now.' Only the word 'chair' had suggested something other than this reclining object little better than a bed.

'Aye – once that lift's constructed, I'll be all over t'house again. Good to see you, Frank lad.'

The sincerity of his greeting made the difference. Frank sat down, quite at ease and fished in his pocket for the dark carved figure.

'By, but that's grand!'

'It's Othello,' Hester announced, standing beside them.

'You didn't need to tell me – I've got eyes, haven't I? Well, Frank, you've made a good job of this.'

'It was a good design to work from.'

'Hester knows already what I think of her work, doesn't need telling. I want you to know Frank, that I think you have it in you to be one of the best carvers and engravers in the trade – and there's not too many as is good at both.'

'There you are, Frank, what did I tell you?' said Hester, dark eyes gleaming.

'What did your mother say when she saw this?'

'Well, as yet, she hasn't actually seen it.'

'Not seen it?' Abel's expression seemed as dark as his brows. 'Do you mean the pair of you've connived to produce this behind her back?'

'It wasn't like that, Father,' Hester protested.

Frank coloured, then paled just as quickly.

'No? Well, I suggest that that's just the way it was, young lady! And I don't like it, not one little bit. What right have you to come to me with this, making me tell you it's good, while all the time you've been producing it in an underhand way?'

Hester was so distressed she could weep, but she wouldn't though, not in front of Frank.

'There hasn't been much time. Frank only put the finishing touches to this tonight, after Mother had left.'

'I daresay. You'd want her out of t'road first.'

'No, no. What I meant to say was Frank's only worked on this in his own time, after hours.'

'That's right, Mr Falgrave, and I don't want a penny for it.'

'It might be right, but it's not *all right*, not in my book it's not. I'm not blaming you, Frank. It's our Hester who's in the wrong.'

'We've not had a chance to show Mother!'

'Nor to tell her, eh? What about the designs you drew – hid them from her, did you?'

'No. I think she's seen them. She just . . .'

'Happened to be conveniently absent whenever they were brought out? Nay, Hester, I expected better of you.'

'I didn't know we were supposed to consult her through every stage – cutting the jet to size, and then all the painstaking carving and engraving. To say nothing of the polishing.' She had watched Othello developing stature, then his features taking on character under the tool that even rendered expression in each curl on that Moorish head.

'It's because you're not in charge there, can you understand that? You're nobbut a lass of seventeen. When you've a few years on your back and a bit of experience, happen you'll be capable of making decisions as to what we'll sell. Until then, you'll toe the line.'

Hester took the figure from Frank. 'We'd best forget this then. I'm sorry, Frank, that I had you wasting your time.'

'Where are you going with that?' Abel demanded. 'Have I said it'll not be produced? You'll ask your mother's opinion first, though, and you'll couple the request with your apology for leaving her out.'

Hester hurried from the room. If she'd stayed in there a minute longer she'd not have held her tongue. Her father had humiliated her. In front of Frank. And she couldn't bear his anger.

Frank was following when Abel called him back. 'Don't you go, Clough, an' all. What have I said? It's not you I

163

blame. Yon's a damned good jet figure. Sit down again, Frank – please. I want to talk to you.'

'Yes, Mr Falgrave?'

'You like our Hester, don't you?'

The question was a shock, made his colour rise again. 'She's a nice person to work with. Doesn't – fill herself with airs, like.'

'Despite her being so independent that I've found it necessary to lay into her with my tongue? Hard on her, is that what you think me?' When there was no response, Abel smiled wryly. 'She'll learn. I'm not surprised she tends to forget she's too young for asserting herself, we forget that as well. Fact is she's taken that natural to the jet, from the start, that she does know a good thing even while it's just a mass of lines on a bit of paper.'

Frank nodded his agreement and Abel beamed. 'Our Hester's going to be the best thing that's ever happened to the works. But not for a while yet.' He paused for a moment, glanced across at Frank.

He saw a tall, pleasant-faced young fellow with the steady Clough eyes that always looked at you straight and saw more than he sometimes let on. Scrubbed of all that jet dust, his cheeks were a little pale on account of too many hours indoors, but well-defined by the bones beneath them.

'Hester's a mite headstrong, but that's her worst fault. Keep an eye on her, will you, lad – for me?'

'I will that, be glad to.'

There was a smile on Frank's face when he emerged from the room. He'd always liked Abel Falgrave and today he'd been delighted by that final request. He was forgetting already how embarrassed he'd felt when Hester was being criticised. He wondered where she was now, though, as he hurried along to descend the stairs.

He didn't notice her at once. She had retreated to a windowseat where the shadows cast by the gas-lights on the walls concealed her from all but a searching glance. Huddled into the corner between the cold panelling and even colder glass, she was struggling against the lump in her throat.

Hester had scarcely been able to answer Mrs Richmond

when the latter had approached to inquire when she would eat. And she had startled the housekeeper by asserting that she wanted nothing. It was all Lambert's fault, she decided, before silently acknowledging that it was her own. Even without his concept of the Prince Consort figurines she'd have been reluctant to consult her mother about the Othello.

She felt sick of the whole business. If she'd anywhere to go, she'd leave Whitby right now. She had antagonised her father, and no one knew how deeply that upset her. All she ever caused was trouble.

Frank startled her, appearing at her side while, with her back half-turned to him, she was too preoccupied to notice. Wearily, she rose.

'Ay, Frank – I'm sorry. I got you into this, and I'd have given anything to not have it happen. He's been telling you off an' all, I suppose. Was it very bad?'

He was smiling when he shook his head. 'As a matter of fact, he didn't say owt of the kind.'

'Oh, what was it then?'

'Something between me and him.' *And I can't tell you, mustn't let on that he's given me cause to hope.*

'So I'm the only one in disgrace.' Her spirits had lightened slightly on learning that Frank hadn't been reproved. But being the only wrongdoer left her feeling as alone as she had the other day walking along the quay. 'I'm beginning to think there's no place for me down yonder.'

'In the workroom?' He was incredulous. 'That isn't how your father talks.'

'No? Well, I just wish he'd tell *me* what he's thinking.'

'He won't, will he? You're his daughter and parents never do say . . .'

'Parents?' She looked up at him. 'Happen you're right.'

There was so much she wished to do – some days she was filled to bursting with ideas. The Othello figure was only the beginning. She'd been planning a whole series of Shakespeare characters, then some from Dickens. Then there was her greatest concept of all . . .

'Mother will stamp on the notion from the start,' she complained, half to herself.

Frank pictured the small, indomitable woman crushing

every mortal suggestion of Hester's. So in character he was compelled to smile.

'It isn't funny, drat it! Nay, Frank, I thought you understood.'

The tears welled up in her eyes now as the second man she cared about threatened to distress her.

'Come here . . .'

Rather clumsily, he held her. 'I'm not amused, Hester – or only by your mother ruling you like she rules us lot at the works. I know what matters to you. You ought to realise it matters to me, an' all.'

'You don't know, do you? Not all the things I was planning. Othello was only the start . . .'

'And when you've obtained consent for going ahead with that, it'll be all the easier to consult her and your father on your next design.'

'Crawl to her, you mean – *crawl?* Never in a million years. My designing's getting crowded out, any road, with the day to day running of the place. I'd best concentrate on that.'

'And throw away your creativity?'

'I might as well. She'll never approve. Because I'm not Lambert.'

The tears were of rage now, and streaming over her cheeks. Frank kissed them away, could not ignore her lips. When she kissed him back, and went on kissing, he willed his concern to strengthen her.

'You'd better go,' she said unsteadily when he drew back from their embrace.

'Aye, I think I had.'

They could not know what time Maud Falgrave might return. And if he doubted Hester's judgement on how her mother would react to her drawings, he was certain what she'd make of finding them kissing here.

The hardest thing was leaving. While Hester was so distraught, how could he simply walk out through that door?

The trouble was, he reflected, turning up his collar against the blast of icy wind from the sea, he was another Othello. He loved not wisely, but too well.

Chapter 9

Maud took no persuading that the Othello figurine must join their range of carvings. Hester was as relieved as she was surprised, and more grateful than ever to Frank, recognising that his skill in interpreting her ideas was responsible for its acceptance.

Less easy to swallow was her mother's attitude to her personally, which swung from critical to downright aggressive. Whatever Hester did, it seemed there was no satisfying Maud. Her irritability appeared to be due simply to Lambert's return to his regiment.

Construction of the lift, though, was completed quickly and once Mrs Richmond had put Falgrave House back in order, aided by a team of extra cleaners brought in especially, Hester believed they might all be happier.

For the first few days when family or staff or even Nurse Clapper seemed only too pleased to wheel him to and from the contraption, Abel was highly delighted. And Lambert came home for a short weekend leave.

He walked through the door unannounced on the Friday afternoon, and exclaimed with pleasure on finding the lift completed and his father in one of the ground-floor rooms.

May Thorpe was sent in with tea and they talked, mostly about the business, for although Abel was proud of his son's army career he'd little interest in military matters.

'Glad you've come back to see us so soon, Lambert,' he admitted with a smile. 'The days seem very long. And your mother fair pines for your company.'

Lambert smiled and nodded, feeling troubled since it wasn't really to see them that he was in Whitby. He had arrived in the town more than an hour ago, and had already visited the Flowergate shop. Sally Drinkwater's reaction was all that he had hoped, and more. There had been several customers between the door and her glass counter. Across their heads, her gaze had linked with his immediately, delighted astonishment shining in those eyes that were even bluer than his own.

When at last they were alone and she was looking up at him, he'd noticed a gleam of joyful tears. He'd felt moved then, far more than he'd ever expected. Whatever he'd first intended with Sally, her response to him was steadily deepening his regard for her.

'I was so afraid I wouldn't see you for months,' she exclaimed straightforwardly. And that had mattered. She'd seen Jamie Skelton twice since Christmas, but that had been no more than a bit of company that briefly eased the pangs of missing Lambert.

'I'm only here until Monday evening,' he told her quickly. 'But we'll make the most of it, I hope. Can you get away today when you close the shop?'

'Oh, yes, yes. But I'll have to let them know at home.'

'What'll you tell them, Sally?' It was early yet to bring their friendship into the open, but having her deceive her parents still gnawed into the part of him that hated duplicity.

'Same as I did before, I suppose – that some of us from Falgraves' are going out.'

'And tomorrow . . . Tomorrow, Sally, I want you to come with me to a house-party. You know the friends of mine whose home we visited? Crispin's wife is twenty-one, and they're celebrating all weekend. I was wondering – would your mother permit you to stay there the night?'

'All night, but why?'

Lambert smiled. 'Well – you know how it is with house-parties. The guests like to laze over breakfast on the Sunday, walk the dogs, that kind of thing.'

Sally didn't know, but she adored the prospect of being with Lambert for such a lovely long time, especially in that beautiful big house.

'I'll tell them there's a lot of us have been asked to this party and 'cos it's a fair distance away we've been invited to sleep there.'

Lambert was so elated by the ease with which these arrangements had been made that now, sitting with his father, he could scarcely contain his high spirits. Even when his mother and Hester came in from the workshop, both looking tired and on edge, he still felt exhilarated.

Maud was less than cheered when he disappeared the moment they had finished their meal. Rather than admit her annoyance, though, she turned instead on Hester.

'There, you see – that's the sort of life you should be having. But then, Lambert always was so personable. A credit to me, that's what he's been since the day he was first put into breeches.'

Inwardly, Hester sighed. Her mother was so predictable in her opinions. And half-blind to the reality of working such long hours.

'Now, if you'd smartened yourself up and worn a decent gown with your crinoline frame beneath it, I'll warrant Lambert could have considered taking you with him.'

'Wherever he's going, I shouldn't think Lambert'd want his sister along.'

'And why not? He's lost touch with most of his friends in Whitby, hasn't he, since going away with the Grenadiers?'

'From what he was saying, he must know some people round here well enough for them to invite him to their home.'

'Yet, you're here all the time and who asks you to call? Nobody.'

It was true, but the reason was different from what her mother supposed. Except for friendships with girls she had known at school, and they had dwindled, most of her visits in the past had been to the Skelton home. And once to the Cloughs'.

Why she should recollect that, Hester had no idea. She had been cautious in her daily contact with Frank ever since the occasion when her father was so vexed. Whatever anger she invoked upon herself, she wouldn't readily expose Frank to similar awkwardness.

She wasn't particularly interested in socialising for its own sake. And her old companion Jamie was frequently away for long periods at sea. When he was in Whitby, she'd heard tell, he lodged with a fellow seaman and visited the house near the harbour only to take money that would help pay off his debt. Happen that was why she didn't see him.

Suddenly, she was overcome with the ache for their easy friendship, for the knowledge that, no matter what disturbed her, there'd always be Jamie the next day, or the one after, and no opportunity for remaining glum when he was about.

'You've never done it right, not from the word go, have you?' her mother persisted. 'Befriending that ragamuffin from down yonder till decent folk wouldn't look twice at you.'

Refusing to listen to any more, Hester went to sit with her father who was finding his return to the rest of the house exhausting and frequently went early to bed. Over Christmas, Abel's interest in local legend had returned and they often read about St Hilda's involvement with the abbey, even her turning to stone a plague of snakes, now reputed visible at the foot of the cliff as ammonites.

'Have you ever watched them planting the Penny Hedge, love?' he asked her today.

'Once, when I was small. You took me, don't you remember?'

'Ay, I forget, Hester lass. Knew I'd taken one on you, wasn't sure if it was Olive.'

'I can remember a lot of people standing round on the river bank, watching. It began as some penance or other, didn't it?'

'That's it, way back. Some say it were in the reign of Henry II, some folk tell it as being Anglo-Saxon. Any road, the crux of it was when a boar being hunted was driven into a hermit's cell, or chapel.'

'Didn't the hunters set about the hermit or something dreadful like that?'

'Aye, so the tale goes.'

'How did the penance come into it?'

'He was a holy man, wasn't he? Instead of the punishment they deserved for sacrilege as well as maltreating him, he decreed that they and their descendants should plant the Penny Hedge . . .'

'Or *Horngarth*, that's its other name, isn't it?'

Abel nodded, pleased that she'd remembered so much after all this time, yet saddened as well because of the countless local occasions which he was now compelled to miss.

'I wish I could go again,' Hester said impulsively. She yearned so fiercely to participate in something that *wasn't* connected with work in this area that she loved.

'There's nothing to stop you, is there?' You're not manacled here, he thought.

'It's at something like nine o'clock in a morning, isn't it?'

'Aye. On Ascension Eve. I don't suppose the works would fall down if you took four or five hours off.'

Hester nodded, but inwardly she was sighing. Her father was making no attempt to conceal his resentment of this enforced imprisonment.

'I've got another idea of something I want to design,' she announced, changing the topic. 'It'd be big, and could take several months to complete.'

'Months? Nay, whatever can it be? Summat of that sort'd cost that much you'd never find a buyer.'

'I'm not certain we'd want to sell it.'

'We're in business, lass – that's what it's about.'

'I was standing looking at the shop window t'other day. We've got some lovely stuff there, Father, but it's all – well, much of a muchness.'

'Nay, I'll not have that . . .'

'Will you listen to me, please? We've got masses of necklaces, brooches, bracelets, even quite a few figurines now. What we want, though, is something that'll draw folks' attention from across the road. Something different from what other jet jewellers are displaying. It's time we reminded 'em we're better than most.'

'And you know the very thing, of course.'

There was a bite to his words which didn't miss her notice, but then when wasn't he tart with folk, these days?

'I hope so. A tree – that's what we could have. The trunk and some of the main branches could be carved from the one piece, you know that's possible. Wally Hardcastle would manage that all right.' Her dislike of the man didn't obscure his talent from her. 'The more delicate branches could be worked separately and attached, as could . . .' Smiling, she paused. She observed that she'd won his attention, enjoyed

171

anticipating his reaction. '... As could the scattering of birds, tiny butterflies.'

'How big do you plan on this thing being?'

'Like I said, so's it'll be seen from t'other side of the road.'

'Go on then, you've got me interested. I'll have a look at your preliminary sketches.'

'Now?'

'I might have known. Trust you to make a start, long before anybody's given their approval. You can show me some time. When you come and tell me your mother's in favour of all this, as well.'

There was to be no risking this concept by not observing the accepted code. And Hester couldn't wait to learn her mother's verdict.

She raised the matter later that evening, carefully using similar words to the ones that had aroused Abel's interest.

'I'm not keen,' Maud snapped at once. 'Think of all them hours put into summat that we're not even sure we're thinking to sell. It's proper daft. While you've got most of the men in the workroom laiking with that, they could be producing hundreds of pieces of jewellery.'

'That all look just like stuff that's in the Broadbents' jet shop or Arkwrights' – and maybe not as unusual as that in Greenburys'!'

'I'll have you know we Falgraves always pride ourselves on our originality, as much as any family or individual in the business.'

'Happen so, but a brooch is only a brooch, a ring's just ...'

'Jet rings were sold in Whitby in 1394.'

'Aye,' said Hester dryly, 'for about a penny each.'

'Have you spoken to your father about this notion of yours?'

'Yes. He seemed enthusiastic.'

'I thought you'd have had a word with him first. Think you can still wind him round your finger, don't you? Well, it's me now that has to consider what's best for t'works.'

'Are you saying you won't even study the designs?'

'Been wasting your time already on such nonsense, have

you? If you haven't enough to do, my girl, there's plenty of work down yonder. And if you haven't forgotten all you learnt, there's lots of beads you could be turning. That lad of Dunsdale's hasn't found his feet yet, he'll be a while afore he's use to us for more than sweeping up.'

Hester bit back the retort that she didn't intend returning to an apprentice's tasks.

Maud chuckled. 'After all, you only need a pair of breeches instead of yon skirt and you could be taken for a bit of a lad.'

Thank you, Mother, thought Hester, wounded despite perpetually resolving that such exclamations wouldn't be permitted to penetrate.

'I'm not condemning your notion without giving it attention,' Maud added, her tone reasonable. 'I'll talk it over with our Lambert.'

Hester stared across at her, willing herself not to scream, not even to echo her brother's name. But, heaven's above, what did Lambert know about it?

'He's home again to help, isn't he?' Maud said. 'He spent a lot of time round Christmas thinking what might be best for the shop.'

Yes, I did catch him there once or twice, thought Hester, and wondered again what had interested her brother so greatly about the place.

'He's not considering coming out of the army, is he?' she asked her mother. It was unlike Lambert to return so soon to Whitby. Had he developed the urge to participate in the business? She might make herself even more unpopular by it, but she'd feel compelled to resist his interference.

'He – might,' Maud replied slowly, though with no cause for such a supposition. If Hester kept coming up with these ridiculous schemes she needed somebody to curb her.

'I want a bit of fresh air. I'm going out for an hour or so,' Hester announced abruptly.

'Get Kilner to take you then. You know it's courting trouble to go wandering these streets of a night.'

'I'll not get much fresh air in the carriage.'

'According to you, that brougham's allus full of draughts.'

173

Hester was compelled to laugh. There were times when she envied her mother the swift answers.

'All right, I'll do as you say.'

But now she wondered where she would go. Originally, she had toyed with the idea of visiting the Cloughs. She was shrieking inside with desperation to talk to somebody. All she wanted was to see Frank. The trouble was, with Edwin there, and young Harold all ears for whatever their boss's daughter might be saying to his brother, there'd be no privacy. Having Kilner conducting her there and waiting outside was the proverbial final straw that made the prospect intolerable.

She stopped the carriage instead a few streets away from the Skelton home, at the top of a dingy alleyway.

'I'll not be long, Kilner,' she told him as he helped her down. 'You've maybe time for a drink in the public house over yonder.'

Archie Skelton opened the door to her knock and it pleased her to see that Jamie's father was on his feet again. From his expression, though, nothing about her pleased him.

'Jamie's not here,' he told her, smiling now in satisfaction. 'In lodgings, these days – with one of his mates.'

'Hester, it is, isn't it?' Edna Skelton called, and looking through into the untidy room Hester saw her struggling to haul her bulk from a chair. It fell over as Edna moved away, but no effort was made to right it. 'Come in, lass, come in,' she invited, elbowing her husband aside.

'Folks like her don't want visiting the likes on us,' Archie grumbled, and began closing the warped door after her.

'Hester's never made herself out to be better than anybody else. And it's weeks sin' she were here.'

'Glad you're up and about again, Mr Skelton,' Hester said, turning to look at him as a heave from his shoulder finally shut the door.

'Not a lot of choice, was there?' he snapped. 'Got to see there's food in us mouths. *We* don't have nowt at back on us.'

'Come and sit down, Hester,' his wife insisted, righting

her own chair and proffering one from which she tossed a mangy cat.

'It's strange to see you without any children at all about.'

'Our Jessie's got a young man now,' Archie Skelton informed her.

But she can't be more than fifteen, thought Hester, and refrained from speaking her thoughts.

'You're not married or owt then?' he persisted, and she marvelled that he could be so interested in her personal life.

'Archie . . .' Edna Skelton warned, but he continued nevertheless.

'A fine lass, our Jessie's grown into. It's no surprise to us that someone's after her hand But I suppose getting a husband matters less when your folk want for nowt.'

'So, Jamie's in lodgings now,' Hester said, smiling, to Mrs Skelton. 'I haven't seen much of him lately, not since he's been staying longer at sea.'

'Don't suppose you've lost sleep over that,' his father snapped, still embarrassed by what saving Jamie had cost the Falgraves.

'You're right,' she replied. 'But only because I'm having to work so hard that, most nights, I'm exhausted.'

'And how is poor Mr Falgrave?' Jamie's mother inquired.

'Not very much different, I'm afraid. Except that we've had a lift installed to take him from one floor to another.'

'That'll be a blessing.'

'He certainly seems to appreciate the change of scene. Oh – and Lambert's got him an invalid chair.'

'Short of nowt you've got then, up there, eh?' Archie Skelton remarked. He'd like to believe he owed them nothing.

Except for the ability to walk, to do a job, to live . . . Hester swallowed, willed herself not to let the words tumble out.

'Do you think your family'll be asleep?' she asked Edna.

'Don't suppose the older ones will be yet. Go on up, lass, and have a look.'

The odour of the one bedroom met her before she was halfway up the narrow stairs. The bed that had been taken downstairs while Archie's leg was healing now occupied the space against one wall. Beneath it was a chamber pot, in serious danger of overflowing. A similar receptacle stood in one corner close to one of the two beds occupied by children.

Leaning with an elbow on a grubby pillow at the foot of the girls' bed, Dollie was concentrating, tongue between teeth, on plaiting Joanie's hair. Joanie might have been asleep, she remained so motionless and unprotesting, Her rather vacant, oriental eyes were open, though, and as Hester watched she wiped her nose on the coarse blanket.

'Hester!'

The cry was from Sylvie who shot upright at the head of the bed and extended fragile arms. Maisie's bright hair appeared from the covers beside her, but she sneezed in the chill of the unheated room and pulled the blanket up to her ears again.

With the bed packed as it was with children sleeping top to toe, there was no room for Hester to perch on its edge. When she walked over to embrace Sylvie, though, the child rose to her feet and hurled herself into Hester's arms.

'Our Jessie said you wouldn't come to see us no more, but I knew you'd not forget us.'

Her tiny face and the thin body in a holey shift were dreadfully cold. Hester hugged her against her chest. The instant that Sylvie moved, the ones at the foot of the bed dragged on the blanket until Maisie screeched that she was freezing to death.

That wasn't surprising. If Sylvie's shift was worn, Maisie's was outgrown. And she wore nothing else. Hester ached for them all, loathing on their behalf the indignity of being improperly clothed as much as the cold they were suffering.

Harry and Maurice were regarding her suspiciously from head and foot respectively of the third bed. Beside Harry she could just discern the top of young Nat's gleaming hair.

'Jamie don't live here no more,' Harry informed her.

'I know,' said Hester smiling. 'That doesn't prevent me coming to see you all.'

'Got something to show you,' he continued, and grinned.

'That's nice,' Hester began, feeling pleased that she

hadn't lost the knack of communicating with this group of young persons.

Harry leapt from the bed, stark naked, stalked past her with a saucy look, and relieved himself into the chamber pot.

'I have brothers as well,' said Hester evenly.

With the exception of Joanie and Nat, the other children were giggling.

'I wish I could do it standing up,' confided Sylvie, hugging her. 'Our Joanie tried to once. Mam didn't half wallop her.'

'Jamie does it out of the window,' Maurice informed her, and laughed uproariously.

'Only if the pot's full, or there's someone won't get off it,' Sylvie added loyally. 'And it's only like what they have to do while they're at sea.'

Hester busied herself returning Sylvie to the bed. The child was protesting, providing reason to keep her eyes focused on her while she encouraged her to lie beneath the blanket.

'I can go downstairs with you,' Sylvie announced. 'Mam'll let me. It's scaring up here when it's all dark.'

Hester had been given a rushlight, the only illumination. 'There's nothing to be scared of,' she began.

'There's eyes look at us in the dark,' Sylvie insisted.

'Bad folk that come out of t'walls,' Dollie added.

'Nonsense! Anyway, there's enough of you to protect each other,' Hester continued reassuringly.

'But we're only little,' Sylvie protested, 'and they're 'normous.'

'Tell you what – I'll leave you something to keep you safe,' said Hester, unfastening from round her neck the crucifix and chain of carved jet. 'Do you know what this is made of?'

No one answered.

'It's jet, and it's always been used for keeping evil away.'

In the faint light facets of the cross glittered while she held it for the children to examine.

'I'll hang this on the wall, here, for you. It belongs to you all – that means no one's got to remove it. Now, what have you been learning at school, Dollie?' she inquired, and came to lean on the rough board at the foot of the bed.

'I've forgot.'

'She don't go no more,' Maurice revealed.

'I once ran away,' Hester confided. 'And I got lost walking home. It was your Jamie found me, and we've been friends ever since.'

'When will you and him get married?' Sylvie asked. 'Jess and her Fred'll get wed on her next birthday.'

'Me and Jamie?' Again, Hester was embarrassed. How could she explain to his kin that there'd never be anything but friendship between them? Or would there, she wondered suddenly. So many times in the past she had felt that all Jamie needed was a steadying background. If he should consider that necessary too, if he began displaying his former readiness to trust . . . *if* he admitted that he needed her?

'I'm very busy, these days, with my father having been injured.'

'But you'll want to have a home, you'll want to make babies,' Dollie suggested.

Make babies? However had this child learned to contemplate that? Hester managed a smile. 'It might be nice to have a lot of brothers and sisters – like you,' she confirmed. Despite their rude ways, they were a lovable bunch of youngsters. Avowing affection for them was easy. Much easier than visualising cooperating with Jamie to bring up a family. Even if none of his siblings were in the army, nor likely to be, and none of them would come back to Whitby to ruin life for others by interfering.

The uninhibited nature of the Skelton brood had not turned Hester against them. Instead, her visit had reawakened her old admiration for Jamie. He'd clung to his determination to emulate Captain James Cook, the man he had always idolised. He might be a Skelton, but already he'd freed himself to some degree by finding lodgings. Jamie was earning good money now, from what his mother said, and was gradually recompensing his father for the loss of the fishing smack.

178

Another young lady was equally impressed by Jamie's determination to pay back his father. Unfortunately for Jamie, though, he'd chosen altogether the wrong Saturday for calling in at the shop in Flowergate.

Instinctively, Sally greeted him warmly, beaming when she looked up from putting away several jet necklaces that she'd shown to a customer who'd left a few moments ago.

'Ay, but this is a nice surprise. I didn't expect you ashore for a day or two yet.'

'We came back unexpected, like. The boss's wife is expecting a bairn, and he was uneasy – I think her time's nearly due.'

'Does that mean you won't be putting out again for a while?'

'Don't know. Depends when the baby arrives. But I'll be here today and tomorrow, any road. I'll meet you when you close . . .'

Colour raced into Sally's face, though why she should react like this she didn't know. It wasn't as if she and Jamie had any kind of understanding. They'd only been friends.

'I'm sorry,' she began in a rush, 'I'm going out tonight. It's all arranged.'

'Tomorrow then . . .'

'That's just it,' Sally continued. 'I can't. I'm going away for a night, shan't be back till quite late on Sunday.'

'Oh, aye – where are you off to then?'

'Just – with some friends.'

'Change your mind – come out with me instead, Sally.' He had yearned for her, spent hours gazing across the churning sea, thinking and thinking about her.

'I can't let them down, not at such short notice.' And changing her arrangements with Lambert wasn't to be considered. Last night had been magical, and they'd only been to one of the inns over the moors again for a meal. Going to stay with his friends was generating deep inside her enormous lurches of intense anticipation.

'Did you ever get that jet pendant you wanted?' Jamie inquired, glancing across to the display cases on the wall. The glittering black jewellery appeared to have been rearranged.

Sally grinned. 'No, but I'm not all that bothered now.' Much as she still loved the sparkle of the jet that she sold, her desire to own a piece herself had lost all urgency. How could it matter now, when she was in love with the Falgraves' eldest son? Lambert would deny her nothing.

Disgruntled, Jamie hurried from the shop, crossed the road and set off in the direction of the harbour. He'd been afraid that Sally might eventually tire of his long absences at sea but hadn't believed it could happen this soon. He had thought he could count on her. And although she'd suggested he might call in at the shop on Monday if he hadn't put out from here again by then, today and Sunday threatened to be boring.

Annoyed, he decided to ease his battered pride while he slaked his thirst, and turned back the few paces to the door of a public house. He took his ale to a table near the window and sank on to the wooden bench without a glance at the sandy-haired fellow sitting across from him.

'Been buying summat for your sweetheart, have you?' the fellow asked, wiping his mouth with the back of a hand.

'No.' Puzzled, Jamie stared at him.

'Come out of t'Falgrave shop, didn't you? Don't tell me you buy their baubles for yoursen . . .'

''Course not. No, I happen to be friendly with the young lady what serves there.'

'Sally Drinkwater.'

'You know her then?'

'In a manner of speaking, aye. I used to work for Falgraves' – bloomin' hard graft, an' all.'

'The shop's nice, though.'

'Or the lass that's in there. There's more nor you thinks that, tha knows.'

'Hardly surprising,' said Jamie, while jealousy and disappointment combined to make him pale.

'Some of the young apprentices make right fools of themselves over her – Harold Clough, for one. Not that *he* can do any wrong, nor their Frank, what with their old man being the foreman of the jet works.'

'Does this Harold take her out?' He had to know – if only so's he knew what to do.

'Reckon he does his best – not that you need worry on that score. Soft, he is, all t'Cloughs are.'

'Trouble is I'm away at sea a lot.'

'Even so. To my way of thinking, there's no contest. That Harold Clough'd not know what to do. Reckon he thinks it's for stirring 'is tea with!'

When Jeff Hardcastle laughed raucously, Jamie joined in, glad to be accepted. They exchanged names, bought each other an ale, and then another, both ready to settle to a few hours' steady drinking.

By the time Lambert's hired carriage stopped outside the jet shop Jamie, if not past seeing across the road, was past noticing.

Sally's excitement had increased with each hour. As soon as she saw Lambert's red tunic, she rushed to the shop door.

'Won't be a minute,' she gasped. 'I've locked up the back. Haven't had one customer in the past hour. Thought them hands on that there clock had got stuck.'

He smiled, charmed by her evident delight, elated by her eagerness. He could rely on his friends the Stansfields, to provide a situation conducive to romance.

All the way out to that home on the cliff, Sally chattered, first about the weather which was abominably cold but, thankfully, with no threat of snow, then about her day in the shop. She told him about Jamie Skelton's brief call; after all, she wanted Lambert to understand that nothing would have tempted her to miss this house-party.

Rather than reassured, he was somewhat disconcerted. He would have claimed to no one that Sally was totally committed to himself, but he had so quickly grown attached to her that there'd been no time for him to wonder if there was some serious rival. Maybe it was as well that he should declare his love for her.

They kissed in the shadow of the carriage before Lambert took her hand and led her to the front door.

Crispin Stansfield was only a few paces behind the maid who admitted them. A hand extended to each of them, he gave a gallant little bow to Sally as they were introduced. Their outdoor clothes were whisked away, together with their overnight bags. With Lambert's hand on her arm, Sally followed their host through into the room she remembered so well from Christmas.

She'd never seen so many lovely people. Two more of the men were in military uniforms, the rest in dark coats and trousers with pleated shirts such a bright white that they dazzled your eyes. The ladies were the most splendid of all, naturally. For a second or two Sally wished she possessed something more exciting than her white dress.

All at once, though, what she wore mattered not at all. Crispin's wife, Emma, came forward to meet them, turned then and announced their names in such a way that even 'Sally Drinkwater' sounded special. Glasses were passed to them and, because she was too elated to sip, Sally felt the alcohol rushing to her head.

Immediately, she issued herself a silent warning to be careful. She'd be mortified if she did anything to let Lambert down in front of all his friends. But she'd drunk enough to make conversation easier, and soon was feeling far more at home than she'd expected.

Dinner that evening seemed to last for ever, but Sally had no complaints. She'd been seated across the table from Lambert, which had alarmed her, but only for a moment. Sitting like this, she was able to look straight into his eyes, and nearly every time she glanced from her plate it was to meet his gaze.

There was a new element in the looks he gave her tonight, a possessiveness that made her heart surge. It affected other parts of her also, not that the deep inner pulsing was unfamiliar. Combined with the sensation of belonging to him, though, it felt right somehow. As if this was destined for them.

Destiny, she reflected, meeting his glance again – that's what it was. Hadn't her friendship with Harold, and with Jamie, been a search for someone of her own? And now there was Lambert.

One of the ladies present could play the piano, one of the other guardsmen the flute. After the meal was ended they returned to the room where they had first gathered, and couples began dancing.

The wine taken with their meal had increased the slight intoxication that Sally had experienced earlier. But Lambert's arm was firm about her waist and she'd never felt better supported. Indeed, any dizziness only enhanced the thrill of it all.

There were whirling dances to leave her breathless and laughing, then dreamy waltzes that sent all her pulses tingling. When at last the music stopped Sally felt blissfully, gloriously happy.

No one seemed to have even one eye on the clock, but then she thought with a private smile, they hadn't been on their feet in a shop all day. Not that she'd permit that to dim her enjoyment, she'd not earned a name as a game little thing for nothing. So long as Lambert kept going, she'd be at his side.

And very much at his side was the way she walked at long last up the curving staircase. It was only when they reached the landing that even his arm about her failed to quiet her sudden panic.

'I don't know which room's mine,' she gasped. 'I don't know where they've took me things.' Not having given a thought to these matters made her predicament all the more alarming.

Lambert's arm tightened about her, he concealed a smile. 'Don't fret, sweetheart, *I* know.'

'I'm daft, aren't I? I should have thought . . .'

'You're adorable.'

And so she appeared, with the flickering light from the gas jets turning her pale curls to silver. Tiredness had painted mauve shadows beneath her eyes and the heat generated by dancing had moistened their lids, rendering them near-transparent. The desire coursing through him these past few hours adopted a new dimension. As strong as the longing to possess was the urge simply to hold her.

He opened the door of her room. Still with an arm about her, he led her inside. Behind them, the door shut with a click.

'What a lovely fire!'

Sally rushed to the hearth, extended both hands to the

183

blaze. His side where she had been pressed felt icily cold. Slowly, Lambert followed until he was standing behind her.

'You're beautiful,' he murmured, was surprised by his own intense emotion, so overwhelming he could scarcely speak.

His hands went to her shoulders, then down over her shapely breasts. Sally felt his lips on her hair, his breath fluttering its strands. Leaning into him was instinctive. Eyes closed, she sighed in ecstasy.

'Love you, I want to love you,' he said huskily.

She turned in his arms, reached up to find his mouth with her searching lips. Her arms were about him now, drawing him closer than ever. Their kisses grew more fierce, demanding.

In the firelight her white gown gleamed, bridal, alluring. Beneath his fingers its fabric felt silky, fragile. Any but the lightest touch would tear it from her body. Its delicacy increased his awareness of her vulnerability. Slowly enough to allow her to check him, he began unfastening its tiny pearly buttons.

The undergarment she wore scarcely covered her breasts. A groan imprisoned in his throat, he bent his head to kiss the skin that was silkier even than her gown.

She was stroking his hair, uttering his name repeatedly in a voice appealingly tender. Affection surged, stronger than any he'd experienced towards anyone in his life. Startled by its force as well as distracted by insane desire, he couldn't order his fingers to cope with the rest of the buttons.

Smiling, Sally took over, holding his attention with steady eyes that revealed consent to his unspoken intention.

The gown was laid aside, the ungainly crinoline cage discarded. And Lambert pulled her against him, pressing her to the yearning that multiplied by the second. Her response was immediate, a stirring that removed his final doubts about proceeding. Was it her fingers or his own that began on the fastenings of his uniform?

There were pauses to kiss and to cling, but soon they stood skin to skin, too needful of each other to experience awkwardness.

184

'I didn't know it was like this,' Sally murmured, surprised by the intensity of the love that accompanied her body's urgency. Until tonight, desire had seemed an adventure, not quite allied to commitment.

'Nor I . . .' he answered fervently.

She had thought him experienced, and maybe he was, but not in the ultimate sharing between man and woman. Recognising this endeared him to her even more fiercely. When they embraced again it was her arms that locked around him, her lips and tongue that tested and tasted, then invited.

Utterly absorbed with each other, both started when coals shifted in the grate. Together, they smiled; together, walked towards the bed, hardly drew apart even to settle between icy sheets.

Sally clung to him for warmth, relaxed in his affection, smiled against his mouth when kissing continued. In each pore, and every nerve and pulse she was aware of him. But no less aware of herself, of the now familiar drumming that flared in some internal space, soared through every vein, or did it begin in her heartbeat . . . ?

His hands were on her now, slow at first then swift, tracing her spine then swerving over one hip, increasing her need of him until she couldn't restrain a moan.

'Love me, Lambert.'

His touch grew more intimate, escalating longing. And he could wait no longer, tried to govern this great intensity, and succeeded only in ensuring that he entered her.

Her cry made him fear that she was hurt, her body told him differently. Reassured, he permitted the clamour that feelings demanded.

Eventually, both grew still, held each other in peace that grew from desire's waning. He kissed her smiling eyes.

'You're mine now, Sally. The separations will only be for a time, then you'll go everywhere with me.'

'And you'll come to Whitby often until then, won't you?'

She was childlike in her need of him, and he had needs as well. There would not, there never could, be lengthy intervals between sating this massive passion. And nor could he survive away from her loving ways that assured him of enduring understanding.

'You may count on that, my love, on every possible occasion.'

Chapter 10

Lambert kept his word and returned as often as he could to Whitby. On each visit, he contrived to meet Sally in places where their lovemaking remained not only exhilarating but unrevealed. They took each other greedily in the bedroom of a moorland inn, awkwardly in the Falgrave carriage, and urgently when desire shook them while they walked in the moonlit abbey ruins.

Sally was elated, so happy that her family and everyone she met remarked on her good spirits. With her parents and brothers, she was sorry to be unable to divulge anything at all of the cause; but she agreed with Lambert that their love was too precious to share with others until they were ready to solemnise the marriage which, for them, had already taken place on that night in the Stansfields' home.

Hester was less pleased by her brother's frequent visits. He annoyed her with seemingly ill-informed interrogations and criticism.

'Are you sure you can't obtain a higher quality jet?' he asked one evening after inspecting other jet shop windows.

'Cousin Isaac's *is* the best round here,' she retorted. 'Other folk might have to compete for their supplies but we're fortunate to have another Falgrave looking after us.'

'Is it the final polishing then that's not sufficient?' he persisted. 'Our things need some extra refinement to put us ahead.'

'There's nowt wrong with any stage of our production. You can examine how it's done any day you like. Look, Lambert – you've got to realise that we're up against lots of highly-skilled craftsmen all over the town.'

'That's the very reason I'm advocating improvements.'

'Do you think I'm not constantly looking for ways we can do even better? But any development does take time.' If she'd been willing to relinquish her involvement with the

187

jet works, she'd have told him to try *his* hand at running the place.

Their mother's attitude towards her was still regulated by Lambert. There had never been any room in Maud's heart for much outward criticism of her favourite son, but when his unexplained absences from the house vexed her, Hester watched the blue eyes darken, saw the stiffening of Maud's short body and steeled herself for an onslaught.

The day tempers flared over her friendship with Frank Clough, Hester resolved to harden herself against Lambert and her mother. It all began when Hester was minding the Flowergate shop. One of Sally's brothers had called with the message that she had wakened that morning with a sore throat and unable to speak. Maud arrived in person with a newly-completed bodice ornament for one of the local gentry.

'This was promised for today, be sure you have it to hand, but not anywhere that it'll be seen by casual customers walking in off the street. It was particularly requested that this remain unique.'

'I know,' said Hester, well aware of the circumstances. Aware also that it was Lambert who'd suggested modifications to her design. Although the changes, upheld by her mother, would be of no consequence to the client, who'd so little discernment she'd accept anything that she'd see on no one else, Hester had yet again felt diminished.

Maud lingered there, convincing Hester that she doubted her ability to deal with the customers coming at pleasingly short intervals.

'While you're in charge here, you might take a look at that window display,' her mother bade her. 'It's too ordinary for my liking.'

Together, they went out into the spring sunlight and stood on the narrow pavement regarding the range of jewellery on show.

'You see – that'd catch nobody's eye,' Maud sniffed. 'You call yourself a designer, yet you can't manage to make our stuff look any better nor our competitors'.'

'I did suggest a centrepiece,' Hester began.

'That tree thing, you mean?' Maud shrugged. 'Lambert

thought like me that there's more sense in employing the men on things that'll sell.'

'All right, then. Tell me what you want, and I'll see we produce it. We could have more figurines . . .'

'Them Shakespeare things? This is Whitby, not London. How many folk living round here even know who his characters are?'

'The ones we've done have sold. We could do more carved card trays as well, or inkstands. Frank did a lovely one with a man's head . . .'

'It's always Frank, isn't it? He's the one who's so good at those figurines, isn't he?'

'And the ones of Prince Albert as well – several of the men are.'

'It's Frank Clough I'm on about – and because *you're* always on about him. I hope, young lady, that you're not becoming overfond of the fellow.'

To anyone else, Hester would have denied it. With her mother, she experienced only a massive desire to rebel. Instead of answering, she clamped her lips together, and forced a smile into her eyes. Her mother might, and did, curtail her work but she'd not have her curtail friendships.

They were still standing like this, implacable as the street itself which had endured since Domesday, when Lambert came striding along Flowergate.

Disconcerted to find them in the vicinity when all he wanted was a loving tête-à-tête with Sally, he bit back a surge of irritation.

'What's this?' he inquired pleasantly. 'A deliberation on what we're selling?'

'Amongst other things,' snapped Maud. 'All of which hinge on your sister's judgement – apparently.'

'Well, surely this might be settled at the works,' he suggested.

'Not today. Hester's running t'shop. The girl's not in.'

'She's not ill, I hope?' Already picturing Sally in a decline from which even he could not save her, he struggled to level his voice.

'Bit of a sore throat or summat. Doubtless she'll be in

189

tomorrow. Like as not she fancied a day off. I only hope she realises she'll have her pay stopped for it.'

'Then why don't we continue the discussion inside?' said Lambert evenly. 'This is hardly the place for business matters.'

Maud was surprised she hadn't thought of that herself. Especially while their Hester's tight lips revealed their disagreement to every passerby. Much more of this, and the whole of Whitby would have it that the Falgraves were falling out.

'We were discussing the window display originally,' Maud announced.

'Sally keeps all the shop very nicely,' Lambert said very quickly.

'Aye – but what goes on show isn't up to her. And I've just been saying as, *if* Hester's as artistic as she makes out, she ought to be able to come up with summat better than this.'

Hester followed her mother as Lambert held the shop door open for them. She was burning to demand that she be given a free hand. She'd prove then that her beautiful carved black tree would work. That people wouldn't be able to keep their eyes off it.

Swallowing, she gripped the edge of the glass counter top, looking down but seeing nothing of the rows of necklaces, the bracelets and brooches. She was seized by an emotion rarely experienced – the intense yearning to break free of Falgraves'. To go to some other workshop where her designs would be granted their just consideration, where she might create all the magnificent pieces filling her mind. Pieces which she was *certain* would appeal.

Only she knew she would not leave. Somehow, she'd achieve everything that she intended, and for Falgraves'. She just wished that working here in these circumstances wasn't breaking her heart.

Hester's distress lasted for weeks, for there was no taking time off to regain her perspective. The sound of a train drawing into Whitby station and the sight of boats putting to sea irked her with their reminders that she had no freedom. On good days, she acknowledged to herself that she cared too much about the family firm to contemplate leaving. When things went badly and her mother was as critical as ever, she believed she'd gladly go anywhere.

Always, though, the reality of what such a move would do to her father brought Hester up sharp. He had so little, confined as he was to the house, she mustn't consider bringing him further anguish. And through her, these days, he was taking some part in running Falgraves'.

On Abel's insistence, once Christmas was over, they had got together around his invalid chair for a fresh discussion on how the works should be administered.

'I've left a lot to you two, ever since November. That can't be allowed to continue. One of you's going to start bringing home the weekly accounts, and t'monthly ones an' all. We'll go through 'em together. There's nowt to stop me adding up, you know.'

Maud stifled a sigh. Did he really think she wanted to spend her evenings struggling with figures when she'd passed the best part of the day in the workshop, and still had to supervise the running of their household?

'What's up?' he asked, seeing her expression. 'You want to be glad I'm not leaving everything to you.' He'd go insane doing nowt!

'Nothing. I just – well, I can think of better ways of spending my time while I am at home.' Between them, she and Hester had kept the books in order. And at the same time had been on the premises keeping an eye on the workers.

'I'll do what you suggest, Father,' Hester volunteered, smiling at him.

Abel had his mouth open to respond, but his wife cut in swiftly.

'You?' she demanded of her daughter. 'You will, if we say so. What authority have you got to be into the ins and outs of it all?'

'She helps now, doesn't she?' Abel snapped. 'And she'll have the authority I bestow, won't she? There's no suiting you sometimes, Maud – you refuse to cooperate, then object when our Hester offers.'

'I haven't refused, I was only thinking . . .'

'You as near as dammit did. Any road, it's decided. Me and Hester will have charge of accounting.'

'Happen you'd like her to buy in t'rough jet an' all. Why don't you send her to your Isaac next time? See if she can beat him down over t'price.' She hated any change, felt threatened by it.

Quietly, Hester rose. 'I'll do whatever you both agree on, just tell me what you want.' Outwardly, she was composed; inwardly she had wept for weeks. If she gave in to emotion, she'd never be able to work at anything. She went steadily towards the door and had it closed behind her before either of them spoke.

'Now look what you've done,' said Abel.

Maud sighed. 'Aye – well, she'll come round, she always has afore.'

For a moment or two both remained silent. Abel could understand his wife's reluctance to hand over important jobs to a bit of a lass who was barely eighteen. But he'd not say owt, not even that Hester had the maturity in business matters of some women twice her age.

Maud was thinking for the hundredth time how much had changed, in their home relationships as much as at the workroom. Abel had been such a tolerant man, and a loving one. Nowadays he flared that readily there was never a day without some disagreement.

'Do you really want to handle the accounts yourself?' he inquired at last. He was aware of his wife's dislike of arithmetic.

'There's many a day when I'd rather have nothing to do with the place at all, if you must know.'

'Ay, love, I'm sorry.'

'So am I. We all know it's a far from ideal arrangement, but we opted to carry on. I daresay our Hester will do well enough, working with you on all the figures. She didn't frame so badly when she analysed the shop takings. It won't hurt now for her to do more on that side than collecting up the few bills as wants paying.'

Maud knelt impulsively beside his chair, leaned over to kiss him. No matter how badly incapacitated Abel was, he was still the man she'd married and she was still desperately in love with him.

'We've too little time for each other,' he said huskily. 'We'll start giving Nurse Clapper more evenings off. A few early nights wouldn't do you any harm.'

Maud nodded, didn't trust her own voice. It wasn't only work kept her from the master bedroom until all hours. The passing weeks had made it no easier to live without the love of this once-virile man. Many a night she lay rigid on her side of the bed, anguished by the need that gave her no rest. Once or twice, she'd been on the point of asking if there wasn't some way they could still be man and wife to one another. Each time she'd abandoned the idea. Weren't things bad enough for her husband – how could she let him know that she could hardly endure the absence of their lovemaking? She'd not make anything any better, would she, by forcing him to admit they might never be close in that way again . . .

Although Hester was interested in ensuring that Falgraves' was run efficiently and profitably, sitting with her father over the accounts grew to be most pleasing for the contact with him. Hours seemed to race by while she called over figures to him, and sought advice on keeping the books.

Feeling that, at long last, he was performing some function, Abel became less disgruntled, and showed renewed concern for every member of the family. Both Bernard and Olive were busier with their schooling now and spent more time with their friends. But Hester noticed his greater warmth, and grew more content again.

It was Abel who had reminded her again about the Ascension Eve ceremonial planting of the Penny Hedge and encouraged her to go there. He even raised the matter with Maud, and was prepared to insist that Hester deserved a few hours at least away from the works.

Hester had watched her mother's expression, noting how the blue eyes narrowed as if she were about to condemn so frivolous an outing. But then she had smiled, looking up at Hester and nodding her fair head.

'You go on, lass – it's a poor do if we can't manage for half a day while you do summat you want to for a change.

Mind you put on a decent gown, for once, an' all. Nobody'll miss you for a few minutes more if you have to come back here to get into your working dress.'

The morning dawned with mist swirling about the Esk, obscuring some of the houses clustered on its banks so that first one conglomeration of red gables appeared and then another. Beyond the harbour wall the sea also was hazed, the homecoming fishing cobles appearing like toys from this distance, no more substantial than the ethereal seascape.

Hester had intended to stay in bed late, free from the need to rise early and rush to the works by six. But she had no regrets now about sleep that might have been lost. Up and about, she enjoyed the rare pleasure of lingering to watch the mist dispersing, and town and harbour growing increasingly visible as the sun strengthened its gleam. And she would need longer to dress her hair properly and put on her best lilac and white gown.

Her mother was crossing the hall to the front door as Hester hastened down the stairs. Scarcely pausing, Maud gave her a look. And then she did stop, motionless, gazing towards her daughter.

'By, Hester, you look a treat today, love. You've not worn that since Christmas, have you?'

'There's been no suitable occasion.'

'You certainly look bonnie in it. Be sure and see your father when Nurse has finished attending to him.'

'Of course.'

On impulse, she ran across the few paces separating them, astonished Maud by bending to hug her.

'I'll not be all that long,' she promised, smiling. And made a mental note to purchase another attractive dress, since it so evidently delighted her mother. She was wearied by their differences, and had begun to suspect that she herself was growing entrenched in *not* conforming to what was expected of the elder daughter.

By the time Hester was leaving Falgrave House, the sun felt quite warm if the breeze that had dispelled the mist remained chill. She walked out quickly towards Boyes Staith where the Horngarth would be planted, feeling strange to be going alone to somewhere other than the workshop or St Mary's church.

I must go out more often, she thought, well aware that she frequently felt nearer twenty-eight than eighteen. By living as an old maid she was developing into one. And that wasn't what she wished. Ever since she'd been twelve or so she'd visualised having a home of her own and children in it.

Others were hastening in the same direction towards the shore of the river. Groups of girls and others of young men, families with their children, several gangs of boys. Briefly, Hester wished that she had company. But then she was nearing the point where the crowd assembled, and was too interested to be concerned about her solitary state.

'Hester!' a girl's voice shouted excitedly, and there near the water's edge were Sylvie and Joanie Skelton, and Jamie with them.

His sisters clinging to either hand, he strode towards her. And then, freeing himself of Sylvie's grasp, he took Hester by the shoulder and embraced her.

'I've missed you,' he announced unashamedly. 'It's been too long, this time, far too long.'

Smiling into his hazel eyes after he'd kissed her cheek and was standing back to gaze, Hester nodded.

'It's my fault perhaps, Jamie. I don't know. But I'm that glad to see you!'

She went down on one knee to fuss over Joanie, although the child's round face seemed more than usually impassive.

'She wanted to turn back when we got halfway here,' Jamie explained. 'Even as she is, though, it's not good she should have all her own way. And this was intended as a treat.'

'You're good to your brothers and sisters, Jamie.'

'Sometimes.' He laughed. 'There's long absences now. Any road, I heard tell you've been kind to 'em an' all – going a-visiting.'

'I told him you'd come,' said Sylvie who had been dancing about on first one leg then the other, tugging at Hester's skirt as she waited while poor Joanie received attention.

The young men appointed to construct the hedge were

195

moving through the crowd now, assembling the stakes and osiers which would be planted below the highwater mark and interwoven in the hope that they might withstand the necessary three tides.

Smiling with sheer enjoyment, Hester glanced sideways at Jamie, glad that she had worn her new gown and a smart little coat, fitted to the waist and of a slightly darker lilac.

'You're a lovely lass, you always have been,' he murmured.

The manor bailiff blew on the ancient horn, making them jump and sending Sylvie into shrieks of excited merriment. Joanie loosened her hold on Jamie to cover both ears.

'Out upon ye! Out upon ye!' the bailiff cried.

'What did he say that for?' Sylvie demanded, pulling on Jamie's arm.

'I'll explain on the way home. Just watch for now.' He turned to Hester again. 'Do you remember all the story?'

'I think so, I'll have a try later on.'

After the bailiff had sounded his horn several more times, and the osiers were securely attached to the stakes, the adults among the crowd began gathering their children to them. Only the lads who appeared to lack parental control remained at the edge of the water, investigating the newly-constructed Penny Hedge.

'Why is it called "Penny"?' Sylvie wanted to know.

'They have to use a knife that's cost a penny for cutting the stakes and osiers,' her brother told her.

'Are you sure?' asked Hester. 'I thought it was the hammer that cost that much . . .'

He laughed. 'Maybe we're both right, and they were each a penn'orth.'

'It's all legend, anyway, isn't it? The details vary with the telling.' She squeezed Sylvie's hand which had seized her own. 'You'll have to ask your teacher to tell you for sure when you get to school.'

She sensed Jamie giving her a look, and turned to see him shaking his head in warning.

Even Joanie had joined in their insistence that Hester go back to their home for a second breakfast. Hester couldn't refuse when Jamie told her he'd taken in kippered herrings, more than sufficient for the entire Skelton family.

The children who had remained at home had long ago eaten theirs and were playing in the grimy alley that was so narrow it seemed the sun's rays must never enter. They stormed the house as a boisterous group, surrounding Hester and Jamie and making such a noise that when Edna greeted them her loud voice was drowned.

The welcome, though, was obvious and when the rabble subsided as one or two of the youngsters ran back outside again, Jamie's mother reiterated her delight.

'It's best like this, while my man's at sea. T'last time you came I felt fair shamed that he hadn't a good word for thee. He's like that wi' everybody, tha knows. You mustn't feel offended. Any road, the childer said what a nice time you all had upstairs . . .'

Hester glanced down at her plate, concentrated on extracting the smokey fish without too many bones. Nice? All she could recall was the way the lads had relished embarrassing her. And not only the lads, either. She hadn't expected an interrogation about her relationship with their eldest brother.

When eventually they finished breakfast, Hester thanked Edna Skelton and stood up, explaining that she'd have to get off home to change ready for work.

Jamie offered to walk her to the house, and she was glad of the opportunity to talk as they had in the past. First, though, she asked him about the younger Skeltons and school.

'That stopped when my father broke his leg. He said they'd no brass for sending all t'family to the dame, so none of 'em would go. Then at after, when I started bringing a bit in, he still wouldn't let them. Said that were my fault an' all – maintains as education did nowt to make me any use.'

'Oh, Jamie . . .'

He grinned at her, and shook his head. 'Nay, Hester lass, don't look like that. He don't bother me none – not any more. I go my own way, earn good money, these days. And

I'm paying him back, bit by bit, every last penny to replace that damned boat.'

'I just wish he could appreciate you, that's all.'

'Don't matter, honest. I don't care *that* for him any more. There's only one thing I wish – that money'd buy a better life for your father, Hester.'

'Aye, aye.' Eyes misting, she stopped walking and looked at him again. 'It wasn't anything you could help.'

'How – how is he now?'

'Physically, not much different. But we've had a lift built so's he can get about the house – in an invalid chair, Lambert got him that.'

'He's been helping out, has he – Lambert?'

'When he's at home, yes.'

'Seen him once or twice, going back and forth to the shop.'

'I hope you didn't see me and Mother there an' all, last time he was home! Quite a to-do we had, some of it out on the pavement. Until Mother bethought her that that wasn't exactly the thing for Falgraves'. I don't quite fit in, you know, not with what she'd have me be.'

'Why ever not? Ay, Hester, you're lovely-looking, clever . . .'

She laughed. 'You don't see me when I'm dressed for the workshop. That doesn't go down at all well. But I'll be hanged if I'll ruin my good clothes in that place.'

'And after all you do there . . . I'd have thought she'd have just been very glad.'

'Now and again. It's – well, when our Lambert's in Whitby nowadays that Mother becomes so difficult to please. And then there's the way she encourages him to interfere.'

Hester paused, reflecting that revealing so much was being disloyal to her family. When she sighed, Jamie took her arm.

'What you need, lass, is somebody to talk to. Good thing I thought to take Sylvie and Joanie down to the Penny Hedge making.'

'Well, I'm certainly glad you did.'

'I'm off to sea again on t'evening tide, but I'd like to see you when I get back – like to see you regular.'

'It was good in the old days, wasn't it?' There'd been no occasions then when she'd felt all alone with her problems. And it certainly was true that she no longer considered Jamie in any way responsible for the tragedy overshadowing the Falgraves.

'How'll I let you know when I'm back in Whitby again?'

'You could leave a message at the Flowergate shop. Sally's a reliable girl, she'd see I got it.'

Jamie's hazel eyes darkened, and furrows appeared in the brow that was tanned by North Sea winds. 'No – I don't think I'll . . .'

'Jamie? What is it?'

He shrugged. 'Don't let on I said owt, not to anybody, least of all to her. But I was quite fond of Sally before I had to get work that took me to sea on longer trips. Don't know what happened while I were away. She's not the same somehow – still friendly, like, but not the same.'

'She's very young. There's time enough for her to think seriously about your relationship, if that's what you're hoping.'

'*Was* hoping, more like. No, I'm over whatever it was I felt for her. Besides, I've a deal of money to earn before I can settle with my father. Till then I'll be content with the friends I've got.'

After they had said goodbye Hester found herself dwelling on what Jamie had told her of his affection for Sally Drinkwater. She'd felt surprised, but couldn't see any reason why she should. Sally was a bright lass and exceedingly pretty. She would like to see him settled. Maybe the girl was an ideal partner for him.

As soon as Hester emerged at the top of the workroom stairs she sensed that something was amiss. Her mother and Edwin Clough were closeted in the office, and even through the dust-streaked window the gravity of their expressions perturbed her.

'What's to do?' she asked Frank in a whisper, pausing beside his bench as though to inspect the cameo ring he was carving.

Frank only shook his head. If he knew the source of the difficulty he thought better of telling.

Hester hadn't long to wait. Seeing her daughter in the workroom, Maud opened the office door and beckoned. 'Have you a minute?'

The door was closed after her. Edwin Clough nodded a greeting and her mother resumed her seat.

'I want your opinion of this,' she said, handing across a portion of rough jet. 'You see enough of the stuff in the process of being worked, you ought to be able to tell if it's been handled properly.'

Hester took the piece, turning it this way and that as she scrutinised each face.

'Well?' Maud prompted.

'It's obvious this has shattered.'

'Anybody can see that. Was it because there was summat up with the jet itself?'

'I'd say not, but I don't want . . .'

'To get anybody into trouble?' her mother interrupted. 'That's nice, but it doesn't help us much.'

'What's it all about?' Hester looked from Edwin Clough to her mother, then back again.

Edwin sighed, continued only when Maud indicated that he should. 'Wally Hardcastle had just started on this when it broke into smithereens. I hadn't watched him all that sharply, mind, there's too much going on for that, but I could have sworn as he was trying to rush the job.'

'He ought to know by now when to take care.'

'Aye – that's what I told him. He didn't take kindly to that. Said he'd have all the men downing tools if I didn't drop my insinuations.'

'Father might be able to tell whether this has been tackled wrongly.'

'And Cousin Isaac would know for sure if it was flawed jet. And he's the one whose opinion I'll have,' Maud added. 'That were new in the other day, could be first of a bad seam. If it is, I'll not have the men wasting time that I pay for on any more of t'same.'

'When are you seeing Cousin Isaac again?'

'We're not waiting for that. Somebody'll have to go over

there. *I* can't, not with Hardcastle being awkward again, he needs keeping an eye on.' She suspected he was trying to stir up trouble again.

Hester was told to hire a carriage from around the corner which would be far quicker than walking all the way up to the house for Kilner and the brougham. It was quite some time since she'd last visited her father's cousin and his wife at Sandsend, and she'd never before been to the mine.

She went straight there now, and was right in assuming that it was where Isaac Falgrave would be. But her hope that she might find him in the outbuilding that served as his office on the site vanished as soon as she tried to obtain an answer at its crude wooden door.

'The master's in yonder,' called one of the men wheeling out a barrowload of the spoil ready for sorting. He jerked his head towards the mine entrance.

'Could you get him for me, please? I'm his cousin's daughter – Hester Falgrave.'

'You mun wait if you expect him to come to you. He's attending to summat as can't be left without his say so,' the fellow called over his shoulder. He rapidly trundled the barrow towards two men with very fine rakes who were recovering jet from amongst the shale.

'Then I'll go to him,' Hester resolved, and began walking swiftly towards the opening gouged into the side of the hill.

'Mind where you're putting your feet, love,' warned another man with a barrow which he had just emptied. 'Sithee – these here grooves is for t'barrows. You'll see nowt once you're inside. That's why we has to have a track to follow on us way in and out.'

It was indeed dark once she had moved only a few paces from the entrance.

'How about hanging on to my shoulder,' the man with the barrow suggested. 'I'll slow down for you, I know it's far fro' easy when you don't know t'road.'

The sound of picks driving into the rock face reached them long before even a glimmer from the miners' candles. Reverberating about them the noise was intense, more alarming than Hester liked to admit even to herself.

'Have you worked here long?' she asked her guide, when

she could make herself heard above the sounds of hewing and the trundling barrow.

'For t'master, aye, many a year. This seam's fairly new, though. A good 'un, and all – providing the shale don't start shifting.'

'Does that happen often?'

'More than we'd like. Proper tantalising it is sometimes – knowing the jet's there and you can't get at it.'

They had almost reached the level being worked. Hester couldn't have been more relieved. Even the flickering light from the pair of candles was a vast improvement on total blackness. She'd lost count of the number of times she had stumbled on the uneven floor, and each occasion that she'd strayed only a little to one side had wricked an ankle staggering on one of the grooves. And that was with the men's boots she still wore to the works. In anything else, she'd long since have crippled herself.

There were three men hacking into the jet seam. The one nearest to them faced them, lowered his pick with a clatter.

'Well, I'll go to heck – it's a lass!'

The other two turned and she recognised the man farthest from her whose face was no less smothered in dust than those of his companions.

'Don't tell me Maud sent you here . . .'

'Hallo, Isaac. She sent me to see you, yes. Though I doubt if she intended I should come looking for you in the mine.'

'What's to do then, Hester? Not a crisis with your father, I hope?'

'No, nothing like that. We've been having a bit of bother at the works. We want your opinion on some of this jet.'

'Is it from here? No – no don't tell me that. Let's have a look at it first.' Isaac turned aside to instruct his miners, then passed Hester and the man who had escorted her to the face and was now swiftly filling his barrow, creating yet more dust.

'I'll lead the way, love. I didn't expect to see you in here.'

'I didn't expect this morning that I'd be here.'

The amusement in her voice delighted him. 'It's champion of you, any road, not to baulk at searching me out. Your father'll have summat to say when he hears, I'll be bound.'

They spoke of Abel then, until the light of the bright May afternoon appeared ahead of them.

In the mine office Isaac took the piece of jet that she carried with her.

'It is from here, isn't it? One of the last lots we let you have. And somebody's made a right mess of this, haven't they?'

'It wasn't a flaw in the jet itself then?'

Isaac inspected the fragment more intently. 'No, I don't reckon it was. And I'd not say no different if it were from somebody else's mine. Some daft beggar's started on this without watching where the spar begins . . . I thought you employed good craftsmen?'

'We do an' all. I suppose even the best on us makes the occasional mistake.'

'Were it one of your best workers?'

'He's good at his job, normally.' There was no point in going into Wally Hardcastle's shortcomings.

'And he's had you coming all this way. Glad though I am that it doesn't seem to be my jet that's at fault, I'm sorry you've had the trouble.'

'We had to have an answer. Thanks for giving one. And how are you, Isaac – and your wife?'

'Not so bad, thanks. As you saw we were having a bit of a problem in t'mine, but nothing that can't be rectified. But why don't you go on up to the house now you're over here – Bess'd be pleased to have a word with you.'

'I'm afraid I haven't time. I've already had a few hours off this morning.' She told him about watching the Horngarth planting.

Isaac Falgave inquired after the rest of the family, then walked with Hester to where the carriage was waiting.

'You're doing a grand job, you and your mother. Never thought as how two ladies would manage to keep the workshop going.'

'Father does what he can from home, as well, keeping the books up to date and so on.'

'That'll do him good.'

'Yes, I believe it does.'

When Hester arrived back at the works, Maud smiled to herself on being told what Isaac had said.

'I'm not surprised. From Edwin Clough's telling, Wally Hardcastle might have been trying to break that piece of jet.'

'But why would he? Doesn't make sense.'

'It's been quiet enough here for weeks, hasn't it? If we accuse him of bad workmanship, he'll think he's justified in calling on the men to support him. There's been nowt no more said about him having got a union going, but then he's not had cause to use it against us.'

'Are you saying he could have shattered that piece deliberately?'

'I wouldn't put it past him.'

'What are we going to do, then?'

Her mother smiled. 'Nothing. And say nothing, either. That ought to fox him. His pay packet will suffer, of course. We don't give our brass away without it's been earned.'

'He'll try again, won't he, if he does mean to stir things up?'

'Aye, but he's reminded us we have to watch what he's about. Edwin Clough knows what he has to do.'

That evening when Edwin and Frank arrived home, though, Alice soon learned that keeping an eye on Wally Hardcastle was something Edwin would prefer to avoid.

'I know what it'll be,' he told his wife. 'Wally'll manage to split the workforce. He's had his heart set on that since Mr Falgrave was injured. Today's effort were a feeble attempt, but I haven't forgotten as we were sure it was him beat Bob Dunsdale up.'

'You still think that was the way of it then?' Alice asked them sceptically as she ladled water into the bath for him. 'Has he shown any animosity since towards Bob?'

Frank laughed wryly. 'He wouldn't, Mother, not now. Bob's lad's an apprentice, and he might be nobbut young but he's big for his age.'

His parents laughed with him, and he went out and through the bit of a courtyard to the privy. On the way, he was stopped by Ida and Lydia who were being tormented by their older brother Alfred and a couple of neighbours' boys. The little ones, Herbert and Maggie, were scratching about trying to make a sandcastle out of the mixture of earth and dust which, along with stones, formed the area between the closely-packed houses.

When Frank went back indoors, Harold had just walked in. He was late because of taking a delivery round to the shop. Normally, Harold had more to say for himself after he'd seen Sally Drinkwater. Tonight he was quiet even for him, his green eyes had lost their lustre and his ready smile had disappeared.

'All right?' Frank asked him.

'Aye, aye.' He refused anything to eat, though, and went upstairs to lie down.

'I hope he's not sickening for something,' Alice remarked, serving a meal to the others.

Harold's sickness had more to do with his spirits, rather than any indisposition. He'd had such a shock he didn't rightly know how to carry on.

It had begun as soon as he walked into the shop in Flowergate. Sally had been by one of the glass showcases, standing sideways on to him. They'd greeted each other as usual. He'd seen straightaway how plump she was getting, even her crinoline didn't conceal that. When he looked into her face he wondered how he hadn't noticed before how that was filling out, too. And as for her bosom . . . she'd never been small, not since he'd known her and suddenly just looking at her made him itch to touch her.

He had placed his hands to either side of her waist which was as much as he dared, turning her while laughingly, he squeezed.

'You're getting bonnier every day,' he'd begun, slightly breathless.

It was closing time and he didn't often get the chance to be here at such an opportune moment. The clock struck as soon as he'd spoken, and his glance shot straight towards the back room. For long enough, he'd been determined to pick up where they'd left off, when his own hesitance had combined with circumstances to suspend any kind of intimacy between them.

Sally, however, had gently removed his hands from her waist. 'Better not,' she'd said, going to lock the shop door.

'Is it something I've done? I used to think – well, you were the one always after kissing and that . . .'

'Aye, well – I'm not now.'

'What is it, Sally?'

For weeks now she'd been so vital, sparkling with life, as if there was so much it couldn't be contained inside her. Today, her blue eyes were shadowed with some intense anxiety.

There was somebody else, he ought to have seen that earlier. He was going to ask if it was Jamie Skelton. He watched her walking through the shop to go and lock up the rear. And he knew. He'd seen his mother time and again when she was carrying, hadn't he? He'd have to be proper daft not to know what ailed Sally Drinkwater.

Chapter 11

Hester was walking through the narrow Whitby streets, savouring the warmth, the sun slanting between tall buildings and glinting off the water each time she caught sight of the harbour. She had felt too uneasy for remaining indoors.

Jamie had put to sea again, would be away for some undefined period that depended upon the speed with which they made a good enough catch to satisfy the owner of the vessel. Ordinarily, she accepted his absences along with the days he was in the town. The summer evenings with him this year, and occasional Sundays, had helped renew her for coping with life at the works. They did nothing special, for wasn't he desperate to pay off that debt to his father for the boat? But they walked a lot, talked a great deal, the way they always had. Yesterday, he'd even kissed her.

There had been kisses before, long ago, when they were both as curious as they were eager to try the experience. This was different.

They were up near the abbey, strolling, until they sat down to watch the sun dropping low in the sky behind the ruins. No one else was around, and no one needed. His lips on hers had been friendly at first then grew hard, demanding. When she was kissing him back the gasp that sounded in his throat might have been her own yearning. While she was with him, she recognised that attraction was all that generated these kisses. Alone, she wondered if that were true, was perturbed about the extent of her feelings towards him.

The parting had been hard this time, the lack of surety concerning the date of his return a burden. And she was annoyed with herself. Jamie was a friend, she hoped he always would be, she'd not have their friendship changed. Not in any way. She was fond of his brothers and sisters in that tiny house in the alley, but she'd no wish to produce their like with him.

Was that what was wrong, she had wondered during the long night, while moonlight revealed the blue and white delicacy of familiar bed-hangings and curtains, and silhouetted dark, burnished furniture against pale walls. Jamie had acquainted her with reality, causing her to think again about her emotions.

He had told her, and she'd tried to keep her flaring face impassive while fragments of earlier knowledge fitted together, how he had caught their Jessie and her young man, lying in the heather of the moor, her with her skirts above her legs and him thrusting as if his life depended on it. Never mind the life of any bairn he might bestow.

'My mother says they're to wed now, before Jessie's birthday,' Jamie had concluded, 'whether or not their action's produced a youngster. I suspect that's what our Jess is after, any road. She's talked of nothing but having a gold band on her finger since the day she found this fellow.'

Hester had been saddened by the knowledge that Jess would risk bringing a child into such unpromising circumstances, but she'd kept the thought to herself. Jamie had said it all.

'She never has had much sense, that one. But I felt like throttling him. I've no patience with men that use a lass that's too young to know what she's about.'

'What's age got to do with it?' Hester had asked, only too aware that she might so easily have been content to go on supposing that parents only had to *choose*, quietly, when they considered the time for a baby was right.

'Not age, happen – maturity. A lass that seeks only to trap her man that way isn't fit to be a mother. Not that I'm saying the fellow's any better. Spawning a child doesn't make a father of anybody.'

'You don't approve of their marriage then?'

'I don't approve of any folk clamping themselves together in a bit of a hovel when, by him controlling himself out of respect till they were decently wed, they'd be off to a good start.'

Learning to deal with embarrassment, Hester had begun to suspect it might be good to speak so freely with someone on such personal matters. No one at home ever hinted at what went on between couples, and she'd never felt sufficiently at ease with friends remaining from her schooldays for there to be this kind of conversation.

And she liked Jamie all the more for being so opposed to gratifying needs at the expense of someone else, was glad also that he thought so well of her he could be entirely frank. Perhaps this augured well for their renewed relationship.

There was only one other person who'd ever induced in her the ease that might result in such uninhibited conversation, and opportunity never arose these days for that to develop. Her infrequent meetings with Jamie would have to suffice.

Now, she entered a smart tea-room farther along the street, smiled at the young lady who appeared when the bell jangled, and followed her to a corner table.

Hester was ordering when she heard the name Falgrave whispered, but not so carefully that it did not carry from another table. Four ladies had their bonnets close to touching over their silver teapot, the feathers and ribbons bouncing as they exchanged details. When they simultaneously stared towards her, she was extremely annoyed, although she knew most certainly that there was no cause for them to make her the subject of gossip.

Her own tea arrived, but the glances and bobbing heads continued, if more covertly. She made a conscious effort to steady her hand in order to pour.

'I'll not enter their shop again,' one of them announced severely. 'That Drinkwater girl's so brazen, it'd shame me to be seen there.'

Hester couldn't believe what she was hearing. Sally was a sweet girl, nicely brought up despite straitened circumstances. She'd earned her position behind their counter by her love of jet, by being obliging, and by maintaining this innate courtesy which exceeded that of many persons in far more affluent circles.

'I stopped my daughter shopping there only last week,' one of the woman's companions stated. 'There's plenty more jet shops in Whitby, where no one'll be contaminated by her goings on . . .'

Appalled, Hester itched to approach their table and

demand an explanation of what they meant. By doing so, however, she would make a spectacle of herself before a teashop full of the town's matrons and young ladies. She lacked both the skill to avoid a scene and authority to dismiss their gossip. She would tell her mother, maybe her father as well once Nurse Clapper was out of the way. Since Christmas the nurse was neglecting to take her permitted days off, there seemed no getting rid of her. Private conversation was limited. I'll have to talk to somebody afterwards, she resolved, it's the only way I'll keep quiet in this place while I drink my tea.

Maud was prepared to be philosophical about the rumours, even hinted that Hester might have misheard.

'I'm not deaf, Mother. And I have eyes as well – they began by remarking on my being there, they stared more than once, then they began picking Sally to bits.'

'What do you expect me to do?' Maud wanted to know. 'I can hardly go to the girl and ask her if she's said or done summat that customers haven't liked. Not without something to go on.'

'I can see that, but . . . well, we can't just let this rest, can we?'

'That's the quickest way of stifling gossip, in my experience. Refuse to fuel it by the attention folk expect, and it just disappears.'

Unfortunately, ignoring the teashop episode was of no use. On the following Monday Maud was accosted in the street by the lady for whom they recently had fashioned the elaborate bodice-ornament.

'I'll be straight with you, Mrs Falgrave, I'm taking my custom to the Arkwrights. And I'll have you know that, with my mother-in-law on her deathbed, that'll be a considerable loss to you.'

'I'm sorry to hear that,' Maud responded. 'I'd like to hear your reasons. I hope you've no fault to find with our craftsmanship, and that Miss Drinkwater has always been civil towards you . . .'

'I'll not fault her on that, nor anything else towards myself. It's the way she is that's causing the unpleasantness. I'd not have expected anybody with the Falgraves' reputation to continue employing her. Especially where any member of the public can't help but notice.'

'Notice? Notice what, exactly?'

The woman snorted. 'Where's your eyes, these days? Have you not seen how she's rounded out lately, and only in particular areas of her . . . her person.'

Maud sighed, shook her head. 'Oh, she isn't . . . ! Are you sure you couldn't be mistaken?'

'Mrs Falgrave – if the girl was married, it'd be indecent to have her on show in that way, in her condition. Without a ring on her finger, it's unfair to expose her to the speculation, to say nothing of the effect upon decent folk who're brought face to face . . .'

'All right, I'll speak to her. See what I can do.'

'I hope so too – it's the talk of our chapel, and a scandal throughout the town. I'm sure you knew better than to display yourself to all and sundry when you were carrying your four.'

But I hadn't even guessed about Sally, thought Maud, couldn't credit it when I was told Falgraves' was being talked about. Maybe I shouldn't have depended so much on Hester to watch over the shop.

Harold Clough heard Mrs Falgrave telling his father that she was going round to Flowergate immediately and read in her eyes that she knew. I'll stand by Sally, he decided in that moment. No matter who's given her the baby that's the cause of all the trouble, I'll see they're both looked after. She'd be grateful that someone would take on the responsibilities so evidently neglected by the bairn's father. He'd make Sally that happy she'd forget who'd brought this upon her.

Sally's happiness was the first thing that struck Maud as soon as she accepted the witness of her own good pair of eyes and spoke up.

'I think there's something you've been keeping from us, Sally, isn't there?' she began, wishing not for the first time that she'd a few more inches that would preclude her looking up to the person she confronted.

'Aye, I'm afraid so,' Sally admitted. 'I was wondering how I were going to tell you that I'd be having to leave, eventually, like. My mother guessed on Saturday night. Not that I was sorry about that – I'd been worrying myself to death wondering how to tell her. She took it very well. Mind you, that were only because he's a better class of a fellow.'

'I see.' Maud was astounded. 'But on the matter of your leaving, it will have to be sooner rather than later – like the end of this week. I really cannot tolerate a situation that is losing us custom. Since your – the father is in a position to provide for you both, I trust that he will assume responsibility at once.'

'Oh, you don't know!' Frowning a little, Sally checked, but then she smiled again. 'No, I don't suppose you would.'

'Who is this lad – er, *young man?*'

'Like I said to my mother, I'll have to tell him first. 'Tisn't right to let on to anybody else afore he's heard. He'd be that upset. Trouble is he's away so much, and I can't get in touch with him.'

'He's at sea, maybe, with the herring fleet?'

About to shake her head, Sally stopped, drew in a deep breath, smiled again. 'It's not fair saying, not till he gets back.'

'Let's hope then that he's not absent too long. You'll need medical care, as well as things for the child.'

'Oh, he'll be here long afore it's born.'

'And when exactly do you think that'll be?'

'I don't rightly know.'

Maud closed her eyes. Did the girl understand nothing of the time of her confinement? Or had she indulged more than once in the circumstances that were its cause?

'Look Sally, it's unfortunate that you can't yet obtain assistance of your future husband, but you must understand that you can't leave all medical care until the actual birth. Especially while you seem so uncertain as to when that might be. I believe your family are scarcely in a situation where they can help, I'll speak with our own doctor. We'll see that you receive all the treatment that he deems necessary. You must see him at once – Dr Jon Davidson in Royal Crescent.'

Sally was delighted about this suggestion, if not by the prospect of giving up her job in the shop.

'She gave me the impression that she welcomed this in order to retain the link with our family,' Maud confided to Jon Davidson whilst informing him of Sally Drinkwater's condition, and requesting that he render the relevant accounts to Falgrave House.

'She obviously knows you for a good employer, one can understand her reluctance to leave,' the doctor observed.

Maud smiled. 'That's all very well, but I hoped to sever her ties with the family. Since people are so indignant about the mess the girl's got herself into, I don't wish to think of her going around Whitby announcing how attached she's become to us Falgraves.'

'If I hear any such talk, I'll try to stress that your kindness to the girl now is only of the nature of what you'd do for any employee.'

Maud laughed. 'If that's so, we must be extremely thankful that the rest of our workers are men.'

Jon Davidson was pleased to see her in such good spirits and said as much. 'You seem very resilient, these days.'

'I have to be. All Abel's got now is his interest in the business. I've got to see that keeps going, or he'd just give up.'

'There's the family, as well . . .'

'Yes. But they're all growing up. Olive and Bernard talk to Abel, and read to him, when they can. But they have their schoolwork, their own friends.'

'And Hester's as busy as you yourself.'

'Aye. She's very willing, even went right into the mine after Cousin Isaac the other day. That's something I've never done.'

'She's a remarkable young lady.'

'I suppose she is.' Maud's lip quivered. 'If there's one thing I regret it's the way I treat our Hester,' she began, and suddenly was sobbing. 'Can't seem to stop myself. I'll be annoyed with somebody or disappointed, and there I go – criticising her again.'

'Knowing Hester, I feel sure she wouldn't harbour any grudge.'

'I wish I could be sure of that. But I shouldn't be troubling you with my conscience, you've enough to bother you. How is your wife nowadays, any better?'

The doctor's blue eyes darkened with pain. His genial smile evaporated.

'I'm afraid there's been no progress in response to the treatment her doctor has tried. He's admitted to me that he's baffled.'

'Ay, dear. What is it that ails her?'

'Some kind of intestinal obstruction. Short of surgery, which Ruth won't contemplate, there's not much we can do to prevent her from slowly starving.'

'Oh, but surely – since chloroform was introduced, operations aren't so painful?'

'And nor do they induce such a state of shock. Unfortunately, Ruth's mother died under the anaesthetic shortly after chloroform was first accepted in our hospitals.'

Maud left Royal Crescent feeling so concerned for Jon Davidson's wife that she experienced no relief on having arranged things satisfactorily for young Sally.

She arrived back at the works, however, to find Hester's dark eyebrows nearly meeting in a scowl, and Harold Clough also looking gloomy. The rest of the men appeared their normal selves, singing for some of the time, despite her presence. When she tackled her daughter, asking what was wrong she was told, 'Nothing.'

The truth emerged as Kilner drove them home that evening. Settling into the brougham, Hester revealed that one of the men trying to sell the rough jet gleaned from the seashore had called.

'And what do you think, he says as it's all round Whitby that Jamie's the father of Sally's baby!'

'Jamie Skelton, you mean?'

'Aye. Didn't I say?' She was too perturbed to know what she was doing or saying.

'I see. Well, if he is, I can't say I'm surprised. I know the lad's always been a friend of yours but he's always been a harum-scarum, as well.'

'In some ways, maybe. But he'd not do anything dishonourable.' Hadn't Jamie said, only so recently, that he deplored the way some men took their pleasure with a girl? She needed to believe him.

'I didn't realise that he knew Sally Drinkwater – have you ever caught him hanging around the shop?'

'Ay, I don't know.' But she did know that Jamie had fancied Sally, he'd told her so himself.

For days Hester was depressed by the interest of the local people in the paternity of Sally's unborn child. Hardly a day went by without some mention of the matter reaching her ears.

In the end she asked Frank Clough if he'd heard more than she had. It was one evening when they were working late together. Her mother had finally consented to a proper start being made on the large jet tree that Hester had been itching to try for ages. She resented all the more this disturbance about Sally and Jamie: without it, she would have been ecstatic about this job.

'You know about Sally Drinkwater leaving, of course, and the reason. Have you heard an' all who they say's the father?'

'I've heard about nowt else, if you must know. Our Harold thought a lot of Sally, didn't he? Now he reckons he'll give Jamie Skelton a right good hiding next time he's ashore.'

'That won't help anybody, will it?'

Frank grinned. 'True. But I wouldn't get too agitated about that myself. Harold's full of talk, that's all. You know us Cloughs – there's none of us ever spoiling for a fight.'

'I hope you're right.'

'You're fond of young Skelton, aren't you?'

'We've allus been friends. But it's more that I just can't credit it's him.' She told Frank, without mentioning names, what Jamie had thought of his sister's behaviour.

'Happen everybody's got hold of a wrong tale then,' said Frank reassuringly.

'I wonder.' Hester sighed. She couldn't believe now that such a thing was possible. If Harold Clough had been seriously interested in Sally, and Jamie no less keen on her, it wasn't likely there'd be a third young man in her life.

'She's only eighteen this summer, same age as me,' she added, half to herself.

Frank was smiling, thinking that it was an age he found particularly alluring.

'We'd better get on, I suppose.' She spread out her design for the carved tree, glanced sideways along the bench to Frank. 'My mother's saying *she'll* deal with Wally Hardcastle over this. I'm afraid she thinks I'm not capable. Still, we are going ahead, so I mustn't grumble. What we want from you, Frank, is the tiniest butterflies and bees you can manage, things of that nature. Happen one or two of the birds, an' all, but some of the others are able to carve those. To my way of thinking, it's what we show on the tree that's going to make it impressive. The tree itself is what started it off with me, but . . .'

'Was it a very long time since that you conceived the idea of a tree?'

'Aye, Frank, I sometimes believe it were over ten years ago, at the Great Exhibition. But that's daft talk, I didn't even know what I was going to be then.'

'You're an amazing girl, Hester.'

If the expression in his green eyes had been less intense she might have laughed. As it was, she could only gaze back, thinking how nice he was, how *genuine*.

'Thanks,' she said. 'I needed that today.'

'Because of Jamie Skelton? Are you in love with him, Hester?'

'I love him, in a way. But I don't feel for him like I would for somebody I was going to marry. We've been friends since we were little, haven't we, and we've always talked a lot. Even when Jamie . . . *you know*, and my father was injured so dreadfully, it didn't take all that long for me to realise Jamie and me were still friends.'

'And now – if he marries Sally Drinkwater?'

'Oh, they'll be just right for each other, only . . .'

'Yes?'

She grinned ruefully. 'Oh, I had some fancy notion I was going to be the one that got Jamie to settle down to being a responsible young man. I don't mean settle *with* me – or I don't believe I meant that.'

216

'Are you sure?'

She nodded. 'I only wanted to see him better himself.'

'But you'd make a wonderful wife – for some fortunate young fellow. You would bring out the best in anyone.'

They rose simultaneously, holding each other with eyes that were full of affection. Disregarding her position as a Falgrave, and his own dust-streaked face and working clothes, Frank drew her to him.

His lips felt gritty with particles of jet to which Hester paid no heed. She was conscious only of a sudden need to be enclosed against his chest, and to have his arms around her.

'I'm always here, Hester,' he said urgently into her hair. 'Happen I haven't known you all that many years, but there's none could care more greatly about you.'

'Oh, Frank, you're so good to me, you always have been.' It was good, as well, to know someone who didn't have to have her encouragement to be sure of shaping up to being straightforward and honourable. A man who made her feel cherished as well as attractive.

He was kissing her as no one ever had, his tongue plunging deeply between her teeth after its initial tentative probing. Inside her she was coming alive, a strange sensation combined of burning and an unfamiliar tugging.

'Oh, Frank,' she gasped, astounded by how exciting he'd become, and how attractive. She felt his hands at the back of her waist, crushing her to him, and all the while his mouth was delighting her own, one moment with featherweight kisses the next as though to devour her.

They went slowly towards the office – the workroom seemed too drab for their glorious emotions. As the door closed behind them they looked at each other yet again, lingeringly, as if to affirm the depth of feelings permitted no other expression.

A grave smile in his eyes, Frank took her hand, walked to the desk and leaned against its edge. He pulled her towards him then, sealing her lips at the same moment as his fingers anchored on her lower spine. His body felt firm through the silk of her gown, insistent as the stirring recommenced between them.

I need you Hester, he thought, it seems I always have. And there's no way I'll tell you. Not while things remain as they are.

'I'm always here,' he reminded her nevertheless, his voice breaking a little with the passion he felt compelled to contain.

'I know, I know.' Now she was kissing him, the scent of her entering his nostrils as she penetrated all his senses.

The need of her touch was pain, so fierce he took his mouth from hers to grit his teeth on the words that mustn't be spoken.

'What is it?' Hester asked, her gentle concern warming him till resisting his own urgency grew even more intolerable.

He shook his head. She stilled it with both hands, slowly brought her lips to his own. The gesture eroded more of his command, energised the muscle and sinew which, with some will of their own, exerted pressure against her.

'You're magnificent,' she exclaimed. 'How will we ever go back to being the people we were?'

'By knowing that owt else'll be disaster. There's no room, is there, in the works for folks that give way to what they're desiring. Your family would have me out . . .'

'I'd not let them,' she interrupted fervently, and hugged him. Didn't he know she yearned to prove how loyal she could be?

His arms wrapped her shoulders till he felt her heart's rhythm at his chest, its pulsing a duplicate of the beat journeying his veins.

'You're not yet of age, have no real say over your own life, let alone other folks'. If this is to survive, Hester, it'll require a deal of sense. I'll not let you ruin your future by surrendering to needs that are created for them as are wed.'

'I'll not exist if I have to keep you at a distance, Frank.'

Her lips sampled the corners of his mouth, the point of her tongue began probing until he no longer held out and felt its contact with his teeth. She was pliant in his arms, the thin stuff of her gown no substantial barrier to guard her breasts from him, its skirts no real insulation that might disguise his need.

'You'll have to trust me then,' he said, 'to – to keep myself back.' His face fiery with embarrassment now, he struggled to articulate matters he'd never expected to discuss. 'You know what I'm saying?'

Hester swallowed. She knew all right. Jamie'd condemned his sister's lover, the entire town condemned Sally and *whoever*. Was this yearning her own punishment for considering herself above desire's claims?

'It'll be private between ourselves for – for as long as necessary. There'll not be much opportunity, I'll warrant, for occasions like this.'

Will that make it easier, thought Frank ruefully, when I've but to see you across from my bench and there's nought can appease the passion you stir? That, though, was his penalty, the price to be paid for continuing in daily converse, for working in close proximity. He'd not complain, even should the outcome be her marrying within her own class. There was always their work – carving, polishing, creating to her designs was satisfaction, privilege even.

'You'd better kiss me again,' she murmured into his neck. 'If this has got to last us a fair while.'

The day Jamie next came home from sea, Hester met him at the quay. He hugged her the way he had in the past, and they kissed. She recognised at once the massive divide between the emotions he aroused and those experienced with Frank. Jamie, however, was still her old friend and learning of his return she'd felt compelled to warn him.

'There's talk in the town,' she announced when she'd asked how the trip had gone. She still loathed the possibility that he'd contradicted with actions all his fine words, but they had always been allies. 'I thought you'd better know that there's a rumour that you're responsible for the bairn that Sally Drinkwater's carrying.'

If she had meant to hurt him, his reaction would have satisfied her. As it was, the distraught look that drained his face of all pleasure in their greeting was like an arrow going through her.

'I'm sorry,' she said at once. She'd wanted the truth to substantiate her belief in him, but not like this. 'I can see you have no connection with her state, that you're as shaken as I was.'

'She's *expecting*? Who is it that's started the tale as it were me? One of the Crabtrees?'

'I don't know – I really have no idea, love.'

'Their dad saw us once, but I've never done owt as I shouldn't with the lass. Thought you knew I don't hold with suchlike.'

'Whoever started the rumour's done a thorough job. From the gentry that used to patronise the shop to folk that mix with our workers in Whitby's inns, news of Sally's condition has been chewed over.'

'I'll face every one of 'em, make sure they believe who it *wasn't*. Though I'm bound to admit I'd far rather go straight back to sea.'

At first, he'd doubted Hester's motive for shattering him by relating Sally's news and, worse, suggesting that he was the cause. Now, though, he saw that she'd come here today, to prevent him learning in other, less favourable, circumstances.

'Has she told you who the fellow is?'

'So far as I can tell, she's revealed that to no one. I think that's what has increased the speculation.'

Jamie sighed. 'I thought there were summat up the last time I saw her. Now I know.'

He was more disappointed than he would let on even to Hester. While they stood there with the breeze rattling the rigging of nearby boats and the smell of fish enveloping them, he felt his own future darkening. Until today there'd always been the thought at the back of his mind that he and Sally might end up together, eventually. Unable to make any kind of conversation, he muttered some sort of excuse and strode off up through the town towards his lodgings.

Hester wasn't sorry she'd seen Jamie and told him. What she did regret was her own inner certainty that the news had changed something within him. He'd been keener on Sally than he'd ever hinted.

Feeling utterly weary, she hurried in the direction of the Flowergate shop. Susan Blakeborough, the new girl they had set on, was an experienced shop girl, but she knew very little about the jet trade. Fortunately, she was eager to please and after spending time in the workroom was growing enthusiastic about their jewellery. For the present, though, she needed quite a lot of supervision and, as usual, it was Hester's designing that had to take second place.

Wondering despairingly how on earth she was going to keep up with creating patterns for routine items and also get on with her ideas for the carved tree, she didn't notice that the uniformed figure emerging from their shop was her own brother.

'Where's Sally?' Lambert demanded, without preamble or explanation of his sudden arrival in Whitby. 'The girl in there says she was asked to leave.'

'Lambert!' Hester exclaimed the minute she glanced up. 'We didn't expect you home just yet.'

'Evidently not, or you'd not have got rid of her. Why, Hester, why? She was a good worker . . .'

'It was nothing to do with her work,' she interrupted, furious with him for implying that he had some right to interfere yet again in the running of the business.

'Then nobody had any right to make her go. You must be wrong in your heads, all three of you.'

'I'll explain, if you'll only give me half a chance,' said Hester, thrusting into place strands of glossy dark hair that had been loosened by the wind down by the harbour. 'I'll just have to check that Susan can manage for a bit. If you wait there, we'll . . .'

Lambert seemed to grow another three inches as, inhaling harshly, he straightened the shoulders beneath the scarlet tunic.

'I'm not waiting for your explanations. I'm after the truth and I'll have it, or somebody'll be sorry.'

I did offer, thought Hester as she entered the shop. If he goes to the works Mother will only give him a sharp account of Sally's condition. Although maybe their mother would stop short of telling Lambert to mind his own business.

Desperately alarmed as well as angry, Lambert went straight to hire a carriage. He directed the man out beyond the town to the lane end which had been their rendezvous, then up to the only house in sight.

'I'll find my own way back,' he stated, and settled for the journey. Only then did he wonder what he would do or might say should Sally not be at home.

The place was as unprepossessing as anywhere he'd visited, but the living room opening immediately from the door that Mrs Drinkwater had answered was clean and bright.

'I'm Lambert Falgrave,' he announced, and was compelled to wait while the woman recovered.

'Would you please step inside, sir,' she began. 'If it's about our Sally, she's . . .'

'It is indeed about Sally,' he said. And then he saw her, through the back in the stone-flagged kitchen where she was hauling wet clothes up and through a mangle.

She heard his voice, ceased her task and stared. A reddened hand flew to her mouth, wet clothes slithered back into the tub while blue eyes regarded him in consternation that appeared to match his own.

'Oh, my love . . .' he murmured.

Though the living room was but small, the quantity of furniture and knick-knacks took some negotiating. It felt like minutes rather than seconds before he was standing beside her at the washtub, with steam rising between them, coarse soap a harsh scent that caught the back of his throat.

'Sally, what have they done to you?'

Even following their lovemaking, he'd not seen her so dishevelled. The beautiful fair hair had grown lank in the damp air, her face appeared to have swollen. Her slender figure was distorted . . .

'Oh, Lambert, I knew you'd come!'

He drew her to him, kissed the top of her moist head, an ear, her throat. His lips met hers in the minute that he recognised the bulk which was holding them apart.

'You never said. You didn't let me know. Why, Sally, for God's sake, why?'

'I wasn't sure for a long time. Then you'd gone back to the Grenadiers, and I didn't know where.'

'Was that the reason they took away your job?'

'They had to, love, your mother explained it to me. Folks were talking, you see. Falgraves' were losing custom.'

'I'll not forgive them, ever. I should have been told.'

'Do you think I'd tell anyone you were going to be a father before you knew yourself? Ay, Lambert, you've a lot to learn.'

He grew aware now of Sally's mother, a justifiably-interested spectator from through in the other room. Still holding Sally, he glanced towards the older woman. 'There's no question about my willingness to wed your daughter, providing she'll have me, and if you and her father give your consent.'

'Well, I – well, naturally, I'd be very pleased. Don't know, for sure, what her father will say, but he'll likely be in any minute.'

She told Sally to leave the washing, and make a pot of tea then sit with her young man.

'I'll finish t'rest of this lot,' she explained. 'Sally's been a big help to me, though, since she's been at home. And washing's one of the jobs that'll always bring in a few shillings, specially in a port like this with lots of lone fellows coming off the boats.'

Lambert couldn't keep his gaze from Sally, while she was brewing the tea, and afterwards. Although troubled by the absence of her normal daintiness, he couldn't help but be moved by the evidence of the child she was expecting.

'When's it due?' he whispered when they were seated on their cushions of Berlin woolwork at the table with its patterned chenille cover.

Sally shifted on her chair. 'Dr Davidson thinks I'm in my fifth month, not that he can be certain.'

'Davidson, eh? A good man. Our doctor, you know.'

Sally smiled. 'Your mother got me to go to him, she's paying.' She saw his look and gave her head a tiny shake. ''Course she doesn't know, not about me and you. Didn't I say – I've told nobody. Mrs Falgrave – er, your mother was just being very generous.'

Or paying you off, he wondered. But he'd breathe no word of that. When he and Sally were wed there'd need to be some kind of relationship with his family.

And it was the potential reaction of his family that now created the greatest havoc in Lambert. By the time he left the Drinkwaters' home he had the approval of Sally's parents for the marriage, and her agreement on a suitable date. He wished with all his being that he would encounter as little opposition at Falgrave House.

Chapter 12

'Are you sure that's what he said?'

Maud was mystified, a situation which she despised. If only *she'd* seen their Lambert she'd have found out what he was doing in Whitby, and where he was going.

'Well, I took it to mean he was calling in the workshop to see you,' said Hester, 'but he was off that fast there was no time to find out.'

'You always were too slow.'

'Nay, that's not right,' Abel protested from his chair. 'You don't have to go on at everybody, just because Lambert's done summat you don't like.'

'Don't like, don't like . . . What do *you* think of his behaviour then, eh? He's been in Whitby best part of a day by now, and have we seen him?'

'Happen he's asserting his right to live his own life without consulting us,' Abel ventured, taking a wicked delight in rubbing in the fact that Lambert was going beyond reach of maternal influence. 'Should have thought you'd have been thankful to have one less to worry about, any road . . .'

'You know nowt about it. I'm a mother, aren't I? Mothers don't stop caring. I only want what's best for him, for them all. I've got Mrs Richmond to cook his favourite steak pie tonight.'

Hester concealed a smile. Her father laughed, a rare enough sound which didn't delight his wife.

'Maybe his taste in food has changed, an' all, over the years,' he suggested. 'Have you asked him?'

'Are you trying to be funny?'

Amusement glinting in his dark eyes, Abel shook his head. 'Just think it's time you faced the fact as he's changing.'

And not the only one either, thought Hester grimly. Her mother had been irritable all afternoon at the works, because Lambert hadn't appeared. This evening, she'd banished Olive and Bernard to the schoolroom the minute they'd finished eating; ever since, had done nothing but carp. But then, *was* this a change in her mother? Hadn't she always reacted in this way when Lambert displeased her?

Hester felt the impact of Maud's keen blue eyes. 'Why didn't you think to ask how long he was here for? Hadn't you the sense, just this once, to find out what he's doing?'

The drawing room door opened and Lambert stood there. Slowly, he unbuttoned his tunic, ran a hand over the fair hair which wasn't quite so immaculate as usual.

'Don't blame Hester, Mother,' he said evenly. 'It was I who didn't give her any opportunity.'

His gait controlled, he crossed to Maud, leaned over to kiss her cheek. He kissed Hester also, more fervently, and squeezed her shoulder. Turning to his father, he grasped his hand, went down on his haunches to ask how he was, took time to hear out the reply.

Maud was bubbling up inside her with a conflict of pent-up emotions. Relief that Lambert had arrived was tempered by the hour of his coming, and by her awareness that he was just failing to conceal some terrible tension.

At last, prepared to give attention to more than his father's well-being, Lambert straightened up and went to stand behind a hardbacked chair, his hands on its rosewood frame. His knuckles whitened as he gripped the carving while he began to speak.

'I would like you to know that I am to be married – in four weeks' time, once the banns have been read. That'll be on Saturday, August the ninth, at St Mary's. I hope you'll all be present. I'll make arrangements, Father, to ensure that's possible.'

'Here, steady on,' his mother interrupted. 'Married, you say – who to?' Before Lambert could respond, she went on again, even more agitatedly. 'You could have brought her here first, introduced the girl, whoever she is.'

'There's no need of any introduction.' Somehow, despite the turmoil inside him, he was still speaking calmly, facing them square on, his back rigid. He might have regrets but he'd not display anything that might be interpreted as

226

shame. 'Sally and I have been in love for some months now, have known that we wished to make our future together.'

'*You* . . . it was you!' Maud flared. 'Heavens above, if I'd only known! To think that there she was, serving on as nice as pie, and all the time she was trying her darndest to trap you.'

'I think we should be realistic, don't you,' Lambert suggested, his voice its quietest yet. 'There's nothing any naïve little Whitby miss might have tried that'd have made me act against my own inclinations. You can't be that blind that you fail to see I'm the one with some knowledge of the world, and all Sally's done is make me fall in love with her.'

Hester smiled at him, rose, and walked over to stand at his side.

'I'm glad it's you,' she said. 'And, curiously, I'm not sorry it's Sally who'll be my sister-in-law.'

'You're not surprised?' Lambert inquired, astonished.

'Oh, I'm that all right, astounded. But sorry? Never.'

'Bless you,' he murmured.

His mother, though, was off again, in a tirade that drowned all speech but her own. 'I'll not acknowledge the girl, not after what she's done.'

'You'll risk the future of our relations if you absent yourself from our ceremony, Mother.'

'If you get me there, I'll wear my deepest black. There'll not have been a greater cause of mourning in that church since young William Scoresby took the service for the lifeboat disaster nigh on eighteen months since.'

'Maud, my dear,' Abel protested at last. 'We reared our family to accept their responsibilities with good grace – you'd not have Lambert neglecting his?'

Maybe the side of his wife that was long accustomed to seeing no fault in her eldest son was already inclined to relent; whatever the reason, her animosity suddenly collapsed and with it her onslaught. And even though it was evident that Maud wouldn't take warmly to her daughter-in-law, she'd not oppose the wedding.

The conflict, as Hester might have supposed, emerged in their daily contact. Knowing of her mother's deep disturbance, however, she made allowances, otherwise she could not have endured the constant stresses.

'Half the time she doesn't know what she's doing, poor soul,' she confided to Jamie during his next stay ashore. And in this way she came to tolerate Maud's changes of mind as well as mood. It was fortunate that biting her tongue had grown instinctive in cooperating with her mother to run the jet works. The ability stood her in good stead during those few weeks preceding the wedding.

Life was made all the harder by the fact of this unusual pairing having developed within the close community of works and shop. No matter how much she yearned to talk through the matter with Frank Clough, there wasn't the remotest possibility that she might do so.

Frank knew, of course, as did all the workers, if not the entire town. Wally Hardcastle had enjoyed announcing the news, though no one could be sure how he'd obtained the information. For all the service was planned for St Mary's, a bride whose gown and crinoline must be specially designed to disguise the child she carried was hardly eager to invite all the town's citizens.

Hester, for one, wasn't entirely sorry to have the fact out in the open at the works. Watching what she said to her mother was bad enough, without other restraints to trouble her so greatly that creating designs would grow impossible.

Away from the workroom, she saw Sally from time to time, Jamie rarely, and for the rest was left alone to brood.

It was Jamie, not the forthcoming marriage, that most alarmed her. The times that they met now, she liked him less for he'd grown sharper, more superficial, soured by the final removal of Sally from his life.

'I'd have wed her, you know,' he told Hester one day, 'even with this bairn your brother's fathered.'

'Have you been drinking?' she asked incredulously. 'You say over and over again that you'll not spend on yourself while you still owe your dad for his boat. And where would you get the brass for a home for a wife and child?'

'I'd earn it, of course.'

'By longer trips at sea, leaving her on her own? That's not what Sally needs.'

'Who'll look after her, in any case, when that brother of yours joins his regiment? Is she moving in with you, in t'great house up on yon cliff?'

'Lambert's taking her with him, naturally.'

Jamie hadn't thought of that. He stared at Hester who was stating it all so calmly, excluding him by being a part of the family closing around Sally.

He looked so dispirited that a lump developed in Hester's throat. He appeared pale, despite his seaman's tan, and even his hair looked washed out. Could all that glorious red be draining through its roots? They all were changing: her mother, now Jamie, perhaps most of all herself.

And he *had* been drinking. Stepping nearer to sympathise, she smelled the ale on his breath.

'I'm off now,' he announced abruptly, and she noticed his glance swivel from her to someone across the street. A young man raised a hand to greet him. It was Jeff Hardcastle.

'It was you told him about our Lambert and Sally,' she accused.

'So?' he said arrogantly. 'Them as wants to keep stuff hid, should learn to keep their parts to themselves.'

'That's gross,' she snapped, intensely embarrassed. 'How can you be so crude with me?'

'Not much so special about the Falgraves, as I can see. Not when they behave no better than fellows as go seeking it round t'back of some public house.'

'Jamie, Jamie, don't . . .'

'It's all round Whitby already, lass. Don't come complaining to me. There's one thing I hope, and I mean this sincerely – I hope you manage to keep t'extent of the talk from your father. He's got enough to contend with.'

If he hadn't left her then Hester would have wept, in fury and humiliation, and despair. As it was, while Jamie walked jauntily over the cobbled street to clap Jeff Hardcastle on the shoulder, she raised her chin, straightened her back and hastened away up the nearest ginnel.

But tears, albeit unshed, filled her eyes. Blinking determinedly, she felt compelled to lower her head, concentrating fiercely on each foot as she placed it before the other.

Heedless of passersby, she let them go their way, moving aside out of her path when necessary. Cannoning into the bulk of a large man was a shock all the more intense for her oblivion to everyone else. When he spoke, surprise and relief gave her the confidence to look him in the face. The blue eyes were kindly, blessedly familiar in their concern for her.

'Jon! I mean – Dr Davidson.'

'Don't correct yourself,' he told her gently, smiling. He had steadied her by grasping both of her arms, was holding them still. 'Hester – what is it?'

She shook her head, but he'd not be put off.

'Come now – don't conceal anything from me. I've seen and heard the worst that this life does to folk. I'm sure you're not about to shake me.'

'Oh, it's . . . well, you know our Lambert's to wed Sally?'

'Aye, she did tell me, only a day or so since.'

'I've just been told the whole of Whitby's talking.'

'Is that a fact? Well, tomorrow it'll be someone else'll be making waves inshore among public houses and tea-rooms.'

'But I never for one minute thought . . .'

'That the Falgraves would feed such gossip? Tell you the truth, nor did I. But I'll tell you something else – from what's come to my ears, it'll not do much harm. There's many a soul rejoicing that you've proved yourselves human.'

No matter how disturbed she'd been feeling, Hester couldn't remain unamused. Smiling back at him, she raised a dark eyebrow.

'Is that true? It sounds as if folk think we're a stuck up lot.'

'It comes with position, my dear, surely – the certain distance at which business people are held. Doctors, as well, you know.'

'I've always mixed with everybody,' she asserted quite hotly.

'I daresay.' His smile was deepening now, warming with approval. But she was the first of the Falgraves to dismiss barriers of class.

Although aware of little more than his apparent regard for her, she recalled what he'd said about doctors experiencing similar distancing from folk. Maybe that was why she often thought of him, bearing alone the declining health of his beloved wife. She asked after Ruth, then wished instantly that she hadn't.

The light went from his eyes like someone turning off the gas. The ginnel in which they stood was no more shadowed than a moment ago, yet it felt far darker. Hester shivered, glanced from side to side at the buildings so tall and closely-packed that the sun never penetrated.

'No better, I'm afraid,' he answered at last.

His hands hadn't left her arms; he seemed now to be frozen in position, then all at once his fingers slid down the silk of her sleeves. He held both her hands, gripping tightly.

'If there's anything at all that I can do,' she said softly, yearning to put her arms around their old family friend, to give some kind of comfort and support. Gravely, he nodded, thanked her.

The workshop seemed over-noisy, too cheerful. The men were singing at their benches, pausing now and then to laugh. All except Harold Clough, who was another that had taken it hard that the lass he might have courted was being obliged to marry. Happen it was as well their Lambert was the bridegroom, Hester thought. If Jamie had been the man concerned and Skeltons and Cloughs almost neighbours down by the harbour there, Harold would have had less chance of forgetting.

For a time at least, Lambert and Sally would be living wherever his regiment took him. And if they ever did settle in Whitby it would hardly be in the area a Clough might inhabit.

Minutes later, the significance of that thought hit her, and with it the realisation that there *did* exist a yawning gap between any Clough's circumstances and her own. No matter how attracted she was to Frank, whose helpfulness and concern for her were equalled only by their passion, difficulties could arise which might be too great to be surmounted. Her own personal disregard of class differences wasn't sufficient, and after Lambert's disgrace . . .

It was Edwin Clough who prevented her from dwelling overlong on these gloomy thoughts.

'Have a look at this, Miss Hester,' he began, and called her over to inspect the latest delivery of rough jet. 'Isn't this the sort of size might be of use for t'main part of yon tree you're planning?'

The hunk was far larger than many pieces that came their way. Lifting it, Hester guessed it must weigh around eight pounds.

'That'd be champion, Mr Clough. Make sure it's set aside, will you?'

There was too much on her mind now until after the wedding, but once that was over she would get them all working on this centrepiece for the shop window. Even today she was glad of this reminder that there'd always be the jet willing her to tackle something different and show it to even better advantage.

For the present, Bob Dunsdale's son Silas was making his first attempt at hand-engraving, coached by Frank. Pausing near enough to see without disturbing their concentration, Hester watched.

In his rather serious quiet voice, Frank finished explaining what the apprentice had done wrong, then told him to turn the jet piece over.

'Have a go again now, on t'other side, lad. And don't be afraid to make a mark. You were nobbut scratching it afore. Take it nice and slow, like . . .'

Some men in the trade were known for reservations about passing on all their skills. Those who were better than average craftsmen might be forgiven for wishing to guard their right to the most interesting jobs. In the Falgrave works, though, there appeared to be little or no such reservation. Certainly, Frank, his father and brother seemed as glad as any apprentice himself when a particular aspect of the work was mastered.

He was smiling now, nodding his approval as the simple design gradually was etched into the jet.

'By, Silas, tha's coming on a treat – that's grand.'

The apprentice glanced sideways at him, beamed, and paused to wipe perspiration from his hands.

'It'll not take so much out of you, once you've done a

few like that,' Frank murmured kindly to him. 'Have a change for a bit, eh – see how you frame with polishing.'

Frank was good with youngsters, Hester noticed, firm enough for them to be sure there'd be no nonsense, but as kind with them as he always seemed towards herself. He'll make a lovely father, she realised, and felt her cheeks warming with a heat that had nothing to do with the strong sun penetrating the black dust coating the windows.

There were several long windows in the wall that overlooked the street. Her father had had them enlarged when the window tax was repealed, and he maintained they soon paid for themselves in what was saved in gas for lighting. Certainly, on a day like today, they brightened the workroom a great deal, even if they did show up the dark glinting powder that stirred in each slanting beam and formed a layer, rough beneath the fingers, on everything you touched. In wintertime she was less sure about any saving. Especially with winds and snow and sleet of the kind you experienced here in Whitby. Many was the time that she'd seen the men huddled over their benches, as far as they could get from the draughts afforded by the glass. They also contrived frequent trips to toss a handful of jet chippings on to the coke bogey stoves that heated the special ockamatutt glue as well as the building, and had ugly pipes to conduct smoke through the roof.

Frank had a hand on Silas' shoulder now, and they laughed together over some mishap that made the apprentice shake his head.

'Have another go, that's t'only way tha'll learn. If you do summat wrong, it's best put behind you – except to learn you not to make t'same mistake next time.'

Philosophy, as well, thought Hester. But if the Dunsdale lad only applied the concept to his work here he'd do nicely. And the training any apprentice received at Falgraves' was thorough. Throughout the trade there were no specific factors laid down as compulsory for training. Indeed, apprenticeship for a given number of years was not obligatory in every workshop. Here, they spent time on every facet of producing jewellery and figurines, and also received instruction in fashioning their own tools to see them through their working lives.

And the workers turned out well. Most could turn their hands to any task required of them, and all had at least one particular skill which had been honed as carefully as the jet itself.

Sometimes, on occasions like this, Hester longed for the greater breadth of ability which a fuller training would have given her. She'd have loved to sit for a day, creating perfect features in cameo or engraving monograms to personalise jewellery for some wealthy dowager.

'Is there something wrong that makes you stand motionless over yonder?'

Her mother's question, from the top of the stairs, made Hester start and wonder how long she had remained immobile, thinking. She shook her head, hurried across to her side. And that, she thought, is just what's wrong with my place here. I'm neither a craftsman with a skill that is to be exercised day long, nor yet a manager in charge of administration.

'If you want to do some more at that tree design you've set your heart on, I don't suppose the place will go to pot for want of you standing watching t'others working.'

Hester beamed. 'If you're sure . . . I was afraid I'd not have the opportunity to concentrate on that, at least until after this next week or two.'

'I've been taking stock of what we have in the shop, and other folks we send our stuff to seem to have plenty in hand. So long as you're prepared to set that job aside if a crisis occurs, I reckon there's nowt else needing urgent attention.'

Working on this special undertaking put Hester in a happier frame of mind which seemed to spill over into the hours away from the workroom. On a sudden impulse she got Kilner to drive her out to the Drinkwaters' house, and while she and Sally sat over a pot of tea put her suggestion to her.

'I know you and Lambert aren't planning a big wedding, but have you thought of who'll attend you?'

'There'll not be anybody, will there? Not with me only

234

having brothers, and our Dennis' wife has turned all stuck up now she's heard the way I am.'

'Will you have me for an attendant?'

'You? Oh, Miss Hester . . .'

Hester laughed. 'You're not going to go on calling me "Miss" after you're married to my brother, I hope? Any road – what do you think of the idea?'

'I think it'd be perfect. More than I deserve.'

'Don't talk that way. I daresay our Lambert knows how to be persuasive. He always did know his own mind. And maybe if I'm going to be a bridesmaid our Olive will take it into her head to do likewise. Will that be all right?'

'Wonderful. Thank you ever so much, Hester.'

'I'll have to arrange for you to get to know Olive, or have you met her and Bernard?'

'Once or twice last year, when your – er, Mrs Falgrave brought them into the shop.'

The gown Hester chose was similar in style to the lilac and white which was so flattering, but in a gorgeous shade of blue which reminded her of the sea beneath a summer sky – especially since it was of a taffeta that gleamed with every movement.

I'm going to enjoy this wedding, she decided, no matter what anyone else feels about the occasion.

When the second Saturday in August dawned, Whitby was obscured by a sea fret that had drifted up the Esk to fill the entire town from the West Cliff to the East. Even the massive Royal Hotel across the harbour from the Falgraves was virtually obscured in the dismal cloud of moisture. Not that Abel minded not seeing that particular edifice. Despite its being constructed as a recent part of George Hudson's scheme for attracting visitors to Whitby, he couldn't wholeheartedly approve an addition of such dimensions. Smaller establishments, less obtrusively designed and integrated into the ancient town, might surely just as effectively have accommodated those who arrived on Hudson's railway link from Pickering.

'You're awake then, Abel?' Maud remarked, hurrying along from the bathroom which had been installed two months ago. 'Nurse Clapper's filling your bath.'

Abel sighed. 'Lambert's at home, isn't he? Haven't I said as I prefer . . .'

'Lambert's busy already, so I'm afraid you'll have to put up with things the way they're arranged. It is *his* wedding, after all. He's got plenty to see to. And he has promised to get you to the church ahead of everybody else.'

'After this week I'm sending that blessed nurse packing. You've all kept telling me since the day she walked through yon door, that she'd improve. And she's not a damned bit better, not one scrap. And who is it has to put up with her nursery treatment, day in and day out – none of you lot, is it?'

'No, dear,' said Maud placatingly. She was needing iron-hard determination to get through this day at all. Well, if she'd to commence by appearing to humour her husband, it was good practice. There'd be a deal of saying only what people wished to hear, if she was any judge. And she'd rarely found her own judgement to be lacking. Some things, in any case, were patently evident. She'd only met Sally's parents the once, for instance, quite sufficient to convince anyone that they were even more naïve than the girl.

Nurse Clapper clomped into the room, transferred Abel to the invalid chair and conveyed him out and along the landing. Maud allowed herself a small smile. Abel might create about the woman but she was efficient, did all that was necessary with the minimum of disturbance to the rest of the household.

May Thorpe came in to dress Maud's hair. The girl had progressed these past few months, slimmed down a little, perhaps by long hours spent moving about the extensive house. Her original impulse to perform tasks at a run had at long last been curbed.

Now there was a new girl, three years her junior, and May took this as encouragement to develop a few more skills.

'This is the hat I'll be wearing,' Maud announced when May had greeted her with a neat bob. An elegant concoction of feathers, lace and satin bows it was in an exquisite shade of grey-green exactly matching her gown and long-sleeved bolero, which had a fine bright blue trimming.

'That's a beauty, Madam,' May exclaimed.

Maud nodded. It was rather larger than current fashion dictated, but suited her well, and without an impressive hat today she'd never survive.

'Quite plainly is how I'll wear my hair, parted in the centre as always then drawn back over the ears. Any curls will be restrained so as to fall at the nape. It's from the rear, after all, that most folk will be inspecting me.'

Her hair arranged, Maud was finishing dressing when Abel reappeared, bounced along in the invalid chair by an indignant Nurse Clapper.

'If your son's so determined to take over, Mr Falgrave, I'll leave you to get on,' she snapped.

Bosoms heaving with indignation, the nurse turned with military precision and strode off towards the staircase. The clomp of her feet revealed that she was disappearing en route for breakfast.

'Just the person I want, May,' Abel began amiably. 'Find Mr Lambert will you, at once? Tell him I'm ready to dress.'

Maud gave her husband a sideways look as May left everything to comply. She could understand Abel's dislike of being dependent upon anyone, or thought she could, but he seemed to delight in rearranging everyone's routine.

Lambert arrived with commendable speed, even though he seemed singularly unready for the day's ceremony. The trousers he had on were uniform ones, but Maud doubted they were what he'd wear to the church. And his shirt was old, civilian.

Maud still found the necessity for Abel to have help with even the most basic of tasks greatly distressing. Now that Lambert was here she collected up the gold jewellery which she would wear and hastened, almost at a run, through the door.

Hester was emerging from the next room, exquisite in her blue gown which rustled so deliciously as she moved.

'You look lovely in that, Hester,' her mother approved. 'Haven't I told you before that you can make yourself nice if you take the trouble.'

The 'if' rather took the shine off the compliment, but Hester smiled her thanks nevertheless. For once, she and her mother were united in presenting a contented front to the world.

'I've asked the Drinkwaters to come here first,' Maud announced. 'It's one way of ensuring they're none of them late or anything, and that they turn up at the right church. If they do arrive afore Lambert has set off with Kilner to get your father installed in our pew in plenty of time, there's enough rooms here. We shall be able to shove Sally out of sight to avoid them two getting a look at each other.'

Hester nodded, smiling inwardly over such precautions when bride and groom were already wed in all but name, and complimented her mother on taking such thought for the Drinkwaters.

'Aye, well – since we've decided to acknowledge the union, there's no point in being petty. And it'll help 'em to feel a bit easier, like, when we all come back here afterwards.'

For once, Hester admired Maud's behaviour. She knew how difficult it must have been for her to accept first of all that her favourite son could fall from grace, and then that he'd neglected to select a girl from the local gentry.

'Your father'll get on well enough with them, any road. He's got that many friends among fisherfolk I was only surprised he didn't know them already.'

There were hired carriages in addition to the Falgrave brougham to convey the family and all the Drinkwaters to St Mary's. It was lucky no one was expected to struggle up the Church Stair in this, thought Hester some time later, glancing from the windows while Sally was putting the final touches to the fair hair beneath her veil. The sea fret had disappeared, but only because it was driven off by a deluge of thundery rain.

'It's a terribly wet day for you, Sally love,' she observed. 'I hope it lets up before we come out of the church. Our Bernard's learnt how to use one of the latest cameras, and he's determined he'll have pictures of you and Lambert.'

Today the church when they entered certainly needed the rows of cabin skylights in its roof to prevent the interior looking gloomy. Once her eyes adjusted, Hester smiled, delighted by the masses of flowers which Mrs Richmond and May had arranged there. They softened the effect of the box pews and had been twined around the barley-sugar columns supporting the great Cholmley pew which straddled the main aisle.

'If the squire's descendants get to hear of me decorating their pew and don't like it, I'll whip 'em off after t'service,' Mrs Richmond had confided when Hester called into the church yesterday to check their progress.

There were flowers of various kinds in garlands over the three-tiered pulpit, multicoloured cascades spilling from the top, normally reserved for a visiting preacher, to the minister's deck and finally fanning out and nearly concealing the parish clerk's lower tier. No expense had been spared by the Falgraves if the appearance of the church bore witness. And Mrs Richmond and May had tackled the work with enormous enthusiasm. Hester had only just succeeded in restraining May from slipping roses into the ear trumpets attached to the pulpit in the time of one vicar whose deaf wife might otherwise have escaped his sermons.

It seemed to Hester that the flowers set the mood for the ceremony, despite her father's being trapped in the invalid chair beside their front pew, despite Sally's pallor and the curious cut of her gown, and despite the wind now wailing across the top of the cliff to thrash the windows with rain.

And there was no denying that her own mother was an asset to the occasion. She glided towards the Falgrave pew without a trace of hesitation. And that took some doing, thought Hester, noticing what an unexpectedly large congregation was gathered. They had invited no one beyond the two immediate families, yet the church held close on two thousand people when full, and over half the pews were occupied.

Lambert, with Crispin Stansfield to his right, stood rigid in his military dress uniform. And was far more nervous than ever in his life before. There'd been no time for adjusting, that was the problem, no time for accepting that from this day forward he'd be answerable to someone other than himself, and soon to two people.

Sensing his apprehension, Crispin smiled. 'It really is quite simple to adapt,' he said from the corner of his lips.

'Especially with the regiment. Life goes on, and there's always some reason for not spending all one's time at home . . .'

The line of Lambert's mouth tightened, his shoulders grew even stiffer. Crispin simply could not comprehend. He loved Sally, utterly. This might seem a mismatching, but they'd all see very soon that he'd be a model husband. And father.

His glance strayed to the invalid chair just within his line of vision when he allowed his head to turn a few degrees. He'd hone himself in his father's image, though perhaps with a fraction more discipline towards his offspring. He himself had gone his own way, by one means or another, had learned only since going into the army that he responded best within guidelines.

Sally'll not understand that, he reflected, without regretting the differences in their natures. Hadn't he grown to love her ingenuity that had found ways of circumventing parental strictures? Didn't he rejoice that it was for him that she'd risked disgrace?

She was coming now, the music not quite disguising the swish of fine fabrics, the tread of soft shoes that contrasted with the steady step of the minister and Mr Drinkwater. Within moments she stood beside him, agleam in a gown of palest peach, her smile radiant behind her honey-toned veil.

Lambert smiled back, felt emotion filling throat and eyes. Against the dull black of her father's clothes and the rest of her kin over the aisle there, she glowed. How she'd emerged from that ordinary fisherman's family with so much loveliness he couldn't imagine. That she was his seemed scarcely believable. He must mind not to voice *that* sentiment, though, in his mother's hearing.

Sally was entranced by her bridegroom who'd never looked more handsome and impressive, by the people who'd ignored the downpour in their honour, and by the fact of their imminent marriage.

Within her the child stirred, making her catch her breath, yet creating no other disturbance. She'd wondered many a time these past few months if she was wrong in failing to experience the regrets so readily voiced by her mother. But all she had felt, other than at times of sickness, had been this steadily-increasing joy. Hadn't she and Lambert belonged together since that first time he'd delighted her with caresses? Today, all Whitby would know they were joined.

Abel quelled a sigh as the minister began speaking. They'd brought him here early to simplify matters; now he ached in every bone – the familiar soreness of a body unable to shift for itself and too long restricted to one position. From his invalid chair, now that its back was raised as much as he could tolerate, he could see the chief participants, though not his own wife. Neither he himself nor Lambert had thought to ensure that the chair be placed to enable the limited movements of his head to allow eye contact with Maud. He couldn't even see the side of her skirts. All that was visible, by forcing round his head until effort made him bite on his lip, were her gloves draped on the edge of the pew and her left hand with the rings he had placed there.

Withdrawn by frustrations, he'd missed one half of the ceremony, but he attended as his son bent to place the gold band on that girl's finger. Briefly, he resented Sally for her background. He'd made friends of many of the town's fisherfolk without wishing any for his kin. But then his glance focused on his own daughters. Hester, tall and too slender, these days, from long hours of working. And Olive, growing swiftly, reminding him of both Hester and their mother, yet not really resembling either. He'd not deny any lass the satisfaction of parenthood. Sally was neither bad nor stupid and she'd be a sensible wife to their Lambert, for all her fun-loving nature. She'd make a good mother.

Hester sensed the faint movements possible by her father, was distracted by concern for him from events before the oak Communion table that had existed in Queen Elizabeth's reign. And she wasn't entirely sorry to avoid dwelling too intensely on this ceremony.

Walking down the aisle, beneath the roof fashioned by men more accustomed to building ships, she'd had the fanciful notion that the ambience was appropriate to the life on which Lambert and Sally were embarking. Even the wind and rain beyond the Georgian windows presaged the

241

storms that no pair avoided – though she'd be the first to admit that Sally's disposition would weather most *contretemps*.

It wasn't doubts about their future which troubled her. It was reminders of the inadequacy of her own. She'd loved the children when Olive and Bernard were small, enjoying their development to a degree that equalled their parents'. These past few months, she'd worked harder than ever she'd thought possible, but not always extinguishing a certain restlessness. She might contemplate no life without room for designing jet ornaments, but she'd no wish to exist solely for that workshop. And Frank was here.

A few pews from the rear, with his father and others from the works, the shape and the tilt of his head were too familiar now for any mistaking. In this moment, as in all the others since walking past him, she was aware of his gaze on her, of her own response to his notice. The other day she'd thought fatherhood would suit him.

She might have considered, once, that Lambert and Sally could be confronted with differences greater than their love, but their potential inequalities would be evened out in a life away from here. Their problems were as nothing beside a man who wanted his own boss's daughter and could not fail to grow to resent that she was the one who gave him directions. And Frank hated coming to Falgrave House.

It was all *her* fault. She was the one who had gone willingly to his arms to fulfil her need, if only for affection, with no thought that she accelerated his own. A matter of weeks ago, she'd been so *innocent*, still unsure of the details surrounding conception. All that had changed in being confronted with this girl now becoming a wife in her dainty gown and ungainly body.

They'd all been scarred by it: Mother vexed and Father silently made to surrender dreams concerning family heritage. And she herself brought to see the reality behind what might have been rapture. She'd bear this in mind, even against her deeper inclinations, even if her life became yet narrower, more restricted.

Hester, for one, was relieved when the register was signed and the organ took up its triumphal melody. She seized hold of her father's chair to follow behind the newly-wed couple.

'What a lot of folk turned out,' Abel exclaimed out in the open with the recently-lapsed rain glistening on the grass in a burst of sunlight.

'Aye – inquisitive creatures,' snorted his wife. She was glad that her gown and especially the hat had outshone everyone's. She was infinitely thankful also for the discipline ensuring she'd come through it all without that smile wavering.

'I'm not waiting while our Bernard plays around taking photographs,' she told Hester. 'You can do as you think fit, your father and I are off home. Not that we have much choice over that, any road, for who else will host this reception while Lambert has eyes for nobody but that bit of a lass. And as for her people – they'll be tongue-tied, I expect. They'd little enough to say afore we set off.'

Hester pushed the chair as far as the space where Kilner waited with the brougham. She helped the elderly man settle her father into the carriage, but shook her head when Maud suggested she ride with them.

'I'll just keep an eye on what's happening back at the church. Olive and Bernard might take it into their heads to dawdle.' And Sally and Lambert couldn't be relied on to think of the time.

'You look absolutely beautiful, especially when you forget to be so worried about everybody else.'

It was Frank behind her; he was standing smiling, having detached himself from the other workers. He wore a white shirt as he had that other time. With the dark cloth of his coat and trousers, he was as smart as any man she knew. Her earlier resolve drifted with the wind away from the cliff, inland, and dispersed.

'You look very well yourself when you're dressed in your best – pity we work in such a mucky place, isn't it?'

Frank gave her a knowing look. 'You're ignoring what else I said.'

Hester laughed. 'I'm the eldest living at home, aren't I? If I don't keep an eye on things, who will?'

His smile faded. 'There's no point in answering that, is

there? Because you will worry, and see to what needs doing. I only hope it isn't going to be many a year before you pause while you're getting on with that. You might find then that you've had no life of your own.'

I didn't need reminding of that, she thought in the silence developing between them. And I just wish I could believe you have it in you to ensure that I do live my own life. But that might require that you become someone altogether different, a person who could share my life in all its aspects, including my father's incapacity.

Chapter 13

'Where's Nurse Clapper got to?'

It was Maud's first question as soon as they were back inside the house. At first, she was too perturbed to notice her husband's smile. When she did see it, it would have taken more than his disability to shield him from her annoyance.

'Abel – what have you done?'

'Told her to go.'

'*You've done what?*' Hadn't today been enough of a strain, without him dismissing the nurse and no prior serious discussion with her. 'We can't manage without her.'

'For the rest of the day we can. I only sent her off to her sister's for an hour or two.'

'You're developing a very peculiar sense of humour,' Maud told him sharply. Her heart had pounded wildly at the prospect of coping without Nurse Clapper.

Abel nodded, compelled to agree. But ever since he'd elected to be shot of that woman for a while he'd relished the idea of having them all on that he'd sacked her as threatened. His wife's reaction had put a stop to that. He'd not wish to worry their Hester, she took too much on her shoulders as it was. And all he'd really wanted was to ensure that they couldn't pack him off with the nurse, in case he became a nuisance, while they enjoyed themselves.

'Well, you've only yourself to blame if you're kept waiting for our Lambert to give you any help you need.'

'What help do I need, just to loll about i' this thing?'

Before Maud could reply the new maid hurried to open the door to the Drinkwater family. And there could be no regretting the interruption – another minute and she'd have gone all soft, weeping over her husband because having him immobilised seared into her.

By the time Sally's parents had come into the hall and

were discarding their outer garments, Maud's smile was in place, her will underpinning her sociability.

'Do come this way, won't you,' she invited, leading them towards the dining room.

Lambert arrived next, with Sally on his arm, both beaming as they paused to lean over and speak with Abel.

'I've got summat for you, young lady,' he told her, smiling back. 'You'll have to take me upstairs, though. I'll tell you how to operate yon lift.'

Sally had been awed by Abel Falgrave's incapacity, and only with Lambert beside her had she managed even a few words with him. The prospect of being on her own with him petrified her. He was the boss, wasn't he? Yet now he was so *reduced* she hardly knew what to say or do.

The lift, however, was a splendid construction, and manoeuvring his chair inside, then sending them soaring to the upper floor demanded concentration. When she pushed the chair out on to the landing Sally was feeling better.

'You managed that champion,' he told her, then felt guilty when he remembered her condition. 'I hope pushing won't do you any harm, it's only along here . . .'

Inside the master bedroom, he asked to be conducted to an inlaid chest of drawers.

'Open t'bottom one, will you, lass. See what's inside.'

There was one item only in the drawer, and it was wrapped in aged tissue paper.

'Aye, that's it,' he prompted her. 'Get it out.'

Unwrapping the tissue, Sally tried with her fingers to identify the object. And then she was smiling again, widely, and so was he as they examined the simply carved cross. It wasn't new but it was of jet.

'It's for your home, when you get one. Do you know what it is?'

'I do that!' Sally exclaimed. 'It's to fasten to the witch-post.'

'Ah,' said Abel, nodding approvingly. 'Didn't suppose you'd have come across one afore.'

'Not long since, actually,' she said, loving the feel of the cross as she ran her hands over its glossy surface. 'My grandmother had one tied to a piece of wood by the beam supporting the inglenook fireplace. I'd never paid any heed to what it were till I was clearing the place out.'

'Was the wood rowan?'

'Eeh, I don't know. I'm not well up in suchlike.'

'Rowan's traditional – as much so as jet, for warding off evil.'

'Well, thank you ever so much. I'll always look after this, and it'll be t'first thing we put in place when we have somewhere of our own to live in.'

'Glad to hear it.' And he was glad to think of his jet cross surviving to protect future Falgraves, long after he was gone.

The gathering proved pleasant enough, despite the disparity between the circumstances of Sally's parents and her parents-in-law. Maud dispensed tea and Lambert handed around stronger drinks while Hester and her younger brother and sister passed overladen plates which were frequently replenished by Mrs Richmond and May Thorpe.

Sally's parents and her brothers didn't know when to leave. Long after Lambert had departed with their daughter for the train to Pickering which would connect with one for London, they sat on, looking and feeling uncomfortable now, and unable to extract themselves with anything resembling grace. Eventually, Hester suggested that they might wish Kilner to take them home.

They seized the offer so eagerly that their relief could not be questioned. And relief was Maud's strongest emotion once the Falgraves were alone again. Even when Nurse Clapper appeared a quarter of an hour later she was ready to accept that the nurse should prepare Abel for the night.

'I hope you're not as done-up as I am,' she exclaimed, when she finally joined him in the big brass bed. 'It's many a month since anything's taken so much out of me.'

'I'm not so bad. But you were magnificent today, Maud. I'm right proud of you.'

'None of it was easy, that is for certain.'

'Nobody'd have guessed, though. You carried it off as if that lass would have been your first choice, and as if they hadn't gone and behaved as though they were married already.'

'Having so many folk in the church made it all the harder.

I was that surprised . . . there must have been at least a thousand there.'

Aye, thought Abel, and all seeing how useless I am now.

'By the time Sally's family left I thought my grin was etched that deep it'd never disappear. I swear my jaws ache with smiling.'

'Never mind, you did smile and that's what counts.' And he hadn't even attempted to, some of the time. Then there was the way he'd tried to provoke her over Nurse Clapper.

'I'd not get rid of that nurse, you know – not without your agreement,' he announced suddenly. Maud was the one who'd bear the burden if he responded to the impulse.

'I suppose we could get somebody else,' she ventured wearily.

'Happen so. One day.' The trouble was he didn't believe he'd think any better of anyone in that capacity; because of the reason they were here, the shaming things they had to do for him.

'I'm afraid the reaction's setting in,' Maud said in a soft voice, quite unlike her own. 'Even my thoughts took some managing, you know. When we were in church my eyes seemed to be drawn to the jade's pew – and I couldn't help picturing Sally there, shrouded for penitence, instead of wearing her finery. And then I had to be nice to her.'

'She's not an unpleasant girl,' Abel observed, wishing he could draw his wife to him.

'She's not a person who'll ensure our Lambert gets on, either.'

'I believe he has enough about him to manage that for himself. If he hasn't, there's not much anybody can do.'

'A good wife can make a lot of difference to a man.'

'When they're like you, aye.'

'I just – wanted it to be different . . .' She was weeping now, letting tiredness and stress drain out of her. No matter that she had got through this day, now she felt inconsolable.

'Come here, Maud love, don't take it all so much to heart.'

During the ensuing weeks, though, it was Abel himself who grew downhearted – more so than at any time since the accident. He invited the Etheringtons to the house and the Crabtrees, solitary Leslie Melbeck as well. If he subconsciously hoped to restore the genial good humour prevalent over the Christmas period, the effort was a failure. His friends came and talked convivially enough but, unfortunately, they always went away again, leaving him no brighter than on their arrival. With Hester and her mother at the works, and the young ones at school, he pined for a life that had some purpose.

One month followed another in listless repetition. Hester showed him the sketches for the carved tree she was planning, afterwards brought home samples of the minute butterflies and birds which would decorate its branches. All he felt was the perpetual ache to be there in the workroom, to see what was going on, to manage the place himself.

On his insistence, Nurse Clapper was wheeling the chair out on to the terrace beyond the drawing room on fine days. Feeling no better out there was an enormous disappointment, but one he wouldn't admit. Perversely, he continued to sit out there with the cool breeze freezing his veins, well into the autumn. He was finding the confines of the house intolerable – the improvement he sought must be out here.

The town itself seemed to taunt him, though, every well-loved aspect of houses, shops and alleyways, the West Cliff facing him, the harbour. This was the place where he'd been born, had grown, matured, then married. The scene of his success, the area kindling his hopes.

It was but a few days short of a year that he'd been just sitting or lying about like this, near enough senseless – certainly, there was neither sense nor purpose in his existence. He'd had enough.

All it needed was some means of starting this chair rolling. Once in motion it would be propelled over the edge of the terrace, down the slope of the lawn, past the rustic gardenhouse, across flowerbeds of zinnias, dahlias, lobelia. It would bypass the shrubbery, that gloomy mass of laurel, yew and holly. The drop was sheer then, into space.

The chair would be smashed to smithereens against one of the houses down yonder, and him with it, if he hadn't been hurled from the damned thing long before then. They'd all think it was another accident, and if they grieved there'd be the business to run still, too much to think about to give grieving its head. And afterwards they'd run the place unimpeded.

Lacking the ability to apply this remedy didn't prevent Abel from dwelling on it. There was little enough otherwise to occupy him, even though Olive and Bernard were making great efforts to interest him again in folklore and in his favourite authors. Hester was working longer hours and Maud, these days, seemed strange.

He wakened frequently of a morning to find her out of bed already, wandering the house on some pretext, for all he could tell. He suspected she was unwell, though she denied any such thing, but she tired easily and looked shorter than ever as she dragged herself about the place, shoulders hunched and the spark gone from her blue eyes.

Anxiety for her, for Hester as well, and annoyance with his own inability to aid them made him scour his mind for a way to relieve them of one responsibility.

He was dour with them all, but did those two even notice, he often wondered, coming home as they did, filled with their doings in the workroom. When Hester wasn't too tired she went on and on about this tree they were making, how fine the carving of its branches and trunk were, how exquisitely *his* men were fashioning the leaves.

The day he'd decided he could endure no more put him in mind of the morning of that cliff fall. Overnight fog had lifted, leaving Whitby bright under the November sun. He went down in the lift which never had made the difference he'd expected to life, and prayed that some fault might plunge the thing through the cellars.

Nurse Clapper was patronising, as normal, steering the chair away in the direction of the dining room and breakfast. Maud and Hester had left for the workshop long since, of course. They had agreed many a month ago that there was no sense in his rising early.

The food appeared, specially prepared so it might be fed to him with the minimum of fuss. He could not swallow the first mouthful: it gagged him. Despair swirled up from the heart of his being, overtook his mind, everything.

'There's a letter for you,' Clapper declared, her gaiety as false as the emphasis of her every sentence.

The letter was opened for him, held so that he might read.

'*We're calling the baby Abel*,' Sally announced in her childish script. '*He arrived just a few hours ago, at three in the morning. I planned all along that I'd be the first to tell you . . .* '

And that he'd be the first to hear. He read again those first few words, read on to learn his grandson had weighed a little over eight pounds, that they would visit Falgrave House as soon as she was recovered and had been churched.

He could read no more. Tears raced unchecked down cheeks which for too long had been fixed in one expression – or lack of expression – in order to contain what he was feeling.

Later that morning, he sent Kilner to the works so that Maud might read for herself how their family had grown. And he decided finally that there'd be no more thoughts of suicide.

Hester was no less pleased than the rest of them that Lambert and his pretty wife had a son. But the summer had brought innumerable visitors to Whitby, diminishing their stocks and convincing her that they must increase production in readiness for next year's season. There would be the normal demand for mourning jewellery in the meantime, and now that the tree she had planned was almost completed she must try to conceive some other novelty which might distinguish the Flowergate shop from other jet shops, of which there seemed to be more each month.

And Christmas was all but upon them once again. She wasn't looking forward to the festival. Over these past months, she had once more grown isolated. When she saw Jamie on his infrequent sojourns in the town, he interested her as much as before, but pleased her rather less. He made no secret of his new liking for ale, and although he was just as attractive she'd been quick to acknowledge that the feelings he aroused in her were no deeper than desire and friendship.

From the day of Lambert's wedding, she had ceased to

consider her emotions regarding Frank Clough. It might have been that the marriage which could be made to work between her brother and Sally only emphasised the unlikelihood of a similar match succeeding. And, being the eldest one at home, she grew increasingly aware that she'd never wed anybody who wouldn't share her concern for her father.

She wished she was more like her sister-in-law, or her own brother, able to yield her heart while her head was protesting caution. But she'd been formed with more than her share of introspection. And there was much around her to invite serious contemplation, with her father now into the second year of being immobilised – a situation which warped their family life. And their doctor, on every visit, bringing worse news of his failing wife. If Ruth Davidson lasted into 1863 it would be surprising. By the time Christmas Eve dawned all Hester hoped for was that it would pass without trauma.

With Sally, Lambert and baby Abel arriving the atmosphere changed. Maud became a besotted grandmother, forever taking up the infant, cradling it as though it were her own. She appeared more lighthearted and carried the rest of the family along with her, so that by their return to the workshop afterwards, she was the indomitable little woman, full of spirit again, ready to drive them all to make this another successful year.

The impact of the shock that was to devastate Hester began one day while she was waiting for Jamie outside the Flowergate shop. She had promised him some cast-off clothing for his many brothers and sisters, and he was late. Because the day was fine and she'd no desire to meet him under the watchful glance of their new shop girl, she was standing out on the pavement. This was no hardship – she was still too delighted with the tree created in their workroom to tire of gazing at the window where it fulfilled all she'd anticipated as the dramatic centrepiece.

Jamie arrived at last, swaggering and accompanied by Jeff Hardcastle. Hester was appalled to see her friend's companion and searched her mind for something to say while all she really wished was to ignore him. The words

252

that emerged following their greetings came out in such a rush, she was thankful they were at least coherent.

'I hope you've noticed this carved tree we've got in the window? We're doing all we can to gain attention.'

Both Jamie and Jeff gave the display a perfunctory glance, then looked significantly at each other and spluttered with vulgar laughter.

'I did hear summat o' the sort,' Jamie snorted.

'So that's the reason, is it!' Jeff exclaimed, and guffawed again.

'You've both drunk that much, I can't make head or tail of what you're saying,' snapped Hester. 'And don't you know it's ignorant folk that laugh at humour they're not intent on sharing.'

'I'll tell you quick enough,' Jeff volunteered, but Jamie checked him.

'I can't see what there is to laugh at,' Hester complained when the silence of the other two was shaken by sniggering. 'If you haven't heard, the jet business is becoming highly competitive these days. Them that don't progress won't survive to make a good living out of it.'

Jeff Hardcastle grinned knowingly. 'I expect t'Falgraves'll need all t'brass they can lay their hands on now.'

Jamie nudged him into silence again, making Hester even more livid. She held out the bundle of clothing.

'Here – take told of this, you daft thing! I've got something better to do than stand listening to your rubbish.'

Jamie looked uncomfortable. 'Can't you just leave it in the shop or summat for me to collect. I've had a bit of an argument with Dad, and I happen to know he's at home.'

'Oh, I'll take it myself. Maybe there'll be somebody there with more gratitude, and more sense, than you.'

Without another word to either of the lads, she bustled past them, along Flowergate, then down the turning that led to the Skeltons'.

Young Maisie opened the door, smiled at Hester and beckoned her inside. Archie Skelton and his wife were both asleep on chairs to either side of the fire. Both were open-mouthed, snoring, and Archie had unfastened the waistband of his trousers.

From the scullery at the cellar head, Sylvie and Joanie appeared, the former shrieking Hester's name so wildly that their parents wakened.

'Bloomin' heck, what's to do?' asked Archie, sniffing then dragging the back of a hand across his nose.

'Hallo, Hester love,' his wife said slowly. 'I don't know where our Jamie's got to . . .'

'It's all right, thank you, I do. I've only brought you a few things, any road. Just some stuff that might come in for the family.'

'Eeh, thank you, lass. Will you have a sit down, now you're here?' Her sleepy gaze crossed the room to the only other comfortable chair, then riveted on her husband's undress.

'Archie Skelton, look at you! Just you go upstairs and make yourself decent.'

'It'd take more than that to make me fit to mix with some folk,' he muttered. 'At least t'would have done,' he added, recalling recent news. 'Happen things are going to be different now, and them as looks down on t'rest of us will be brought up sharp.'

When he had stomped off upstairs, Edna repeated the invitation to Hester to be seated.

'And how *is* your mother?' she inquired avidly. 'It must be taking it out of her at her time of life.'

'You mean working every day, running the business?'

'That as well, of course. I wonder how long she'll be able to carry on – now.'

'Now?' Hester was compelled to ask. Still sore from one conversation in which she'd been disadvantaged, she'd not embark on another where she remained totally in the dark.

'With her carrying again, specially after all this time.'

'Oh, I see,' Hester heard a voice not quite her own responding, while the room plunged about her like a boat on the nearby sea. 'Naturally, we're not permitting her to overtax herself.'

'Be nice for your brother's little lad, won't it, having a playmate just that bit younger in the family . . .'

'Very nice,' said Hester, swallowing down agitation, and rising so she wouldn't be detained on her way to the door.

In the filthy alleyway, she leaned against the wall, inhaling deeply, time and again, fighting to regain composure. Eventually, she walked unsteadily to the top and its junction with the street. A part of her itched to run straight back to the workroom and confront her mother with the news she had heard. Another part, though, felt humiliated by the fact that it was Jamie's mother who had told her, not her own. She felt she might never bring herself to speak of her mother's condition. She ached to stride up the hill to the road that led out of the town, to walk up and over the moors, to go on walking until she made some kind of sense of things.

There was no choice – she was expected back at the works. Somehow she must summon enough self-possession to remain silent on this matter until she and her mother were at home and alone. First, however, she must permit herself a few moments to recover. She passed one teashop because of its unpleasant associations with first learning of Sally's misdemeanour, and hastened towards another that was less fashionable.

Thankful that the place was half-empty and graced by no one that she knew, Hester ordered a pot of tea and sat nibbling at a biscuit while she willed the encounters of the past hour or so to the farthest corner of her mind.

By the time she emerged she felt relatively equipped for facing her mother, believed she knew exactly how she was going to behave. There were several partly-completed designs on her desk, and if they did not fill the whole of the rest of the day she'd been meaning to have a word with her mother about the Dunsdale lad. Silas was a keen enough apprentice, but too unsure of himself by half. He needed encouraging or he'd never develop the guts to produce anything on his own. With Frank, or any of the Cloughs and with his own father, he could turn out reasonable jet pieces now. Superintended by any of the other men, he grew so nervous that he ruined most things that he touched.

Speaking on this subject, she'd be able to behave normally with Maud. Otherwise – she really did not know. She felt mortified at being kept in ignorance of her mother's condition, and it would be a long time before she felt ready to discuss it.

Still reluctantly, she climbed the worn stairs to the workroom. The first person she saw there was Frank and the sight of his head, bent again over his engraving now that he'd acknowledged her, made her stand motionless for several seconds. She couldn't bear it if he were as embarrassed as she felt.

But why should he be, she reflected, moving in a daze to hang her cloak in the office. It was a normal event for a married woman to conceive a child, after all. Why should people be astounded?

Sickened, she remembered then every word that Jeff Hardcastle and Jamie had uttered, the innuendos and the accompanying laughter. This was neither the time nor the place for working out the significance of this miserable business. Soon, though, very soon she would be compelled to unearth the cause of the disproportionate interest this matter was arousing.

Her mother was sitting at the desk, matching delivery notes to invoices, and looking rather tired but other than that little different from usual.

'You've been a long time,' Maud snapped, as if to confirm that nothing had changed.

'I'm sorry. Jamie was late, then I had to take the things down to his mother myself.'

'And she kept you talking, I suppose. Couldn't you have spared a thought for the jobs that're waiting for you here?'

'I've said I'm sorry.' And why the heck I should, I don't know; when it's because you've done something to make tongues wag.

'Well, now you're here, you'd better start thinking. Bob Dunsdale's had a quiet word with me . . .'

'About that lad of his?' When her mother nodded, Hester continued, 'I was going to mention him to you, any road. I think he needs something to give him confidence.'

'That's what his father said. According to him, the lad's all right some of the time, the rest he makes a right muck of things.'

'How would it be if we kept him with Frank Clough all

the time, at least until he's grasped all the processes Frank's best at?'

'That'd waste time – slow Frank down a lot.'

'It wouldn't waste so much of the stuff young Dunsdale's turning out. We could see what Frank thinks . . .'

'See what he thinks?' Maud slammed down the flat of her tiny hand on the desk. 'Nay, drat it, Hester, we don't ask the workers, we tell 'em.'

'Not . . .'

'Not Frank, eh?' Maud interrupted. 'We all know you think t'sun shines out on him, everybody talks about it.'

And that's a relatively innocuous matter for general discussion, thought Hester ruefully, unlike some of the things I've been hearing.

'I'll inform Frank of our intention,' her mother stated. 'Tell him to let us know if his output is greatly reduced.'

'He'll do that if he has any sense – his pay packet is what'll be affected.'

'If not his pride, when he doesn't have quite so much opportunity for tête-à-tête collaboration with t'boss's daughter.'

'It isn't because of *who* I am that Frank wants to work with me, Mother. That doesn't enter into it,' Hester began, then suddenly stopped. If she said one more word she would break down. Was there nothing fair about this life of hers? How had they reached this situation where her mother was carping at her friendship with Frank, and all the while, she herself . . .

Unable to stay in the house that evening, Hester went for a walk as soon as they had eaten dinner. Rain was falling from a heavy night sky, and whenever the wind let up she could hear the sea churning, its waves beating upon the rocks at the foot of the cliffs. Somehow though, the open air did her good and although her cloak, bonnet and shoes were soon saturated she paid the discomfort no heed.

She had crossed to the far side of the harbour from where she could discern the lights of Falgrave House and, above them, the silhouette of the church and abbey ruins. Tonight, she felt like staying away from home; at least until she sorted in her own mind the conundrum about her mother. There had been some measure of conversation during their meal which had, she supposed, been much as normal. And all the while she herself had been wondering if they were close enough as a family to endure, no matter what was said by outsiders.

There had been times in the past year and more when she'd longed to work for some other jet manufacturer, with the freedom that might bring her. Now, all she felt like was getting right away.

For the first time ever, she envied Lambert, for his ability to live his own life freed of obligations, and of involvement with family affairs.

And I'll have to be getting back over yonder, she reminded herself. She had told no one of her purpose and her father wouldn't settle while she was out of doors alone.

Choking down her sigh, she set off along one road, then down the next, across at an intersection, then down again where a steep ginnel led towards the streets near this side of the harbour. Approaching a public house, she steeled herself to walk past. At this time of night, she hated such places, was rather frightened by the raucous laughter and the shouting. And, as if drawn by her fear as she hastened past, a man emerged, but not on his own feet.

He had been hurled out through the door by an irate landlord who grinned at her before returning indoors.

The man was sprawled at her feet, near-enough unconscious with the drink he had taken. His forehead had fetched up against a gas-lamp with the impact and blood was trickling already from a long gash. With every part of her being, Hester longed to hasten past him and run, and all she could manage was to stand, staring down, appalled. Because she knew him.

'Jamie,' she said quite loudly, and then again. '*Jamie* . . .'

He did not move at all. The flow of blood was increasing, trickling down one side of his face and neck to soak his collar. Rain was saturating the rest of his clothes, seeping up from the black puddles as well as bucketing down out of the sky. Reluctantly, she bent down, said his name again, shouted it.

258

'He'll not heed thee, lass. He'll have to sleep it off.'

She straightened her back, gazed up at the wizened features of an old deckhand. 'He can't sleep here . . .' she protested foolishly.

'Yourn, is he?'

'No. But I, he's – I do know him.' God forgive her, but she'd no wish to claim friendship with Jamie this night.

'Aye. So do I, an' all. Getting a reputation for himself, whatever his name is. He were chucked out of here last night. Night afore it were out of one of them low places i' bottom end of town.'

Jamie shifted slightly and Hester, alerted, made as if to bend over him again.

'Mind out,' the old fellow cautioned, 'mind thy shoes, lass.'

Just in time, she stepped sideways. Vomit gushed from Jamie's mouth.

'Happen that were what he needed.'

The man was gone, striding away into the darkened area between this lamp and the next.

'Lord, what am I going to do?' Hester breathed.

Jamie was solidly built, would be heavier still she thought, when insensible. And the upheaval from his stomach had disturbed him far less than it had troubled her.

She was still standing over him when the inn door opened again. The laugh was familiar and followed by a cry just as swiftly recognised.

'Well, I'll go to hell!' Wally Hardcastle shouted gleefully. 'Here's Miss Falgrave, looking for her man.'

'I'm not, I just chanced to come this way,' she began furiously, before realising what an idiot she sounded. 'Was he drinking with you?' she asked, this time of Wally's son.

'Aye, he was that,' Jeff responded, grinning. 'Are you going to tell me off?' he derided.

Although far from sober, he was at least able to stand. His father appeared to be in rather better condition.

'I couldn't care less what any of you do, so long as you make yourselves responsible for getting Jamie to his lodgings now.'

Wally snorted. 'Reckon he'll not be much use to you tonight, *Miss* Falgrave? Going home without him, are you?'

'I never for one moment considered going anywhere with him tonight, didn't know where he was,' Hester protested, and realised she was making everything worse. These two were more experienced than she'd ever be, would twist any sentence she uttered.

'Funny she just happened to come along this way, in't it?' Wally observed to his son. 'Know what I reckon – we've come across a family failing! T'Falgrave women have taken to hanging round in t'streets to see what they can catch . . .'

'You'll regret saying that,' Hester began.

'Oh, I think not. What do you say, Jeff? Time achieves marvellous things. We'll not have to wait long afore none of you'll be in a position to tell decent folk what to do.'

'You're only wasting time, and if that lad doesn't die of what he's taken inside him today, he'll catch pneumonia.'

Instead of helping, though, both Hardcastles walked in a wide arc to avoid their drinking companion and, staggering now and again, made off into the distance.

I'll have to get help, decided Hester and, bracing herself, pushed open the inn door. Standing on the threshold, she noticed for the first time that the rowdyism had ceased. All she could hear was the sound of someone sweeping up broken glass. The only people left in the place were the landlord and a serving girl, scowling now as she used a bucket and mop.

'Can somebody give me a hand?' Hester pleaded.

The landlord stopped sweeping to stare curiously at her. 'You still here, lass? If you want my advice, you'll leave him to stew.'

'But he'll be ill, he . . .'

'Look, lass,' he said, laying aside the brush and striding towards her. 'I'm not a hard man, but I do have limits. See that lot over there? That's his doing – fighting, smashing glasses and pots. Threw a table, he did – the ale folk had left on it, the lot . . . clear across the room. Then when somebody punches him what does he do – pukes over everything and everybody i' range. If you've a mind to help cleaning up after your man, well and good. Otherwise, I'm afraid you're holding us up.'

'I'm sorry you've had such an upsetting time, but I'm sure Jamie didn't mean . . . he's not accustomed to having a lot to drink.'

'Jamie, you say? Jamie Skelton?'

'That's it, he's at sea a lot and . . .'

'They were right then,' he called to the girl, then faced Hester again. 'Some of my regulars – they had the tale that he'd assaulted a landlord on t'outskirts of Whitby. I only know he's lost me my best customers for the night. Cleared out they did, the back way. If he survives this, there's one won't have him in here again.'

If? Hester turned on her heel, plunged through the door into the deluge.

Jamie had moved slightly, was clutching with one hand at the lamp-post, had vomited again.

'Jamie, listen – I'm going to fetch the doctor. Just stay where you are, keep off the road, for heaven's sake. I'll run as fast as ever I can.'

Jon Davidson's home in Royal Crescent wasn't all that far distant, but it was uphill most of the way. By the time Hester had reached the beautiful house she was too breathless to speak, and perspiration was spreading through from her fiery skin to meet the rain soaking every garment.

The housekeeper had long since gone to her room, and the door was opened by the doctor himself.

'Has your mother taken a bad turn?' he demanded anxiously, as she felt his warm hand on her arm, drawing her through the door.

Speechless, she shook her head.

Jon Davidson groaned. 'Is it your father?'

'No,' she rasped, from a throat that felt as though skin and flesh were peeled from it. She swallowed, willed herself not to weep with pain, or not until she'd told him. 'Jamie Skelton – not far from here, I'll show you. He's – well, drunk, sick. He'll die if we don't do something.'

'Drunk! For God's sake, you come to fetch me for a lad who's drunk. Calling me out when . . . Oh, never mind. Wait there, I'll get my bag.'

261

She hadn't listened properly. When he turned and went back through the door that had been ajar she followed.

She had never seen anyone who was dying before. Especially not anyone so obviously dying as Ruth Davidson from the growth relentlessly devouring her from within.

'Hester . . .'

Her own name came thinly from pale lips in a sallow skin that was stretched over bones that surely were several sizes too large for her. Eyes too haunted to bear were smiling, but only for as long as one might draw breath before another pain darkened them.

'I'll not be long, Ruth,' said her husband, gathering his bag and coat. 'Shall I get Mrs . . . ?'

Ruth interrupted with a shake of her head, lowered it against the pillows. 'I'll be fine, Jon, fine.'

'You don't have to come,' Hester ventured as they reached the doorstep.

'And how will you shift him on your own, eh?'

She didn't know, what was more she cared not at all. She had witnessed a sight that drove concern for any but these two people right out of her mind.

And she was badly shaken. For many a week now she had privately been strengthened by the knowledge that Jon Davidson was to hand. It was only now that she acknowledged how massive her reliance upon him threatened to become. A situation which she must curb . . .

It was common enough, she knew, for women to learn to lean too well on doctors and clergymen. Was it two years now, or three, since the whole of Whitby shuddered when Leslie Melbeck's wife grew overfond of their local vicar? He had been compelled to resign his living. And Leslie, crushed, estranged from his wife, was left to exist alone in that cold, gaunt house, aged beyond his years by the harrowing shock.

Chapter 14

Jamie had moved again, and was now leaning against the base of the gas-lamp, his head stirring from side to side. Blood was congealing around the gash. He moaned when Jon Davidson took him firmly by the chin and commanded that he open his eyes.

'Can't . . .' he mumbled as the doctor inspected his forehead.

'You'd better learn how,' said Jon sharply. 'You're darned lucky I've turned out for somebody's who's not ill. If you don't cooperate while I examine you, you'll be left as you are.'

Gingerly, Jamie opened his eyes, put a hand to his pulsing head.

'I've a good mind to leave you here for the law to pick up. I'll not have you occupying a hospital bed that someone who hasn't bought their suffering is needing. And I can't think your mother'll be pleased to see you in this state.'

'He's in lodgings,' Hester told him.

'Not surprised. From what I've heard, young Skelton's taken to causing havoc anywhere that there's drink available. Where are you biding, lad?'

Jamie only moaned again, shook his head, then clutched either side of it where the temples were threatening to burst open.

The doctor grasped each hand and hauled them away, then shook Jamie slightly to try and drag him out of his near-unconscious state.

'You've two choices, Skelton – direct me to where you're living, or sleep the night here with your own mess.'

Jamie raised heavy eyelids again, and tried to focus on the doctor's face.

Jon turned to Hester. 'There's no cause to look so anxious, love. There's nothing wrong with him that won't be cured by a good clearing out and uninterrupted sleep. And it looks as though the former's begun some while since.'

'I just wish he could be made to see how daft he's been.'

'More money than sense, that's his trouble.'

'And he's supposed to be saving up to recompense his father for that boat.'

'Fat chance of that when he's out carousing like this each time he sets foot in Whitby.'

'I don't think it's that often, is it? Happen this is one of the first occasions . . .'

'*You* don't get fetched out to patch up folk that's been in every fracas where the likes of him congregate. There's a nucleus of troublemakers, and he's getting to be as bad as any.'

'I work that hard at sea, I earn a few drinks,' Jamie mumbled.

'Oh – coming round, are you? Let's be having you . . .'

'Do you need a hand?' asked Hester.

Jon grinned, shook his head. Slipping a hand under each of Jamie's arms, he dragged him upwards until he was more or less standing, but still supported by the lamp-post. He picked him up then, bodily, and taking him over his shoulder headed towards the landaulet.

'Just steady the horse, will you, Hester?'

Jamie groaned and sighed, and declared that he was dying as they set off through the town.

'All right,' said the doctor, smiling wryly. 'Just do it quietly, eh?'

Somehow, he managed to keep Jamie sufficiently alert to direct them to his lodgings. He left Jamie where he was until they had obtained an answer at the door, then carried him again all the way upstairs.

'Makes you wonder, doesn't it?' he remarked when he had got his breath back and they were on their way again. 'There's your father the way he is – and that's what he saved the lad for! There's no justice, Hester love, I hope you've accepted that.'

'I believe I'm beginning to.' Her sadness, though, was more for this man and his ailing wife than for her father. How could there be anything worse than devoting your life to healing folk, yet being unable to do a thing for the woman you loved?

'Thank you ever so much,' she said when he let her out at Falgrave House. 'Can I offer you a hot drink or something?'

'No, thank you, my dear. I'd best be getting home. If there's been anyone else wanting me, Ruth'll be growing uneasy.'

'And she needs you herself, if there's no other calls on you.'

'Aye, lass, aye.'

'Well, thanks once again. You'll charge Jamie, I hope?'

At last, Jon laughed. 'You may depend on that.'

'Let me know if he doesn't pay up.'

Maud was waiting just inside the drawing room on her favourite Great Exhibition chair which was velvet-upholstered mahogany with a Worcester porcelain plaque depicting Prince Albert. Her blue eyes were shadowed, and her normally pretty lips drawn tightly together.

'What time do you call this, young lady? Where've you been?'

'I'm sorry, Mother, I only went out for a walk, but . . .' She was cut short by another abrupt question.

'Why didn't you tell us?'

'Because I was only going to be out for a short while.'

'Why do you always have to cause us so much anxiety? Especially with me in my condition.'

Hester's protest froze on her lips. Was she about to learn the truth? 'What condition, Mother?'

Maud stared at her for several moments. 'You don't know, then? I wondered.' Her tone had levelled. 'You'd better sit down so's we can have a bit of a talk.'

There was a fire dying in the grate, and Maud stabbed at it with the poker which she then returned to its brass stand. Hester sensed that she was weighing her next words.

'You know I'm fond of children, always have been. Well, I'm going to have another, before I'm too old.'

Hester didn't know how she bit back the words asking if Maud wasn't too old now. She certainly looked it.

265

'That's nice,' she said. It seemed to be what her mother wished to hear. Her own sentiments wouldn't be of interest.

'You don't seem very surprised.'

'If you must know, I'm not. I had heard tell.'

For once her mother's disconcertment wasn't concealed, but Hester was the one who felt she ought to say something.

'It'll give you and Father a new interest. When – when will it be?'

'Oh, not for a long while yet.' She didn't want Hester knowing how long she had kept her in the dark. 'And when he or she arrives it'll not make a lot of difference to you. For a time, naturally, I'll be at home. But I shall still administer some aspects of the works. We might appoint somebody, temporary like, to work alongside you.'

'I think I could manage without that.'

'Well, we'll see. We'll see . . .'

Maud had risen. Automatically, Hester stood up as well. She noticed now that her mother was, indeed, putting on weight. Her exhausted brain struggled to unearth some reason why the people of Whitby should be so fascinated by the fact that she was expecting a baby. She abandoned the matter because she discovered she was literally too tired to think.

'What did hold you up tonight, any road?' Maud inquired, glad to recall something that prevented questions being directed at herself.

'Oh, it was Jamie Skelton. Made a right fool of himself this time. I came across him just as he was thrown out of a public house.'

'Had he been fighting?'

'Among other things. He was drunk.' She'd no need to conceal the fact from anyone. She'd no intention of sustaining the friendship between herself and Jamie now. As far as she was concerned, he'd finally disgusted her.

'You didn't try to look after him?' her mother asked, torn between horror that *her* daughter might become involved in anything so degrading, and grudging respect if she'd tackled such a task.

'Not really,' said Hester, wearily walking towards the door. 'I fetched Dr Davidson.'

'I bet he was pleased.'

'I felt terrible about it. His wife's very ill. I saw her.'

'Aye, poor soul. He was telling your father the other day. She hasn't got long.'

The following morning, Maud announced that she wouldn't be at the workshop until later; an event so unusual that Hester was compelled to reflect on the fact of the expected baby. The previous night's rain had continued, so she wasn't sorry to have Kilner and the brougham to take her to the works.

She arrived to find Frank and Harold Clough looking worried, and their father nowhere in evidence.

'Thank goodness you're here,' said Frank. 'Father's got the influenza, he's sorry he won't be in today.'

'We'll manage,' she assured them both. 'But tell him I'm sorry to hear he's poorly. You two had better give me a hand while I dole out the jet.'

Some of the men already had items which they had been crafting the previous day. To the rest, she gave out pieces that she considered most suitable for their individual talents.

Bob Dunsdale grinned at her. 'Thanks, that looks good quality stuff,' he remarked, turning over the rough jet on his bench.

One of the older men, who rarely said a great deal, also gave her a smile. 'That's a grand bit of jet, Miss Hester, just right for yon double locket I've been told to get on wi'.'

Wally Hardcastle, as she might have anticipated, had no word of approval, merely a sarcastic grin which had nothing to do with their work.

'Did you get your young fellow home with you all right last night?'

'The doctor and I got him to his lodgings,' she informed him coldly, mortified because Frank was at her side, holding the box of rough jet and staring at her in amazement. 'And when you drink with Jamie Skelton again you can tell him from me that I'm disgusted with him.'

'Nay, you'll be seeing him afore me, I'll be bound,' Wally continued and winked.

About to rise to his bait, Hester felt a firm hand beneath her elbow. Frank had more idea than she how to deal with the likes of Wally Hardcastle.

Later, when the jet was distributed and everyone was either treadling away to drive their wheels or engraving by hand, she paused beside Frank's bench.

'There's something I want to know about your father, it won't take a minute,' she said. 'Will you come into the office, please?' Once inside it, away from the men, she admitted, 'It's not about him at all, Frank. But there's enough talk goes on in this place, and in the town. I want to know what's going on. What are folk saying?'

Frank hesitated, coloured from his blue smock up to the brim of his dusty hat, then paled alarmingly.

'Hadn't you better sit down?' he suggested.

'What for? I'm not scared of learning that Jamie's earning a reputation for hard drinking, and knocking folk about. Dr Davidson told me as much last night.'

She read the relief in his lovely green eyes, and understood that he'd been about to answer a totally different question, regarding someone else.

'Aye, aye,' Frank agreed. 'I've seen him on the odd occasion myself when I've gone for a sup of ale. Mind you, he is away at sea a lot.'

'And that entitles him to be blind drunk while he's in Whitby, eh?'

'It's not really my business . . .'

'Nor mine, Frank. Believe you me, I don't care any longer what he does.'

'Ay, lass – I'm sorry.'

His genuine concern made her smile. 'In a day or two I might start missing the way he and I were such pals. You can save your sympathy till then. Today, I'm that mad I just want to find out how serious this is and confront him with it. Make him see as he's letting himself down.'

'Hester – don't. Don't do it, please. He's got a right temper, has that one. He might set on you.'

'So it's true then. The landlord said last night that he'd smashed the place up.'

Frank nodded. 'Our Harold saw Skelton start a fight t'other evening. Didn't wait to watch, though, did our Harold.'

'Last night I blamed the company he's keeping, but only to myself. You know he's thick with Jeff Hardcastle?'

'I've seen 'em together, aye.'

'Today, I've come to realise it's Jamie himself. He's always been a bit of a rebel – and to think I used to admire him for it.'

'Take care, Hester, please – you can't think you'll avoid him for long. Whitby's not that big.'

She sighed. 'I know, I know.' After a moment or two she managed to smile. 'Thanks, Frank.'

He had reached the door when she quietly called him back. 'What else was it that you were going to say, in the first place?'

Again the high colour sped up across his face. How could he speak to her of what he'd heard, first in the inn where a lot of the jet workers gathered, then when he'd gone with his mother to carry home her provisions from the market . . .

But if he said nothing, though, left Hester to find out, mightn't it be even worse for her? When folk are intrigued by gossip, especially when it concerns people of some local standing, they aren't choosy over their words. Already, he'd heard several crude interpretations of Mrs Falgrave's condition. He could tell Hester now, gently, and try – God knows how – to offer some sort of explanation.

This time, she sat down in readiness, making him even more aware that she was having to steel herself.

'Can't it wait till tonight,' he suggested, 'after that lot have gone home?'

'I can't think waiting is going to do a lot for my concentration all day, Frank, nor for yours. And, again, I think I do know half a tale . . . It's my – my mother we're talking *around*, isn't it? It's her condition that we're finding too embarrassing to mention properly.'

Frank nodded, swallowed.

Hester smiled wanly. 'You'd better sit down an' all. They're all gawping in through t'window, any road. Your Harold'll fall off his stool any second.'

He sat to her left, went to rest his hands on the desk, saw they'd already acquired a layer of black dust and placed them awkwardly one on each knee.

'You must be prepared for a certain amount of interest, I'm afraid Hester.'

'Aye, I reckon that's right. I'm pretty curious myself.' Only 'curious' was a massive understatement and gave no hint of the extent of the hurt she'd suffered because no one had considered her worthy of being told.

'It – it might have staggered everybody a bit, in the ordinary course of events,' Frank plunged on. 'With young Olive and Bernard being . . . well, whatever age they are.'

'Olive's getting on for fifteen now, Bernard's just gone thirteen.'

'But, with the way things are . . .' He swallowed, shrugged helplessly, coughed.

Despite her own embarrassment, Hester had to help him out. She'd got them into this acutely difficult conversation.

'Since my father's not moved a muscle for well over twelve months, and everybody knows he can only get from the bed to that there chair if he's lifted, how the blazes can he be the one who's – who . . . Oh, God, now I'm crying.'

She blew her nose determinedly, then blinked. 'I'm all right now. It's just . . .'

Frank nodded understandingly. He hadn't realised it until just now, but Hester had been blissfully ignorant about physical matters. So, this had been a double if not triple shock. First learning of her mother's pregnancy, then being astonished to consider that Maud Falgrave still wanted relations, and then wondering . . . ceaselessly wondering. He blessed his own life in that crowded little house where they'd each in turn soon gathered what was happening when the creak of bedsprings and other sounds came through the paper-thin wall dividing off their parents' bedroom. And, after the appropriate length of time, another little Clough appeared.

'Frank – what are you thinking?'

Initially, he wouldn't say, but others would – and with no consideration for her long-sustained innocence.

'About you and the way your home will have kept you insulated – yes, insulated.'

'From learning what man and wife do together, aye.' She sighed, shook her head. 'I'm thick, I suppose, dense. I believed what I were told when I was little, when our Olive was born. They said she was chosen, *chosen*.'

He couldn't entirely discipline a faint smile.

'Happen if we had a good laugh about it, I'd feel better,' she told him. 'We must look ridiculous to the rest of the town. My mother's turned forty, Frank.' She paused, gritted her teeth. 'Who are they saying the father is?'

He gave her a look. 'Nobody's gone that far.'

'They just speculate, eh? Same as the rest of us.' She gulped. 'I'd have sworn on the family Bible that there was nobody. Apart from anything else, when does she have the time?'

'Look, love.' Checked by his own endearment, he paused then resumed swiftly because there were problems far greater than the means of addressing her. 'So far as I'm aware, there's nobody in the whole of Whitby has attempted to name anyone. All you can do is the same as your mother's doing – let them talk till they tire of the matter, and don't let it go home. I know it's easy for me to say it, but Hester, you're not alone in this – you're not alone.'

Frank had helped. She wasn't sure how, but maybe simply by being there to share her dreadful misgivings, he'd strengthened her to endure.

Many times during those next few weeks, Hester recollected every word that had been said, and reflected on some that hadn't, as well. And she expected that she would cope as the birth of the latest Falgrave grew relentlessly nearer.

At home the atmosphere was better than she'd anticipated. Whatever the circumstances leading up to this situation, her father appeared unperturbed. He was still impatient with his incapacity and sometimes with those on whom he was compelled to rely, but he'd behaved this way ever since that day in November 1861. Towards his wife he seemed more genial. Hester noticed he rarely ranted at her for the purpose she served at the works, and which was denied him. And Maud did still work there, if for somewhat shorter hours.

What Abel did not know, and Hester would be the last to enlighten him, was that her mother was doing less and less actual running of the business. Hester herself was required to go over and agree delivery terms for the rough jet with Cousin Issac. Not that she objected to visiting Sandsend, provided it didn't involve entering the mine again. And she was obliged to maintain contact with the wholesale dealers who took their completed jewellery, figurines and set pieces.

If her mind had been left free to devote the rest of her time to designing, she'd have felt better, but nothing alleviated the intensity of work. Once, a short while after that terrible night when he'd been thrown out of the inn, Jamie appeared outside the Falgrave works, apologised and begged Hester to overlook the misdemeanour. Sadly, she was unable to consider any such forgiveness. He had degraded himself, and she couldn't forget that there'd been previous occasions: there would be others. She told him how she regarded such degradation, and afterwards saw him not at all.

Most weeks, the only place she went, other than in connection with work, was to St Mary's. And there her concentration seemed minimal. The glances of other parishioners revealed that they were as well aware as the rest of Whitby that Maud Falgrave was drawing attention to herself in a scandalous fashion. Maud herself never attended service now, claiming that no one in her condition should appear publicly, but making Hester believe her sins weighed too heavily.

Two months before the baby was due Maud took Hester aside one evening, leaving Olive and Bernard talking with their father.

'I'm getting rid of Nurse Clapper,' she announced fiercely. 'Your father's greatly elated, but I shall get someone else in, someone accustomed to dealing with infants as well. I don't see paying two nurses if one will serve,' she added, with characteristic Yorkshire thrift.

Hester was too exhausted to be particularly interested. Wally Hardcastle had been inciting the men to agitate for a gas engine instead of treadles to power the wheels, and only her intervention along with Edwin Clough's had prevented the workroom from coming to a standstill. She had been determined not to raise the matter of new equipment with either her mother or father. All the Clough family, Bob Dunsdale and some of the older men insisted that the treadles were adequate, and that Hardcastle would always be casting around for some cause for his so-called union.

'You haven't asked why I'm ridding us of that woman.' Her mother had been regarding her keenly for over a minute, couldn't bear having aroused such minuscule interest in a matter meant to introduce her own statement.

'She abused me, that's what – in my own home. Verbally, to a degree bordering on profanity.' Clapper hadn't used the word harlot, or only by implication but, already almost defeated by gossip, Maud had been incensed. 'In case you're in doubt, this child I'm carrying *is* a Falgrave, fathered by the man I've loved and will go on loving till the day I'm carried up Church Stair to the graveyard in my box.'

The words were meant to assure. Maud's utterance emphasised the talk there'd been throughout Whitby – where William Scoresby, presenting the town with a pump, had it inscribed with a Latin text that when translated read: *Water for the use of all. Draw it. Drink it. But don't stay gossiping.* What had she herself believed in the secret recesses of her soul, during the long night hours devoid of sleep?

Despite her tiredness which seemed to increase daily, the nights when Hester lay awake gnawing at her problems were many. She grew pale, thinner even than before, completely lost her appetite. If she ate of an evening, to pacify her mother, she wanted nothing more than an occasional cup of tea through until the following evening. Now that she alone was leaving the house to reach the works by six of a morning, who was about to care that she ate no breakfast? Mrs Richmond and May Thorpe might fuss for a time, but eventually accepted that they could not make Miss Hester eat, even for her own good.

Frank noticed, of course. How could he cease to observe every change in Hester's appearance, the worsening of her pallor, the dreadful shadows beneath her lovely dark eyes? But since their discussion about her mother, weeks ago now, she seemed to avoid every opportunity for private conversation.

He was there, though, the day she collapsed. He it was who went running through the town to bring Jon Davidson.

The men had carried Hester into the office, had lain her on the floor, for where else was there space to stretch an unconscious person flat? She didn't rouse until the doctor had been kneeling beside her for fully five minutes. The instant she saw him, the anxiety gnawing into her nerves for weeks emerged as panic.

'What are you doing here? What's happened? Is it Mother?'

'It's you, lass, that's unwell. And by the look of you that's the way you've been this past month or more. But you're not to be worried by that, you'll pull round once we stop you neglecting yourself.'

His examination, after he'd cleared Edwin Clough and Frank from the doorway, was gentle and thorough.

'It's home to bed for you, Hester. A long rest and then we'll start building you up . . .'

'No, Jon, not home, not yet. No, please, no.'

His blue eyes registered his perplexity. 'You can't lie here, love.'

'I'll be all right. Just let me get up and sit for a minute.'

'Hester, I'm your doctor. I'll not heed your arguments.'

'But it's at home where I feel worst.'

He took her to his surgery. He wasn't seeing patients there that day. Helping her through the door, he led the way to his examination room and told her to lie on the couch.

'You'll take some tea in a while. First, though, what's bothering you?'

She could contain the appalling anxiety no longer. 'It's my mother, of course – all the talk. And I can't believe any differently. Father can't have given her this baby, can he?'

Jon assisted her up on to the couch, drew out a chair and sat facing her. 'Have you never found one thing to marvel at in all your life?' he began, astonishing himself by the tenor of his words, today of all days. 'Nay, Hester, you'll

274

be telling me next that there's nothing unexpected where folk are concerned.'

'But he can hardly move, you know that better than anyone . . .'

'His spine and his limbs are virtually immobilised, agreed. But that isn't to say that his becoming a father again is a medical impossibility. When your mother confided her condition I saw no reason to utter any of the questions that you are asking.'

'You think I should mind my own business, don't you?'

'If I did, lass, I'd have been direct with you and said so. No, Hester, I simply believe you're causing yourself a deal of unnecessary anguish by not accepting the facts as they are, and getting on with your own life.'

'That might be easier if the whole of Whitby didn't seem to be agog.'

He smiled sympathetically. 'Aye, well – I don't suppose any of you enjoy hearing the Falgrave name bandied about. But if your mother can weather this you might at least stand by her.'

'Yes, but she *knows* the truth, doesn't she?'

'And you don't want to believe her.'

'That's not fair, I . . . Oh, I'm just so tired and confused. I wish I could get miles away from it all.'

Why did he look so shocked, Hester wondered instantly. He'd seen the state she was in – wasn't it obvious that she needed to escape?

'You'd not leave Whitby?' he asked, frowning. 'Your – your family will need you, Hester. And what about the jet works?'

What response could she make, while he appeared so concerned that his blue eyes had a frantic look she'd not read in them before.

'I don't imagine I'd desert before one of the others showed any aptitude for the business.'

'Do Olive or Bernard show any inclinations in that direction?'

'Nothing definite. Father wishes them to prolong their education, anyway.'

'Which keeps the weight squarely on your shoulders. I

275

know it's far from easy, my dear, even without this latest trouble. But I'm certain that if you gave your mind to enduring it, you'd manage very competently. And I'll see you pay more attention to your general health and well-being.'

'There's nothing wrong with me,' Hester began, then saw his expression and nodded. 'Thank you, and you always so busy, and your wife so ill . . .'

'I'm afraid Ruth passed away in the early hours this morning.'

'Oh, no! Oh, I am sorry. But you shouldn't have let me go on and on about my selfish anxieties when . . .' She reached out and grasped his arm. He glanced down at her slender fingers then faced her again.

'It's done me no harm to be freed of my own company. I had to cancel surgery today, but that didn't mean I was any better for sitting idle.'

They drank the tea that he had promised, although now Hester felt she ought to leave the doctor's house at once.

'You'll have plenty to organise between now and the funeral,' she said sympathetically. 'Are there lots of relatives on their way here?'

'No, nothing like that. We both were only ones.'

Hester represented the Falgraves at Ruth Davidson's funeral service. She felt out of place when almost all of the other people paying respect were male, and the doctor's wife, looking strangely peaceful in her coffin, was the first person she'd seen dead. In the windswept graveyard, though, Jon grasped both her hands.

'Thank you for being here, Hester. This day hasn't been easy.'

'Don't forget there's always somebody in at Falgrave House, and Father especially enjoys your company.'

It seemed after that short while in the churchyard on the cliff that the sea breeze buffeting their clothes might have dispersed her longing to escape all the local gossip about her family. She returned to work later that day determined that if her friend and doctor could survive such a dreadful loss she could, at least, overcome her few difficulties.

By the time Maud's baby was imminent Hester had willed herself to ignore the talk she still heard in the town. Wasn't she far too busy by now to allow any distractions to divert her resolve from making Falgraves' the best jet workroom?

Since her mother had been compelled to cease visiting the works, Hester had been free to introduce whatever new designs might be approved in brief consultations with both parents in their home.

Her father seemed to enjoy overseeing the accounting side, and she'd not dream of taking that from him, but she was thankful to have more of a say in administering the works.

The day that Cecil Arkwright appeared at the top of the narrow dusty stairs there, she was astounded. She also felt apprehensive, but tried to conceal that as she invited him into the tiny office and indicated that he should be seated.

As he had on earlier occasions with her mother, Mr Arkwright remained on his feet, appearing to draw himself up to his full height.

'I understand there's to be a happy event in your household, Miss Falgrave,' he began. 'In case you're unaware of it, I'll explain that I have suggested in the past that it could be advantageous to combine the resources of our two companies.'

'I had heard,' she said dryly, 'but do go on . . .'

'I can't believe you're eager to yoke yourself to a business that'll keep you worked to death for the rest of your days.'

'There's worse fates,' said Hester, and meant it. She'd been sobered by Ruth Davidson's death.

'And prevent your having time for a life of your own – marriage and so on,' he persisted.

'My mother married, didn't she, while she was working here.'

He smiled slightly, smoothed his lovely white hair. 'From what I hear, you're integrated more fully into the running of the place, to say nothing of your designing. And she, of course, had first a father and then her husband in the business.'

'My father is still involved, you know. Just because you no longer see him here, it doesn't mean . . .'

He silenced her with a gesture of one elegant hand. Hester could have struck him.

'You're evidently here with yet another offer to buy us out,' she said sharply. 'Did you hope maybe that you'd wear me down more readily that you could grind down my parents? I can't speak for them, of course, though I'll pass on your interest. But whatever they might conclude about the future of Falgraves' I'll obstruct you with every ounce of my strength.'

He departed almost immediately, and left Hester smiling to herself. When she eventually had the opportunity for a private word with Frank Clough, he remarked on her satisfied smile.

'I trust it's not because you've agreed a deal with yon Arkwright.'

'You should know me better than that by now. What's more, I hope you're all of a mind to give of better than your best. I want to see Falgraves' with a Royal Warrant, and taking trade from folk like the Arkwrights.'

That evening as she walked up the hill to the house in a cold drizzle, Hester was fired by ambition and determination to oppose any person, even from her own family, who thought the time had come to relinquish the business.

The doctor's landaulet was by the front steps. As she hurried indoors May Thorpe came running down the wide staircase, her plain face fiery with agitation.

'Eeh, Miss Hester, thank goodness you're home. The doctor's with Mrs Falgrave, and he's warned us she's in for a difficult time.'

'Oh, dear – I must go and see her!'

May clutched her arm in a manner normally forbidden. 'Oh, no – they won't let you in there, Miss.'

'Where is she?'

'In the master bedroom, but . . .'

Hester prised each of May Thorpe's fingers from her arm, raced up the stairs and along the landing. She tried the door of the master bedroom but it would not yield.

Jon Davidson heard the commotion and opened the door. 'Is it right,' she asked, 'can't anyone come in?'

Sighing, he grasped her shoulder. 'I'm sorry, Hester.

Your mother's been given medication to ease her pain. Look – I have to make sure one of you understands, and your father's scarcely in a state to bear the truth. Your mother's condition is grave, and there is concern also for the unborn child. A colleague is on his way here now. If he agrees, we'll maybe operate.' We might save either the mother or the infant, he thought, but could not bring himself to darken further those exquisite brown eyes by telling her.

'Operate?'

'With the introduction of chloroform, remember, operations have become far less dangerous. But I must return to my patient. Be assured that we will do everything in our power.'

'I know you will. I do know.' But sometimes no amount of wishing or skill could achieve a thing. Wasn't that why he'd suffered the devastation of losing his wife?

'Your father is in one of the guest rooms. When you've had a bit of something to eat, you'd best see he doesn't brood too much on his own.'

She went to her father at once, kissed his anxious face, then sat as close as she could beside his invalid chair. She took in her fingers one of the hands that always felt so lifeless and too cold.

'The doctor says they're doing all they can. He's got one of his colleagues coming to assist, they'll not be long then.'

Abel sighed. He'd grown to know Jon Davidson well, especially these past few weeks since he'd come so often to Falgrave House for company.

'Nay, Hester, I've not lost my faculties, you know. Jon's worried sick about your mother, do you think I can't tell? And another thing – he's not the sort to call in some other doctor to help if it were a straightforward job that he could manage on his own.'

Neither of them could have eaten. When Olive and later Bernard appeared, Hester and then her father attempted to cheer the strangely subdued young people. If they succeeded in convincing them that Maud would be all right and would eventually produce a healthy baby, they themselves remained unconvinced.

The other doctor was heard driving up. As the carriage

slowed at the front steps Hester thought to run down and greet him. But then she remembered that delaying him might prove crucial, a fact which was confirmed by the haste with which Mrs Richmond was heard to conduct him up the staircase and along to the master bedroom.

The housekeeper came to the room where Hester was sitting with her father and offered them a meal, but accepted their refusal without demur. Mrs Richmond's uncharacteristic response added to the feeling of abnormality, increasing their apprehension.

Beyond the windows early darkness, brought by the rain which had intensified to a downpour, gathered about the house, isolating them with their alarm. The wind wailed in the chimneys, rattled every pane of glass, and sighed under many a door.

'You can hear the sea,' observed Hester, thinking that it seemed to churn against the rocks in echo of her tormented thoughts.

'Aye, aye,' said her father wearily.

'I do love Mother, you know,' she asserted suddenly.

'Folks that live on top of one another can't be expected to get on all the time.'

They were silent once more, both reflecting that the night would be long if they found no better than this to fill the hours of apprehension, neither knowing what else there was to say.

It was almost four in the morning, and still no word from the master bedroom when Abel turned his head to his daughter.

'If your mother doesn't survive, I'll swear it's a judgement on my vanity. From the day she told me she was expecting again I've blessed the knowledge that there'd be some proof I wasn't quite dead.'

Hester felt tears slipping down her cheeks and spilling onto the working gown which she hadn't changed. Before, she might have prayed for proof that the gossip mustn't be heeded. Now that proof hung in the strained atmosphere of this room, in words that only seemed to presage grief.

Chapter 15

The wet and windy dawn brought Mrs Richmond to draw back the heavy curtains on a familiar aspect of rain-lashed houses and sea. Hester released her father's hand and stood up on legs that felt wooden.

'If there really is no news, Mrs Richmond, I'm going to have the reason out of somebody. With two doctors in the house, there must be something they ought to be doing.'

'Ay, Miss Hester love, don't you know they've struggled night long both of them. The midwife who's attending told me not an hour ago that the bairn's so weak it'll not make its own way into t'world.'

'Then why weren't we told?'

Fleetingly, the housekeeper's glance flicked towards the invalid chair where Abel's dark eyes were smudged with grey shadowing, his cheeks haggard and sallow.

Hester stepped out of the room with her, drew the door closed after them.

'And Mother? I thought they were going to operate?'

'We'll all have to be very brave. The poor mistress is not much better herself. Her age is agin her, you know, and her being so tiny. It didn't matter as much when she was more supple, but now . . .'

'But Jon – Dr Davidson said something about taking the baby away.'

'Aye, but only as a last resort.'

'They don't think Mother'd withstand an operation, you mean?'

'Sounds like that's it . . .'

Her father's shout startled them both, brought them running back into the room.

'Am I not master in my own home, now I'm not able to master any one of you! I'm not an imbecile that you must talk in whispers of matters concerning *my* life, *my* wife . . .'

'I'll be about my duties, Miss Hester,' murmured Mrs

Richmond, only too anxious to escape. 'You know where to find me if there's anything you need.'

'You'd best tell me what all that muttering was about just now,' Abel snapped at his daughter. 'And I'll thank you to mind in future that you'll not be in charge of what goes on here even if, God forbid, I be left without your mother. So long as I linger on I'll be treated like the man who's provided this home and . . .'

He was interrupted by the door being flung open. Jon Davidson stood there, his face florid with exertion, tiredness dulling his eyes, though nothing had diminished his assertion.

'Abel, don't be so damned stupid, man! Your wife needs rest, and how'll we ensure that while you're ranting like a bull! We had to operate, in the end. It's taken it out of her, it'll be touch and go for some time.'

'But – but she is hanging on?'

'Aye, just about.'

'And the child?'

'A girl. A frail bit of a thing, but her breathing's regular enough.'

'We'll name her Ruth,' Abel announced. 'Whatever else Maud wants her called, one of her names'll be Ruth.'

Watching the doctor's exhausted features, Hester saw his slight smile, and then the tears that filled blue eyes.

'I'll tell you the minute they've both been cleaned up.' The survival of both mother and infant depended now on a higher authority, but he'd not deny his friend the opportunity of seeing them both. If they delayed over-long it could well be too late.

'I'll take your father in there myself,' Jon told Hester when he returned to the room where they were waiting. *He'd* been alarmed by how ill Maud Falgrave looked, he'd not expose the girl to such distress.

'Just as you wish,' she said coolly. They owed him a great deal, but that didn't mean she automatically agreed with all his instructions.

She was surprised when, leaving Abel with his wife and infant, the doctor reappeared in the doorway of the room.

'It was to spare you,' he began. 'You've endured a lot

this night, remaining with your father. Insisting on seeing your mother at this moment will only make you feel worse.'

'She's that bad, is she?'

Gravely, he nodded. 'But a few hours may see some improvement. We can only pray that it will.'

'Then I'd better get ready for work. I'm late as it is . . .'

'Hester – take the day off. You've not had a wink of sleep, I'll be bound.'

'And how many times have you worked a full day when you've been called out in the night? I shall be all right.'

'You're a good lass, Hester. Take care of yourself, mind.'

'I shall have to, shan't I? There'll be no one else to run the works for some while now.'

It was nearly Christmas before Maud began to regain some measure of her normal energy, and longer than that before little Ruth Falgrave was thriving.

'Christmas will be a quiet time, this year,' Abel announced to the family. 'Though we'll have one evening when the door stands open for friends.'

Hester didn't find that prospect particularly appealing. Who was there whom she might invite? She'd suggested once or twice recently that Frank should call on her father but, although still as friendly towards herself, he was reluctant to visit the house even on a quite ordinary occasion.

There was no one else. Jamie Skelton had contacted her again the last time he was ashore for any length of time, but she hadn't been able to believe his claim that he had moderated his drinking. He still frequented the public houses of the town, along with Jeff Hardcastle and his father, and none of them cared that they earned reputations as hard-drinking seekers of trouble.

A rest was the most Hester expected of the change from daily routine, and maybe the opportunity to spend some time with her tiny sister. Lambert, Sally and young Abel would be there as well, although Sally had grown so many airs as a Grenadier's wife that Hester wasn't entirely certain she liked her quite so well as previously.

By Boxing Day evening, Hester was feeling rather out of place in her own home. Olive and Bernard had their friends

Belle and Cedric Jenkins there. The two girls were enchanted with the baby as well as little Abel. Sally, in turn, basked in their approval of her offspring and was content to keep an eye on Ruth whilst joining in the fun as her son took advantage of an appreciative audience.

From the sitting room drifted the voices of the men – whose company automatically included Bernard and the Jenkins lad, both highly delighted to share in the yarning. Leslie Melbeck had arrived first, always glad to forsake his solitary abode when the season dictated he should find company. Sidney Etherington had left his wife Sadie chatting with Maud and could be heard holding forth now on some outrage generated by his mother-in-law.

Suddenly, though, Mrs Richmond appeared, sent by Maud to interrupt the men's tale-telling. Everyone was to gather in the drawing room. Charades were to be organised while Nurse Scott, who was already well established at Falgrave House, whisked Ruth away to her cot.

'Isn't it young Abel's bedtime an' all?' asked Maud, smiling firmly in Sally's direction.

Sally hadn't altered sufficiently to oppose Lambert's mother, and meekly went upstairs carrying her son.

As the men came through from the sitting room, Hester was surprised to see Jon Davidson among them. She knew he'd been told he was welcome here at any time, but she knew also that he'd appeared reluctant to attend.

'Do think anyone would notice if I slipped away?' he whispered now, after they'd exchanged greetings. 'I never was one for games, and these days . . .'

Hester smiled sympathetically. 'You can take me with you if you're leaving. I've been feeling decidedly uneasy.'

'But this is your home,' Jon protested, concern for her superseding his own feelings.

'I don't suppose that has to mean it's synonymous with everything I happen to like. And, anyway, I suspect I'm fast developing into a bore who is interested in nothing but work.'

'There are worse enthusiasms.'

'Still, happen we ought to humour Mother today – if only because she finally does appear to have regained spirits as well as strength. Could you bear to pretend you're enjoying these silly pastimes?'

As it turned out, neither of them had much difficulty in pretending. Before the hour was out they were laughing as much as anyone, if not entirely with those present rather than at them.

Supper was served and with it a quantity of wine which helped both Hester and Jon to behave as though they had no cares. Some while later she chose him for her partner in a treasure hunt quickly organised by Bernard and his friend Cedric.

'Come on, we're to search the entire house,' said Hester, smiling as she seized the doctor by the hand and hustled him up the staircase.

Although scarcely serious about the task, they finished ahead of all the rest and laughed together as they collected their prizes.

Somehow, the laughter continued as they went out into the hall to recover their breath. Suddenly, Jon Davidson was gazing at her. He drew her to him with the slender hand still locked within his.

'Do we need mistletoe?'

She shook her head, moved by the realisation that their enjoyment had encouraged him to begin to forget his bereavement.

His lips were firm over her own, the arm which went about her waist crushed her to his chest. And the kiss continued on and on, a tender expression of affection gradually gaining intensity as it indicated their mutual need.

'With someone like you, Hester,' he told her eventually, 'I begin to believe I might survive.'

She remembered then all that he'd once said about doctors remaining a little aloof. How lonely he must feel since losing his wife.

'It's strange you should say that; earlier today I was wishing I had someone I could invite here.'

'Happen you'll invite me again one day.'

'Happen you'll realise you don't have to wait to be asked.'

Jon Davidson did come more frequently to Falgrave House,

and reproached Hester more than once for exhausting herself by overworking.

'Tell me a better way and I'll try it,' she answered him one evening the following summer. 'There's times, you know, when I'd gladly chuck the lot.'

His anxiety developed different roots, no less strong. 'You wouldn't leave Whitby?'

'Maybe not, but I have to believe the chance exists.'

'Is the work really that gruelling? I know jet working's dirty, but . . .'

Hester interrupted with a short laugh. 'If only that were the limit of the trouble! It's never been the dirt that's bothered me. No, it's the frustration gets me down. It's obvious now that Mother will never do more than pop in now and again since she's had the baby. And my time just seems to vanish into the air with all sorts of daft little jobs that keep the place running. I don't know when I last sat down and worked on an important new design. Most of the stuff we're producing hasn't changed in long enough. It's as well it's still selling, but there's not much stimulation in it for me, and I suspect not much for the workers.'

Jon sympathised but at the same time he was concerned for Hester's health. She was too young to shoulder so many cares, and to come home each night to a house arranged about her father's incapacity.

'Do you never think of taking a holiday?' he suggested.

'Oh, aye – and who would keep the workroom going while I was away? Should you take my father's chair there and haul it up the stairs?'

'You know I don't mean that. There's a foreman, isn't there – one of the Cloughs?'

'Edwin, the father, yes. He's a good foreman, an' all. But it'd not be fair to expect him to manage the place.'

'Are you being fair now, to yourself?'

Hester grinned at him. 'Don't tempt me, Doctor – I might take up your suggestion. And I might put it to you that you try your own medicine. How long is it since you went away anywhere?'

And if anyone needs a break, it's you, she thought, watching him later as he walked slowly towards his landaulet. She only hoped her concern for him might help, in the way that his anxiety for her made her determined to survive.

It was through Frank Clough, though, that Hester began to experience a renewal of energy and enthusiasm. She had been over to Sandsend to confirm a new deal with Cousin Isaac and was returning through Whitby's narrow roads when she saw Edwin Clough and called to Kilner to stop the brougham.

'You're late finishing! Do you want to ride the rest of the way home with us?'

'That's civil of you, Miss Hester, thank you. But I'm in my dirt, mind . . .'

Kilner beamed down at him. 'I've cleaned out jet dust afore, Mr Clough. You want to take advantage of the offer.'

'I must admit I'm glad of a bit of help,' Edwin confessed. 'Alice'll be wild because I'm late, she likes the four of us to sit round the table together. Frank and Harold set off a bit since, but I were held up.'

'What was wrong this time?' Hester inquired, knowing that Edwin only mentioned problems that he'd not succeeded in solving himself.

'I caught Wally Hardcastle lambasting young Silas Dunsdale – out in t'street it were, not in the workroom.'

'Not him again!'

'We never proved it were Wally, not that time Bob were beaten over t'head.'

'I know – I wish to goodness we had. We might have had good reason to be rid of him once and for all. What happened today, then?'

'Summat and nowt, as it turned out. Young Dunsdale had been giving Wally plenty of lip, even his father admitted he deserved a bit of a hiding.'

'You don't think Bob was too scared to say otherwise?'

'Not really, no. Any road, I'll know more when I get home. Wally were insistent that our Frank heard the beginning on it. Happen you'd like to come inside with me, hear what he has to say?'

Alice Clough greeted them at the door, alarm draining colour from her face when she saw Edwin arriving in the Falgrave carriage.

'Whatever's up – has there been an accident?'

Hester reassured her at once. 'Nothing like that. It's just that your husband suggested Frank might explain something that happened at the works.'

Frank was emerging from the wash kitchen, towelling his hair, his clean shirt unfastened almost to the waist where he'd just finished tucking it inside clean but old trousers. His embarrassment would have made Hester smile if she'd cared less for his feelings.

'Don't forget I've got brothers of my own,' she told him quickly, brown eyes sparkling. 'I promise I won't go into a swoon at the sight of a bit of manly chest. And it's you I want to talk to, so don't go hurtling off upstairs. I understand from your dad that you heard Silas Dunsdale cheeking Wally Hardcastle.'

'We all heard him – those of us that weren't busy taking stuff into the office,' he added with a nod towards his father. 'I reckon the lad timed it so's it was only us lot overheard. He'd got hold of some tale about Wally going home worse for drink and finding half his clothes chucked out of t'window. From what he said, I gather that Wally's young missus accused him of taking so much liquor he wasn't any good to her.' Realising what he had said, Frank coloured again as he abruptly stopped speaking.

His father laughed, revealing that as one detail that *hadn't* emerged from Wally's telling. 'Happen he were justified then in standing up for his name. Though I made it clear to him as we'll not tolerate him throwing his weight around, specially with apprentices that don't allus have the bulk to fight back wi' somebody the size of him.'

Hester nodded. 'Unless there's any further trouble, I think we can let it rest at that this once, so long as it was young Dunsdale who's big enough to hold his own, and wasn't really hurt.'

'I think he dodged most of the blows, he's nippy on his feet.'

Alice asked Hester if she would care to join them for a cup of tea. While it was brewing, Frank came across the room to her.

'Since you're here, there's something I'd like to show

you,' he said and offered her a chair while he went up to his bedroom.

'It's just a few ideas I had,' he explained, coming to her and unfolding sheets of paper. 'Yon carved tree that you designed triggered it off, like. Now I hope you don't think I'm getting above myself trying to jot down a few sketches . . .'

'It's the reason most of the men are encouraged to learn drawing while they're training, isn't it? Though I hadn't realised you were this good.'

'No, well – when I were starting off it were a bit before your time, weren't it?'

Hester laughed. 'Go on – you'll have me convinced you're ancient. Now, let's have a proper look . . .'

'I thought if we could have a tree with birds and so on, like we've got, we might have summat else with branches.'

'Only stylised, as you've drawn here, and each one bearing a tiny frame – all of it in jet, naturally. What's to go in the frames, Frank?'

'Oh, didn't I say? Photographs, of course. Or miniatures, if folks have 'em. I thought it might catch on for widows and such. People that have a large family, then lose somebody and want to keep a reminder by them . . .'

'You're a genius! These'll sell, all right.'

'You'll have to smarten up my designs a bit.'

'I don't think I shall – anyway, we'll have another look at it together. Do you mind if I take these to show Father? Only because he'll be interested, not because we need anyone's confirmation to go ahead. I wanted summat new to get us out of the rut of producing established lines, and I'm certain we have it in front of us here.'

Abel was delighted with Frank's concept and insisted that he come to Falgrave House so that he might have a share in its development.

For several evenings he looked on approvingly while Hester's dark head and Frank's lighter brown one bent side by side over a table.

'You'll not get it no better nor that,' he said at last when they showed him what they considered the final drawing.

289

'Is Wally Hardcastle still a dab hand at turning out bigger things like the main section of this?'

'I suppose he is really,' Hester admitted, exchanging a look with Frank.

'Which is why we've kept him on all this time, eh?' Abel observed. 'Aye, well – he mun show his worth. And it'll free those of you that's more skilled with intricate work for getting them tiny frames right.'

Some short while later, Abel grinned, adding: 'Once you've sold the first of these, you'll doubtless be thinking to do variations – giving the frames different carvings on each set you turn out.'

The whole team engaged in producing these new lines found the work enjoyable, but best of all, Hester seemed to have been stimulated to work closely again with Frank in producing other ideas.

And there could be no denying that she was still attracted to him. She often found concentration difficult, simply because he was sitting so near to her.

Inevitably, emotions too long ignored grew too powerful to remain in the background. They had worked all evening at the table in the Cloughs' living room. Earlier, Hester had been pleased and not at all distracted to have the family about them. Alice and Edwin had a good relationship which seemed to set the mood of their offspring. The two youngest, Maggie and Herbert, loved any attention she could give them but never behaved badly or cheeked her. And the older children could be relied on to admire their work without touching, and often seemed content simply to stand there and watch.

Gradually, the entire family had retired to bed until finally Edwin and Alice had said goodnight as well, bidding them keep an eye on the clock, for wasn't it work again tomorrow.

Alone with Frank, Hester would have felt entirely at peace if it hadn't been for this ceaseless attraction that reminded her constantly that he'd always be more to her than just another worker. And all at once she sensed without looking that his attention had left the paper before him, and was riveted on her.

'You're very lovely, Hester.'

She grinned. 'Like this? When I've come here in my working clothes and haven't thought to put a comb to my hair since we left there at teatime?'

If he had his way, he'd loosen her hair of whatever constrained it so tightly away from her face. He'd run his fingers through its glossy black strands, would press it to his nostrils, breathe in her fragrance.

Slowly he rose, took her by the arm and drew her to her feet. Holding her gaze with green eyes that seemed as mysterious as the River Esk where it passed beneath trees, he pulled her against him.

Without a crinoline's support, her skirts and petticoats were flattened to nothing. And Frank was warm and lean and hard, so insistently alive that awareness of him compelled a gasp from her. And this was wrong. Whatever there'd been between them once, it wasn't enough now. Because she cared far more for Jon Davidson.

'You feel it an' all, don't you?' Frank said huskily. 'I wish to God it were right between us.'

'Only it's not, is it, though? We work together, don't we, and work well. But there's not enough besides to justify . . . to justify this.' I need more, don't you understand, more than being attracted, she thought.

'I can't offer you enough, is that it?' he snapped.

'Just because I was born in a big house? Is that how you think I measure what I want in the future?' I want the man with whom I would belong, the man whose love would be entire, near-perfect. The man, grown dear through his care of my family, who perplexes me by never seeming to see how I might be concerned for him.

'Because you're the one who, to all intents and purposes, is running the works now! What does that mean for us? *Not*, I am sure, that you'd readily continue in that position if you threw in your lot with one of t'men on your payroll.'

'It's not that, Frank. As you well know, I've never been bound by any convention that segregates folk.'

'True. And I've admired you for it. I daresay I allus will. But I'm not that daft I can't see there's some way I'm disappointing you.' He'd not have admitted that to anyone else, would ensure now that he regained enough pride to show her one day what he was worth.

'No, Frank, it's not that.' But how could she explain when all the time all she wanted was to be with a man who was mourning the wife he'd adored.

'I'll walk you home,' he said, his voice raw.

'Not yet...' She wasn't ready to be alone with this intense yearning, and with the knowledge that even the physical release that Frank offered would resolve nothing.

Wordlessly, he took up her cloak and placed it around her shoulders. His hands were warm and tender through the cloth and she longed to keep him with her. She needed his friendship, but must not invoke that or she'd risk their deeper involvement.

The narrow streets down by the harbour were icy. Snow came on the strong wind tearing in from the sea, the flakes scattering as they fell past lamplit windows.

Hester shivered and his arm went about her, hauling her against his side. Out here, Frank appeared easier with her, in control again. He talked of the designs they'd tackled that evening, of the rough jet pieces in store which might be suitable. His words made sense, but conjured no response, except the surging within her that reacted to his voice.

She had no will to protest when they kissed in the lee of the walls surrounding the Falgrave House gardens, with only the screeching seagulls to notice, and their desire's heat to counter the increasing blizzard. The length of him trapped her against the rough stone, sweet pressure that forced each nerve to echo the pulsebeat of their need. Feverish, his lips travelled from her mouth to her throat, savoured the tiny hollow at the neckline of her gown.

'No, Frank. Not now.' And not ever, for that would betray the real person interred somewhere within this hungry body. If I care at all for Jon, I'll learn to live with this tumult which keeps impelling me to heed instincts ungoverned by reason.

How *could* she feel this way – could long so fiercely while all her heart and most of her emotions were committed elsewhere? And they were committed; this need tonight seemed empty of all but desire.

292

After a long, lingering look at her, Frank turned and began running. She heard his feet ringing on the frosted setts, growing fainter with distance, disappearing into silence.

Behaving normally towards him the following morning demanded even more of Hester than she'd feared. Through most of the night she had lain restless, tormented by a need which frightened her because of its force. And alarmed her the more for being generated when she was not in love with the man concerned.

Frank was adept at concealing his feelings, had been conditioned by an inherited belief that revealing too much to those in charge could be dangerous. And in the cold light reflecting in off the snow-covered town there could be no doubting the situation.

Hester appeared almost regal today, her demure dark grown buttoned to the chin, its skirts descending over such a quantity of petticoats that they did the work of the crinoline cage they replaced. Even his avid thoughts would be taxed if he hoped to relive in memory their erotic, crushing embraces. Her back was ramrod straight, giving an imperious tilt to her head. He wasn't to know the immense effort she exerted to appear unperturbed.

The next few days made pretending indifference easier for both of them, though they did nothing to ease the intensity of the attraction still drawing them together. At times, Hester longed for the passing of years that this need might wane, then despised herself for having so little control over physical feelings. She was appalled by her own body which seemed unable to discriminate between men who were merely friends and the one she wished to love. And Frank had distressed her by saying it was her snobbery prevented any relationship between them.

Isn't it plain to everyone that I don't even consider a person's social position, she thought, walking home one evening. I could have made such a relationship work – *if* it had been what I wanted.

Preoccupied, she didn't notice the young man striding through slush that was rapidly melting in the heavy drizzle.

'Hester, how nice . . .'

It was Jamie Skelton, a rather different Jamie now, matured in his approach to others as well as in his smartly-dressed person.

'Hallo, Jamie,' she responded quickly, certain now that she'd no wish to extend the encounter. Nothing could eliminate the memories of that dreadful night when he'd been drinking.

'You're in a hurry,' he observed, and his smile waned a little.

'It's been a long day.'

'I was on watch from three this morning, have just been off to change since we put in here. But I'll not brush past a friend . . .'

'I wasn't trying to.'

'You've no time for me now. Go on – admit it. You've said from the beginning that you didn't resent that accident on the cliffs, your actions ever since have told a different story.'

'No, Jamie, that's not true.'

'You've grudged me my health, on account of your father.'

'No, no, never.'

'You can't bear to see me on my feet, can you?'

'That's not justified.' Hadn't she, initially, struggled against all such feelings. Overcoming them had taken only as long as coming to realise that Jamie was too good a friend for her to feel anything but thankful he'd survived.

He dismissed her words with a sideways jerk of his glorious flaming head. But he didn't persist, trying instead a different tack.

'Then I'm not good enough for you, not now you're managing yon jet works virtually unaided.'

'For heaven's sake, Jamie, stop this. I'm not turning into a snob. In fact, I'm no different, it's you that's changed.'

'Being good at my job, an' all, that what you mean? Don't you like it now I'm dressed decent and have a bob or two in my pocket?'

'There's one thing I don't like about you, and only one

– and that's the way you go filling yourself up with drink till you're senseless and start causing trouble.'

'By gum! We are high and mighty, these days, aren't we? Where's the lass who used to insist that rules were made for breaking? What happened to that girl what enchanted me each time she got away from Freda Blake who was supposed to be keeping an eye on her? You were fun in those days, Hester, you had spirit.'

'Any spirit I possess is used up making Falgraves' a success.'

'That's not spirit, it's blind obedience to what's expected on you. Your mother coped at first, and I had to admire her for it. Then you thought as you'd better do likewise. That's the trouble wi' folk like you, you can't see beyond conforming.'

'I've only tried to do whatever was necessary.'

'And it's turning you into a dried-up thing, like fruit that's been left in t'sun till even the core's withered. I'll tell you one thing, though – you'll not slight me again. I'm finished wi' you.'

Hester made as though to hasten past him, but he caught her savagely by the arm. She read anger in his hazel eyes, felt dismayed rather than afraid.

'Walk away from me, that's easy, i'n't it? You'll be sorry, though, one day – when you wake up to what you're about. I cared about you, Hester Falgrave, you're the one that's destroyed that. You're incapable now of treating folk right. All the time you're saying they're the same as you are, your pretty ways are proving otherwise.'

'I don't have to listen to this from you . . .'

'No, but it's time somebody told you. By, but I pity the poor fellow you marry. The minute he puts a toe wrong, never mind a foot, he'll get what for . . . !'

The encounter was unpleasant; Jamie had said a lot of hurtful things. They would have mattered less if she hadn't suspected that they contained a few grains of truth. Had she failed so desperately all along to ignore differences of status? Was she as priggish and patronising as he maintained? And had Jamie unearthed the reason why she experienced this private dread that she'd spend the rest of her life unloved, existing only for the jet works?

Could it be that no one would countenance marriage to her because it would entail permanent submission to her will? Because of who she was?

There was no way of dismissing what Jamie had said. His words plagued her by day and interrupted her sleep at night. If there'd been someone to ask, she'd have demanded if his assessment of her were true. As it was, she attempted to analyse her motivation, grew awkward through this self-absorption, and worsened relationships with everyone she met.

Even Frank Clough's patience was tried. Her enthusiasm was gone – where were the times they'd enjoyed, working in total commitment to Falgraves'?

By the time Hester realised her introspection was achieving nothing of worth, Frank had concluded that her withdrawal indicated a deep regret of having allowed him to share her confidences.

Hoping to right the situation between them, she stayed behind one day when his father had left him to lock up so that he might go and have a tooth extracted.

'I'm glad we've a chance to talk, Frank,' she began, leaning against his bench. 'Our Bernard's just told us he wants to come into the jet business.'

'That's nice for you all.'

'Aye, Father's particularly pleased. Any road, it won't be for a while yet as Bernard's to complete his schooling.'

'Naturally.'

She gave him a look, but his face remained impassive.

'Once he does start here, though,' she persisted, and was interrupted by Frank, smiling determinedly.

'You'll have the future assured,' he snapped.

'That's not what I was saying,' she protested, reeling from the animosity, sharp as an unexpected slap. She'd been going on to say that Frank himself must take a large part in Bernard's training, must pass on his craftsmanship. She swallowed, gathered in breath to say just that.

Despairing now, he forestalled her. 'It's bound to be uppermost in your mind. You've said all along that Falgraves' is going to the top. Now there's another on you coming up, to be groomed for licking us lot into shape.'

'I hope that's meant as a joke, Frank?'

'I don't see owt to laugh at.' All he saw in prospect was more of the family coming in till she was surrounded with them, enclosed by a ring of Falgraves, impregnable. Happen young Olive would fancy taking on accounts, then there'd be Abel's grandson, the one named for him . . .

'Haven't I shown that's not the way we run this place?' she asked, dejected by his attitude.

Frank did not reply.

Hester was appalled, broken by his misinterpretation which had staggered her so much that she couldn't begin to rectify matters.

I cannot live like this, Hester resolved. I've got to show him and everyone else that I haven't an ounce of arrogance in me. I'm an ordinary lass who wants to do a good job of work, to make something of my life, there's no harm in that. And I want to be loved, for what I am, and that's not being a patronising, ambitious boss. I'll have to prove this one day, or I can't carry on. I'll have to prove it, if it takes five years, or ten . . .

Chapter 16

By the year 1870, the Falgrave family business was booming. The workroom had expanded, their Flowergate shop had been extended and now employed a young girl as well as Susan Blakeborough who had taken over from Sally Drinkwater years ago. The entire jet trade was proving just as profitable, with fourteen hundred Whitby folk employed in the business.

During the past few years, Jamie Skelton had noticed the new prosperity in certain areas of the town, and in particular had seen how well the Falgraves were doing. A part of him felt better for their increasing success, for didn't it prove he needn't cling to any remaining regrets? They had survived, despite what had happened to Abel. There was, however, another element in his emotions. He'd not have acknowledged envy for their evidence of success, but nor would he deny that he'd have relished some similar proof of his own importance. He'd worked damned hard, often in lousy conditions, for something like nine years. And all he had to show was the boat he'd finally managed to purchase for his father.

Still, he thought, as he again prepared to put to sea, he had friends who were in a position to ensure that he set that right. He'd begun earning real money now, over and above his seaman's pay. In another year or less he'd again be investing in a boat, and this time for himself. He'd no longer be employed at the whim of someone else, he'd be his own master. And not before time.

Despite the way Jamie or anyone else saw Falgraves', Hester wasn't satisfied yet; they still hadn't achieved the Royal Warrant that she aspired to, and they were into 1870. It had become a sort of family joke by now, and she'd had to reprove Bernard only the other day. If he didn't take progress seriously, what could he expect of the workers? Bernard accepted criticism from her with the good grace that made him popular in the works and approachable wherever he went in Whitby.

Even now that he was almost of age, the lad had a likeable way of deferring to anyone his senior by more than a couple of years. Hester supposed this was what eased his relations with the experienced men who'd remained loyal to Falgraves' to this day. He even managed to get on with Wally Hardcastle.

'How do you do it?' she asked one June evening, as they walked up towards the house through alleys where sunlight alternated with deep shadow cast by the tall buildings. 'Neither Mother nor I ever had anything but complaints from him.'

Bernard laughed. 'I just listen to what he has to say, nod now and then, sympathise when he goes on yet again about having a gas engine so's we can do away with treadling . . .'

'But you don't do anything. How is it he puts up with it, instead of ranting on?'

'But that's it, Hester, don't you see? I don't do anything because I can't. He understands that. I haven't the authority.'

'And I have. They know, don't they, that while Father might have the final say he's not on the spot.'

'You are, and if you recommend something it's as good as happening already.'

'I don't like it, you know. I don't believe I have all along, though I couldn't see that at the time.'

'But think how you've made them look up to you. There's not many women manage that in a lifetime. You're certainly the only one in our line.'

'There was Mother.'

Bernard grinned. 'Before our Ruth came along, aye. And didn't I resent her working every day!'

'Did you? I don't remember you grumbling.'

'Not after a while. There wasn't any point. And Father made up for it, by being interested in whatever I did.'

'I reckon that's what's kept him alive this long. Caring about folk, sharing what he knows about the Whitby area, and about jet.'

'Will you want to ease up, do you think, when I've finished my training?'

'Trying to get rid of me, are you, Bernard?'

'You know me better than that. It was you I was thinking of, Hester. Don't you want a life of your own?'

'I have my own life, down yonder.' It was the answer she always gave now, to herself as well as to others. And it did all seem to be work. Her only social life seemed concerned with family; and to involve no one new. For a time, after Lambert's marriage, Sally's people had been invited over, but their patent unease had formed a barricade that eventually defeated Maud's resolute hospitality.

Whatever there might have been once between Hester and Frank Clough, he no longer attempted to rekindle any passion. And if she regretted the warmth lost from their friendship, she was relieved by the absence of complications. For many a year all her affection had been for Jon Davidson, even though he appeared to exist on memories of Ruth.

Falgrave House seemed alive with people the minute they entered. Lambert was on leave and he and Sally had brought their three children for a visit. Young Abel was an engaging child, solemn when relating something that he'd learned at school, but given to sudden fits of laughter. He had grown so quickly that Hester lost track of how old he was, but it must be eight or nine.

His younger brother and sister, Samuel and Polly, had colouring as fair as his which was lighter even than their parents'. Samuel was seven – Hester never forgot his age since they shared a birthday – and Polly had been born two years after him. The three of them were so attractive, with their mother's lovely features and this remarkable hair, that people stopped in the street to admire them. However justified that might be, it hadn't done a lot for the two little ones.

She could hear them now, rampaging through the kitchens, driving Mrs Richmond to distraction. Their housekeeper was ageing now, took longer over every task as she moved about the large house on arthritic legs. May Thorpe had stayed on, but Hester doubted that she'd ever succeed if left to run the place. She still was amiable and willing, but somehow lacked the acumen to shoulder more responsibility.

May met them now in the hall, and greeted them with her mistress's instructions to join them in the drawing room after they had changed.

'Tell her we won't be long,' said Bernard.

Hester was thinking that her mother never credited her with the sense to bath and change without being so directed. Haven't I been doing this year in and year out, and never a break in the monotony?

By the time that Hester came hurrying down the stairs again, nursery tea was long past and the children were being marshalled for bed, with the exception of young Abel who'd been conducted to sit with his grandfather. The bond between the pair was stronger by far than their shared name, and grew with the years. A fact which didn't always delight Hester's mother.

'You take more notice of him than you do of your own little lass,' she frequently complained.

And although Abel might deny this, even a casual observer would have noted the partiality. Hester suspected that Ruth tired him. She had developed from a weakling into a wiry little thing, but with a restlessness that didn't combine well with her dissatisfied nature.

Maud doted on her, to the extent that the child's every whim was indulged, a circumstance which might have been avoided if it hadn't been Maud alone who was responsible for her upbringing. Nurse Scott, who'd been employed to tend Abel as well as caring for his smallest offspring, had soon made it plain that attending to Ruth's swiftly changing demands wasn't to her taste.

Fortunately, Abel had taken to the woman, and they had progressed to a state of mutual respect, generally expressed in daily banter.

Hester could hear them now, using young Abel as an audience while each tried to outsmart the other.

'Ooh, Grandfather, that was rude,' exclaimed the lad, who managed to extract enjoyment from what would seem to others the repetitive chiding of a dutiful nurse by her dependent patient. Nurse Scott was giving as good as she received now. Whatever Abel's remark had been, she evidently capped it. But only to be answered by hoots of derision from grandfather and grandson.

The woman was smiling, nevertheless, and greeted Hester with a cheery, 'Good evening,' as she entered.

'Two of them to torment you today, eh?' said Hester, and crossed to kiss her father.

'She looks well on it, though, don't you think?' Abel remarked. 'She'll never admit it, but it's attention she craves.'

'Aye,' said the nurse dryly, 'that much that I'm glad now your daughter's here so's I can go to my supper.'

'She's late again, bless her,' Abel confided, glancing towards the clock as the nurse left the room. 'That woman never takes off half the time she's due.'

'I think it's because she finds you irresistible, Grandfather,' the youngster announced gravely.

'Do you now? You'd best keep quiet about that in front of your grandmother then.'

'But *why* should I? Having two people love you must be twice as good – won't Grandmother be pleased for you?'

'I think she might at that, but not for your reason,' Abel observed a shade tetchily. Maud would welcome anything that freed her time for spoiling Ruth.

'Everything go smoothly today?' he asked his daughter when she was seated beside him.

'More or less, I think. Our Bernard's coming along very well, you know. The men have taken to him, and he's quick to learn. There's not much more he can be taught, except by applying himself to different aspects of the work.'

'He says he's best at engraving, is that what you reckon?'

'So far, but he'll be able to make a good job of owt he tackles there. He reminds me a lot of Frank Clough when he were that age.'

'My, that is a recommendation! Well, I won't pretend I'm other than suited to death. It's time we had one of us own in the business again.'

'And what am I then?' Hester pulled him up, smiling to belie the sharpness in her voice. 'I always thought I was yours . . .'

Abel grinned, rather shamefacedly. 'You know what I mean. There's no guaranteeing you'll always be a Falgrave . . .'

'I'm twenty-six, Father,' she began.

Before she could say any more her nephew interrupted, his face a delight of utter astonishment.

'You're not, are you? You aren't really that old?'

'And feel it, young man, many a time.'

'Don't worry, soon as I'm old enough, I'll see you're all right at the works. I'm going to be apprenticed there, you know.'

'Are you really?' said his grandfather. 'I thought yesterday you said you were after going into t'mining?'

'I shall do both. You did, didn't you?'

'There you are,' Hester said, laughing. 'Answer that one.'

Both knew, though, that young Abel's future was unlikely to have any connection with jet. Hadn't his father elected to leave Whitby as soon as he could, and never at any time had considered bringing his family back to live in the area.

Later that evening, when the family had dined and all the children were settled for the night, they started at the sound of carriage wheels and the clang of the bell by the door.

Olive came rushing in, her face as flushed as the rose taffeta gown she wore. She had married in 1866 and into the jet business, but to the only son of a rival company. Her greeting, as she strode past May Thorpe, was perfunctory and addressed to all in general, and only the prelude to her agitated question.

'What have you heard of this new jet works that's opened up, and is undercutting everyone's prices?'

'Steady on, lass,' her father began. 'What works, and where?'

'Across on the West Cliff, somewhere near the Royal Hotel. Right where they'll attract all the summer visitors.'

'Are you sure about their prices? I've heard nothing about them,' Hester said.

'It's a fact, right enough,' Olive persisted. 'They call themselves "Best Jet" and have their own shop underneath their workroom, and such a display in the window as never!

Paul and his father have arranged an urgent meeting with Cecil Arkwright, we can't have this carry on. I've had two customers all day in our shop, *two*. They're taking trade off us already.'

'Now, just a minute,' Abel put in, 'slow down a bit. Tell us what it is your father-in-law and Arkwright are hoping to do.'

'Well, it's obvious, isn't it? Ensure that folk don't go cutting us out of the market by . . .'

'Fixing prices, is that what you're about?' her father interrupted. 'Nay, lass, that's not right. There's allus been fair competition in the trade, and if folk decide to sell a penn'orth or two cheaper that's up to them. It never lasts, can't do.'

'This is more than a penn'orth. And it's going to affect us all.' She turned to Hester. 'Do you really know nothing about this?'

'I did hear tell of a new shop that'd set up. But not what they were doing.'

'There are that many in the town now,' said Maud. 'It's not as if there were just one or two families in the same line.'

'All the same, I'd have expected Falgraves' to be wise to what was going on. Haven't you noticed a drop in the shop takings, Hester?'

'They might be down a bit, but we know business fluctuates, especially with so much of our stuff being for mourning.'

'And don't forget we sell more to wholesalers, these days,' Abel reminded Olive. 'We aren't looking to t'shop for all our trade.'

'You might be glad of that before very long,' Olive continued. 'Though I don't see as that should prevent you banding with us to stop this somehow.'

Hester and her mother both looked towards Abel. 'Say what you like, I'll have no hand in anything that stops competition. It's never done us any harm. Look at it this way, Olive – we all start off with the same raw material. Mining costs a certain amount, and quality rough jet has always fetched a better price nor poor stuff. Then there's

304

the men in the workroom. You'll not find much difference in wages from one works to the next, else the men'd be chopping and changing till nobody knew where they stood.'

'These new folk must be cutting costs somewhere,' Olive remarked.

'Yes – in what's left, their own profit. And they'll not keep that down so far and stay in business, will they? As I see it, tha can stop worrying. It's no more than a ruse to trick people into patronising them. Give it a couple of weeks – I'll bet by then they're upping their prices beyond everybody else's.'

At the end of two weeks, however, the new jet shop had reduced their prices for every item they stocked. By the end of the following month no one in the trade could deny that their own sales had been hit.

'I've a good mind to pay Best Jet a visit,' said Hester to her brother one wet morning while Kilner was driving them to the workshop.

'And do what?' he asked gravely. 'You know what Father thinks about folk being free to fix their own charges. You can't tackle them about prices.'

'I can at least see what they're offering.'

When they arrived at the works, however, the new rival shop was driven from Hester's mind. As soon as she followed Bernard to the top of the stairs, she knew something serious was wrong.

Frank Clough and his brother were standing by their father's bench, but Edwin himself was nowhere in sight.

'Can I have a private word with you please, Hester? First, though, I'm afraid Father won't be in, so is it all right if our Harold gives out the rough jet? He's been told how it should be allocated.'

Hester nodded. 'Carry on then, Harold, if you will.'

Without removing her cloak, she turned to Frank as the office door closed behind them.

'What's to do? You look shaken up – there hasn't been an accident, has there?'

'No. But Father hasn't felt too great for a while. He's had to go under the doctor, and he says it's consumption.'

'Oh, Frank, I am sorry. My parents will be as well. Do tell him and your mother how upset I am.' She felt all the worse because she hadn't really noticed that Edwin Clough looked any different.

'He asked me to tell you that, providing they've caught it in time, he hopes to get back to work eventually.'

'Let's hope he's able to.'

Pensively, Hester took off her cloak and hung it behind the door.

'He also said to tell you that he does realise you won't be able to keep the job open for him.'

'I certainly don't believe we can manage without a fore-man for any length of time.'

Seating herself at the desk, she found she was gazing at Frank while half-formed ideas jostled in her brain.

'For a day or two, I'd like you to be acting foreman,' she began slowly.

He was astonished. She saw the incredulity in his green eyes, and then beyond that ill-concealed delight.

'I'll be glad to do owt I can to help.'

'Thanks, we've always been able to take your word that we could rely on you. Supposing it did become a lengthy business, how would you feel about being appointed fore-man? That's assuming my father would approve that, and I think he would.'

'Me? Ay, I don't know. I'd like to have a go, and naturally I'm very pleased that you think as I could do it, but . . . well, there's lots of others senior to me.'

'I know. Well, we'll have to see. Happen your father won't be as long as we fear getting back on his feet.'

She knew already, though, that having Frank as foreman would feel good, would fulfil her as-yet unrealised ambition of their working more closely together to develop Falgraves'.

Her father listened that evening while she explained the situation and put the suggestion to him. He was frowning before she had finished speaking.

'You can't do that. There's mature men down yonder that have worked in jet all their lives.'

'Frank's a better craftsman.'

'Maybe. And maybe he's somebody you've taken a shine to, eh?'

'What do you mean?'

'I'm not daft, Hester. I've still got eyes in my head. You fancy him, and have done for many a year.'

'It's you that's talking daft now. When have I ever said anything of the kind?'

One dark eyebrow raised knowingly. 'You'd be the last to tell anybody, so don't pretend otherwise. I still say you fancy him – and I don't blame you for wanting to promote him. We have to think of the works, though, and antagonising t'others won't do.'

'You can't tell me any of them would make such a good job of being foreman. Bob Dunsdale, for instance, is a lovely person and a good worker, but he hasn't got enough about him.'

'I wasn't thinking of Bob – I'm inclined to agree with you there. But there's always Wally Hardcastle.'

Anticipating his name didn't prevent Hester's heart from thudding down inside her.

'Do you honestly believe he has Falgraves' interests at heart?'

'You've got to believe it, haven't you? Look how long he's stayed with us.'

'But he's always finding fault with something. Then there's the way he's tried to get a union going.'

'I think that union idea died a natural death, years since. When did you last hear him whipping the men up about some cause or other?'

'I never heard him in the first place; he took good care of that. He generally made sure there were no Falgraves on the premises before he started agitating.' And there was that occasion, years ago, when she and Frank had been certain it was Wally who attacked Bob Dunsdale – not that mentioning it to her father after all this time would do any good.

'I'm going to see what your mother says,' he announced at last. 'She was there long enough on a regular basis, at one time, to form a shrewd idea of the lie of the land.'

Hester wasn't surprised that her mother opposed Frank

Clough's serving more than temporarily as foreman. Not that she would approve of Wally Hardcastle in the role, either.

'We might have to bring in an outsider as the only means of preventing resentment,' she added.

Her daughter didn't like that notion. If they couldn't agree on either Wally Hardcastle or Frank, there still were other candidates among their own workforce.

Within days there could be no doubting who considered he should be foreman. On the second morning that Frank doled out rough jet and checked that every craftsman and apprentice knew what he should be engaged on, Wally Hardcastle set his lips and his greyish complexion took on more than its normal complement of furrows.

As soon as Hester went out to the Flowergate shop, he stopped treadling and, when Bernard's gaze was drawn to him, glowered back.

Raising his voice, Wally addressed the workroom as a whole. 'You've all seen as how Edwin Clough's not here and I hope you're all taking heed that his family's sticking to his position. Now, is that fair, I ask you? Where's the appreciation that the rest of us has earnt over the years? Wouldn't you have thought there'd have been some acknowledgement?'

Bernard cleared his throat. 'I feel I must point out that it is only as a temporary measure that Frank Clough has assumed his father's duties. And . . .'

'By Gum, and it'd better not be permanent,' interrupted Wally swiftly.

'And,' Bernard persisted firmly, although he felt colour rising over his neck and face, 'it is with my father's full approval.'

Hardcastle snorted. 'I daresay. Happen he needs a bit of a reminder, like. So's he doesn't forget them of us who've given good service for many a long year. You can get back to your treadles, lads – for now. I'll call you together when we lay off at dinnertime.'

Returning to his own bench, Wally smiled to himself. Even if he didn't create too much havoc that way, there was more than one means of paying the Falgraves back for disregarding him. He'd be justified now in putting into practice a suggestion that had tempted him.

Afterwards, when Bernard told his sister what had occurred, she played down the incident.

'Threats, that's all it is, love. We've had 'em before, and they didn't amount to much.'

This time, however, she was afraid – for Frank's safety. She made a point of remaining behind after the others had left and while he was securing the place for the night.

'I understand from our Bernard that Wally's up to his tricks again. Did you gather what he'd said to the men at dinnertime?'

'Nay, you could guess I weren't in on it.'

'No, but didn't any of the others let on?'

Smiling slightly, he looked down at her. 'Ay, Hester, I thought you knew me better nor that by this time. I didn't ask. I'll give nobody the satisfaction of thinking they've put the wind up me.'

'You and I know what we suspected Wally Hardcastle of doing all those years ago. I'm not going to stand by and have him making you the next victim for a beating.'

'I can look after myself.'

'Happen so – if folk are fighting fair. This is serious, Frank.'

Reading in her exquisite brown eyes the concern which he had feared had waned, triggered feelings that he'd been suppressing for longer than he cared to recall. He'd tried going out with other young women but always, to his parents' disappointment, there had been some reason why their friendship never lasted more than a few weeks and never seemed more than friendship. He still wanted Hester Falgrave, and only her; was that so unsuitable? They had shared so much over the years, from development of new jewellery to a keen interest in the Romans who had mined jet locally, and in the ancient jet beads excavated in 1867 at the old monastery of Streonshalh. He needed every part of her.

'You're a lovely lass.' He reached out to draw her against him. Immediately, he felt her go tense, resisting him. But gone were the days when he'd relinquish everything without some effort.

His kiss was at the same time familiar and remarkable for its new maturity. There was authority, these days, in Frank Clough. And today, decisiveness.

'I'll take care,' he announced, 'you may be sure of that. Because somehow – I don't yet know how – I'm going to prove that you and me finishing up together isn't as impossible as we once thought. Things have changed a lot at home – there's more on us bringing home a pay packet. Once my father's back at work, I'm going to go into the matter of our future.'

'*Ours?*' Hester asked him, alarm because he still considered such a relationship possible making her voice shrill.

Frank grinned. 'I see. I should have consulted you, should I – before entertaining owt of the kind?'

'It's not that simple, Frank,' she began, and wondered how she could have spent so many years working among men and still know so little about their way of thinking. And even less of how to cope with this situation.

He was a personable young man, so attractive that her own response could hardly be ignored. But ignore its demands she would, or otherwise she'd soon despise her weakness for succumbing to base desire.

'As I see it,' he persisted, 'there can't be anybody else you're keen on, or you'd have been wed before now.'

'That doesn't necessarily follow.' He didn't know, no one even suspected, that she was capable of loving where scarcely any outward signs of affection existed. And when nothing had occurred to justify her even dreaming of marriage.

'We've never given ourselves a proper chance, that's half the trouble,' Frank continued. 'There couldn't be a less romantic place than a jet works. If we could only start meeting regular . . .'

'I'm sorry. I'm afraid I don't think that would be a good idea.'

'Because of how unsettled things are here, at present? Aye – happen it wouldn't be diplomatic, not yet awhile.' Suddenly his frown had vanished and he was smiling again,

310

his green eyes glittering in the light from outdoors where the day's rain had ceased and Whitby stood washed in sunlight.

May God forgive her, but she hadn't the heart to wipe that smile off his face by telling him, as she ought, to give up hoping. He was the best friend she'd ever had, was it her fault that she dreaded hurting him?

'If I don't get off home, they'll be thinking either Wally or somebody's had it in for me!' she exclaimed abruptly, and left Frank staring pensively towards the workroom stairs.

She walked swiftly along streets and up narrow alleyways, taking the quickest route to Falgrave House, yet all the while wondering how in this world she would disguise her agitation when she arrived there.

Its stone walls mellowed by the evening sun, her home appeared so welcoming that she breathed in a massive sigh of intense relief. As she rushed indoors, Jon's voice was the first sound she heard.

'He's remarkably well considering his disability, Maud. We can only expect that he experiences the occasional headache, like the rest of us.'

Just inside the drawing room doorway, he turned on hearing Hester's approach. His blue eyes lit and he smiled as he walked unhurriedly to greet her.

'I'm just reassuring your mother that I'm not unduly put out by being denied your father's company tonight. As you probably heard, he's resting with a headache – more than likely the product of this stormy weather we've had.'

'You're not leaving just because Father's laid low, I hope?'

Jon's visits were invariably on the pretext of sitting yarning with Abel, but that didn't preclude her enjoyment of every encounter. Today, perturbed by events at the works, she needed to have him here.

'You must eat with us of course, Jon,' her mother insisted, coming to join them.

To Hester, the invitation appeared as cool as the hall where they stood. But Jon was accustomed by now to lack of ceremony, and was content to abandon his half-hearted show of departing.

'I'll be with you in five minutes when I've changed,' she

311

declared, smiling, and felt the day's difficulties slipping from her as she hastened upstairs.

Five minutes was all she took to have a rapid wash and don a clean gown of sea-green silk, a shade once favoured by her mother and which she'd recently discovered also suited her.

Jon was standing beside the sideboard, replacing the sherry decanter from which he had just poured himself a glass. 'Your mother declined, claiming that she must disappear to the kitchen. Am I to drink alone, or can I persuade you this is very civilised?'

Hester smiled up at him. 'You can convince me very easily tonight that I need something to take away the tension!'

His answering smile was grave. 'I thought as much. You might conceal your weariness from some, but you're not very adept at hiding it from me, Hester.'

As they sat down together on the sofa and Hester began to outline the current problems at work in Jon's attentive ear, she secretly vowed that nothing must ever prevent her coming home to his concern for her . . .

Ever since she had come of age, Hester had found that time disappeared without her feeling that she put it to best use. So, when Edwin Clough's ill-health did not improve and the prospect of his return was postponed, she wondered how she'd neglected to ensure that Wally Hardcastle didn't cause trouble.

This time Wally lined up all the workers except Frank and Harold Clough, and had them standing idle when Hester returned following the midday break.

'We've decided as enough is enough,' he told her when she stared anxiously towards them on reaching the top of the stair. 'There's several on us have worked here twice as long as Frank Clough. We'll form a deputation, demand to see Mr Falgrave about the foreman's job.'

'No, don't do that please,' she said swiftly, walking towards the line of dusty-clothed men. 'Go back to work now and you have my word that I will speak to him, on your behalf. I think you'll find he'll agree with your recommendations.'

She mightn't like to accept that Frank would't yet be put in charge, but at least Frank himself was prepared for the position proving temporary. And if she herself spoke to her father it would avoid having the men turn up at the house in protest. That would have made it look as if she'd let things get out of hand.

As it was, Abel was displeased by the fact that such a threat had been made. 'I told you them that had been there years would know it weren't right to keep young Frank Clough in charge of them for even a short while. Resentment's built up, and they don't forget so easily neither.'

'I don't think much harm's done,' she said quietly, looking at her father's set face. 'Once one of them's been put in charge they'll be that pleased with themselves there'll be no thought of any more bother.'

'Let's hope so. It'll be Wally, of course. He's a natural leader and even though we all know he likes a grumble he does know jet working.'

Hester's spirits dropped to her shoe soles. She would have asked if her father was sure had he not already indicated whom he would select. And she knew in her own heart that, with the exception of Frank, none of the other workers had it in them to do more than labour conscientiously on the tasks set them.

'You can tell Wally Hardcastle tomorrow to come up to the house to see me. And I'll see Frank, an' all – we don't want him feeling he's getting his nose pushed out.'

That's up to you, thought Hester. I know you like to keep your finger on what's happening in the workroom. But I shall explain to Frank – the minute Wally gets to know it'll be all round the place, he's not one to play down the promotion. She wanted to thank Frank, as well, for standing in as foreman so effectively.

She was surprised the following day when she took Frank aside in the office for a private word. Instead of reacting as she'd expected and accepting as inevitable that one of the older men should be made foreman, his green eyes narrowed and he frowned.

'I didn't know you weren't satisfied wi' the way I've seen

to everything since my father were laid up. You might have said summat!'

'Frank – what did we say at the time? You knew you were only stepping in for the present. Doing us a favour, in a way.'

'Hasn't got me very far, has it?'

'It's proved you can do the job. With a few more years on your back, you'd be ideal for it.'

'You sound just like your father,' he muttered, still annoyed.

'Is that a bad thing? He always was a good boss.'

'Happen so. But I thought you were different, Hester, that you believed in folk bettering themselves regardless of their age.'

'I do, but . . .' Her voice trailed off in a sigh. She could hardly reveal to Frank that she had supported his being promoted, and had lost when opposed by her father.

'It's funny, isn't it, that it's all right for you to be managing the business at three year younger nor me, but when it comes my turn I'm told I'm not experienced enough even for coming second to you.'

'If that's how it appears to you then I'm sorry.'

'I'm not on about appearances, it's facts as counts. And once again it's all down to whose family you chanced to be born into.'

'Nay, Frank, if I didn't know you better I'd think you were jealous.'

'Happen I'd be justified. I need that job, Hester – for the time being, so's I can help out a bit more at home. Aye, and for the future an' all. And that won't happen while you and your family are keeping me down.'

'There'll be other opportunities. Wally mightn't be all that long before he packs it in.'

'He's got a good ten years before he thinks of retiring. And I'm none going to wait ten year to see some result from my hard work.'

'Having a bit of authority isn't the only reward, surely? Is there no satisfaction in the way you and I collaborate on some new line?'

'Happen there is, and happen it's beginning to pall. Either

way, that's all academic. Do you honestly think Hardcastle will have me involved in any developments now?'

'He'll not have that great an influence, you'll see. He'll only be the foreman.'

'Aye – and the way him and his cronies will change things, it'd take somebody stronger than you to resist.'

Hester had been horrified by Frank's attitude, and totally unable to turn around his thinking. All day long she found herself reflecting on how she'd managed to antagonise him. She might blame her father's inflexibility over the appointment of a foreman, but she suspected her own mishandling of the matter was responsible for Frank's sudden antagonism.

Aching for the opportunity to talk over the difficulty, she longed for finishing time and the walk home with her brother which would provide opportunity for a private word.

When, one by one, the treadles ceased and the men collected together tools and tidied their benches, she went to wash her hands.

Bernard was in the office when she returned.

'Come on, let's get out of here,' she said quietly. 'I've had enough today.'

He grinned. 'Like that, is it? You'd better get off home then. I've told Mother not to expect me in for a meal. There's a girl I've been seeing, I'm having dinner with her family tonight.'

'Are you now?' Despite her ill-humour, Hester grinned back at him. 'You've kept that quiet, how long have you known her?'

'Since we were at school. You might as well know, it's Belle Jenkins.'

'Jenkins, I seem to know the name . . .'

'You do know her. Nay, Hester, you used to be quicker than that. She was at school with our Olive, and her brother was in my class.'

'Well, I don't know! And are you getting serious?'

'Don't let on at home, but I've asked her to marry me.'

'And will she?'

'When I'm twenty-one. We think she'll get her parents to agree then.'

'You don't think that's a shade young for settling down?'

He laughed. 'We aren't all so devoted to Falgraves' that we can't see life beyond it.'

And whatever gives you the idea that that's the way I am, his sister thought but she wished him well and hoped he was right in believing no one would oppose the match.

Privately, though, the news depressed her. The awkwardness between herself and Frank today had shown her that the relationship with him wasn't nearly so amiable as she had supposed. The suspicion that she might indeed be destined to remain single grew from a niggle somewhere at the back of her mind into a prospect that threatened to gnaw into her. The trouble was that she met too few people. And when she grew fond of someone they weren't sufficiently interested to notice.

Chapter 17

Jon Davidson was at the house that evening. He had been called in earlier in the day, when Ruth's persistent cough had again prevented her attending school, and Maud had invited him to join them later for a meal. His old house-keeper had died several months previously and her successor was proving more effective as someone to usher in patients than at keeping house.

Although he amused the Falgraves with stories of the newcomer's shortcomings, Dr Davidson found the lack of domesticity most trying. It increased the difficulty of keeping up with a heavy workload and of accepting the solitude to which he'd never adjust.

When Hester arrived home, he was sitting with her father, listening while Abel described the latest achievements of his grandson. 'I'll always be proud they named him for me, you know, Jon. My only regret's that the regiment keeps them all away from Yorkshire.'

Seeing Hester, the doctor rose swiftly with a smile. 'Hallo, my dear, do come and join us.'

'I will in a minute,' she said, smiling back, although she'd have appreciated a word from someone in the house informing her that he was here. She could have changed then, instead of appearing like this in a three year old gown with the hem encrusted in jet dust.

She kissed her father, inquired how he was and asked after the doctor's health.

Jon beamed. 'I'm all right, thanks, love. And you always make me feel that matters, there's not many folk think to ask.'

'And all the while they make you sorry whenever you put that particular question to them,' Abel observed wryly.

The doctor laughed. 'Thank goodness for friends where I don't have to maintain any pretence.'

Hester nodded. 'Aye, I daresay you've been in and out

of this place that much over the years that it might be considered your second home.'

'It might at that, Hester, and an agreeable thought it is.'

She bathed hastily and changed into a dress that she'd worn only once before. For all the talk of this being like home to him, she'd not have Jon Davidson believe she took no care over how she appeared in front of him.

Sitting before the mirror in her room to attack her hair, she nodded approvingly to herself. The closely-fitting bodice was in a rich taffeta, dark red in colour, its round neckline plain and emphasised now by the black of one of their own carved necklaces. She took out matching earrings and set them aside until she had dressed her hair. Still long, dark and glossy, she swept the back into a heavy coil, anchoring it so that its lower curve nestled above her nape. The front and sides were smoothed away from her face, covering the upper rims of her ears in the fashion that she had adopted for years now. All at once, she recognised the style's severity and experimenting, loosened a few strands and left them to fall softly in waves outlining her cheeks. With the earrings in place and a final check in the glass to ensure that the bustle at the back of her gown was draped correctly, she went out and along the landing.

'Being denied your company for several minutes is amply recompensed by the result!' Jon was pushing her father's chair towards the dining room. Pausing at the foot of the staircase, his blue eyes echoed his approval.

'Thank goodness for that!' Her dark eyes glittered with delight. 'I have to admit I came home in a foul mood, not really fit company for anyone.'

'Had a bad day, have you?'

Abel answered for her. 'She's been crossed, that's all — by me. She wanted Frank Clough for his father's old job as foreman, because she's taken a shine to him. I thought differently.'

'So, it's Frank Clough who takes your fancy, is it?' Jon asked, his expression inscrutable.

Hester snorted. 'Whether it was or not, that all ended today. He didn't take kindly to our decision. But I came home to forget the unpleasantness.'

318

But you'll not forget him in a hurry, thought Jon, and quelled a sigh.

Having the doctor there in Bernard's place enlivened the evening. He was a good raconteur and wasn't above sharing his amusement about some of his patients, so long as he could conceal their identity.

'This is one thing I miss, you know,' Jon confided later when Maud was checking that Ruth was in bed and he was relaxing with Hester and her father. 'There are few people now in Whitby who are close enough to be trusted with even discreet discussions of my work.'

'It can't be good for you to keep so much to yourself,' said Hester, 'particularly when a great deal of it is distressing.'

'You're very understanding, my dear.'

'And haven't you always been understanding of us,' her father put in. 'I know of no other doctor who'd call so regularly over so many years, when there's nothing can be done for me.'

Later, after Jon had left, Hester reflected on what had been said, and realised how grateful they should be for so many visits. Without them, her father would have been denied the satisfaction of a friendship based on mutual respect. And she herself might have missed the warmth that she always experienced whenever Jon was present. A warmth which sustained the deep regard she'd always felt for him.

With Wally Hardcastle as foreman and Frank merely coolly polite towards her, the following weeks passed uneasily. She was compelled to acknowledge that Wally made an effective foreman, a fact which surprised her if it gave no pleasure. Among the workers, there seemed no real opposition to the situation apart from the natural reaction of Frank and his brother. But there remained for her an edgy feeling that all was not well.

They were no less busy than usual, and Hester even after all these years still hadn't devised a routine which allowed sufficient time for designing new pieces as well as attending to the running of workroom and the shop. Most days began with resolutions as to what she hoped to achieve, and ended with more than one item still awaiting attention.

One such matter was investigating the new jet business that had set up and was conscientiously undercutting prices. When first approached by Olive, Hester had been determined to discover more about the company. When more immediate problems arose, she told herself there were plenty of other jet works in Whitby that weren't run almost single-handed, and surely someone would have concluded an investigation.

When Olive called a second time, it was on a Thursday afternoon at the works. Hester was astounded when she turned away from checking some engraved beads produced by their newest apprentice, and saw her sister approaching across the area from the top of the narrow stairs.

'What's happened?' she asked, trying to keep her voice low, as soon as they had greeted each other. 'Is somebody poorly, or something?'

Smiling slightly, Olive shook her head. She was looking particularly becoming today in an elegant striped gown of emerald green trimmed with black. Briefly, Hester wished herself running a shop rather than perpetually surrounded by all the dust and dirt of creating jet jewels. But she shook her head at her own momentary vanity, and invited her sister into the office.

'What is it then?' she asked, offering a vacant chair and remembering just in time to dash the layer of dust from it.

'You remember what I said the last time I saw you, about the new folk that's set up on the West Cliff in our line of business?'

When Hester nodded Olive continued heatedly, 'It's getting worse. Best Jet have lowered their prices even further now, and their shop window's full to overflowing. We can't make out where they're obtaining so much rough jet on the cheap – they must be getting it for next to nothing, or they'd not be able to charge so little.'

'Have you asked around within the trade? I have to admit I meant to try and find out more, but I haven't had time to do a thing.'

'Falgraves' is about the only one that isn't up in arms

about it all. That's why I said I'd come and see you again. I couldn't believe you didn't care.'

'You were right, it's not that, Olive. I've just got so much on my plate, these days. I'm sorry I've let this matter slide, though. I don't agree with it of course and I'll make time somehow to take action.'

Looking relieved, her sister smiled. 'I know Father put you off an' all, when I was on about everyone getting together to fight this.'

'I daresay that did make me think I didn't have to do anything straight away. Any road, now you're here you can tell me what's been tackled so far. It sounds as if your husband's involved.'

'As you may recall, Paul and his father were meeting Cecil Arkwright. They came away with various ideas for enlisting the help of all the other jet businesses. Mr Arkwright was going to contact every company that worked jet.'

'He certainly hasn't been in touch with us.'

'No – well, since his brother's retired and he's not as young as he was, they've been having a bit of trouble in their own works. They had a very strict foreman who was throwing his weight around whenever Mr Arkwright himself wasn't in. Evidently, the bother they had getting rid of the man upset him so much that he took to his bed for a fortnight. Naturally, when he got back to work he'd enough to do catching up. And setting on a new foreman.'

'Well, I don't know! Who'd have thought Cecil Arkwright wouldn't be able to keep things on an even keel. Still, he must be getting on, as you say. So, what's the latest then?'

'Paul and his father are leading a sort of investigation. We're trying to learn from manufacturers like yourselves where they obtain their rough jet, and if the prices are fluctuating unduly. So far as anybody in the trade can make out, though, there's no one supplier that's prepared to pare down his rates for anybody, let alone them that haven't been in the business for long.'

'We're certainly paying enough, I can tell you. If we get away with a pound per pound weight I think we're doing jolly well, and most times we're laying out just over the pound.'

'And that's from family, isn't it? You do still buy from Cousin Isaac?'

'The biggest part of our jet, aye. He always has driven a hard bargain, mind. But it's only very occasionally, if we want something particular that he can't supply in a hurry, that I have to turn to somebody else.'

'The trouble is there are so many sources.'

'That's true enough, from old-established mines like the Falgrave one to them as goes scouting for raw jet washed up by the tide.'

'Then there's the rough jet dealers – it's hard to keep track of some of them, and to find out what they're charging. They travel about wherever it's to be had, and will take all sorts of sizes and in any condition.'

'What do you reckon, Olive? Are these new folk managing to charge so little just by shopping around for the cheapest jet, maybe inferior quality?'

'You'd answer that better than me. Look how long you've been involved with it. I only know what I've learned in the shop, and from Paul and his father. They reckon, though, that it's impossible to sell at those prices jewellery that's been manufactured from jet obtained anywhere round Whitby.'

'I wonder if Isaac could come up with any ideas. I'll go and have a talk with him if you like.'

'I'd come with you, only it would mean getting somebody to mind the shop. I've had a job finding a girl to take over for today.'

'Don't worry. Going on my own doesn't bother me, not like it used to. I've been over to the mine often enough these past nine years.'

Isaac Falgrave was inside the mine again when Hester arrived at Sandsend the following morning. She had the self-assurance now, though, to ask one of his men to tell him she had arrived. And the standing to bring him out immediately to greet her.

'Well now, Hester, this is a surprise. I hope there's nothing untoward? Nowt up with that last lot we sent you, is there?'

'Nothing like that. As a matter of fact, it was a lovely supply of jet. Even Wally Hardcastle had a good word to say for it.'

Isaac chuckled. 'How's he framing as t'new foreman?'

'Very well,' Hester admitted as they walked towards his office. 'I'm not sure whether to be pleased about that, or not. Anyway, it's to pick your brains really that I'm here today.'

He grinned wryly. 'Let's hope that's as profitable as t'digging that goes on over yonder. What's to do, lass?'

She asked if he had heard about the newcomers to the trade and what they were doing. And learned he knew there were rumours. When she outlined what Olive's father-in-law and others were doing, Isaac nodded seriously.

'They've set themselves a task trying to discover what folks are paying locally, as you doubtless understand. Still, I'm not saying that can't be done. They may come across somebody as is selling very low, though I've not had wind of it. Certainly, this is summat as wants watching.'

'Don't I know it! If folk like that keep offering a shopful of stuff cheaper than any of ours, there's nobody who will stick to old-established jet shops.'

Although Isaac had offered no concrete help, just visiting him made Hester feel better. She had given these few hours to initiating her own investigation of this new threat to the trade, and the action helped clarify her own intentions. As soon as she could be spared again for an hour or so she'd go over to that new shop, take a look at what Best Jet were offering.

Arriving at Falgrave House that evening, Hester was dismayed to find a horse-drawn hearse in the drive. Rushing indoors, she immediately located May Thorpe but the woman was so tearful and distraught that the only coherent words she uttered were, 'Oh dear, Miss Hester, isn't it terrible.'

Abel heard his daughter questioning the maid and called from the drawing room.

At least he's all right, she thought distractedly and hurried through to him.

'Who is it?' she demanded. 'Whatever's happened?'

'Mrs Richmond, I'm afraid. She's just – gone. One minute, she was standing by the range, checking the broth they were preparing, the next she'd collapsed.'

'Oh, how awful!'

'You've not heard the worst. As she fell, she went across the fire. Her face was badly burned and most of her clothing. Kilner was there, fortunately, taking a pot of tea. He's to be commended for his presence of mind. Dragged her off the fire he did, wrapped her in the rag rug to beat out the flames. Not that he could do owt for her poor face.'

'How ghastly! Was Kilner hurt in the process?'

'His hands are singed, of course. Jon was called in, naturally, and recommended hospital treatment. Unfortunately, our Ruth heard the commotion and went tearing along to the kitchen. May Thorpe tried to hold on to her, but the child saw it all.'

'Oh, God, no!'

'Jon sedated her, your mother's with her now.'

'And Mrs Richmond had – had just died, like that, without any warning?'

Her father nodded. 'So Jon says. Her heart gave out afore she fell on the fire. Apart from being burned, of course, it were an ideal way to go. For the person themselves.'

Not for the rest of the household, though. Mrs Richmond had served the Falgraves well and for a long number of years: she belonged with the family. No one would replace her. And for many a month nothing would ease the distress of her sudden, tragic ending.

Chaotic was a mild way to describe the ensuing days. When Maud wasn't keeping an eye on Ruth who was greatly shocked she was trying despairingly to encourage May Thorpe to organise everything. Poor May was totally disorientated. All her years at Falgrave House, Mrs Richmond had been there to see to everything. In the early days, May had been indoctrinated into the tough regimen to which any new maid was heir. But the housekeeper had been just and, in time, May had come to regard her as the mother she had never known.

Her grief now was genuine, rooted in true affection, and

her loss was so intense she literally could not command herself sufficiently to think.

'I had high hopes of you, you know,' Maud told her on the day before Mrs Richmond's funeral. 'If I ever thought about something like this happening, it was with the expectation that you would take over as housekeeper.'

May only wept again, profusely, convincing her mistress that there wasn't a chance of her being of any use.

'You'll have to help out till we get somebody reliable,' Maud told Hester that evening.

Hester was astounded, couldn't credit that her mother did not see that she already worked to capacity in the business. Abel, who had heard his wife's statement, intervened to point this out. Maud, however, merely paused for a second as if surprised, then shrugged.

'No matter what, I have to have help.'

'Are you trying to kill the lass?' Abel inquired.

'Hard work never hurt anybody,' snapped Maud. 'You're surely not suggesting I should do it all myself?'

'It's all right, Father,' said Hester. 'I'll do what I can. We'll manage somehow.'

Jon was making demands on her as well, expecting her to go with him one day when he called on one of their former workers, now long retired. For anyone but Jon, she'd have refused. As it turned out, the day was anything but a chore and she thoroughly enjoyed the outing.

The man ailed no more than advancing years and a chest that had been choked by too much tobacco. He was cheerful still, despite living alone, and was delighted to see Hester. On the way home Jon insisted that he was hungry and they must stop for tea. He'd already thought out where this would be, and smiled to himself when Hester's evident pleasure confirmed his taste of a village teashop. Their easy conversation was proving how right he'd been to get her away.

They took the rest of the journey at a leisurely pace while Jon relished her company, and she grew accustomed to letting go of cares.

Hester smiled when he pointed out several large pale

weathered discs on the hillside. 'I've seen those before around here. What exactly are they, do you know?' he asked.

'Mermaids' dining tables.'

Jon chuckled, and she grinned at him. 'That's what local folk call them. My father'd confirm they're useful landmarks for miners, help identify the site of jet deposits. It's a band of limestone – the Top Jet Dogger – and when the adits are dug into the hillside it also gives them a substantial roof.'

'You certainly know jet!'

'With my background, how could I not? Father always made a study of its formation. Did you know jet originates from trees – according to him, they'd be something like our monkey puzzles. Don't ask me how he knows.'

'Strange, I was under the impression jet was some form of resin. I've heard workers refer to it as "black amber".'

'Yes, most folk still believe that that's what it is. And they've the Romans to thank for that idea.'

'I'd be inclined to back your father's theory.'

Hester laughed again. 'You've come to know him pretty well, haven't you? But don't we ever bore you with our fixation about the jet?'

It was Jon now who laughed, and struggled for words to express the extent to which she constantly delighted him. Suspecting that she'd be startled by such a revelation, he spoke instead of his curiosity about the substance providing her livelihood.

'Have you ever heard anything to support the notion I read somewhere that jet cures toothache and even dropsy as well?'

Hester gave him a teasing look. 'Are you becoming a *witch* doctor?'

Smiling, he shook his head. Only bewitched, he thought, as I always am when I ease you away from your responsibilities.

'Well, you've certainly used a magic touch today,' Hester continued. 'I felt entrenched in gloom and unrelieved work – I'm thankful there's still a bit of pleasure to be found.'

She was strengthened to carry on. So long as he wasn't too far away, that was how she'd continue.

*

The workshop would have to be left to run itself for the time being, Hester decided. Fortunately, Wally appeared to be coping. Until they found someone as a substitute for Mrs Richmond at Falgrave House, she would endeavour to get some sense out of May Thorpe. She and Hester had always got along very well.

Hester wished yet again that Frank was foreman at the works: she'd have been completely satisfied then that the place was being run along lines of which she would approve. As it was, she could only give her attention to organising household matters – from Fitch's Patent Fire Wheels to ensure every fire was lit to Glenfield Starch for the maids who did the laundry.

The day of Mrs Richmond's funeral was bright, dawning to a watery sun glimmering through clouds which were quickly dispersed. Maud wouldn't leave Ruth, who was making the most of her first encounter with death. Not for the first time, Hester was the sole female representative of their family at such a sad gathering, and she didn't relish being conspicuous among the male mourners. Not that there would be many of those. Mrs Richmond's only relatives were an aged brother and a cousin who was travelling along with him from their home beyond Pickering.

The only good thing about it was Bernard's insistence that he would accompany her. 'I've got to face funerals some time, haven't I?' he said when Hester seemed surprised by his attending.

It was only afterwards that she recalled having been much younger than he was now when paying her last respects to Ruth Davidson.

The doctor was there today, waiting near the first of the resting places specifically constructed at intervals on Church Stair to permit bearers to rest the coffins they carried. He smiled, if somewhat gravely, towards Hester and her brother, fell into step beside them as they followed the slow progress of the coffin.

She asked him to sit with them in the Falgrave pew which was only one removed from where Mrs Richmond's relations were seated. Very aware of him beside her, she was conscious of his outward composure and that it concealed an unforgetting personal sorrow.

Alone with him back at the house while May Thorpe and the young maid scurried about with refreshments, she wasn't surprised to hear Jon's admission that each death brought back the loss of his beloved wife.

'I'm sure it must do,' she sympathised, and considered how dreadful this must be for a doctor who became involved in the demise of more people than anyone she could imagine.

'Normally, I'm adept at excusing myself from a funeral. Who can it help, after all, to have my presence? The person himself is past our assistance, and normally relatives are too distressed to know who is there.'

'It helped me today,' she told him simply.

Jon nodded. 'I felt certain you would be there.'

Once the funeral was over May Thorpe seemed to gather herself, and approached her mistress to request that she be considered for Mrs Richmond's post.

'I do know I've been useless since the day she passed on, Madam, but I won't allus be like it. I was so flabbergasted when she dropped all of a heap and died. It made a right mess of me, straight it did.'

'We could see that, May. You will understand why I'm not eager to rely on somebody who hasn't proved herself to have the necessary steadiness. However, I will allow you a short period in which to show us what you can do.'

Hearing the news, Hester was relieved but her mother soon dampened the rise in her spirits.

'We're not over the worst hurdles yet I fear, not with that one. If she can go to pieces once, she'll do it again. We may well have to search for a fresh housekeeper eventually. In the interim, Hester, I shall have to count on your support.'

Maud did indeed still expect Hester to assist in the home, and since her idea of testing May Thorpe's ability was to initiate a round of entertaining there was always some occasion demanding her daughter's time. Hester wasn't aided by the fact that May, realising she was on trial and less at ease with the mistress than with herself, took to consulting her on any matters which remained unclear.

Unable to spend much time at the works, Hester adapted one corner of her bedroom for designing new figurines, jewellery and any other items which she thought might effectively be created in jet. Incessantly interrupted by May in order to haul herself back to some humdrum aspect of entertaining guests or organising the household, she grew so frustrated that she came close to screaming.

The evening that she finally gave in to the increasing pressure should have been a celebration of Bernard's intention to marry. Although not yet engaged, Belle Jenkins and he were regularly seen together now, and on this occasion her parents also were invited. Sidney Etherington and his wife Sadie were present and Jon Davidson as well.

Also at table were Olive and her husband, a rare-enough event for Abel to observe tartly that he hardly knew he had a third daughter, these days.

'I'm not your third daughter, I'm the second, and if I've been absent so long that you've grown confused it's because *I* take an interest in what happens to the jet business.'

She glared across at Hester who only then recalled all that she had meant to investigate before the domestic crisis.

'If that was directed at me, I can only apologise, Olive – and to you, Paul. We've had so much on here, and I still have to keep the workshop running.'

'We have a home to run as well,' retorted Olive, ignoring her husband's cautioning glance. 'I'm on my feet all day long in our shop, but that doesn't stop me attending to other things that matter.'

Hester had had more than she could take. 'It's all right for you, you're not stuck at home with Mother demanding that you help out, and nor are you weighed down with responsibility for that place down yonder.' She just checked herself in time before adding that Olive wasn't trapped for the rest of her life watching their father exist as a mockery of the man he'd once been. Too appalled by what she'd said already to be thankful that she'd stopped short of saying worse, Hester broke down in uncharacteristic tears and rushed out into the entrance hall.

Jon sought her there, taking her to the windowseat where, years ago, he had spoken with her about her father's injuries.

'I think you'd better leave me alone,' she murmured huskily, recognising that kindness would completely dissolve what little composure remained.

'I think I'd better take you in hand,' he corrected her gently. 'As your doctor, if not as the friend that I hope you consider me.'

The appeal in his tone astonished her into looking at him. 'I hope you are my friend – I seem to be at odds with the rest of the world.'

Jon smiled. 'If that's a rare experience so far, love, you must have been fortunate. It's not an agreeable feeling though, I know, and in your case it's undeserved. Your mother taxes you too heavily here when you should be free to give your attention to running the workshop. And then there's your father . . .'

'I never said anything about him.'

'You bit the words back.'

His knowing this startled her so much that her eyes widened beneath dark lashes drooping with tears.

'Do you think I don't know, Hester, how much it hurts you to see him the way he is? Hurts you, maybe, more than any of the others. Especially since your mother had young Ruth. You're the one on whom so much depends, the one who links him with the business that was his life, the one who endures the stress of keeping it going. Because any other way would be unthinkable. And you are well aware that he envies you.'

She swallowed, gulped, blew her nose. But still another onslaught of tears refused to be contained.

The bearlike strength of him provided refuge for the woman who had supposed she had mastered the ability to stand as firm as many a man. He let her cry out her grief that had never quite been allowed full expression all those years ago, and along with that the frustration of eternally trying to cram too much into too few hours.

'I'm giving you medication that'll sedate you,' he told her

when at last she was snuffling wearily against his shoulder. 'And the one place for that is in your room.'

'That's not necessary,' she began, and was taken securely by the arm.

They went up in her father's lift, which allowed less time for argument and continued opportunity for Jon's grasp to support her.

In her room he set down his bag on the dressing table, strode to the bed and threw back the covers.

'Come along, Hester, I'm going to see that you're resting.'

'Then please leave me for a few minutes,' she said with as much dignity as she could manage.

He grinned. 'For heaven's sake, lass – I am a doctor! And was married for years.'

He went out just the same, and called back to her from the landing. 'I wonder what you possess that's so different from other females!'

Instead of returning downstairs, he waited on the landing, gazing out over the rest of Whitby. Not having noticed quite this aspect of the town before, he was interested in the conglomeration of roofs, jammed in all anyhow, it seemed to him, to embrace the harbour.

This cliff was very different from the west side and his own home which now felt so comfortless despite the elegance of the Crescent. He could understand how this spot had nurtured Abel's love of old Whitby and his affection for local history, legends as well. Granted the time, he'd take up similar interests himself. Medicine and science had provided him with sufficient stimulation but he longed often enough, these days, for a change that would engage his curiosity and his attention.

He'd allowed her time to undress, and went with more eagerness than he'd have admitted towards her room. He couldn't recall a time now when he hadn't cared for Hester Falgrave. Seeing her so distressed was disturbing, but being able to demonstrate his concern generated warmth deep inside him.

'You look better already,' he said immediately. She had brushed out her hair which contrasted sharply with her porcelain features and long slender neck.

331

'I know,' she responded swiftly. 'I feel a fraud, here in bed, though I'll admit to you I've no desire to return to that dining room after my outburst.'

'Do 'em the power of good,' he told her, smiling. 'It's good to have folks you can rely on, but even the best of families need the occasional reminder that relying shouldn't be synonymous with taking for granted. What was your sister on about, though, some sort of trouble in the jet trade?'

'Aye – sounds like it's getting worse as well.' She told him about the shop that was competing unfairly by ridiculously low prices, and how she'd got no further than beginning to ascertain where they were getting supplies of rough jet.

'That'll wait for another day, that's for sure. And as for the problem of a housekeeper here I'm surprised your mother's not promoting May Thorpe.'

'She's permitting her to have a try, but I don't believe May's sufficiently prepossessing for Mother's liking.'

He laughed. 'I'd trade her any day of the week for the woman I've got across the way there. Do you believe your mother would do a deal with me?'

'I shouldn't think so at all. Though if you showed interest in May that might just convince her that she's precisely the person we need.'

Jon gave her medication to ensure that she slept. He surprised her then by recommending at least two days away from home.

'What would I want to do that for? Isn't Whitby a holiday town that draws people for its beneficial air and all that?'

'It's also the place where you've taught yourself never to let up from work. I'm serious about your needing a change, Hester. Have you no friends you could visit?'

'Friends?' She shook her head. What had become of her friends? There'd been Jamie once, years ago, before he proved himself a disappointment. Then there'd been Frank, hadn't there, until he'd flared up because he couldn't bear to wait for the promotion he deserved.

'I've a cousin in Scarborough, Hester. She's been widowed five years or more now, and takes in guests during the season. I've promised her a visit – why don't you spend a day or two with her?'

'But – but I don't know her. She knows nowt about me.'

He laughed again. 'You'll find she's much like myself, though I hardly dare hope you'll consider that a recommendation.'

'You're being foolish now . . .'

'*I'm* not. But if you refuse to accompany me there . . .'

Mist was filling the town right from the West Cliff to the East, swirling about from upriver, across the harbour, to the sea. Moisture beaded Jon's brown hair when he took up the reins of his landaulet after stowing her belongings, and minute droplets hazed the flanks of his grey horse.

Nothing, however, could diminish the quite disproportionate excitement which Hester felt simply because she was going somewhere unconnected with work.

'Tell me about your cousin!'

'Susan's roughly the same age as myself – you'll find her motherly. She lived abroad for some years as her late husband was a tea-planter. After he died she couldn't resist returning to Yorkshire. I don't believe it was need made her take in summer visitors, not the need for money, anyway.'

'But you say she's made it pay?'

'Aye, she has an' all. With railways opening up all around us and improvements to the roads, our East Coast resorts are doing good business. But then I don't need to tell you that.'

'If your cousin's doing so well, I'm surprised she can spare us the rooms, especially at short notice.'

Jon chuckled. 'We're to live as family, I understand. When I drove over to enquire, she said as her Mabel and Billie have left home now. She keeps their rooms ready, but isn't above letting them to folk that she knows.'

Susan Walton was a handsome woman, big-boned like her cousin, but with hazel eyes and fading gingery hair. She beckoned them through and into her large kitchen, laughing as they passed the parlour door.

'You'll not be wanting to be mixing with that lot in there.

Mining folk, biggest part of 'em, not known for taking their pleasures quietly.'

'You'd better watch what you're saying, Susan,' Jon warned her. 'Hester's father used to be in mining.'

His cousin paled. 'But I thought . . .'

'Jet was what he mined,' Hester explained. 'And that was long since. Up until his accident he'd run the jet carving workshop.'

'That's what I gathered.' She turned to her cousin. 'There you go again – picking me up afore I've fallen. I don't often forget what I've been told about folk.'

'That's only the truth,' he admitted to Hester. 'As far as family goes, anyway. Susan has all the history off pat.'

'Well, it's no good expecting you to have, is it? You're too busy to take heed of yoursen, never mind t'rest of Davidsons.'

'Are there many of you still around these parts?' Hester inquired, smiling when the doctor took her coat.

'We're the last two of our generation surviving within a hundred miles of this coast,' he told her.

'There's some half-cousins or something went to live near Liverpool – our Billie's written to them once or twice.'

Although slightly smaller than the kitchen at Falgrave House, Hester was reminded of childhood mornings spent 'helping' Mrs Richmond. Together with this family gossip, the comfortable atmosphere instantly made her feel at home. She and Jon sat half-turning from the scrubbed pine table, drinking tea and absorbing the heat from the big iron range, while Susan talked about some of the more extraordinary visitors whom she'd entertained.

'I daresay you'll have as much variety in your patients, Jon – though I reckon they'll all put on their best behaviour for you.'

He raised an eyebrow at that. Hester laughed.

'Is that what I'm supposed to be on now?'

'You're supposed to be learning to relax. Or teaching me the way,' he added ruefully.

'Father seemed to consider you'd be adept at curing my tension. He jumped at the idea of my accompanying you.'

'Was your mother less pleased? She didn't say overmuch when I called for you this morning.'

'Mother was being obliged to look in at both the works and the shop this morning. She's grown away from the business since our Ruth came on the scene.'

'At least that's given you some freedom to organise the day-to-day running without criticism.'

Hester gave him a look. He'd noticed then that Maud Falgrave's hand wasn't always any too light.

'Still, it's escaping the lot that's intended,' he continued. 'And here I am already, letting you think of your responsibilities.'

Escape was what the two-day break from work became. When Susan had shown them to their rooms so they might freshen themselves after the journey they strolled as far as the nearby North Bay, and returned to a late luncheon with strong appetites.

They walked again in the afternoon, ambling sometimes among holidaymakers, sometimes away from crowds with only the sea birds for company. Jon was garrulous away from their home surroundings, telling Hester all about his long medical training and the dramatic results of Joseph Lister's introduction of carbolic acid three years before: it was sprayed inside operating theatres to disinfect the air.

'There have been many other advances, too. Now we perform operations that were once considered impossible.' There had been mistakes as well, though. For instance, carbolic could burn a patient. 'We're working on that – it's being used diluted.'

'You sound as though you'd be more interested in experimenting,' she observed.

He smiled. 'I fancied myself once in something of the kind, but I love the work I'm doing. I still have my small laboratory at the house, though, gathering forbidden dust.'

'I suppose we all have things we set our hearts on, only to have them crowded out.'

'You're young to talk that way.'

'Am I?'

She'd not thought of herself as young since goodness knows when. Happen the time that Lambert's youthful unconcern earned him a wife and children. It was from that period certainly that she'd grown more serious. *Too* serious, she wondered today?

She couldn't ever remember considering what Jon's age might be. Clearly he was nearer her father's age than her own. Or was that so? Did a doctor's calling imbue him with sufficient authority to make him appear older?

'I'm forty-five tomorrow, Hester.'

'Tomorrow? Why didn't you say?' She'd have presented him with a card, a gift of some kind. 'We'll have to celebrate!'

'We are. We came away from Whitby. And you're not to tell my cousin. I thought we might leave Scarborough early, make our way back then stop and eat at some agreeable inn when we're but a stone's throw from home.'

'I'll love that.'

Dining with him was a delight, an exquisite ending to a weekend which had relaxed her as much as intended.

The inn was high on the moors with coals ablaze in a large open fireplace, taking the chill out of the wind that rattled at doors and windows. No words were adequate for wishing him the birthday he deserved, if only for his great kindness in bringing her away. Hester tried, nevertheless, to express the good she wished him, even though she felt afterwards that anyone with a bit of gumption could have said far more, far better. But Jon minded not at all. She wasn't the only one who'd benefited from taking a brief pause in a busy life.

Pleasantly tired, both companionably at ease, they talked only intermittently during the rest of the ride into Whitby. For Hester it had been a significant interlude, in which Jon had become the one person she could depend on. He'd always been so understanding especially since her father, against all his inclinations, had been compelled to rely on his offspring. Tonight, she'd begun to believe there was mutual benefit in Jon and herself being together.

It was as well she couldn't know then that she would need every single ounce of support – to say nothing of her own fortitude – in order to survive the next few months.

Chapter 18

A message was awaiting Hester at the works. Olive's neat script on the envelope sent her heart plummeting even before she extracted her note. I'll not let her destroy the good that lovely weekend in Scarborough's done me, she determined. Her jaw taut, she began to read.

> Dear Hester,
>
> *I hope you are recovered as a result of getting away from Whitby. Those of us less fortunate have been confronted by further difficulties which, I am sorry to relate, concern Falgraves'. I therefore urge you to notify either myself or Paul the instant you are returned in order to arrange a discussion without further delay.*

There was more to the letter, no less overbearing. Hester locked it in her desk drawer, and willed herself to dismiss it until the evening. Although she had been absent for only the Saturday morning shift at the works, she felt that she had been away far longer, and had an inward suspicion that she might not have too firm a grip on proceedings here.

Wally Hardcastle had been stirring matters again, she was sure. Bob Dunsdale and his Silas both wore fixed expressions of grim concentration and Frank and Harold Clough seemed watchful of Hardcastle's every move.

In the past, she'd have taken Frank aside and inquired what had occurred – but with his loss of the foreman's job still like a wall between them, she could depend on no one.

'Was my mother here for long on Saturday?' she inquired of Wally Hardcastle.

His shrug was dismissive. 'Mrs Falgrave looked in for a time, but she took herself off to Flowergate.'

Yes, thought Hester, and while she was checking out the

shop were you up to your old tricks, sabotaging the smooth working of this place?

Just then, she heard the sound of slow feet ascending the narrow stair. Standing motionless, as if sensing already the import of the visit, she looked towards the top of the steps.

Cecil Arkwright had aged, even though with his prematurely-white hair he'd never seemed to her anything but elderly. Now, his cheeks had hollowed and the once determined chin seemed hatchet-sharp. His eyes remained just as keen, though, and were threatening to pierce through the bone of her skull.

'Miss Falgrave. You'll grant me your attention, I trust. I come on a grave matter.'

Her own response was smoother than she might have feared, and she silently congratulated herself on her outward composure as she conducted him towards the office.

Even seated, and despite showing his years, Arkwright possessed a commanding presence. A week ago, she might have permitted her alarm to surface. Instead, she merely swallowed to ensure that her voice emerged on a lower octave.

'I have been away from Whitby for a day or two and returned to a note from my sister, Mrs Broadbent. I haven't yet, of course, managed to speak with her, but she did mention a matter of urgency involving Falgraves'. Am I to take it that you know of its nature?'

Every gesture measured, he felt in an inner pocket of his coat, then with the other hand in an outer one. Abruptly, he slammed the contents of each down on the desk. A handful of engraved buttons scattered in several directions. An intricately-carved ring rolled for a moment then settled.

'Are these of your designing?' he asked.

More perturbed than she would show, Hester gathered up the buttons one by one, scrutinising each before placing them to form a row close beside her sleeve. She took longer over the ring, examining it minutely, trying to still the agitated pulsing in her throat.

'Yes, they do appear to be made from my designs.'

'But not in this workroom.'

She might have been surprised, had she not been so

338

familiar with the work of the craftsmen they employed that she'd have identified their jet anywhere. And she'd used the time whilst inspecting these pieces to calm the panic that menaced her grip on the situation.

'I can see that.'

'You're not astonished to learn these are from that new Best Jet place that'll put us all out of business if we don't act now?'

'Appalled, is the word, Mr Arkwright. I can't claim to be very astonished – the second you showed me what you've obtained, I feared the worst.'

'That you're discovered?'

'I beg your pardon?' Involuntarily, she had sprung to her feet. There was no place here for deference to the man's years, not when he'd come with accusations that barely bore mentioning.

'You admit they're your designs, and they were bought in yon upstart's shop. Speak for themselves, don't they?'

'They might to you, to somebody who wants to believe the worst of me, without permitting me time for explanation.'

'You can talk from now till the last trump, you'll never excuse what you've done. How *could* you, lass – and you Abel Falgrave's daughter!'

'I protest most strongly, Mr Arkwright. Your attitude is totally unwarranted.' Inwardly, she seethed because of this misjudgement.

'Mine? Do you honestly think it's only me? All the jet trade is up in arms, has been for long enough. And who's the one person who's consistently neglected to join with us in getting to the bottom of this?'

This time when Hester swallowed it was on a despairing lump that refused to vanish from her throat.

'They must have bought stuff out of our shop, copied it.'

'Oh, aye – for every item? That would cost a packet, they'd have no profit left. Nay, you'll have to come up with a more likely tale nor that. There's many a score of things as they have on show that even you will see have come from your patterns.'

'I've had nothing to do with them, I swear it. I – give me time, and I'll prove how they're getting away with this. Do

339

you think *I* don't want to know how they've achieved this – this fraud?'

'I think you know already,' he interrupted. 'And believe me, I'm not the only one. Somehow, from somewhere, you've acquired large quantities of cheap jet, and you've deliberately set out to get one over on the rest of us.'

'No, no – oh, please . . . Let me work this out, I ought to be able to discover how they've managed . . .'

She was interrupted yet again. 'You'll have to be quick about it, and you'll have to convince a lot of us. So far as the rest of the trade is concerned, you've played the most shabby trick of all time.'

Hester immediately went to the new shop herself, saw in the window evidence that the majority of goods displayed were unmistakably of her own designing. Still disbelieving of what sight told her, she entered and strode towards the counter.

The girl was someone she'd not encountered in Whitby before, and her accent certainly wasn't local.

Hester began with a few general inquiries about how long they had been in business and who the owners were, and received a smiling response that they were long-established elsewhere in jet working.

'I find that hard to believe,' she replied, but without explaining how her own family were involved, feeling it inadvisable – could not go on to tell how close the jet community was.

Instead, she purchased samples of as many different items as she could without arousing too much interest. There must be something about one or more of these pieces which would give her a clue as to where their production had begun.

Olive was waiting for her back at the workshop, tapping an elegantly-shod foot that raised a dust of jet particles.

'You received my letter?'

'I did indeed, and a call from Cecil Arkwright. You'd better come through to the office.' If their workers were still in ignorance, she'd prefer them to remain that way, until the story was announced around the whole of Whitby.

'It wasn't me,' she told her sister. 'I've never been near that Best Jet shop until just now, to obtain samples. And I've had no contact whatsoever with the owners, whoever they are.'

'If you don't know who's running the place, you can't be certain it's nobody you're involved with.'

'Thank you, Olive,' she said tersely, paused then recovered. 'Oh, sit down, lass. I've no quarrel with you. I'm just – shattered!'

At last, the look in her sister's eyes was sympathetic. 'I can see now that you're not involved. Thank God for that. I'll tell Paul, of course, and his father.'

'But if they believe you no one else will. I'm going to prove it's nothing to do with me, Olive. I don't know how, but there must be a way.'

'We had somebody round from the *Whitby Gazette* on Saturday. They'd got wind of trouble in the jet industry. I managed to put them off, I think, but if they're short of news at any time . . .'

'This'll creep in. But we've got to keep the rumours of my involvement from Father. I won't have him upset by this.'

After Olive had left Hester decided she must overcome her reluctance and have a word with Frank Clough. If his father was up to it, he might be able to help. Edwin's long experience in the trade could produce some lead as to where exceptionally cheap jet might be obtained. And intuition kept hammering at her that the raw material used by these people would provide the information they needed.

Frank had watched her covertly all day long, first when she reacted to Cecil Arkwright's arrival and later her own sister's. He'd seen the look on her face, as well, after she'd been out on that errand.

He'd never seen her more perturbed – and that sickened him. All week, talk in the public houses where jet workers gathered had centred on this new shop, and he was tired to death of being told the designs were just like Falgraves'.

He'd discussed the matter with his father last evening. He could see them now, sitting either side of the hearth while his mother left the kitchen sink and her washing-up to listen.

'Once, Frank, I'd have sworn on oath as it couldn't have owt to do with Hester Falgrave,' Edwin said seriously.

'I should think it couldn't indeed,' Alice had put in, only to have her husband check her.

'Just a minute, Alice, afore you go sayin' that. In recent years, I've begun to wonder if the whole family were being – well, *warped* by Abel's disability. Nowt's same there, is it? And look how they made Wally Hardcastle foreman. I'm not saying it necessarily should have been thee, Frank, but they could have picked somebody better nor that.'

Frank had been trying hard to contain his prejudice, but couldn't resist a remark. 'Well, you know I felt I'd been smacked in t'face by it. Specially when I'd been appointed temporary foreman. Looked like I'd made a mess of t'job.'

'Which you hadn't, I am certain,' his mother asserted. 'There's nobody in this town more conscientious.'

'You don't think they chose Hardcastle because you were too close to what were going on there?' Edwin suggested.

'I wish I didn't think that.'

'You were getting very friendly with Hester Falgrave at one time, weren't you, Frank?' his mother said.

'I'd have bet my last shirt that she had nowt to hide,' Frank responded.

But that had been years ago.

When Hester asked him to step into the office, he sensed their Harold and some of the other men gazing significantly towards him. He'd always felt uneasy when the relationship he'd hoped to further between himself and Hester was under his workmates' scrutiny. Today, expecting that she was going to confide the reasons for what she'd been up to, he yearned for anything that might be a different cause for this interview.

'Please take a seat, Frank,' she began, trying to muster her agitated thoughts sufficiently to render conversation coherent. 'I've asked you in here because I need your help. First, though, how's your father getting on?'

'Not much different, thanks,' he answered tautly. Why

didn't she get on with the business, instead of pretending she cared about any of them any longer?

'You've heard about this new jet works and shop that's set up?'

'Aye, I have. It'd be hard not to when there's talk of nowt else in all the public houses where jet folk meet.'

'Have you seen the stuff they're selling?'

'I've been told. I know enough.' One or two of the men from other workrooms had actually accused him of engraving the things on sale there. He'd put them right, but hated the nasty taste that remained. 'It'll destroy the rest on us,' he added. 'You know that, don't you?'

It was his eyes that did it – sharp and green, and accusing. Whatever she said, he'd not believe she wasn't involved. Just like everyone else, Frank required proof of her innocence.

They hadn't had much of a friendship for some while now but its sudden final disappearance felt like bereavement. And the day had provided enough trials.

Hester glanced at the clock. 'It's nearly finishing time,' she observed quietly, and decided to say nothing more: if she expressed her disappointment in him, it would escalate into an irreversible quarrel. How wrong she had been: she couldn't ask help of somebody who no longer believed in her.

She couldn't face any of them. Taking her coat from the hook she walked straight out of the office, down the stairs and out into the street.

Too disturbed to go home, she continued walking up through the town and off in the direction of the moors. The wind that hardly ever dropped for more than a few hours together was sighing through the heather, heavy as her own thoughts.

She had counted on Frank to assist with her examination of the jet pieces: he might have spotted something she had missed, some clue in the manufacture that would help trace the source. He'd have been there also while she conducted tests – what kind of tests she hadn't yet ascertained, but she'd seen them both in her mind's eye, working together as on more constructive ideas, and emerging with a solution.

As it was, she'd been so distressed by his evident suspicions of her that she wasn't even certain now what she'd done with the package brought from the shop over on West Cliff, nor with the items Cecil Arkwright had tossed down in front of her. If she didn't go back to the workroom she couldn't begin tonight.

The sea glittered in the hazy distance. The rooftops of Whitby, red-tiled and a mass of angles, stood out against the green of the cliff-edge with the darkened stone of the abbey ruins silhouetted against a cloudless sky. And for the first time in her life she felt exiled from this place that she loved, reluctant ever to return there.

Turning her back on the town, she pressed on further, hurrying now, bent into the wind that buffeted her head and whipped at her wide skirts making progress difficult.

Was it only last night that she'd returned to Whitby, refreshed as much by Jon Davidson's concern for her as by the change of scenery? If only it hadn't been *Frank* who'd revealed by a glance that he doubted her . . .

Time passed without her paying any heed. Only when the sun dropped nearer to the horizon and the wind grew stronger and more chill did Hester think to head for home.

The fresh air and wild surroundings had done nothing to clear her head. She was still obsessed with that wretched new jet shop, and her supposed crime. Maybe if she re-examined the items purchased there, inspection might reveal something.

The workroom was eerie in its twilight silence, with the treadles idle and neither chatter nor the men's singing in the dust-laden air. She opened the office door swiftly – she'd be glad to pick up those jet pieces and be away from here.

They were where she had left them, though she didn't recall opening the package from Best Jet. She collected up all the buttons and the jewellery, and added to them those brought by Cecil Arkwright.

'I thought you might be back . . .'

The voice behind her in the doorway startled her so much she gave a harsh scream, and dropped everything in her hand.

Buttons rolled and bounced on to the desk and then the

floor, larger items clattered as they fell. A large ornamental brooch split in two as it hit the edge of the desk.

It was Frank, and he came into the room now, wordlessly gathering up every item that she had dropped. When he had them all he held them towards her, green eyes challenging while she took them in her hands.

'Thought you'd come to remove the evidence.'

'One day, you'll know,' she said, and prayed that she was right as she walked past him.

The brooch that had broken intrigued her; all the way to the house, she was fingering the halves as they lay in her pocket. As soon as she reached her room she removed and scrutinised them.

She'd never seen jet like this before. The inner core was black, not the brownish colour of jet. She looked again at some of the buttons and beads . . .

Pausing to eat a meal that evening couldn't be avoided, but was a tantalising process, separating her from the urgency of her task.

As soon as they had finished dinner, she asked her parents if it was all right to use the brougham.

Kilner reined in and the carriage stopped with a tiny jolt just as the doctor was emerging from the house in Royal Crescent.

'At least I haven't missed you entirely,' she said with a rueful smile as he came to help her alight.

'You haven't missed me at all, Hester. I was merely going for a stroll.'

'Are you sure?'

'Will you walk with me?'

'If it's not a dreadful nuisance, I was wondering if I might borrow that laboratory of yours.'

'You've just got yourself a willing assistant as well, if you'll only tell me what you intend.'

As Jon showed her the way through to the room he'd set aside for experiments, Hester told him all that had occurred that day, only stopping short of explaining how, twice now, Frank had as good as accused her of responsibility for the unfair competition harrowing their trade.

'There are tests then, are there, to prove the authenticity of jet?' he asked.

She knew by his tone that there was no possibility of his doubting her integrity. She nodded. 'Father's one of the few folk who've experimented – they're very simple, and don't demand much in the way of equipment. All I need really is somewhere private that isn't Falgrave House or our workroom.'

Although his eyebrows soared, he contained his exclamation. He'd heard last week that her name was linked with contention surrounding the new jet shop, but didn't like to think it was possible she was mistrusted at home.

'I suspected this wasn't jet when it snapped the way it has,' said Hester, showing him the brooch as she set it on his work-bench. 'Firstly, jet has an oily smell when fractured but there was no smell given off when this broke – and internally, it's nothing like jet in appearance. This feels heavy for jet, as well. I think it's some kind of black glass.'

'That's interesting.'

Jon drew out a high stool for her, occupied another next to it.

'Do you have some means of heating small items?' she inquired.

He went to a cupboard and returned with a length of rubber tubing, one end of which he attached to a gas-tap. After turning on the gas, he ignited the nozzle of the apparatus.

'What next, Hester?'

'I don't suppose you have a needle or something similar that I can heat in the flame?'

'A small scalpel?'

'That's fine, thank you.'

She took the scalpel from him, held its point in the flame, then applied the point to one half of the brooch.

'Can you smell anything?' she asked him.

'Not a thing. I presume one should?'

Hester nodded. 'Like burning coal. And this has scarcely marked the substance. I'm positive it's glass.'

She took out the rest of the pieces acquired in the new

shop, and selected two buttons of different designs and several beads.

When she applied the heated point to the face of one of the buttons the reaction was similar to that of the brooch. She examined the button more closely, then inserted the hot scalpel at the side of the piece just in front of its metal backing.

A minute wisp of smoke arose. She and Jon looked at each other.

'That's not the smell of coal either,' she said, while he nodded agreement.

'Wax?'

'That's it, Jon. So – we know already that somebody's hit on the idea of using either black glass or a combination of dark wax with a glass covering to protect and give it the necessary shine.'

'Both cheaper than using genuine jet?'

'I should say so. That might take some proving, though, and how did they obtain my designs?'

'They were yours, then?' he asked gravely.

'You've heard all the talk as well? Yes, as soon as I saw their window display I could tell much of their stock bore a marked resemblance.'

'Don't you keep your designs locked away?'

'We've never felt the need to. Certain patterns might be traditional within the trade, but as for the rest . . . we've simply considered that every other jet works was just as keen as ourselves to develop originality. Until now, there seemed to be work enough for us all.'

Jon took out and consulted his gold watch. 'Have you eaten this evening, Hester?'

'Why – what's the time?'

'A quarter to ten.'

'It can't be! I did have something anyway but what about you?'

'Oh, I consumed some featureless mass presented by my housekeeper.'

'Thank goodness I'm not keeping you from a meal. I'm sorry I've taken up so much of your time, though. And I shall have to be making for home.'

'Well, at least you've had some success.'

'Thank heaven!' She looked longingly towards the other pieces she had meant to subject to tests.

'You may come back whenever you wish, my dear. If I'm in surgery when you arrive or out on call, my housekeeper will have instructions to admit you.'

'You're so good to me. Thank you ever so much, Jon.'

During the following three days Hester returned and carried out tests on every piece of jet that had come from the new shop on the West Cliff. When each item proved to be skilfully faked she went back and purchased further pieces, then hurried to test those.

There was nothing which hadn't been produced from either glass or black wax with a thin glass covering. To the naked eye, though, and even to a skilled jet craftsman, the pieces appeared on the surface to be utterly genuine.

She told Olive first of all, and then Cecil Arkwright, asking to see him in the magnificent office he'd recently had constructed adjoining his workroom.

'This isn't jet, Mr Arkwright,' she told him, just as baldly as he had produced the offending samples on visiting her. 'Some of it is dark glass, some wax . . .'

'Wax doesn't shine like this,' he interrupted cautiously.

'It does when they've used a layer of glass to cover it.'

Slowly, his thin face relaxed into a smile of sheer satisfaction. 'So that's how they've kept their prices this low.'

'What I mean to learn next is how they've acquired my designs.' And she already had a suspicion that she might resolve that without too much difficulty.

'I suppose you haven't discovered who these people are?' she asked him when he'd finished examining the articles that she had brought with her.

'Not yet. I went to inspect their workroom – feigning a courtesy call – and there wasn't one man I could identify.' He smiled at her. 'Now I know why the place appeared exceptionally clean.'

Hester smiled back. 'I'm sure there's nothing produces the dust that jet does.'

'I can see how I was deceived,' he admitted. 'I wasn't

shown from bench to bench, and whenever I approached one of the workers he ceased whatever he was doing. I ought to have been more suspicious, I suppose . . .'

'But you were looking for people – people who seemed familiar, weren't you? And I wouldn't be surprised if that place were only a front, if there were other men working elsewhere.'

'In order to conceal the fact that they work to your designs.'

'And to conceal their identity.'

'Have you any idea at all, Miss Falgrave, where these people might have obtained their raw materials?'

She shook her head. 'I haven't thought about that yet. Is there any glass produced in this part of Yorkshire?'

'To be honest, I have no idea.'

'And wax, in large quantities?'

'Again, this has me foxed. But it won't remain that way, Miss Falgrave, you may be assured. And I can only apologise most sincerely for believing that you could ever have been involved.'

The hours she had devoted to investigating this unfair rivalry within the trade had been taken from her own job. Although Bernard had kept an eye on things at the works, she had done little or no designing for some time. In order to compete with the stuff turned out at that wretched place, she would need to create masses of new patterns, soon.

Ordinarily, she might have discussed some of her ideas with Frank. As things were, she consulted no one except her father. Fortunately, he was impressed by the first suggestion she put to him.

'I've been wondering if we could do something to mark the Education Act,' she began, 'something as a tribute to William Edward Forster.'

'That's quite a notion,' Abel concurred. 'Busts of him, you mean?'

'Or figurines. There have been photographs of him in the newspapers.'

'And he is a Yorkshireman!'

'That's what I was thinking,' Hester added. 'I'll bet quite

349

a lot of visitors to Whitby are from his native Bradford. And happen we could manage to sell figures of him over there.'

Her father chuckled. 'So long as his Quaker background doesn't make him object to them as effigies!'

'Do you think he would see them like that?'

'Ay, lass – I'm teasing you. You get on with some drawings, and see how fast you can begin producing them. Have you done any busts of Gladstone since he became Prime Minister – when was that, two years ago?'

'Round about then. No, I don't think we have. It's some long while since we had any new politicians going through.'

'You'll have some busts of Charles Dickens to hand, though, I'll warrant.'

'It's a regular line, Father. They've sold well since he died, just as they did when he was doing his reading tours locally.'

They were interrupted by May Thorpe announcing that Mr Clough wished to speak with both of them.

'All right, show him in,' said Abel, and turned to his daughter as the housekeeper went back to the hall. 'Edwin, eh? He must be picking up at last.'

It wasn't Edwin. His eldest son's face was ashen, yet his neck above the clean white shirt was deep red, witness to his embarrassment.

'Good evening to you, Mr Falgrave – Hester. I'm glad I've caught you together. I want you both to hear what I've got to say.'

'Come and sit down, Frank,' Abel invited genially.

Frank could not sit. He could no more relax before saying his piece than he could take wings and drift through the window.

'I've come to apologise, Hester, for what I said t'other day. I only had to think for a bit to realise it weren't justified, that it couldn't be . . .'

Hester inclined her head towards him, and tried to cut him off before he revealed more to her father. 'You've heard then, have you, Frank – that the jet the new shop is offering is all faked.'

'No, no – I've heard nowt like that. It's just, as I say, I know you couldn't have been involved.'

'*Involved?*' Abel echoed. '*Hester?*'

'That particular rumour hadn't reached Father,' she said quietly.

'But I thought – well, it was your sister talking about it, surely?'

'Whatever Olive said at the works, while she was here she only ever spoke about the way their prices were undercutting everyone else's.'

'Now, just a minute,' Abel began, 'let's get to t'bottom of this. And do sit down, Frank, for pity's sake. It's bad enough craning my neck to look at folk when they're on a chair.'

'There was a lot more to it than you knew,' Hester began telling her father while Frank lowered himself on to a seat. 'The designs of the stuff they're selling are identical with our own, with what I've drawn.'

'Never! Has somebody broken in then, taken them?'

'I don't know – there's a lot that I don't know as yet, but I shall find out.'

'I'll help you, Hester, if you'll let me,' Frank volunteered, still looking embarrassed.

She nodded. 'Aye, I'll take whatever help I can get. Not that I'm rightly sure what the next step is. I've proved that samples of their stuff is made from glass and, alternatively, wax with a glass coating.'

'You didn't tell me that,' said Frank.

'No, I wanted to have more to go on than that before I spread it around the works that I was investigating. And I'll thank you to keep quiet about it now.'

'But why wasn't *I* told?' demanded Abel.

'I can't speak for our Olive, but I didn't tell you because I didn't want you worrying before I had all the answers.'

'Ah, well – Olive hasn't been here for a good few days, has she? So what are you after finding out next?'

'Where these people get their supplies from. Short of searching their premises, I can't see a way of discovering how many of my designs they've got, never mind how they acquired them.'

'So, we'll concentrate on the raw materials. I must say

you've done well, love, to find out that it wasn't jet they were using.'

'I had a bit of help.'

'Have you thought of t'possibility that they could be bringing in the stuff by sea?' Abel asked.

'It had occurred to me. With Whitby being a port, it's an obvious answer. Then I wondered if it was *too* obvious – and wouldn't it be costly?'

'On the face of it,' said Frank, 'it does sound like that. There'd be shipping charges on top of the actual cost of the materials.'

'It wants looking into, though,' Abel stated.

'I know,' Hester agreed. 'And so do a lot more aspects of this racket. If need be, I'll get other folk in the trade to help out. But I'm going to be there when they get whoever's responsible. I'll see they get what's coming to 'em.'

Frank's appearing at the house and apologising in front of her father meant a great deal to Hester. Particularly when she understood that he'd known nothing of her recent findings.

'I mean what I said,' he told her as she walked with him to the door. 'I'm that sorry I could even think for one minute that you might have had a hand in what they're up to.'

'All right, let's forget it now, shall we?'

'There's a lot that I might have handled better of late,' he admitted. 'Like not being made foreman permanently. It were daft going off at you like that, just because I were thwarted.'

'Yes, it was,' she acknowledged softly, with a glance over her shoulder towards the closed door beyond which they had left her father. 'Especially since I was the one who wanted you to take over.'

He appeared astounded. 'You never said.'

'No. Happen you'll have to adjust to the fact that I'm in a situation where there's often times when I have to keep silent.'

When he began apologising again, she cut him short. 'We'll take that as said, shall we?'

What she didn't admit was that his repeatedly misjudging

her was something that couldn't be obliterated. She had been hurt as well as insulted, and though she might forgive, forgetting was something less readily arranged. And the worst of it was that this was a time when she desperately needed the support of a friend she could trust.

Chapter 19

No matter how far he travelled and, these days, voyages frequently took him to France and Spain, Jamie Skelton always experienced a thrill approaching Whitby Harbour. From the sea, the town hardly seemed to change, despite increasing numbers of holiday visitors and the new railways which facilitated that business.

And he always looked forward now to returning to his lodgings. Even after settling with his father by paying for the new boat, he'd no wish to return to the family home by the harbour. Since he'd more brass in his pocket he'd found himself a good place to stay. Ideal, in fact, as it was a room over one of the liveliest public houses in the vicinity. There was an added attraction as well – the landlord's youngest daughter, a pretty little thing who wasn't reluctant to come to his room, on the nights when he remained sober.

This would be one of those nights, not for the lass's sake – he took his pleasures wherever he was now, no one girl satisfied his needs or won consideration of him – but for the business deal awaiting him.

He unloaded the stuff himself. He'd never let his muscles waste, even though his promotion aboard the freighter meant others did the worst of the manual jobs now. He had the packing cases stacked to one side, well away from the rest of the cargo that was being offloaded, long before Jeff arrived with the horse and cart.

'You could give a hand, save some time,' Jamie grumbled, when his friend remained leaning against one of the bollards on the quayside.

Jeff only grinned which was what Jamie expected. If there had been an answer it would have been a reminder that he must protect his hands, ready for the job.

'We'll have to have help next time I come ashore,' said Jamie, not without satisfaction. 'This is t'last time I work for somebody else.'

'You've got your own boat,' Jeff exclaimed, surprised into smiling, even though he felt a tinge of jealousy.

'Aye – she'll be ready before the week's out. Next time I put to sea I'll be my own master.'

'You'll carry what we ask on you then?'

'So long as t'price is all right.'

'It'll be same as you've been getting for months now.' If Jamie wanted more, there'd be less for the skilled craftsmen.

'I'll have to think about it then,' said Jamie, pausing for breath between humping packing cases. It was daft to admit to Jeff that until he'd built up business he'd be taking every order he could get.

When each item was loaded, Jamie clambered up beside his friend. 'How's the shop going?' That wasn't his concern, but without its healthy trade this sideline of his would cease.

Jeff laughed. 'Better nor ever. It's getting all t'jet works uneasy, can't say I'm sorry. And I've got several of the lads working with me now, instead of in the workroom. I've taught 'em quite a bit, they're making theirselves useful to me. And it stops folk getting inquisitive about what's happening in the works.'

'Are folk poking their noses in there?'

Jeff laughed again, at Jamie's anxious face. 'Only old Cecil Arkwright, and he's past noticing owt if it were stuck in front of him. We've got everybody trained to stop visitors from seeing owt that matters.'

'And the shop girl?'

'*Girls*,' Jeff corrected him. 'We've taken on that lass's sister – she's just as keen to earn good money by keeping her mouth shut.'

'Is she from London an' all?'

'Aye – she were working in Covent Garden market, and there's no question she finds this more to her liking.'

'Where's she living, though?' Jamie still wasn't entirely satisfied that nothing might leak out.

'Same as her sister, with me.'

'You greedy beggar!'

'Aye, they are both . . . accommodating. But from what I hear you do all right yourself.'

They had reached the building on the outskirts of the

355

town where Jeff had his own, very private, workroom and two bedrooms besides, with the minimum of furniture. He had walked in and taken over the three-storey house when its previous owner, a solitary old man who used to emerge on Friday nights to drink a week's ale, had imbibed even more immoderately and sunk into his permanent sleep.

'You've got it looking nice now,' said Jamie, dumping down one of the cases of glass in the curtained-off section where his friend worked.

'Aye, it's not so bad.' Jeff was standing in the middle of his living area, his back to the old range, while he surveyed the scratched table and rickety chairs.

The thing he liked best about the place was its distance from his stepmother. Wally might like a young lass in his bed, but his eldest son had never taken to having her around the house. She was a tartar for having her own way, and wouldn't tolerate any countermanding of her wishes. And if she so much as suspected money was being spent on something which she hadn't sanctioned they all suffered. There was nothing like having his own place, and no one to tell him how to manage his affairs.

To Jamie, a home of his own was a dream scarcely acknowledged. However, once he'd built up business enough to keep his boat at sea, there would be nothing to stop him. He would rent somewhere, or even buy a little place. He'd not take the risk that Jeff had, and expect every knock on the door to bring somebody with genuine right of ownership.

'Does your old man know you've just taken this over, like?' Jamie asked, when he was recovering from hauling the next load upstairs.

'Don't talk daft. He doesn't know where I'm living.'

'Haven't you seen him lately?'

'Aye, last night. We meet over a drink, of course.'

'Not – not over yonder?'

Jeff laughed. 'Dear me, we are frightened, aren't we? Scared somebody'll see you in the bar there same time as me?'

'You do watch who's about when patterns are changing hands?'

'Have I ever given you t'impression as I'm stupid?'

Jamie shook his head amiably, continued stacking the goods in Jeff's rooms, then accepted the amount already agreed.

'Shall I see you over a glass later on?' Jeff asked him.

'You might,' Jamie responded.

First, though, he was away to check progress on that boat of his, and to hand over this next instalment.

The meeting was held at Falgrave House. The moment she had decided that the gathering must take place, Hester had resolved that her father wouldn't be left out. Despite the serious nature of their objective, he was enjoying himself.

Dressed in formal trousers and coat he was ensconced in his invalid chair, propped as high as cushions made possible, in the exact centre of the long wall of the drawing room. His back was to the windows. Notwithstanding the enforced inactivity, he remembered how to disadvantage others. Not that it should be necessary to do anything of the kind. From the day that Hester proved the jet from that upstart company was fake, her conduct was accepted as genuine.

Olive had arrived already, together with Paul and his father, Ephraim Broadbent. They were seated to one side of Abel and Maud, but only until the other jet manufacturers arrived. Hester was determined that they would be asked to sit with everyone else, unless or until any of them elected to speak.

It had been left to her to organise this meeting to clear the air concerning the matter of the fraud: no one else had offered to take over its management.

Cecil Arkwright was next to appear, with his older brother in tow and a young man whom he introduced as a nephew. 'William has recently been taken into the business,' Cecil announced.

William possessed the family erect bearing and a habit of gazing at one down his long nose. Hester decided to keep an eye on him.

The room was filling now, old friends and new acquaintances within the trade coming to greet Abel before choosing where they would sit. Maud's blue eyes narrowed when she noticed some of the company staring with ill-concealed calculation about the room.

It had changed little these past nine years. If they'd had the wherewithal for refurbishing, she'd not had the time to give it thought. And events had resulted in a sorting of priorities which she didn't, for one moment, regret. Friends came as they had all along, to dine with them, to sit with Abel. She really did not have time to spare for considering any who'd chosen to stay away.

This was true also of this evening's gathering. When Hester remarked that a few manufacturers had failed to respond to her invitation, Maud had shrugged.

'They'll learn what goes on, eventually. I've ceased troubling myself about folk that won't participate.'

Hester hid a smile. Her mother seemed oblivious to the fact of her own sudden renewal of interest in the business after years of lack of involvement.

'You'll have to begin on time,' she told her daughter now, unconscious of the reality that Hester had to all intents organised the company for many a year. And might, therefore, be capable of managing a two-hour meeting!

Hester strode past her mother and towards the door leading in from the hall. Several representatives of the smaller jet workshops had come in together and were hesitating on the threshold. She welcomed them, showed them where they would find vacant seats.

Returning to her father's side, she scanned the company. Most of the people she'd expected were here, and one or two that she hadn't anticipated attending. The long-case clock in the hall struck the hour and she nodded towards her father.

'It's good to see you all,' Abel began, his voice firm. 'And to see you joining with us to learn what's gone amiss within the trade. As you all know by now, we're being threatened by unscrupulous folk that think they can put one over on everybody.'

He paused, but only to draw in breath. 'My daughter Hester has concerned herself with testing samples from that shop they've had the audacity to call Best Jet! As some of you already know, she's proved that what these folks are offering *isn't jet.*'

This time his pause was longer, to permit those who hadn't learned this fact to absorb it. 'And so – they might be deceiving their customers but they're not deceiving any of us any longer. In due course, we'll ensure they're in no position to continue in business.'

William Arkwright rose to his feet, caught Abel's eye and opened his mouth to speak.

'Aye, lad – what is it?'

Hester was pleased to observe that being addressed as 'lad' hadn't gone down very well, But this latest Arkwright surprised her by asking a question which obliged her.

'Could Miss Falgrave please explain these tests that she carried out?'

Hester glanced at her father who nodded, and then she stood up, smiling. 'They really were extremely simple. By treating the individual items with a heated instrument, I proved that they did not respond as jet would – by emitting the odour of burning coal. And nor did they give off the familiar oily smell when broken. The fractured surface did not reveal the brownish layer in which the annual rings of the original wood should be visible. And, in the case of the items which proved to be made of dark glass, it fractured all too readily.'

'Thank you, Miss Falgrave.'

Hester looked towards her father who then continued, 'So far, we ourselves have drawn a blank trying to find out where these people are obtaining their raw materials. This is why you've been approached and invited to come up with your findings.'

One by one, every company representative or individual jet carver got to their feet, but before half of them had spoken it seemed evident that nothing conclusive had come to light. By the end of the succession of reports Hester and her father were downcast.

It was then that Ephraim Broadbent stood up. A man in his middle years, he was less dogmatic than might have been supposed from Olive's account of him, and his small stature made him seem anything but commanding. His manner, however, was forthright enough, and had some of those present jerking upright in their seats as though aroused from torpor.

'Since not one of us has come up with a possible source that might be supplying this so-called jet shop, I reckon we're going to have to widen our search. None of us here needs telling that Whitby thrives as a port. I think it's about time we began investigating what's coming ashore here.'

There was a murmur of agreement. No one present would be sorry to learn that it was from abroad that such an iniquitous business was being supplied.

Abel nodded. 'We'll look into that. As a matter of fact, it had crossed my mind more than once – even though it seems an expensive method of obtaining raw materials, taking into consideration that it's by undercutting our prices that they're causing trouble.'

Working parties were organised, banding together in groups of four or five who would patrol the entire harbour area, ensuring that it was covered at every time when boats were offloading.

The task seemed tremendous, but already it was generating so much genuine fellow-feeling that Abel considered they had some reward. His only objection was to Hester's insistence that she take part in the necessary extended periods of observation.

'It's no job for a young lady,' he was still protesting, long after the meeting had dispersed.

'You've enough on with keeping the works going,' Maud added, thinking also of the hours when her eldest daughter wouldn't be available at home.

Hester had astonished herself no less than her parents by electing to go on watch with the Arkwrights. With the exception of the nephew, there was no one in their family who'd be capable of moving swiftly in a crisis. And the desirability of keeping the scheme to those in responsible positions had been mentioned. Who could guarantee, if the rest of any workforce were involved, that their plans would not be leaked?

Cecil Arkwright had claimed the privilege of organising

one of the early watches of the harbour area. Although having some reservations about his methods, Hester was compelled to admit that he was thorough.

It was early one morning, earlier even than jet workers normally left their homes, when he sited each member of his band in the lee of some buildings adjacent to the harbour.

Hester was cold, despite two layers of undergarments, the men's boots she still adopted for work, and as many petticoats as she could cram beneath her gown and cloak.

Laboriously they waited, scrutinising each boat that put in, watching as every catch was put ashore or cargo stacked on the quayside. Nothing untoward occurred, and the next band appeared silently to signal their assuming of control.

Hurrying away into the ginnels and winding streets, they went in separate directions to arrive, tired already, at their jet works.

The fruitlessness of this first lookout duty set the precedent for the succeeding two, disappointing Hester so that she came to dread the next occasion when their turn came round.

The fourth time that she met up with the Arkwrights, however, William had some news.

'One of the other surveillance men I was speaking with today has noticed something of interest. He's courting a girl who lives over on the West Cliff – her father's head chef at one of the big hotels. The other night he was walking home from seeing her when he thought to make a detour round by that Best Jet shop . . . He just missed what he took to be a delivery – a cart was pulling away from their backyard.' William hesitated, to fix Hester with a stare. 'The driver's well-known all over Whitby, specially in public houses, and he used to work for you.'

'Would that be Jeff? Jeff Hardcastle?'

William nodded, smiled sideways at his Uncle Cecil.

Why wasn't she more surprised? Why did she feel deep inside her that this was what she'd been expecting? And why, earlier, hadn't she reasoned out this means by which her designs could have left Falgraves' workroom?

But Wally . . . ? Was Wally Hardcastle capable of jeopardising the success of the works where he was foreman?

'Your mother once sacked young Jeff, didn't she?' Cecil Arkwright asked her.

'She did, that's true.'

'Do you reckon he'd harbour a grudge this long?'

'I wouldn't say that it's something he'd never contemplate.'

'Was it because he was no good that your mother got rid of him?'

'He had the makings of a competent craftsman. It was because he was unreliable that he had to go.' And because he and his father tried to stir up trouble for Falgraves' from the day my father was injured. She wouldn't say that, though, not yet. Time enough for acknowledging they'd been made fools of when the whole truth emerged. Speak too soon, and she'd have their company denigrated for not taking sufficient care.

Again, the discomfort of their watch by the harbour proved fruitless, but Hester's determination rocketed. She took to keeping a lookout down there when other groups were on duty, and made it in her way to walk along the quayside of an evening before returning to the house or in a morning en route for the workroom.

Weeks went by, all the more drearily now that they felt they were nearer their objective but lacked substantial evidence. A further meeting of all those running jet businesses was less well-attended, and reports began coming in of missed surveillances. No one could be blamed – it was an uncomfortable, boring task which could only be lightened by some result.

Hester grew restless, could settle to nothing. She neglected her churchgoing, saw no one other than family, the Arkwrights, and of course the men at the works. It was this restlessness as much as anything that caused her to rise earlier than ever one morning, slip from the house, and walk unhurriedly down towards the quay.

She heard the sound of hooves and the rumble of a cart long before it appeared through the mists preceding the dawn. From the concealing shadows cast by one of the

362

boathouses, she saw Jeff Hardcastle at the reins, and simultaneously noticed the bright new boat heading in through the harbour mouth.

Inwardly, she felt astonishingly calm. Had faced already the dreadful supposition of what the truth must be. As daylight increased, so the boat grew nearer. A little way off, hooves clattered on cobbles and the cart creaked when the horse shifted, impatient with waiting.

The boat was heading farther along the quay to a gap between fishing cobles. Slowly, the horse plodded in the same direction, the old cart squeaking and protesting as it turned a corner.

She heard the voice she'd been expecting, eager and enthusiastic, because he thought himself so clever. Jeff's laughing response floated across the angle of the harbour, conveying his satisfaction without actual words being audible to her.

Walking briskly, Hester left her cover and began hurrying along the quayside. Fifty or so yards from them she paused, watched, making sure that they'd started unloading.

They were conversing softly as they worked, stacking wooden cases in the cart. So absorbed were they that she walked right around three sides of the vehicle before they saw her.

'What price are you asking for the dark glass?' she inquired sharply. 'And the black wax?'

It hadn't occurred to her until that moment that she could be in danger.

When Jeff Hardcastle swung round to face her, his brief alarm turned swiftly to fury. Jamie appeared utterly shattered. His mouth literally gaping, he hesitated, still holding on to a packing case. She could almost see his mind whirling as he eventually stowed the case with the rest.

'She's on her own,' said Jeff wildly, 'let's . . .'

Jamie checked him with a firm hand. 'Nay, we can't. And what's the point? If she knows, she'll have told others.'

'You don't know that,' Jeff protested. 'You can't seriously mean you'll let her finish everything for us.'

Jamie shrugged. He couldn't look Hester in the eye. It had only been a scheme to yield enough brass for setting himself up. He'd a right to make a living of some sort, hadn't he? And now she knew.

'How could you, Jamie? How could you?' By the look on young Hardcastle's face, she'd be lucky if she got away from here intact. But whatever happened, she'd make certain Jamie understood what he'd done.

'Wasn't it bad enough, taking trade from decent hard-working folk? Did it have to be my designs you used?'

'That weren't my doing,' he said hastily.

'But you still aided them that were using 'em! You didn't hesitate over that, did you?'

'Let's shut her up,' Jeff persisted.

'That's right,' said Hester, her intense scorn mustered from somewhere. 'There's two of you, you stand a good chance. But just remember I'm not the only one with a jet shop in this town. Do you really think none of t'others have any idea who's at back of that shop on the West Cliff?'

'Hester . . .' Jamie began feebly.

'Hadn't you done enough to us years since, even if it were by accident, without conniving at this to destroy Falgraves'!'

She turned her back on them both. It was the hardest thing she'd ever done. She could feel Hardcastle's eyes drilling into her back, wondered how long it would be before his glance was followed by a blow.

Her legs and feet had gone numb with dread. Placing one foot ahead of the other was as hard as if they were iron chained to the bollard used for mooring vessels. Inwardly she was desperate to run, yet every step seemed as sluggardly as in a nightmare.

Neither of them followed. Afterwards, she could only assume they had decided that disposing of evidence must take priority. All she knew at the time was the prickling of her scalp and spine as, willing herself not to glance back, she trudged along the quayside, then up one of the alleyways into the town.

People were about in the streets but, although thankful that they might provide protection against attack, she was too troubled to recognise anyone. Occasionally a passing worker from one of the other jet shops would greet her, his voice sending her pulse racing, and her lack of response making him turn and stare.

The old doorway and flight of worn steps seemed only vaguely familiar. Clutching the rough handrail, Hester hauled herself to the top. The men were working already, the clattering treadles welcome reassurance. It was then that she thought of Jeff's father, spotted his unhealthy complexion across beams of sunlight slanting through scattering jet dust.

She made it to the office, sank on to her chair and sat with her head supported on hands that shook like willows in the wind. *Jamie. Why did it have to be Jamie?*

She would not weep. If she sat motionless here throughout this day, she'd not give in to tears. But she felt ill and wretched, physically sickened.

Frank came in without knocking, closed the door and stood gazing down at her. She sensed without looking the intensity of concern in his eyes.

'What's wrong?' he asked gently.

Glancing towards him, Hester tried to speak but couldn't. Then she cleared her throat, inhaled raggedly.

'It was Jamie Skelton,' she gasped, 'and Jeff Hardcastle. I caught them unloading the boat just now. Wally must be in on it, or they'd not have had access to my drawings. What'll I do, Frank?'

'Sit still for a minute, you need to recover, love . . .'

She shook her head, gulped. 'No time. We've got to get the police to that shop over yonder, and more police to follow them.'

'Did you leave them at the harbour now?'

'Aye. And I reckon they'll have to pass this way. I think any other alley is too narrow to take their cart.'

'I'll get our Harold . . .'

'You can't. Wally'd know there's something wrong.'

'I'll tell him you've come over faint. One of us is taking you home while t'other goes for Dr Davidson.'

'No, no. It's not worth the risk. Somebody has to stay, make sure Hardcastle doesn't get clear of the place.'

'I'll get Harold, anyway.'

The three of them arranged that Frank would remain at

the works to keep track of Wally, while Harold would set off towards the harbour. If he encountered the pair with the cart he'd follow secretly and learn where they were heading. Meanwhile, Hester would go and report everything she had witnessed to the police.

Frank protested that she wasn't fit to go anywhere, but she wouldn't be told. By having something to do she just might succeed in not breaking down.

The sun had warmed considerably when she set out. At first, she was thankful to be spared the awful shivering that had overtaken her. Soon, however, she was perspiring, felt close to swooning.

Nay, I'll not give in now, she resolved, breathing deeply to try and energise her brain as well as body. She'd never had cause to call upon the police before; ordinarily, that alone would have made her anxious. Today, she only needed to stay on her feet and get there. Wanting Jamie and the Hardcastles punished would ensure that she did all that she had to.

One of the officers had a brother in Arkwrights' jet works, so he knew something of the current crisis. Explaining about the jet being faked took longer, but required less haste for they had taken her word and despatched constables to bring in Jeff and Jamie.

Seeing Hester's distress they had given her a mug of tea, so strong she suspected it would remain the shape of the mug if it were overturned. The drink warmed her throat and spread downwards to her stomach, settling her nerves.

Sitting in the forbidding interview room which felt cold on account of its stout walls and absence of windows, Hester composed her statement. They insisted that there was no rush now, but she wanted everything set down before they brought those two in. Writing was a struggle, but even harder was marshalling her own recollections. Even without that morning's shock and fright, she'd have been tried by attempting to record everything that had occurred since that establishment began competing so unfairly.

She heard Jamie's voice through the thick door, experienced instinctive regret before quelling the emotion. Happen she'd always known in her heart that he'd a lawless streak in him. And surely it must be right that he'd be made to face retribution for his willingness to deceive.

When she had finished, she found Harold Clough waiting.

'Me and the constables converged on that cart of Jeff Hardcastle's while him and Skelton were just finishing loading it.'

'Didn't they resist arrest?'

Harold grinned. 'They tried to bolt for it. But they panicked the poor horse and it set off at a fair lick into an alley too narrow for yon cart. The beast was rearing and stamping when we caught up with 'em. One of the policemen was ever so good with it – calming it, like – while t'other one made Hardcastle back the cart out.'

'Where was Jamie while this was going on?'

Harold chuckled. 'Legging it in the direction of his boat.'

'I thought he might.'

'He weren't too quick for me, though. He was about to cast off when I caught up wi' him. He got the rope untied and tossed it aboard, made as if to jump on to the deck himself. He were that concerned checking the boat weren't drifting away from the side, he never saw my foot.'

Uncomprehending, Hester looked at him.

'Measured his length, he did! Face forrad. He got up with a nasty bleeding nose.' Harold had relished the moment. He'd never forgiven Skelton for being the second fellow to catch Sally Drinkwater's eye.

Back in the workroom, all appeared to be normal. Wally Hardcastle seemed unaware of any untoward events while Frank gave every impression of placidly engraving a large cameo medallion,

Hester had included in her report the conjecture that Wally was responsible for removing her designs from the workroom. It would be simply a matter of time before the police followed that up. Trying to behave as usual herself would have been difficult following her involvement in the arrest, and being in Wally's presence was added pressure. She spent much of her time in the office, sketches spread out before her, while she willed the clock's leisurely hands to stir themselves towards hometime.

Frank wouldn't think of her walking alone up to Falgrave House. His hand at her elbow, he accommodated his long stride to her weary pace, and talked all the while of everything but the folk who had been apprehended.

Her father was being conveyed by Nurse Scott from one room to another. He greeted them cheerily, called them in to talk with him.

After the nurse had settled him comfortably and departed to eat her meal, Hester prepared to relate what had happened.

Abel, though, was swifter. Smiling, he nodded in satisfaction. 'They've got somebody then, I hear. For that business of trying to undercut all our prices.'

'You've heard . . .' Hester was astounded, couldn't believe he was already acquainted with the facts.

'Aye. Our Olive called in, not half an hour sin' – seemingly, she'd run into Cecil Arkwright, and he'd come from seeing the police. Evidently one of his men is related to one of the bobbies.'

'That's right,' said Hester, waiting rather impatiently to get in a word.

'This particular officer had thought to check with Cecil for verification of what had been going on.'

Hester and Frank exchanged a look. Hadn't the word of a Falgrave been sufficient?

'We've spent a good part of the day ensuring the police had enough to go on. Did Olive tell you that an' all?'

'I don't think she knew, love.'

'But she had heard who it was all the time?'

'If she had, she's not told me. Well?'

Tears were at the back of her eyes and in her throat; tears of complete exhaustion, and for the friend who'd charmed her youth. Grimly, she shook her head.

'You tell him, Frank.'

'It was Jamie Skelton. Bringing stuff in from somewhere abroad. They think Jeff Hardcastle . . .'

'*Young Hardcastle*? Wait till I see his father!'

'You might have a long wait, sir. We believe Wally's involved an' all.'

'Slipping them my designs.'

'Nay, I'll not believe that, our lass. I know Wally always were a bit of a tough nut, but dishonest – no.'

'You'll see what comes out when they go to court,' said Hester, irritated by her father's disbelief. 'Whatever you think about Wally Hardcastle, we've had our suspicions about him for a long time, haven't we, Frank?'

He nodded. 'We have that. It's a great pity we didn't manage to pin owt on him long afore this. We might have prevented that damned shop ever opening up in unfair competition.'

'Now just a minute,' said Abel pensively, 'what's all this? What're you on about?'

'Wally Hardcastle always being a bother-maker,' said Hester sharply. 'Trying to incite the men to form a union and . . .'

'Oh, is that all?' her father remarked coolly. 'That were harmless enough.'

'Harmless, *harmless?*' Hester shouted. 'You'd better ask Bob Dunsdale what he'd call it. He was the one that got his head smashed in.'

'And all his tools destroyed,' Frank added.

'When was this?' Abel inquired tersely, his expression livid.

Frank considered. 'Near enough nine year ago, I suppose.'

Abel turned on his daughter. 'And you kept Hardcastle on? You did nowt? What the blazes do you think you're playing at! You're running a business, for God's sake, woman – haven't you a scrap of sense?'

Chapter 20

'I don't think you should blame Hester, sir,' said Frank, icily calm.

'Since she sought to act – or rather not to act – on her own initiative, with never a thought of consulting me or her mother, she's entirely to blame.'

'I rather think she believed she was sparing you anxiety.'

'Sparing? *Sparing?* Is my name or is it not *Falgrave!* I might be confined to this bloody contraption, I am not confined in the looney house. So far as I'm aware, I've not been deprived of my mental faculties. Well, have I, woman?'

'No, Father, not at all.'

'Then stop talking this nonsense, and give us the truth for a change.'

'I've never ceased telling the truth. And whatever the decision at the time, it was taken with the best interests of the company in mind.'

'Rubbish! Twaddle! What was it – had Hardcastle got you so scared you daren't come to me about him?'

'As I recall,' said Frank with a quiet assurance that Hester envied, 'Bob wouldn't say one word in accusation.'

'And Wally'd already claimed their family was being victimised when Mother got rid of their Jeff.'

'That's no excuse. The pair on you should have had more sense. I'm surprised at you, Frank.'

The implication being that less might be expected of *her*, Hester was riled. 'Frank didn't persuade me one way or the other. I was the one who arrived at the conclusion – as you yourself have just said. And we did keep a watch on Hardcastle afterwards.'

'And very thoroughly!' Abel exclaimed sarcastically. 'So well that he took patterns out of our works and handed 'em on a plate to competitors.'

And who was it made him foreman, thought Hester, but swallowed back the words. As she saw it, the best they could do was pull the business together again now that Hardcastle was out of it for good. Briefly, she wondered who would replace him. She was determined she'd put forward no suggestions.

'How's your father getting on?' Abel asked Frank abruptly. 'Is he improving?'

'I'm afraid he's more or less at a standstill at the moment. All the doctors will say is that he isn't getting any worse.'

'So, we can discount him.' His expression grim, he weighed the matter. 'Well, I suppose it'll have to be you as new foreman. Just mind she doesn't have you getting too soft with 'em all, this time. You know the job as well as anybody there, just see you keep the upper hand.'

'Of course, Mr Falgrave. Thank you, sir.'

It was hardly a flattering way of offering him the foreman's position. Frank was glad, nevertheless, and said so to Hester as they walked together through the hall.

'So am I, you should know that. But I'm terribly sorry, Frank, that I got you caught up in Father's annoyance.'

They had reached the front door and he faced her. He was smiling. 'Don't worry on that score. From his point of view, it must have appeared stupid of us to let Wally continue working there.'

'We never had any proof that he was the one who attacked Bob. With no witnesses and no evidence either he'd only have said we were making yet another unjustified accusation.'

'Aye, I suppose so. Why didn't Bob speak up?'

'I can only assume there'd been further threats. He wanted his son to work with him, didn't he? And there's others in his family – he could have been worried for their safety.'

'Happen so. Any road, it's all water under t'bridge now.' He grasped her by both shoulders and gazed down at her, his green eyes concerned. 'If I was you, I'd have a bit of a lie-down. You look worn out.'

'I'll be all right, thanks.'

'I'm sorry it turned out to be Jamie Skelton as was involved. It'll have taken it out of you, will that.'

371

Grimly, Hester nodded. 'Aye, I'm afraid it has. Maybe I ought to have realised long ago that he weren't much good.'

'But you'd been friends for years. None of us like having to admit our judgement might have been at fault.'

For months on end Hester remained depressed by the whole episode. Although the atmosphere in the workroom grew more agreeable with Wally Hardcastle out of there and Frank in charge, she never seemed entirely happy.

She worked harder than ever, immersing herself in new designs for their jewellery and always seeking ideas for different lines which they might try.

For the summer of 1872 she introduced jet replicas of the abbey ruins, and found holiday visitors converging in large numbers on the Flowergate shop. Trade throughout the jet business was picking up slightly after the way it had been hit by that shop selling counterfeit goods. Somehow, though, she felt less than satisfied by it all, and blamed her job for the dullness of the rest of her life.

Despite the fact that she and Frank Clough collaborated well in running the works, they no longer possessed the relationship that once had existed between them. Not that she wanted anything deeper than friendship with him; she could scarcely believe now that they'd ever embraced with such ardour and so frequently.

Bernard was married to Belle Jenkins who was awaiting the birth of their first child. On occasions, Hester wondered if it was her own childlessness that furthered her discontent. She saw Lambert's growing family during their rare visits to Whitby, and now that Bernard looked forward to becoming a father couldn't avoid awareness of the additional meaning introduced by children.

About the time of charges being made against the Hardcastles and against Jamie, she had begun taking long walks alone in an effort to steady her thinking. Initially, she had been dreading appearing as a witness against Jamie, a prospect which diminished her appetite and savaged her ability to sleep. In the end, she was saved a lot of trauma by his pleading guilty to involvement in the fraud.

What she hadn't anticipated was her own feeling of guilt

on account of the effect of his conviction upon his mother. She went one Sunday to visit the overcrowded house by the harbour and to her dismay, was shown the door by an embittered Edna Skelton.

'If knowing you hadn't given Jamie big ideas, he'd never have been so concerned about making money!'

The unjustifiable phrase rankled; it had remained in her head. Even today it recurred to torment her. On days when problems seemed to crowd in on her this was one more to weigh her down.

From the moment that Abel had condemned her for not getting rid of Wally Hardcastle much earlier, she'd had to work to salvage their good relationship. He'd been tart with her in the past, as he could be with all the family, now she strove to avoid replying in kind.

Strangely, it was her mother who grew aware of this, and tried to compensate. Maud had mellowed considerably in her attitude towards Hester, at last recognising the talent and the sacrifice that were contributed to keeping Falgraves' going. And she was concerned that Hester should not continue always to put the business before all else.

'I know I've been hard on you sometimes in the past,' she acknowledged one Saturday evening when Abel was resting in the master bedroom and Ruth also was in bed recovering from a quinsied throat.

'I did want the best for you, as I do for all the family. Happen I wanted it too much, though, and prevented you settling with anybody.'

Hester's tired smile might at one time have reassured Maud. These days, she recognised it as a cheerful façade.

'Hester love, you're working yourself to death . . .'

'And didn't *you*, following the accident?'

'I daresay, but I was doing it for your father. Who've you got of your own?' She paused, finding the words difficult. 'Was it me that put you off? You seemed very keen on Frank Clough at one time.'

Her daughter sighed. 'I really do not know. I like Frank, there's lots of things I admire in him, but that's all there is to it. You don't have to worry, Mother. I don't think it's anything you've ever said, it's just that we're not suited.'

'It's not easy for him, you know, with you being who you are.'

'All the more reason for me not to encourage him. I'm sure he knows where we stand by now.'

I'm not afraid of being left on my own, she asserted privately, and believed that to be true. Most days, she was too busy to fret about things she might be missing. She wondered ruefully where she would find the time to be courted by anyone.

As the Wednesday in September designated the 'Jets' holiday' approached, Hester caught herself looking forward to the occasion. At least threequarters of the jet workshops would be closed for this annual event. And, because she for one appreciated all he did for the company, Frank Clough was going to enjoy himself. She was confident she could prevent him reading more into their attending together.

Never quite so gregarious in company as his brother Harold, Frank had continued to frequent Whitby's inns and public houses only sparingly. He seemed, as a consequence, to be somewhat uneasy with many of the noisier element amongst the men in the trade. And on the evening before the holiday he sounded less eager than Hester herself to join in the festivities.

'Do you like seeing a lot of fellows drinking more than they should and laying bets on a lot of poor horses being compelled to gallop over them sticky sands?' he demanded.

Hester laughed. Normally, she didn't participate to any degree, viewing the races from the top of the cliff, if at all. But she was determined this year to prove herself one of the jet crowd.

'We ought to show a bit of interest. It's for our folk, after all.'

Frank brightened, captivated suddenly by the prospect of having her company.

'Are you saying we'll go together?'

'Why not? We've earned a change, and we can inspect the horses when they're not actually racing.'

'I suppose there'll be plenty going on besides,' he agreed

and began wondering if he'd previously been too defeatist in expecting so little might come to fruition between them.

Whitby looked especially beautiful that Wednesday. The sea breeze was bearable, and the crowds gathering in brilliantly-coloured clothing on the sands appeared as bright as the red-roofed houses.

Waiting for Hester, Frank had relished the time in which to study the cluster of buildings ranged above the harbour, a multitude of different dwellings, as varied in class and condition as they were in colour. Above them all rested the abbey and St Mary's church; a little below them, Falgrave House.

Contrary to his expectations, he'd been invited there quite often since that dreadful day when Abel had reproached both him and Hester. With this new assurance growing out of his learning to cope with being foreman, he was easier with himself. And, he supposed, more comfortable with other people. He'd maybe discover today how well he'd progressed.

The moment Hester came into sight, he forgot all about his own preoccupations. There'd never be any woman quite like her. Seeing her so frequently in clothes adapted to that mucky workshop, he'd all but forgotten what he'd first admired about her. She was dressed in red, a gleaming gown with discreet black trimming. As she came nearer he saw that its overskirt was caught up at the back in an elegant bustle, emphasising the tiny proportions of her waist. Tall, and slender from continual overwork, she appeared fragile, but her sure stride in elegant shoes with pointed toes and Louis heels convinced him of her vitality. She was wearing a glittering black necklace which he'd recently completed.

As she reached his side the once-dismissed pulse was beginning in his veins.

'Have you been waiting long? I'm a fool, Frank. It's been so long since I dressed up for an outing I'd clean forgotten what an age it takes!'

'The result's well worth it,' he responded, and risked taking her hand.

Hester laughed up at him. 'I'll admit now I was wondering if I'd overdone it a bit. It is only Whitby sands we're going to, not a race meeting. But I like to get my wear out of stuff, and I can't picture myself rigged up in this for Falgraves' workroom.'

'It is very splendid.'

'I had it new for our Bernard's wedding. You weren't there, were you?'

He hadn't been invited, naturally. And he'd passed the stage where he'd go along with the rest of the workers to sit near the back of the church. Still, he'd not let that matter; this was a day for looking forward.

They strolled on the sands and talked, discussing the gathering crowd, the horses being assembled with a certain amount of disorder, and the glint of the sea over to their right.

'Have you placed a bet then?' Hester asked mischievously.

'Eeh, no!' he exclaimed, so seriously that she laughed.

'Your nonconformist upbringing, eh, Frank lad? Isn't it time you allowed yourself a bit of a flutter?'

There's enough fluttering going on now you're beside me, he thought wryly. Still, if he must control that particular excitement, happen he'd be forgiven a lesser indulgence.

'Aye, go on – we will,' he asserted, heading in the direction of one of the men accepting bets.

'Put the same on for me,' said Hester, finding her purse. 'And I fancy that chestnut horse stamping about over there, he looks that eager.'

Frank backed an equally energetic looking grey and when the race started they made their throats raw trying to out-shout one another. Neither won, and they grinned ruefully at each other, shrugged and walked around once more until the next race.

'You're not intending to recoup your losses then, by backing something later on?' Frank teased her.

Hester shook her head, dark eyes glittering with amusement. 'Do consider my careful Yorkshire spirit! I think the way we lost on t'other indicated that we'd better hold on to what we've got. I have a nasty suspicion I'm not one as is going to make money easily.'

'The way you've allus thrown yourself into the job seems

to confirm that's the way you expect things to be – orderly, a natural progression from labour to reward.'

'You're talking very solemn all of a sudden, for a holiday.'

It was Frank's turn for laughing. 'Sorry – I was actually luxuriating in the opportunity to try and make you talk of what you *do* want.'

'How about watching the men over yonder – they're racing now, and I'm sure some of our lads said they were entering.'

Frank gave her a sideways look. 'Did you really think I was talking about this afternoon?'

Hester shook her head, but said nothing. For once in their lives, there was infinite time but she'd not analyse her emotions.

Bob Dunsdale's son Silas was running, and one of their apprentices. They stood and cheered them on, and when Silas came in second went over to congratulate him.

'Hallo, Miss Falgrave – Frank, I ought to have won, but I hadn't enough breath left. Have you seen the chest the fellow that won has got on him, big as a beer barrel.'

Hester turned to her companion. 'Don't you ever enter any of these events?'

Frank grimaced. 'Not likely – I know my limitations.'

'The exercise might do you good.'

'I'll walk you off your feet, any day. Come on – you can choose where we go.'

'Very well,' Hester agreed, and linked her arm in his. 'I hope you don't mind leaving this lot behind now. I'll show you where I like walking . . .'

Over on the cliff, where Hester usually viewed a part of the 'Jets' holiday', Maud was standing with Ruth. Smiling, she nodded to herself as she watched the woman in the unmistakable red gown and her companion.

A short distance from them in the crowd, the man who'd left his landaulet in order to watch concentrated on riveting a smile to his lips. No one would glean his reaction to the scene on the sands below them. Local doctors rarely went unnoticed even in a gathering this size and in the years since becoming a widower he'd perfected concealment of his feelings.

The air was fresher out on the moors above the town, and the noise from the sands too faint to trouble them.

'There's a lot of peace out here,' Frank remarked.

'That's why I need to come here.'

'To escape us lot at the works?' His voice was solemn, his lovely green eyes even more so.

'Not you,' she said swiftly, 'or not most times.'

'But the rest of the job gets you down?'

He was looking at her so concernedly, motionless now, the hand that remained on her arm tightening. When he tried to pull her close Hester knew she'd misled him by spending the day with him. Gently, she shook her head at him, pressed at his chest with the flat of her hand.

'I'd rather you didn't, Frank.'

'There's nobody else, is there?' When she didn't reply, he slowly released his grasp of her arm. 'You can tell me,' he persisted. 'We've known each other long enough, surely.'

'There's nothing to tell.' Because he's a very special person, and once had a marvellous wife who meant the whole world to him. No one will ever replace her.

They were still close enough for her fragrance to stir him. But despite the heat generated by her proximity, the wind had developed a bite, and was strengthening. The extent of his caring exceeded even this massive desire.

'We'd better walk on again.'

They talked again, but more infrequently, and each sensed the other was disturbed. Eventually, finding a tiny hamlet, they chose an inn with a varied table, enjoyed selecting a meal. And then neglected it.

Frank felt in his pocket while they waited for their second course. The tissue package that he slipped on to the table between them contained a jet ornament.

Intricately carved with roses, and exquisitely polished, it was a heart-shaped locket. Opening it she saw that only one half had been filled – with neatly interwoven hair.

'I suppose one could have a photograph facing that,' she concluded, then noticed the shade of the strands of hair and glanced involuntarily towards his head.

She willed herself not to colour, continued on her initial

assumption. 'These would sell very well. Especially with holiday visitors who believe they've met their ideal partner.'

Frank said nothing. She couldn't blame him. In his place, she'd have been desperately unhappy to have this love-token unacknowledged.

What to do with the thing became a massive problem. Their next dish arrived and they took up knives and forks. And the locket which Hester had closed now lay on the white cloth like the stone which she felt her own heart must be.

Had it been but another sample of a new line, they would both by now have been discussing the finer details of its production and presentation. As it was, its presence felled conversation.

Inwardly, Hester struggled with the possibility that she should accept the locket, and with it Frank's remarkable devotion. Might it prove enough, for both of them, that he cared so deeply for her? Or would it be a lie to live with him, if she could not rid herself of this long-standing affection for Jon Davidson?

Frank snatched up the locket, stuffed it carelessly into his pocket as they pushed away their plates.

'Time we were getting back.'

Only a slender moon, drifting in and out of cloud, lit the abbey ruins later that evening. They had walked down from the moors and through the twisting streets of the town where people paused to chat in groups, and laughter and songs enlivened public houses and inns.

And the two of them were still awkward together, even friendship strained by emotions that failed to coincide. For Hester the worst of it was the strong inner turmoil which continued to acknowledge Frank as an attractive man and urged her heart to find a way to love him.

For so many years she had resisted her own nature, had stifled its needs in the daily grind of making the business a success. There could be no pretending now that she was other than a woman, that her desires were any less deserving of respect than the matters with which she had occupied herself. And yet wasn't there more to being a woman than acceding to this urgency? There was the need to care – to care more deeply than for herself, to show concern.

As she said goodnight to Frank and thanked him for his company, she wished from the depths of her being that she could feel all these things for him.

Weeks went by and, even against her will and in the dusty workshop, approaching Frank seemed always to accelerate this internal pulse that nothing extinguished.

I might be going mad, she thought, wakeful in her bed, and longed for someone in whom she might confide.

Advice came, after she had fallen down the last few steps from the workroom into the street. Hearing her fall, several of the men came running down to assist and Jon Davidson was sent for.

He took one look at her as she sat huddled on the worn stair, tested the ankle that she'd twisted, and helped her into the landaulet.

'What were you doing?' he inquired, as he drove through a deluge towards Falgrave House.

'I don't know,' she said agitatedly, 'that's the whole trouble. I don't know anything any longer, and certainly not what ails me.'

'Working too hard again?' he asked, then answered himself. 'You always are, but you're the last person that overwork'll worry. It's others who see you crucifying yourself . . .'

'Is there some other way?'

He grinned. 'The jet that makes a martyr out of you claims to heal as well. Don't you recall our conversation that time we rode out by the mermaid's dining tables?'

'That's all a myth, I'm sure,' she answered sharply. How could she bear the reminder of that blissful day, when there'd been so few occasions since that they'd approached such easy friendship? Without Father sharing their conversation or her sister Ruth bounding in to fuss for attention from the doctor. How could she even hope that if she resisted the impulse to make love with Frank Clough she'd find love with Jon?

'Maybe,' he continued, serious again. 'And maybe if you'd

tell me what was wrong, lass, *I'd* not be as ineffectual as such remedies.' Being unable to help her, of all people, hurt far more than he'd like to admit. When she'd been only a bit of a girl and he'd put an arm round her that'd been some comfort. But she was a grown woman now, and his patient.

Hester shrugged. 'I just don't seem able to concentrate.'

'We all have times like that. What's bothering you, love?'

He'd used the endearment before, and with other people, she'd not be a fool and make something out of it. But she did feel easier with him now, found she was smiling a little.

'I seem so restless, Jon. On edge all the time.'

'Happen there's been some upset at the works, is that it, Hester?'

'Nay – the upset's in me. The wretched feeling hardly ever lets up.' She frowned. 'It's not something I can describe – just an incessant kind of . . . yearning.'

If he'd been less personally concerned, he'd have laughed outright at her appalled expression.

'I rather think, my dear,' he confided gently, 'that there's intent in the way we're constructed.'

She was compelled to smile. 'You must think me singularly lacking in common sense.'

'No. But I'd prescribe a new routine – a way of life that admits you might be human, after all. You should waste no more time before you marry.'

She tested his advice, repeating the words within her head until Jon had stopped the carriage at Falgrave House and was assisting her to her room. While he applied a strapping to her ankle, she still turned over the notion, wished a directive which sounded so simple could be more easily adopted.

Supposing that he must imagine her totally dull-witted, she smiled at last.

'You must charge me for the consultation in your carriage as well as for this treatment, remember.'

'I'll do no such thing.' And you'll never know that the cost to me of that particular advice will never be settled.

Hester still ached to have him interpret her emotions. 'I

381

just wish I could be certain that what you advise were for the best.'

'You'll discover what's right. Most likely, in no time at all. Life has a way of pointing us in the best direction.'

Two days of enforced immobility, and a further week of resting the ankle did nothing for Hester's state of mind. Added to indecision was the suspicion that Jon Davidson now thought her an idiot. The only good thing was her certainty that he would keep his own counsel about her confidence.

Away from the works, she had come to dread her return there. Frank had visited the house, bringing an armful of flowers and his protestation that he loved her. With him at her side, she could not doubt that her need was just as strong. Love, though, was a different matter altogether. By the time she was fit to return to Falgraves', she still did not know.

Braving him at the works had to be faced. Kilner was driving her, of course, which got her there too swiftly for much contemplation.

The first sign that something might be wrong was one of their apprentices haring along the road. The instant she opened the carriage door she sniffed the air, realised what the trouble was.

'Wait there until I tell you, please,' she directed the coachman then, forgetting her injured ankle, ran up the stairs.

Smoke was filling the workroom already, fanned by the draught from the windows. Bernard, his face ashen, was anxiously watching Frank and Harold Clough who were struggling with a damp cloth to quench the flames that were spreading from what had been a small heap of jet dust beneath one of the benches. Two legs of the bench itself were smouldering already.

'Bernard,' Hester yelled, 'Kilner's outside – for God's sake, send him for the fire brigade!'

But Kilner had smelled burning almost as soon as Hester herself. He was behind her now, panting with the combined effects of exertion and inhaling smoke.

'Thank goodness,' she said rapidly. 'Fetch the fire brigade! And Bernard – find the broom,' she commanded her brother. 'Get some of this dust swept away.'

Even as she spoke, though, the dust about them started smouldering, then burst into flame. Spreading like tributaries of a river, threads of fire ran out in several directions. Bob Dunsdale and his son rushed to bring water. The only containers they could find were the kettle used for brewing tea and the men's drinking mugs. The rest of the men were galvanised into action. But water only accelerated the blaze. One bench was fully alight when someone remembered the legend that water didn't quench jet fire. Two panes in a window cracked, startling everyone. Unnoticed while Frank and Harold concentrated on the fire threatening to engulf the bench, another blaze had quietly devoured floorboards, wooden skirting and the lower sill of the tall window.

The sudden rush of air darted a tongue of flame at Harold Clough's head. The greasy cap smothered in lethal dust ignited.

'Christ!' Frank exclaimed, swung round, dashed the cap from his brother's head and with bare hands beat out his flaming hair.

The next bench to the centre of the fire was beginning to smoulder. Hester ran towards it, seized the wooden tray containing rough jet and as much as she could of the finished jewellery.

'Quick, all of you,' she yelled. 'Get all the jet you can out of here. It'll all go up in a flash if we don't.'

Led by Bernard, the men and boys formed a chain on the stairs, passing from hand to hand all the stuff that might fuel the blaze.

'Keep out of the way! If your skirts catch there'll be no saving you,' Frank shouted to her, as he and Harold tore off their blue smocks and tried using them to smother the flames.

Hester grabbed the broom and began sweeping, desperate to clear the dust ahead of the spreading fire.

It was hopeless. The floorboards themselves were burning, encouraging the flame from each bench to its neighbour. Frank and his brother were driven, coughing, to back away from the intensity of the fire.

'Hester,' he began, despairingly.

'I know. We'll have to get everyone out.'

With a lingering backward glance to the growing blaze, she turned and hurtled through the smoke-filled room to the stair.

'Get out, get out,' she shouted. 'Just leave everything and go.'

They might as well have been deaf. Instead of dashing for the street the men came, stumbling in their haste, stomping up the steps and back into the workroom. Scarcely visible through smoke, they pounded towards their own benches, cursing and thrusting aside colleagues who impeded them.

Despite their dread, they'd not abandon their tools.

'Come on, come on,' Bernard called from below.

Scared, some of the apprentices obeyed, but the older men were intent on saving what they could.

'No, no,' Hester protested, *please* ... Get out, get out ...'

Frank took charge. In a massive voice which she wouldn't have recognised as his, he ordered them to leave. Some, particularly the elderly ones, were coughing savagely trying to draw in air.

'Take his other arm, Hester,' he told her as he seized the oldest man they employed.

Together, they marched him to the top of the stairway. Hester encouraged him, step by step, down to where Bernard was ushering people into the street.

'Where's that fire brigade?' she asked her brother woefully.

Grimly, he shook his head. 'What's it like up there?'

'Bad. We can only make sure we save everyone.'

'Want me to go back up there?'

'No, you organise everything out here. Direct the brigade when they arrive.'

She was halfway up the wooden stair when she heard an appalling splintering of wood and a prolonged crashing.

'Whatever's that?' she called, forcing herself to run the last few steps up into the billowing smoke.

'Stay where you are,' Frank shouted. 'Part of the floor's gone.'

By keeping her head low, on floor level, she could just distinguish a gaping abyss where Frank's bench and his brother's had been sited.

'Anybody hurt?' she inquired anxiously.

'Could be,' Harold replied.

He had fallen with the benches and flooring and now was trapped against one of the joists.

'Better send someone for a doctor,' Frank suggested tersely. He was torn, agonisingly, between setting to to rescue his own brother and continuing to usher the rest of the workers to the stair.

Hester shouted to Bernard to send someone for Jon Davidson, then yelled to the workers remaining in the room.

'You see how the floor's giving way. You'll have to get out now, or you haven't an earthly.'

The smoke had grown so dense, she could hardly recognise her own workers as they pushed past her on the stair.

'Frank?' she shouted. 'Are you all right?'

'Fine, but there's some as aren't. Got to reach 'em . . .'

His voice had diminished to a rasp. She wasn't surprised, considering all the heat and the smoke in there, as well as all that he had done. She prayed he stayed conscious until help came.

She was still holding on to the doorframe, staring in the direction where she'd last seen Frank, when she felt someone who had come up from the street trying to push past her.

'You can't go in th . . .' she began, then realised he was a firefighter.

'They're here at last, Frank,' she called, and sank on to the step where she'd been standing.

Within a second she'd been ordered to move to allow the fire brigade access. Slowly, woodenly, she stomped down as far as street level.

'Your brother's ferrying the lads to the doctor's,' Bob

Dunsdale told her. 'One of the other fellows, as well. They've got a couple of hire carriages from round t'corner.'

'Good. How're you feeling, Bob?'

'Not so bad. Chest's a bit tight, but nowt to grumble at. My lad weren't so good, though. But Dr Davidson'll soon attend to him.'

Hester nodded, hoped she appeared sufficiently concerned. Now that most of their workers had escaped, all she could think of was those who were trapped back there. And Frank working himself to the limit, and beyond, to get them out.

Chapter 21

Hester could see him in every stage of their developing friendship. Frank Clough, the youngster who hadn't troubled to conceal his contempt for the selective nature of her own training at the works. Then there was the enthusiastic engraver, as eager as she herself to make her designs reality; the man who'd studied Shakespeare in order to interpret her ideas; the man who'd first attracted her.

And there was Frank sharing the load when Hardcastle generated trouble, just as he eventually shared the blame when her father learned what had occurred. She saw the gleam in his green eyes the day she offered him the temporary foreman's position, the way those eyes revealed his hurt when not permitted to continue. There'd been the fun they'd enjoyed on the day of the 'Jets' holiday', the deepening attraction afterwards, unbelievably difficult to resist.

She wouldn't – *couldn't* leave until she knew that he was safe. He was a vital part of her life, she couldn't contemplate an existence without him.

Most of the panes from the workroom windows were shattered in the street. Smoke still sprang in ballooning gusts from between their charred frames. Occasional shouts from the firefighters rose above the constant rush of water from their hoses.

It felt an age since she had emerged. Bernard was sitting at the reins of the Falgrave brougham. Kilner, exhausted, had been left with Jon Davidson at the surgery in Royal Crescent.

Hester was huddled in a doorway across the street from the works, heedless of everyone's insistence that she seek medical attention, scarcely aware of anything beyond concern for Frank and his brother.

The firemen had rescued the other person who'd been trapped; some were working now to free Harold while their colleagues battled to contain the blaze.

Bernard had told her briefly how they'd all been laughing and talking when the fire broke out. How they'd all been taken utterly by surprise.

Frank should have known the place hadn't been swept. She hoped to God he didn't pay with his life for the geniality that had cared more for the good humour of his fellow workers than for their safety.

He didn't deserve to suffer. Hadn't he more than compensated by his relentless struggle, first against the fire, then to save others? She had liked him a very great deal for many years; today, she'd been impressed by his calm. She'd admired his work for as long as she could recall; now admired his tremendous courage.

He staggered at last out into the street, scarcely recognisable – smoke-begrimed and burned. His brother whom he had helped to rescue seemed in far better shape when he emerged as she ran over towards them.

'No, no – I'll manage, thanks,' said Frank hastily when Bernard offered to help him into the carriage. He was sore everywhere, bruised and grazed, worst of all scorched and singed. He'd not let anyone touch him.

'I can't begin to thank you,' said Hester, clambering aboard after Harold had followed his brother inside.

Frank snorted. 'Well, we got 'em all out.' He'd have given a great deal to have saved the works for her.

'That's all that really matters.' She couldn't feel anything for the workshop – ridiculous really, when she'd devoted over ten years of her life to Falgraves'.

Frank asked to be taken home, but didn't argue when told he was going to the doctor's.

The sitting room in Royal Crescent had been commandeered for the overspill of men being treated. Jon emerged from the surgery, glanced towards them, and told Frank he would be the next one in.

Some of the men and most of the apprentices had already been seen by the doctor. One or two had been taken home by hired carriage, others were sipping hot sweet tea provided by the housekeeper who was flitting agitatedly about, for all the world as though she'd never before seen any crisis.

'Is there a nurse helping in there?' Hester asked her brother after Frank had been called into the surgery.

'Not as far as I know,' Bernard replied. 'They were saying he's on his own.'

'When the next one goes in, I'm offering to help. I can surely wash folk, and hand dressings to the doctor, if nothing else.'

Frank came out after a long interval, bandages swathing both hands and with one trouser leg slashed to the knee to accommodate a massive dressing. He had knelt on a smouldering floorboard, didn't even realise until he was examined that he was burnt almost to the bone.

Jon Davidson had tried persuading him that hospital was advisable, but Frank was stubbornly opposed to the notion. And there wasn't time enough for arguments while others were waiting in various stages of shock.

'If he's not back here tomorrow, I shall be round to see him,' Jon confided to Hester when she went in to offer help.

Harold was called in for treatment. Having been trapped, he could be more seriously injured than the men who were still waiting. Surprisingly cheerful considering his ordeal, he laughed about Hester's presence when Jon told him to undress.

'Get behind that screen with you!' the doctor exclaimed. 'You'll know when I've finished with you that you're not here for a bit of fun.'

Whilst he was waiting, Jon asked Hester to lay out fresh dressings. 'And fill the kettle each time it's dry, if you will, we can't take any chances over infection.'

'Is there anything else I can do?' she inquired.

Jon smiled. 'Stick those instruments in that pan over there – it's a makeshift steriliser. Oh – and before you do, using those metal tongs, take out anything that's in there, set it on that tray . . .'

Until Harold's examination was completed, she could only fill in time as she'd been instructed. And it seemed a long while before Jon emerged from the murmured conversation beyond the screen.

'He's a fortunate young man! There's hardly a mark on

389

him. And so far as I can ascertain there are no internal injuries. As luck would have it, he was trapped by the legs. They haven't broken under the pressure, so it looks as though he might have been a deal worse off.'

This latter applied to many of their employees. Some had incurred bruising and grazes in the rush to get out, others had burns, but with the exception of Frank, none had suffered extensively.

Working side by side with Jon, Hester cleansed wounds as he directed, and handed dressings until every one of their workers had received treatment. At some stage Bernard had come in to say that news of the fire had reached Falgrave House.

'Both Mother and Father are considerably alarmed – I think I ought to go and reassure them.'

'Gracious, yes.' She had been too absorbed with what was going on to give even a thought to how news travelled through the town. 'Do tell them that I'm all right,' she reminded him.

'I'll drive your sister home after we're finished here,' Jon added. 'Is your man still here?'

'Kilner? No. He'd got his breath back, and insisted on ferrying the men to their homes. I'll walk, anyway, the air will do me good.'

Bernard needed to think, as well. He wasn't happy with his own performance today. He'd been so shattered when fire broke out that he'd left too much to their foreman. To live with himself, he'd need to stiffen up his spirit, be more prepared in the future to act like the man he now professed to be. And hadn't he, maybe, been more than partially responsible for the easy-going atmosphere that had permitted jet dust to accumulate in hazardous quantities?

Hester was glad of the simple tasks that kept her from thinking too searchingly. There was satisfaction in passing a clean bandage into Jon's waiting hand; and remaining alert to his requirements kept her mind from her extraordinary reaction some while ago.

It was early evening when they waved off the last of the emergency patients, and Jon closed the door and leaned against it.

'You'll be off to see Frank Clough now then, eh?'

'Frank? But – he'll be resting. You said, didn't you, that until tomorrow that's all he'll need.'

'Aye, aye.'

He was puzzled. Hadn't he seen the pair of them only the other day, so obviously attracted, and disappearing off together? And hadn't she admitted to the passion which he could understand any lass feeling for a young man as attractive as Frank Clough . . .

'I only thought – Hester, you do love him, don't you?'

Her dark eyes had tears in them when she met his glance. 'I wanted to today, believe me I did. When I watched him back there, trying to put out the fire, getting folk out . . . then afterwards when I was outside and he was working so urgently to free the others. Oh, Jon – all I could think of was how Frank had always been everything a friend is, to me. I was desperate for his safety.'

'There you are, then.'

Slowly, she shook her head. 'I'm not in love with him. Otherwise, we'd have overcome his position and mine, would have insisted on having a life together. Love has got to be stronger than differences.' And strong, in this case, for constant care of Father.

Jon said nothing. He was trying to believe the news she'd given him which suddenly transformed everything that he had supposed.

Their reception at Falgrave House was sombre, the only possible enthusiasm in thanks voiced to Jon by both her parents.

'I've said before that we're fortunate indeed in our doctor, you know that, Jon,' Abel said quietly. 'You're always there when we need you most.'

'It is my job.'

'Have you had anything to eat?' Maud inquired. When he smilingly shook his head she insisted that he dine with them.

'You can start without me,' Hester told them. 'Just look at the state I'm in, I'll have to go and change.'

'I'll not die of starvation, lass,' the doctor exclaimed.

'And a few moments interlude before eating won't harm my digestion.'

'You're looking pale, yourself,' observed Maud. 'Are you all right?'

'A bit tired, that's all, thanks.'

Abel offered him whisky, watched while the doctor poured. He'd never cease to wish that he was able to do at least one thing for folk, even the small tasks of being hospitable.

Sipping pensively, Jon came to sit beside his chair. 'Hester helped, you know, Abel – in the surgery. Simply came in, asked what she must do. You've a daughter to be proud of.'

Abel raised an eyebrow, thought for a second, then nodded slowly. 'Aye – we'd not have kept the works running this long without her.' Now, he didn't know what would happen. They none of them knew how much could be salvaged, what restoration might cost. 'It's just unfortunate that she'd let things slacken off, like . . .'

'*Hester* had? Nay, man, she'd been off with her ankle for days, hadn't she, until today.'

'A good boss doesn't have to keep an eye on 'em all every minute. The men learn what's important.'

Jon stood up wearily, walked away to stand with his back to the fireplace.

'I'd not wish us to quarrel, Abel, but I can't hold my tongue. Whoever's fault that fire was, you can't go blaming her. You're not blind, you should have seen what was coming. You've overworked the girl for years, and you've been around to see the consequences in her. Where's the carefree lass that used to charm us all? How has she turned into this solemn, exhausted woman?'

Again, his friend's eyebrows soared. When there was no other response, Jon took another sip of the whisky and continued.

'I'm sure you're as aware as any of us that when somebody's worked that hard they're not able to give of their best. Things do get neglected. The nature of life is such that it isn't always unimportant matters that suffer.'

'By Gum, Jon, you don't hold owt back once you get

going, do you?' Abel exclaimed, meeting his very direct gaze. 'That's me reproved, and no mistake. Aye – and not without cause. Happen I've always expected a bit too much . . .'

'Sometimes that brings out the best in folk. In Hester's case, she drives herself, without anyone else's assistance.'

'Too much like me, I suppose.'

'That needn't be a fault . . .' Jon was smiling again, returned to sit beside him.

Abel cleared his throat. 'There'll be changes, any road, in the way things are done from now on, there'll have to be. If we are able to stay in business.'

Hester and Bernard together had suggested to their mother that she accompany them to inspect the workroom the next morning. As Kilner deposited them on the pavement outside, Maud staggered slightly, shocked. Someone had swept much of the broken glass from the flagstones, but sufficient remained to make them all gaze upwards to the charred frames.

'What a mess, what a mess!' she remarked, her voice awed by the damage, by the fact that this had happened to them.

Bernard took her arm in the stairway as they followed Hester, felt his mother's body slacken as though she might faint when they reached the blistered paint of the door.

Hester restrained them both with an arm extended. 'We'd better not go any further than this. Just look at that floor . . .'

Part of the strength of the wooden floor had been in its completeness. So long as the boards were all intact and interlocked, they aided the supporting joists. As soon as the fire ate into the area where the Cloughs' benches had stood the entire structure had been weakened. In addition to the extensive fire damage many of the floorboards had cracked and tilted, allowing other heavy benches to shift. In this way, several were leaning sideways with one or more of their legs thrusting down into the fractured floor.

'Oh, my God,' Maud sighed, and then: 'Thank goodness your father isn't able to see this, it'd finish him.'

It'll finish *us*, thought Hester, unless we're extremely

393

careful. It did seem like a proverbial final straw, after all the unfair competition from that fraudulent shop, and having to prove that she wasn't involved. They'd lost a lot of trade round about that time, and hadn't completely got over all the trouble.

'Well, Bernard,' said his mother briskly. 'You could turn this into your big chance, if you've a mind. You could oversee the reconstruction, find some way of working, meanwhile, so's you'll keep our men, and when it all starts up again proper it can be on your lines.'

Frowning, Bernard glanced towards his sister. This had been *her* works for many a year – *hers*.

To her utter astonishment, Hester didn't feel like arguing with her mother. She didn't seem to care too much how the place would be run so long as they did manage to salvage the business.

'For too long our Hester's had to make her designing take second place,' Maud continued. 'I think she's earned a chance to work on the job she wants. What do you say, love?'

Hester nodded. 'Yes, yes. It's time somebody else had a go.'

Strangely, the fire, although so devastating, had generated fresh thinking in her. She'd never again feel such total attachment and involvement here. This was no longer the Falgraves' that had seemed a part of her.

They all started when they heard boots on the stair, grinned in unison when they saw Frank Clough.

'You did your best, Frank,' said Maud gently, before he reached the sight that had appalled them.

'Sorry, I couldn't do more,' he began gruffly.

'If anybody's to blame, it's me,' Bernard admitted. 'I wasn't taking enough notice. That'll alter, if we are able to set it all up again. I'll need a reliable team, Frank, can I still count on you for foreman?'

'Aye. Aye, thanks, you can an' all.'

They talked further. Now that Frank was here he was able to indicate some practical ways in which they might avoid gutting the place entirely before they could reconstruct.

On their way out they inspected the area beneath the workroom which ten years previously had been purchased from the inn next door and utilised for storage.

'Once the workroom floor's made safe,' said Bernard, 'we might round up the men, ask if they'll give a hand sorting this lot.'

His mother nodded. 'There'll be some finished and part-finished pieces we can rescue. To say nothing of the rough jet. No sense in letting anybody else in, chucking good stuff away.'

Hester turned to her mother. 'Are you going to take a more active role in running things again?'

Maud was surprised. 'Ay, I don't know. Me and your father's not getting any younger . . . Still, our Ruth doesn't seem to be taking up so much of my time.' More than once recently she had grown bored.

'Have you been to the doctor today?' Hester asked Frank once they were done with the business discussion.

'Not so far.'

'Meaning you didn't intend to?'

He laughed. 'Are you going to drag me there?'

'I think I'd better.' There were things to be said, even more vital than his receiving medical attention again.

'Take the brougham,' Maud told her. 'We've got plenty of stuff to see to, any road, while we're down in the town.'

Jon happened to look out of his surgery window as the Falgrave carriage halted outside. When no one emerged for some long while he began wondering if somebody required his assistance to alight.

Hester had detained Frank, awkwardly, just as he was about to open the door.

'I don't know how I'm going to say this to you, Frank, specially when you were so marvellous yesterday, doing so much for Falgraves'.'

'You don't have to say anything.'

'Oh, yes, I do. You've always been so supportive, the best friend I could have had. I owe you a lot, and most of all being straightforward . . .'

'Hester, you don't need to tell me. If I hadn't known before, I knew last night. If there'd been more than that friendship you speak of between us, you'd have come round home after.'

'I'm sorry. I truly am.'

'Aye, well – it ought to have been more obvious to me long since. If we'd loved each other enough we'd not have turned every small difference between us into obstacles, would we?'

Seeing them alight together and walk, in earnest conversation towards his door, Jon felt his spirits plummeting. Why had he, only so recently, believed what he longed to believe?

Frank Clough was in better physical condition than the doctor had expected. Changing the dressings on his wounds, he marvelled that anyone could begin healing so quickly. But then, he thought, the man was young, a tremendous advantage.

Hester looked tired still but admitted to no more than that when he questioned her.

'Take care then,' he told her, walking with them to the door. He steeled himself to remain there, waving them off.

'I'll tell Kilner to drop you off, if you like,' Hester said to Frank. 'I'm not going straight back to the house.'

She needed time alone, for the wakeful night hadn't provided the inner resources to solve her own difficulties.

'See you when you're ready to start on the workroom then,' Frank responded.

'Yes, either Bernard or I will let you know. Or Mother . . .' she added.

Their eyes met, holding for a moment in complete understanding of Maud Falgrave's foibles.

She stood by the carriage while Frank laboriously clambered aboard, shook her head in answer to some question from him.

'Quite sure. I'm going for a long walk.' Telling Frank her true feelings about him was only half the problem. Learning to live with this new truth about her emotions was something she could only tackle by serious application.

'Does that have to be alone? Or might you accept company?'

Jon had approached so quietly that his presence didn't

penetrate her preoccupation until he was beside her. Astonished into smiling, she gazed up at him.

'I'm not exactly scintillating today.'

He laughed. 'What makes you think I'm any better?'

They walked on unspeaking for a while, heading in the direction of the Royal Hotel on the West Cliff then walking past to the cliff-edge itself.

Glancing across the harbour mouth towards the ruined abbey and St Mary's church with Falgrave House below them, Hester suddenly shivered.

'What is it, love?'

She swallowed, instinctively grasping the hand close to her own.

'Changes, I suppose. I have ached for so long for things to be different. Now that they are, I don't know who I am any more, let alone where I belong.'

Frowning concernedly, Jon remained silent. Speaking up would be unfair, would deny her freedom to find her own solutions.

'Bernard's to take more of a share in the running of the works, if we do start up again. I've been desperate for that to happen, but *now* . . . '

'You've put so much into that jet works.'

'Mm. And now it's over.'

'But . . .'

'It is, Jon – whatever happens, it won't be the place that I worked to advance. And the worst of it is I don't really care.' She paused, reflecting. 'It'd have been different if I'd loved Frank. Making a go of things with him would have filled the void. But that's not a strong enough reason for marriage.' And nor is desiring. If I hadn't learned what love is, I might have settled for a reasoning alternative.

'We shall remain friends, naturally,' she continued aloud. 'Falgraves and Cloughs have depended on each other since long before my time.'

'What will you do,' he asked very quietly, 'besides your work?'

She was a long time replying. Conditioned by her upbringing, by generations of Falgrave women who'd been indoctrinated with ancient tradition, she'd struggled like this for years, suppressing her innermost feelings.

'What will *you* . . . ?' she asked at last.

His astonishment made Hester want to hug him. But his was the first move, drawing their clasped hands against his chest, and then with his other arm encircling her.

'This,' he said, kissing her. 'Repeatedly, and more than this. As long as we both shall live.'

His lips were sweet on hers, and fervent, escalating all the urgent pulses that overtook all other senses. It was like that other kiss, all those Christmases ago, when he'd been grieving for Ruth and she'd felt ashamed for loving him.

'Let's go tell Father, he'll be so delighted.'

Against her ear, his breath was warm, deliciously exciting. His laugh sent tangles of delight coursing down her spine.

'Hester, my love, it's time we rid you of old habits. There really shall be a time and a place when we just consider each other.'

'Am I being unfair?'

'No, because I'll prevent your returning home, at least until we have a small measure of the time we've earned by always being too busy for each other.'

His kisses, mingled with expressions of love, were interrupted only for her own declaration.

'I love you so deeply, Jon, have loved you for years, and in so many ways . . .' With the admiration nurtured by his care of them, affection grown from their mutual concern – and in attraction, the pulsebeat need of him that yearned for their especial harmony.

'Marry me now, Hester . . .'

'Gladly.'

He smiled into her eyes, placed an arm about her shoulders, and walked with her slowly, as though they had all the time in the world, towards his home.